FALKIRK COMMUNITY TRUST

D0657535

~~Heat~~ of Betrayal

Douglas Kennedy's previous novels include the critically acclaimed bestsellers *The Big Picture*, *The Pursuit of Happiness*, *A Special Relationship* and *The Moment*. He is also the author of three highly-praised travel books. *The Big Picture* was filmed with Romain Duris and Catherine Deneuve; *The Woman in the Fifth* with Ethan Hawke and Kristen Scott Thomas. His work has been translated into twenty-two languages. In 2007 he was awarded the French decoration of Chevalier de l'Ordre des Arts et des Lettres, and in 2009 the inaugural Grand Prix de Figaro. Born in Manhattan in 1955, he has two children and currently divides his time between London, Paris, Berlin, Maine and New York.

Praise for THE HEAT OF BETRAYAL

'Romance noir, superbly written'
The Times

'Kennedy is a complete genius when it comes to understanding the minds of stylish but troubled women'
Daily Mirror

FALKIRK COMMUNITY TRUST LIBRARIES

'Kennedy's skill is to send you racing down the slope of sheer story'
Esquire

'A psychological adventure illuminated by the desert sun'
New Statesman

the Heat of Betrayal

DOUGLAS KENNEDY

arrow books

3 5 7 9 10 8 6 4 2

Arrow Books
20 Vauxhall Bridge Road
London SW1V 2SA

Arrow Books is part of the Penguin Random House
group of companies whose addresses can be found at
global.penguinrandomhouse.com.

Penguin
Random House
UK

Copyright © Douglas Kennedy 2015

Douglas Kennedy has asserted his right to be identified
as the author of this Work in accordance with the
Copyright, Designs and Patents Act 1988

First published in Great Britain by Hutchinson in 2015
The edition published by Arrow Books in 2016

www.randomhouse.co.uk

A CIP catalogue record for this book is available from the British Library

ISBN 9780099585183
export ISBN 9780099585190

Typeset in Adobe Garamond by Palimpsest Book Production Ltd,
Falkirk, Stirlingshire
Printed and bound by Clays Ltd, St Ive

Penguin Random House is committed to a
sustainable future for our business, our readers
and our planet. This book is made from Forest
Stewardship Council® certified paper.

FSC
www.fsc.org

Falkirk Community Trust	
30124 03062572 9	
Askews & Holts	
AF	£7.99
MK	

Again for Christine

Run up the sail, my heartsick comrades;
Let each horizon tilt and lurch—
You know the worst: your wills are fickle,
Your values blurred, your hearts impure
And your past life a ruined church—
But let your poison be your cure.

from Louis MacNeice, 'Thalassa'

One

FIRST LIGHT. AND I didn't know where I was any more.

The sky outside: was it a curved rotunda of emerging blue? The world was still blurred at its edges. I tried to piece together my whereabouts, the exact geographic location within which I found myself. A sliver of emerging clarity. Or maybe just a few basic facts.

Such as:

I was on a plane. A plane that had just flown all night across the Atlantic. A plane bound for a corner of North Africa, a country which, when viewed cartographically, looks like a skullcap abreast a continent. According to the Flight Progress Monitor illuminating the back-of-the-seat screen facing me, we were still seventy-three minutes and eight hundred and forty-two kilometres (I was flying into a metric world) from our destination. This journey hadn't been my idea. Rather I'd allowed myself to be romanced into it by the man whose oversize (as in six-foot-four) frame was scrunched into the tiny seat next to mine. The middle seat in this horror movie of an aircraft. No legroom, no wiggle room, every seat taken, at least six screaming babies, a husband and wife fighting in hissed Arabic, bad ventilation, bad air conditioning, a one-hour wait for the bathroom after the plastic meal they served us, the rising aroma of collective night sweats hanging over this hellhole of a cabin. Thank God I made Paul pack his Zopiclone. Those pills really do induce sleep in even the most impossible conditions. I put aside all my concerns about pharmaceuticals and asked him for one, and it gave me three hours' respite from this high-altitude sweat-box confinement.

Paul. My husband. It's a new marriage – just three years old. Truth be told, we love each other. We are passionate about each other. We often tell ourselves that we are beyond fortunate to have found each other. And I do truly believe that. He is the right man for me. Just as, the day before we legalised our relationship and

1

committed to each other for the rest of our lives, I was silently convincing myself that I could change some of Paul's worrying inclinations; that, in time, things would tick upwards, stabilise. Especially as we are now trying to become parents.

Out of nowhere, Paul suddenly began to mumble something in his sleep, its incoherency growing in volume. When his agitation reached a level that woke our neighbour – an elderly man sleeping in grey-tinted glasses – I touched Paul's arm, trying to rouse him out of his nightmare. It was several more unnerving moments of shouting before he snapped awake, looking at me as if he had no idea who I was.

'What . . . where . . . I don't . . .?'

His wide-eyed bemusement was suddenly replaced by the look of a bewildered little boy.

'Am I lost?' he asked.

'Hardly,' I said, taking his hand. 'You just had a bad dream.'

'Where are we?'

'Up in the air.'

'And where are we going?'

'Casablanca.'

He appeared surprised at this news.

'And why are we doing that, Robin?'

I kissed him on the lips. And posed the question:

'Adventure?'

FATE IS BOUND up in the music of chance. A random encounter, a choice impulsively made . . . and fate suddenly has its own interesting momentum.

It was fate that had brought us to Casablanca.

The 'fasten seat belts' sign had now been illuminated. All tray tables stored away. All seats upright. The change in cabin pressure was wreaking havoc with the eardrums of all the babies around us. Two of the mothers – their faces veiled – tried to calm their children down without success. One of the babies was staring wide-eyed at the cloaked face in front of him, his anguish growing. Imagine not being able to see your mother's face in public. She is visible at home, but in the world beyond, all that can be seen is a slitted hint of eyes and lips: to an infant jolted awake by a change in cabin pressure, it would be even more reason to cry.

'Little charmers,' Paul whispered, rolling his eyes.

I entwined my hand with his, saying:

'We'll be down on the ground in just a few minutes.'

How I so want one of our very own 'little charmers' sitting next to us.

Paul suddenly put his arm around me and said:

'Am I still your love?'

I clutched his hand more tightly, knowing just how much reassurance he craves.

'Of course you are.'

The moment he walked into my office three years ago I knew it was love. What do the French call it? A *coup de foudre*. The overwhelming, instantaneous sense that you have met the love of your life; the one person who will change your entire trajectory because you know . . .

What exactly?

Was it really love that made me swoon? I certainly thought so at the time.

Let me restate that. Honestly.

I fell in love with Paul Leuen straight away. As he told me later, much to his surprise he too felt 'a profound change in my *raison d'être*' after walking into my office.

That phrase is so Paul. He loves to ornament his language – something I still find endearing when he doesn't overplay his hand. It serves as an intriguing counterbalance to the spare, hugely controlled line drawings that once made his name as an artist; a talent which, though he's recently been thwarted by self-doubt, still remains astonishing to me.

So Paul also fell in love on the spot – with the woman he'd been sent to in order to sort out his messy financial affairs.

That's right, I'm an accountant. A numbers cruncher. The person you call as a barrier between yourself and our friends at the Internal Revenue Service.

Accountants are usually grouped with dentists as purveyors of a profession that they privately loathe. But I happen to know quite a few other certified public accountants, and most of them – from the grey bookkeepers to the corporate high-flyers – tend to like their work.

I certainly like it – and that's speaking as someone who came to the numbers-and-tax game in her thirties. No one grows up proclaiming: 'I want to be an accountant.' It's a bit like driving down an open road, then veering down a lane that looks staid and humdrum. But then, much to your surprise, you find it has its own intriguing allure, its own singular sense of human narrative. Money is that fault line along which we pirouette. Show me a person's numerical sum total and I can develop a portrait of their immense complexities: their dreams and aspirations, their demons and terrors.

'When you look at my financial records,' Paul asked me, 'what do they tell you about me?'

Such directness. A flirtatious directness, even though – when the question was posed – he was still just a prospective client with wildly disorganised books. Paul's tax problems were considerable, but not insurmountable. His salary at the state university was

4

taxed at source. His problem was that when it came to sales of his artwork, he'd frequently been paid in cash and had never thought about paying tax on it. Though the total was reasonably modest – maybe $15,000 per annum – stretched over a ten-year period that was a not-insignificant sum of taxable income which some sharp-eyed IRS inspector now wanted declared and paid for. Paul was being audited and the little local bookkeeper who'd been handling things for him for the past decade ran scared once the IRS started knocking on the door. He told his client that he needed someone who was skilled at negotiating with the taxman. And he recommended me.

Paul's financial problems, however, weren't simply limited to undisclosed income. His spending habits had landed him in severe cash-flow difficulties. Wine and books were his principal vices. There was a part of me that privately admired someone with such an unfazed approach to life that, while being chased by the electricity company for his quarterly bill payment, he thought nothing of spending $185 on a bottle of Pomerol 1989. He would also only choose the finest French-made charcoals and pencil leads for his etchings and these art supplies alone accounted for another $6,000 in annual outlay. When he went to the South of France for a vacation, though he would stay in a friend's guest cottage outside the medieval village of Eze – which cost him nothing – he would easily rack up another ten grand's worth of gastronomical indulgences.

As such, the first impression I had of Paul Leuen was of someone who – unlike the rest of us – had somehow managed to avoid all the pitfalls of the workaday, routine life. And I always wanted to fall in love with an artist.

We are often attracted to whatever runs contrary to our nature. Did I see in Paul – this rail-thin, six-foot-four-inch artist with long grey hair, his black leather jacket and black jeans, his black hoodie, his Converse high-top sneakers – the possibility of change; a way out of the humdrum that so much of my life had become?

During our first professional meeting Paul made a joke about his financial affairs being somewhat akin to a Jackson Pollock painting, and then said that he was the living embodiment of the French word '*bordélique*'. When I looked it up after our meeting I discovered it meant 'like a brothel' and 'all over the place'. Then there was the way he was almost apologetic about his 'financial absurdities', and how he needed someone to take him in hand and 'turn me into a proper functioning grown-up'.

'The books will tell all,' I said.

What the books did tell me was that Paul Leuen was accruing serious debt. I was direct with him:

'You like to show yourself a good time. The fact is, your income from the state university leaves you – after state and federal taxes – with around fifty thousand a year to live on. Your house has been mortgaged twice. You could be facing a tax bill of sixty thousand plus penalties if the IRS has its way. And since you have virtually no savings . . .'

'So what you're saying is – I am a disaster area.'

He was all smiles as he said this; a certain bad-boy cheerfulness as he acknowledged his imprudence, his need to mess up. I knew this smile: my father was all charm and wit and an inability to get the bills paid. He was a so-called entrepreneur; a corporate guy who could never hold down a job, who always had a get-rich-quick scheme on the go, who made me and my mother move five times during my adolescence in his search for the next executive position, the next business scheme that was going to finally get us 'on easy street' (an expression he used so often). But that reversal of fortune, that manna-from-heaven moment, never materialised. My mother found ongoing work as a geriatric nurse everywhere we went, infirmity and ageing being two of life's great constants. She kept threatening to leave my father whenever he had another setback, another financial loss that propelled us to yet another city, another rented house, a new school for me, a sense of ongoing uncertainty counterbalanced by the fact that my dad loved me and I just adored him. He was the sort of guy who, when he had money in his pocket, would indulge me and Mom relentlessly. God knows I preferred my father's absurd sunny outlook on life to my mother's bleaker perspective, even though I knew that hers

6

had a certain credibility. When my father died of a sudden heart attack the first week I started at the University of Minnesota I was beyond crushed. Phoning me with the news, she masked her distress with steely coolness. Telling me:

'There was a will. You'll get his Rolex – the one thing he never hocked, along with his wedding ring. But don't cry for him. No one – not you, not me – could have saved your father from himself.'

But cry I did, long into that night and many thereafter. After my father's death, my mother and I began to detach from each other. Though she was the parent who got the bills paid and somehow kept the roof (or series of roofs) over our heads, I never felt much in the way of love from her. I still spent part of most major holidays with her and dutifully called her once a week. I remained the responsible daughter. And embraced, in my own way, her rigorous standards when it came to financial caution and saving for a rainy day. But when, just a few years ago, I got together with Paul – and finally brought him to meet her – my mother afterwards was bluntness itself:

'So you're finally marrying your father.'

'That's not fair,' I said, my head reeling from the slap-across-the-face nature of her comment.

'The truth is never fair. If that makes you think that I am being, as usual, merciless, so be it. Don't get me wrong – it's not that I don't find Paul charming. He's charm itself. For a man eighteen years your senior he's not in bad shape, even if he dresses like Woodstock was last week. Still, he does have a certain charm. And I know how lonely things have been for you since Donald walked out.'

Donald was my first husband – and it was me who ended our three-year marriage, as she well knew.

'I left Donald,' I heard myself telling my mother.

'Because he gave you no choice but to leave him. And it destroyed you. And now you are with a man much older and as irresponsible as your father and—'

'Paul isn't as irresponsible as you think.'

'Time will tell.'

Mom. She died a year ago; a stroke from out of nowhere that killed her at the age of seventy-one.

Turbulence in the cabin. I peered out the window. The plane was trying to break cloud cover, and rocking with its downward shift towards land. The man in the aisle seat shut his eyes tightly as the plane did a dangerous lurch.

'Do you think the pilot knows what he's doing?' Paul whispered to me.

'I'm sure he has a wife and children he'd like to see.'

'Or not.'

For the next five minutes the aircraft was like a prize-fighter having a bad night, as it took ongoing body blows from the storm enveloping us. The children's cries hit new levels of discord. Several of the masked women began to keen. Our neighbour's eyes remained tightly shut, his lips now moving in what seemed to be silent prayer.

'Imagine if it was all to end right now,' Paul said. 'What would you think?'

'If you're dead you're not thinking.'

'But say this was the moment before death hit. What would your last thought be?'

'Is this line of questioning supposed to distract me from the fact that the plane might crash?' I asked.

Paul laughed; a laugh instantly silenced as the plane seemed to go into momentary free fall. I gripped the armrests so tightly my knuckles felt as though they just might perforate the skin. I kept my eyes slammed shut until, out of nowhere, order and calm descended on the world. We had hit calm air. Moments later, the runway was beneath us.

I opened my eyes. Paul's fingers remained gripped around the armrests, his face now the colour of chalk. We reached for each other's hands. Then my husband spoke.

'I wonder – is this all a mistake?'

Three

THE IMMIGRATION HALL at Casablanca. Controlled chaos. Hundreds of new arrivals being corralled into two different lines: one for non-Moroccans, another for the rest of humanity. Every historical epoch – from the Middle Ages to our current hyperconnected, cyber-world reality – seemed to be represented. There were sharply suited businessmen and women everywhere, at least half of whom, with their Italian tailoring and their black iPhones, were from North Africa. There were backpacker types, all grungy and twenty-something, looking spaced and eyeing the suits with zonked amusement. Just in front of me was a gaunt man in a dusty brown suit, his teeth blackened by cigarettes, holding a travel document from Mauritania in his right hand.

'What's the capital of Mauritania?' I asked Paul.

Without a pause he replied:

'Nouakchott.'

'The things you know,' I said.

'This line is insane. When I last came thirty-three years ago, there were no computer checks – the world wasn't as paranoid as it is now.'

'Zen, zen, zen,' I said, stroking my husband's face.

'This is Casablanca airport, not some fucking Buddhist retreat.'

I laughed. But he stood there, bouncing from foot to foot, an ongoing fugue of impatience and anxiety.

'Let's go home,' he suddenly said.

'You don't mean that.'

'I do.'

Silence. I felt myself tense.

'How will we go home?' I asked.

'Get the next plane.'

'You're not serious.'

'I think I am. This is all wrong.'

'Because of the long line?'

9

'Because my instinct tells me – go home.'

'Even though it was your "instinct" that told you we had to come here?'

'So you're angry at me.'

'If you want to go home, we'll go home.'

'You'd think me a loser if I did that.'

'I never think you a loser, my love.'

'But I know I am a liability.'

Liabilities. That was the word which ricocheted around my head when I discovered, several weeks ago, the extent of his debts, despite his having promised me, months earlier, that he would curb his spending habits. There was a knock on our door one Friday evening around six. A man from a collection agency was standing on our front porch, asking to speak with Paul Leuen. I explained that my husband was at the gym. 'Ah, so you are Mrs Leuen? Then you might be aware of the sixty-four hundred dollars that your husband owes to the Vintners Wine Society.' I was speechless. When had he bought all that wine, and why hadn't I seen it anywhere in our house? The collection agent was explaining that the Wine Society had sent close to ten letters demanding 'a conversation' about the unpaid sum which had accrued over two years. Now they had run out of patience. If the bill wasn't settled forthwith, legal action would follow, and could involve a lien on our home.

Instead of going inside and getting my cheque book (as I had done on several previous occasions) I simply said:

'My husband is at the Gold's Gym on Manor Street, about five minutes from here by car. Ask for him at the reception desk – they know him. And—'

'But you could settle this matter straight away.'

'I could, but I won't. You need to speak directly with my husband.'

Repeating the address of the gym I excused myself and closed the door. As soon as the collector had driven off I went into our bedroom, packed a small weekend bag, and called my old college roommate, Ruth Richardson, in Brooklyn and asked if I could use her fold-out sofa for a few days. Then leaving Paul a note

– The wine debt must be paid off by the time I am back late Tuesday night – I got into my car and drove the seven hours south-east to the city I had always promised myself I would one day call my own. I kept my cellphone off and spent the next four days trying not to bore Ruth with the cocktail of anger, guilt and sadness that was coursing through me. Ruth – a professor of English at Brooklyn College, divorced, no kids, disappointed in love, wickedly funny and hyper-cultural ('High art is God's apology for men,' she's often noted) – was, as always, a great friend. She steadied my resolve when I suggested that perhaps I should check in on Paul, see how he was bearing up.

'When he landed himself in debt last time,' she said, 'what did you do?'

'I dug into my retirement fund and found the ten grand to get him out of trouble.'

'What did he promise you in return?'

'You know very well. He admitted that he's got a sad pathological compulsion when it comes to spending, spending, spending . . . and he promised to curtail it.'

'A compulsion that is eating away at your marriage. It's all so sad. Especially as I rather like Paul.'

'And I do love him madly, despite this one very bad habit. He still makes me laugh. He is so bright and engaged and intellectually curious. He still thinks me hot – or, at least, that's what he says all the time.'

'Still trying for a child?'

'Of course.'

When I met Paul three years earlier, I was thirty-seven. Within six months of declaring our love for each other, and talking about the wondrous possibilities of a shared future together, I delicately raised the fact that I did not want to pass through life without becoming a mother; that I was entering the now-or-never phase. I knew that I was bringing a certain degree of 'beat the clock' pressure to our relationship, and said I would perfectly understand if Paul felt this was all too much too fast. His response astounded me:

'When you have met the love of your life, of course you want to have a child with her.'

Yes, Paul was a great romantic. Such a romantic that he proposed marriage shortly thereafter, even though I told him that, having been there once before, I wasn't pushed about a return visit. But I was so swept up in the wonder of finding love at my age, and with such a talented and original man, and in Buffalo, that I said yes. He did say that though he realised the clock was ticking we needed some time together before becoming parents. I agreed to his request, staying on the pill until last autumn. At which point we seriously began to 'try' (what a curious verb) for a baby. We went about the task very robustly – though sex was, from the outset, one of the aspects of our marriage that always worked. It wasn't as if we were having to motivate ourselves into making love every night of the week.

'You know, if I don't get pregnant naturally there are other options,' I said six months later when nothing had happened.

'You'll get pregnant.'

'You sound very certain about that.'

'It's going to happen.'

That conversation took place ten days before the debt collector arrived on our doorstep. As I headed south in my car towards Brooklyn, my cellphone off, my piercing sadness about Paul was underscored by the realisation that he was my last chance at having a baby. And that thought . . .

Ruth splashed a little more wine into my glass and I took a long sip.

'He's not your last chance,' she said.

'I want a baby with Paul.'

'That's a definitive statement.'

Friendship is always a complex equation – especially a friendship where it had been agreed early on that we would never sugar-coat things; that we would speak what we felt to be the truth.

'I don't want to be a single mother,' I said. 'If I can get him to just accept that he has certain obligations . . .'

'Paul had problems with money before you. Even though you've tried to organise his personal finances, he refuses to play smart. At the age of fifty-eight, he is not going to have some sort of epiphany and transform himself. He is what he is. Which therefore begs the question – can you weather his ongoing recklessness?'

All the way home that question nagged at me. Life, they say, is a great teacher. But only if we are truly willing to shake off our illusions and self-deceptions.

Love, however, always muddies clarity of vision. And a life without love is a bit like the balance sheets I gaze over every working day: far too concrete, too reasoned. My love for Paul was as bound up in his recklessness as in his talent, his intelligence, his ardour for me.

I got home just after six p.m. to the nineteenth-century Gothic place we'd bought together. His car was parked out front. When I entered the house I was startled to find that order had descended upon chaos. In recent weeks Paul had started treating our home as a happy dumping ground. However, in the days I had been out of contact, not only had he divested the house of his mess, but all the windows glistened, all the wood surfaces were free of dust and had been polished. There were fresh flowers in several vases and I could smell something pasta-esque in the oven.

As the door slammed behind me, Paul emerged from the kitchen, looking just a little sheepish. He couldn't make direct eye contact with me. But when he did once look up in my direction I could see his sadness and fear.

'Smells good,' I said.

'I made it for you, for us.' Again he avoided my gaze. 'Welcome home.'

'Yes, I came back. But—'

He held up his hand.

'I sold all the wine.'

'I see.'

'I found a guy here in town. Big-deal collector. Offered me six thousand dollars for my cellar.'

'You have a cellar?'

He nodded, looking like a little boy who had just been caught out in a very big lie.

'Where?' I asked.

'You know that shed behind the garage? The one we never use?'

The shed was something akin to a bomb shelter, with two folding steel doors that lay flat to the ground. When we were negotiating to buy the house we naturally had it opened for us, and found a damp semi-lined cave. As the house already had a renovated basement we simply put a lock on the two doors after we bought the place and left it empty.

At least, that's what I thought.

'How long have you been building up this wine collection?' I tried to sound reasonable.

'A while.'

He came over and took me in his arms.

'I'm sorry,' he said.

'I don't want apologies. I just don't want another repetition of all this financial mess.'

'And I don't want to lose you.'

'Then don't. Because I do want you, *us.*'

To Paul's credit he became industrious again after the wine incident, spending all free non-teaching hours on a new series of lithographs. It was the first time that he had settled down to serious creative work since our marriage. Though his gallery owner in New York was enthusiastic, the general downturn in the market and Paul's lack of visibility in recent times meant that the sort of prices he could demand had shrunk decisively. Still, he did manage to find a buyer. Though Paul was disappointed with the negotiated price, part of him was clearly thrilled with the fact that he still 'had the chops', as he put it, when it came to his art. After paying off most of his credit-card debts he then took me out to dinner at a most upscale (for Buffalo) French restaurant where he ordered a far too expensive bottle of wine and told me the gallery owner had another client interested in a new series.

'The buyer is willing to plonk down fifty per cent up front – so

14

that should be another ten grand to me in a couple of weeks. What's a bottle of Paulliac compared to that?'

I'm not that into wine. Still . . . why not celebrate? Especially as Paul was making good on paying off his debts. When we got home that night, he lit candles in our bedroom, put on a CD of Miles Davis playing 'Someday My Prince Will Come', and made love to me with the ferocity and sensuality that only he could.

My first husband, Donald, had always had issues about intimacy. He was a super-bright, endlessly anxious man; an old-school journalistic muckraker on the *Buffalo Sun* who covered local politics and was widely considered to be one of the great specialists on municipal corruption in the state. Just out of college, having done a stint on a paper in Madison, Wisconsin, after getting my BA from Minnesota, I was delighted to have landed the job on the City Desk of the *Sun*. Donald was completely committed to Buffalo. I was so smitten by this five-foot-six-inch whirlwind that I too became committed to Buffalo. But the sex – when it happened – was, at best, perfunctory; at worst, it flat-lined.

'Not good at this, never been good at this,' he whispered the first night we slept together and he had what could be politely described as 'performance-related issues'. I reassured him that this happened to all men from time to time, that it was no big deal, that things would come right. The truth is . . . even when he was able to complete the act it was never satisfying. He was endlessly anxious, caught up in his fears about appearing inadequate and inferior, and no amount of reassurance could assuage such ingrained self-doubts. But I chose to overlook the fact that our bed became a sort of cross upon which Donald crucified himself. By the end of our first year of marriage, our lovemaking (if you could call it that) had dwindled to twice a month. I suggested that Donald seek counselling. He agreed and then refused to go. Though he remained brilliantly engaging company, that crucial part of our married life went into permanent decline.

But I continued to reason that, given even more love and support, all those intimacy issues would vanish and our marriage would steady and . . .

It is extraordinary, isn't it, the way we convince ourselves all will be well in a relationship that we privately know to be doomed.

The end of my marriage to Donald came the evening he showed up late from the newsroom, with eight whiskies too many in him, and informed me:

'The fact is, even if I did get counselling or go to my doctor and let him prescribe me something, all the little blue pills in the world wouldn't stop the repulsion I feel every time you come close to me.'

I snapped my eyes shut, trying to tell myself that he had not said what he had just said. But when my eyes opened the look on Donald's face was a strange little half-smile. The sight of him, quietly enjoying the hurt and confusion now ricocheting within me, led me to the following uncomfortable truth: he said that because he knew, once it was uttered, we would have passed the point of no return.

'Now you can really hate me,' he finally whispered.

'I just pity you, Donald.'

I asked for a meeting with our newspaper's editor-in-chief the next morning. I told him that, if the paper was still offering the voluntary redundancy packages mentioned some months earlier during a wave of cutbacks, I would be willing to accept one.

Ten days later – with one year's salary in the bank – I got into my car and drove north to Montreal. I had decided to learn French and live in a city that hovered somewhere between a European and New World sensibility. It was also cheap. I found a small apartment in the decidedly francophone confines of the Plateau, and went to daily French lessons at the Université de Montréal where I worked hard at mastering that challenging and intricate language. My proficiency improved considerably when I started having an affair with a man named Thierry, who ran a used record store on the rue Saint Denis and was intermittently trying to write the great *québécois* novel. His charms and reasonable sexual confidence – especially after Donald – were subsumed by unapologetic laziness.

After a year I was able to renew my student visa. As my prowess in French grew, I began to hatch plans about perhaps moving to Paris and working out some way of landing a *carte de séjour* and reinventing myself professionally as . . .

This was the dilemma. What was I going to do next in my life? I set up an appointment at the French consulate in Montreal and found myself facing a very *petite fonctionnaire* who discouraged me from even thinking about finding work in Paris without a European passport or a French husband. My Canadian student visa allowed me to take on work for the length of my sojourn there at the university. I found a temporary post as an administrative assistant in a firm of bilingual accountants – and started finding myself fascinated by the world of numbers. I knew that, by retraining as a certified public accountant, I was again landing myself in the world of other people's narratives that I had said I would dodge when I left journalism. Nonetheless, after eighteen months in Quebec, I decided to cross over the American frontier again and enter a CPA course in Buffalo. I knew why I was running back there. Buffalo was safe. It was the only place to date in my life where I had put down roots. No longer being at the newspaper meant that my chances of running into Donald were nominal. I still felt a deep lingering sadness about the end of the marriage, coupled with the thought that I should have been able to change him. Just as my need to do something practical or serious with my life was also a larger reflection of all the residual things I felt about Dad. In Buffalo I had some good friends and many contacts – so there was also the prospect of being able to set up my own small accountancy firm and have enough people to reach out to as potential clients.

Just to prove that I was a responsible young woman I found a job with a local CPA while doing the two-year accountancy course. This allowed me to take what was left from the redundancy money and put down a 50 per cent payment on a nice apartment in an old Victorian-style house (Buffalo is so cheap), and even renovate the kitchen and bathroom while furnishing it with funky second-hand items. When the time came – and I was indeed an officially certified public accountant – I had seven clients who joined me on the day I first opened my office.

Then, two years later, Paul walked in.

'I wonder – is this all a mistake?'

His words as we landed in Morocco. A journey that was his idea, his surprise which he sprang on me just two weeks after he had cleared a significant portion of his debts and had sworn off compulsive spending. I'd just come home from my bi-weekly yoga class to find Paul at work in the kitchen, the aromatic aromas of North Africa wafting everywhere. Approaching him at the stove I gave him a kiss and said:

'Let me guess – a tagine?'

'Your powers of observation are formidable.'

'Not as formidable as your culinary skills.'

'Your self-doubt is touching, but not founded in fact.'

As always Paul's lamb tagine was splendid. He made it with preserved lemons and prunes; a recipe he'd learned during the very formative two years he'd spent in Morocco in his mid-twenties.

That was back in the early 1980s – when, having graduated from Parsons School of Design in New York and having tried to make a go of it as an artist in the then still demi-monde world of Alphabet City in the extreme East Village, he decided that a radical change of scene was required. Through the careers office at Parsons he learned that an art school in Casablanca was looking for an instructor in drawing: $3,000 a year for a two-year contract, plus a little apartment near the school.

'They told me it was probably the best art school in Morocco – "though that's not saying much". Still, it would give me the chance to live somewhere exotic, escape the workaday world, travel, and get a considerable amount of my own work done under that white-hot North African sun.'

So Paul quit his job, took the cramped overnight flight to Casablanca – and hated everything about the place on sight. In no way resembling the fabled, mythic city of the movie, it was sprawling, concrete, ugly. The art school turned out to be second-rate, the staff demoralised, the students largely untalented.

'I had very few friends at the beginning – outside of a Franco-Moroccan artist named Romain Ben Hassan who was a rather talented abstract expressionist for such a budding alcoholic. But it was Romain who got me a French teacher and forced me to speak with him in the language of everyone around me. And it was Romain who also got me to stop feeling sorry for myself, and let me into his social circle of local and expatriate artists. He also forced me to get on with my own work.'

Paul had found a life for himself. He had a circle of fellow artists – Moroccan and expatriate – with whom he hung out. He had one or two students whom he thought promising. Most of all he worked rigorously on an amazing portfolio of lithographs and line drawings that chronicled his quarter of Casablanca. Though the art school wanted him to stay on he used this portfolio – which he called 'The White City' – to get himself a gallery in New York.

While on a three-week break between art school terms he headed south to a walled seaside city called Essaouira: 'Like going back to the Middle Ages and landing yourself in the ultimate artist's colony.' Essaouira was always one of Paul's conversation pieces. How he found a room in a fantastically cheap and 'atmospherically seedy' hotel, with a great balcony from which he could see the sweep of the Atlantic and the medieval walls of this strange, alluring city where 'Orson Welles shot his film version of *Othello*' and 'Jimi Hendrix smoked far too much dope while chilling out on the Moroccan Atlantic vibe'. Paul spent his weeks there working on a second collection of line drawings – 'In the Labyrinth' – depicting the spindly alleyways of Essaouira. His art dealer/gallery owner in Manhattan, Jasper Pirnie, managed to sell thirty of his lithographs.

'The money I made from the lithographs could have paid for me to stay another two years in Essaouira, it was so cheap back then. But what did I do? The State University of New York in Buffalo had a position open in their Visual Art Department. The fact that I knew the chairman of the department, who actually rated me . . . well, there it was – an assistant professorship with the possibility of tenure in six years if I kept getting my lithographs and drawings exhibited. But even as I packed my bags in Essaouira, after sending a telegram back to the department head that I was accepting the job and telling the Casablanca art school that I wouldn't be returning to teach there, I knew this was a decision I would come to regret.'

I remember distinctly this was the moment when I covered his hand with my own; the first time either of us had made an intimate gesture towards each other. Strange, isn't it, how I reached out to comfort this man after he admitted to me that he had fenced himself in. Perhaps because I too felt fenced in, and because he was someone with a creative, bohemian streak who would pull me away from my innate cautiousness, my need to make lists in my sleep and keep the books balanced. He leaned over and kissed me as I covered his hand, then threaded his fingers into mine and said: 'You are wonderful.' That was the first night we slept together. After my sad time with Donald, it was both revelatory and heady to be with a man who was so sexually confident, so adept at giving me pleasure.

He made me a lamb tagine the second night we slept together. And he made me a lamb tagine just six weeks ago, to celebrate him paying off his debts. That night he also dropped a little surprise into my life.

'What would you say to spending a month this summer in Essaouira?' he asked.

My initial thought was that we'd already put $500 down on a cottage near Popham Beach in Maine. Reading my mind Paul said:

'We can still do the two weeks in Popham. I've booked us to leave Morocco a few days before we're due in Maine.'

'You've actually bought us two tickets for Morocco?'

'I wanted to surprise you.'

'Oh, you certainly did that. But you could have at least asked me if I was free.'

'If I had asked, you would have found an excuse to say no.'

He was, alas, right about that one.

20

'Did you even consider the fact that I have a business, and clients? And how are we going to afford this trip to Morocco?'

'Jasper sold four more lithographs last week.'

'You never told me this.'

'The nature of a surprise is to keep things secret.'

I was already intrigued. Outside of my time in Montreal and a trip once to Vancouver (hardly a real overseas destination), I had no experience of the world beyond American frontiers. Here was my husband offering to whisk me off to North Africa. But my alleged financial caution was, I knew, underscored by fear. The fear of foreignness. Of being dropped into a Muslim country that – for all of Paul's talk about its modernity – was, according to anything I'd ever read, still locked in the North African past.

'We can easily live for a month in Essaouira for two thousand dollars,' he said.

'It's too long to take off.'

'Promise your staff a nice bonus if they hold the fort for six weeks.'

'And what are my clients going to say about this?'

'Who consults an accountant between mid-July and Labor Day?'

He did have a point. It was my slowest season. But six weeks away? It seemed like such a huge block of time . . . even though I also knew that, in the great scheme of things, it was nothing, and that, yes, Morton (my bookkeeper) and Kathy (my secretary) could manage to run everything very well without me. One of the hardest lessons for anyone with control-freak tendencies to absorb is that the world actually carries on very well without them.

'I'm going to have to think this over.'

'No,' Paul said, taking my hand. 'You're going to say yes now. Because you know this will be an amazing experience which will take you out of your comfort zone and show you a world you've only imagined. And it will give me the opportunity to work on a new portfolio which Jasper assured me he can sell for at least fifteen thousand dollars. So there's a big financial incentive. Most of all, it will be very good for us. We could truly use some time out of here, time to ourselves, and away from all that day-to-day stuff.'

Morocco. My husband was taking us to Morocco. To Essaouira. How could I not overlook my qualms and give in to the idea of a North African idyll in a walled medieval city facing the Atlantic? The stuff of fantasy. And aren't all fantasies rooted in one great hope: that of landing, even temporarily, in a better place than we find ourselves now?

So I said yes.

The immigration line inched forward, slowly, inexorably. Almost an hour had passed since we'd landed and only now were we at the front. The man from Mauritania was being rigorously questioned by the cop in the booth, the discussion getting heated, voices raised; the policeman picked up his phone to call someone, two other plain-clothes officers (guns bulging under their suit jackets) showed up and led the now angry and frightened man into a side interrogation room. Glancing away from this little drama towards my husband I could see that he was regarding these proceedings with dread.

'You think they'll let me in?' he whispered.

'Why wouldn't they?'

'No reason, no reason.' But he sounded uneasy. At that precise moment the cop in the booth called us forward, his hand out for our passports and landing cards. As he scanned them and peered at the computer screen I could see Paul working hard at masking his distress. I reached over and took his hand, squeezing it, willing him to calm down.

'You stay how long?' the officer asked in choppy, cadenced English.

'*Quatre semaines*,' Paul said.

'You work here?'

'No way. We're on vacation.'

Another glance at the screen. Then a thorough inspection of all the pages of our passports, during which I could feel Paul tense even tighter. Then: stamp, stamp . . . and the cop pushed the passports back to us.

'*Bienvenu*,' he said.

And we stepped forward into Morocco.

'See, they let you in,' I said, all smiles. 'Why so nervous?'

'Stupidity, stupidity.'

But as we moved towards the baggage carousels I caught him whispering to himself:

'Idiot.'

Four

JULY IN NORTH AFRICA. Heat and dust and gasoline fumes enveloping the parched air. That was the first aroma which hit my nostrils as we left the airport terminal: petroleum intermixed with arid, motionless oxygen. Up in the sky the morning sun was at full wattage. It didn't matter that Casablanca was on the Atlantic coast. The first sensation on leaving the somewhat cooler confines of the arrival hall was: welcome to the blast furnace.

'We would have to arrive in hell,' Paul said as we waited at the packed bus stop for the coach into the city centre.

'Well, you did once live here in July, right?' I said.

'It will be cooler in Essaouira.'

'And we'll be there in just a few days. No doubt the hotel in Casablanca has air conditioning.'

'Don't be so sure of that. This is North Africa. Discomfort at the cheap end of the spectrum is part of the deal.'

'Then we can find a hotel with AC.'

'Or we can change our plans now.'

'What?'

'Back in a moment.'

With that he disappeared off into the crowd. I wanted to follow him but our four sizeable pieces of luggage were there in front of me. They had clothes for many weeks and all of Paul's art supplies as well as the collection of twelve books I had envisaged myself reading while facing the waters of the Atlantic. Were I to leave the suitcases and pursue my husband I would be inviting theft and disaster at the start of what was already shaping up to be a rather dubious adventure. So all I could do was shout Paul's name. My voice was drowned out by everyone crowded around the bus stop: veiled women, men of varied ages in ill-fitting suits, one or two backpackers, two grandfatherly types in long flowing robes, and three very dark-skinned Africans carrying their worldly goods in cheap canvas bags – making me wonder if they were here looking for work and, judging from the bewilderment sketched on their faces, as adrift here as myself.

Buses, most of them ancient, came and went, belching clouds of exhaust as they heaved away towards assorted destinations. I peered into the distance, but could see no sign of my husband. Ten, fifteen minutes passed. *God, maybe he really has decided to do an about-face. He's probably back inside the terminal building, using a credit card to send us home to the States.*

But then, amidst the crowded theatre of this street scene, a tall man emerged. Paul. He was walking towards me, accompanied by a diminutive fellow who was half-shaven with a small knitted skullcap on his head, a cigarette clenched between blackened teeth. He carried a battered tin tray on which sat two stubby glasses, while his other hand clutched a pot of tea. The man smiled shyly. Placing the tray on the empty space next to me on the pockmarked bench he raised the teapot a good foot above the glasses and began ceremoniously to pour a green liquid into them. The heady, aromatic properties of the tea were immediately discernible.

'*Thé à la menthe,*' Paul said. '*Le whisky marocain.*'

Mint tea. Moroccan whisky. The man smiled, offering me the tray with the two glasses. I lifted one of them. Paul took his and clinked it against mine.

'Sorry to have disappeared like that,' he said.

He leaned forward and placed a kiss on my lips. I accepted it, as I did his hand which he entwined with my free one. Then I took my first sip of *le whisky marocain.* The mint was palatably strong, but undercut by a certain sugary sweetness. I usually dislike anything overly sweet but this tea worked because of its aromatic strength and its honeyed undercurrent. After that horrendous flight and the wait in the sun, it was balming.

'You approve?' Paul asked.

'I approve.'

'Our friend here loaned me his cellphone. There's a change of plan.'

'What sort of change?'

'We're going straight to Essaouira. There's a bus that leaves here in twenty minutes.'

'What about Casablanca?'

'Trust me, you're not missing much.'

'It's still Casablanca, a place you've talked endlessly about from the moment we first got together.'

'It can wait.'

'But Essaouira is . . . what . . . four, five hours from here?'

'Something like that, yeah. I checked just now – the Casablanca hotel doesn't have air con. Nor will they let us check-in until three p.m., which would mean sitting in a café for almost five hours. Why not take that time getting to Essaouira? And the guy who was selling the bus tickets told me the coach we're taking is air conditioned.'

'So it's a fait accompli that we're going to Essaouira? You decided for us?'

'He told me the bus was getting full. Please don't take this badly.'

'I'm taking nothing badly. I'm just . . .'

I turned away, feeling beyond tired after the sit-up-all-night stint across the Atlantic, the heat and the oppressive, toxic air. A further sip of mint tea did wonders for a throat gone parched again.

'Fine, fine,' I said. 'Essaouira it is.'

Twenty minutes later we were aboard a bus heading south. It was absolutely packed, but Paul slipped the guy taking tickets a 10-dirham note to find us two seats right at the back. It was not air conditioned.

'*Ça se déclenchera une fois que le bus aura démarré,*' said the guy when Paul asked – in his rather good French – if the stifling heat inside would be alleviated by cooling air. *It's going to start after it leaves.* But when we pulled out there was no arctic blast from the vents. The bus wasn't very old, but it wasn't very new either. And it was crammed with people and goods. Two women in full burqas sat opposite us with a young girl whose hands were elaborately painted with signs and symbols. Nearby was a wire-thin man well into his seventies, his eyes baffled by dark glasses, rocking back and forth in his cramped seat as he prayed semi-silently, clearly bound up in the intensity of his beseeches to a power higher than this sweat-box. Next to him was a young guy – sallow, peach-fuzz beard, don't-mess-with-me eyes – listening to some pop Arab number on an overlarge set of headphones that leaked sound. He sang along with the lyrics, his loud, off-key drone accompanying us all the way south.

The seats were tightly packed, allowing for little legroom, but we were on the long-benched back seat so Paul could angle himself in such a way as to stretch out. I slid in next to him. He put his arms around me and said:

'So I got it wrong about the air con.'

'We'll survive,' I said, though after ten minutes on the road my clothes were drenched.

'We always survive,' he said, tightening his arms around me and kissing my head. The young guy caught a glimpse of this moment of marital affection and rolled his eyes while simultaneously singing that same toneless lyric over and over again. I peered out the window. North African-style urban sprawl. Chipped white apartment blocks. Chipped white stretches of congested houses. Car dealerships. Warehouses. Congealed traffic. Chipped white strip malls. Chipped white villages. And then . . .

Sleep.

Or an approximation thereof.

I passed out.

Then there was a jolt. The bus must have hit a pothole or something. We were in open country, stony, empty, bleak. Low-lying hills on the horizon. The world vanished again, then woke up when . . .

A baby was screaming. The mother – young, in a multi-coloured headscarf – was sitting in front of us, looking sleep deprived and fearful. She kept trying to calm the child who couldn't have been more than three weeks old. And he was, with good reason, miserable. What little oxygen there was in the bus had been sucked away by the malodour of communal sweat, the reek of exhaust fumes; the heat so curdled it actually felt tactile, weighty and doughy like four-day-old bread.

Repositioning myself between Paul's legs I suddenly had a huge stab of desire – not just for the abandonment of lovemaking with my husband, but also an overwhelming need to have a baby. There had, of course, been women in Paul's past. One was a colleague at the university, with whom he'd lived for around two years. He talked little about her, except to say that it hadn't ended well. Otherwise he made it known that he didn't want to talk much about his romantic history. He did tell me one crucial detail: I was the first woman with whom he could imagine having a child.

As the bus hit another bump my husband jumped awake, finding my hand on his crotch.

'You trying to tell me something?' he asked.

'Maybe I am,' I said, leaning up to kiss him on the lips.

'Where are we?'

'No idea.'

'How long have we been on the bus?'

'Too long.'

'And still without AC.'

'It's not your fault.'

He reached over and touched my face.

'How did I get so lucky?' he asked.

'We're both lucky.'

'Do you really mean that?'

'Yes. I do.'

'Even though I've driven you mad sometimes.'

'Paul . . . I love you. I want this marriage to work.'

'If we can get through this fucking bus trip together we can get through anything.'

I laughed – and gave him such a full and deep kiss that, when the bus hit another bump and disengaged me from my husband's lips, I saw that everyone around us was either embarrassed or disapproving.

'Sorry, sorry,' I whispered to the elderly man sitting just in front of us. He turned away, showing me his back. Paul whispered to me:

'They'll be a little more open in Essaouira. They're far more used to hippy-dippy foreigners.'

'We're hardly hippy-dippy.'

'Correction – you are hardly hippy-dippy.'

I found myself laughing again and causing more disapproving glances by kissing my husband once more. A moment like this – when everything seemed so right between us – was so pleasing, wondrous, reassuring. Paul was right: if we could get through this bus ride we could get through anything.

Around ten minutes later the bus pulled into a tiny concrete depot off the side of the road. The landscape here was rocky, scrubby, flat and uninspiring.

'You think there's a toilet here?' I asked Paul.

'No idea – but that line over there looks huge.'

He nodded towards around a dozen women, all but three hidden by burqas, lining up in front of a single hut.

'Maybe I should just try and hold it.'

'But there's at least another hour and a half to go. We should try to slip around the back of the depot.'

Which is exactly what we did – finding a patch of ground festooned with trash, broken bottles, two burnt-out fires, even a dead mouse charred by the sun.

'You expect me to pee here?' I asked Paul.

'There is the toilet option.'

The stench enveloping us was nothing short of toxic: an aroma of faecal matter and festering rubbish. But I was desperate to empty my bladder. So finding a patch of ground that was free of glass shards and trash, I undid my loose-fitting cargo pants, squatted down and let go. Paul, meanwhile, was standing some feet away, peeing against a wall, laughing.

'Gracious living, eh?' he said.

The driver began to beep his horn. We had to get back on the bus. But as we came aboard we discovered that two young toughs – they must have been around twenty years old, both scowling and menacing, both wearing nylon bomber jackets and black plastic sunglasses – had taken our seats. They saw us heading towards them as we negotiated the tiny aisle, sidestepping all the bags and two very parched dogs (German shepherds, rendered inert by the heat). When we reached the back, Paul informed them in French that they were sitting in our place. Their response was to ignore us. I glanced around. Every other seat on the bus was taken. Paul quietly asked them to move. Their response again was to act as if we didn't exist.

'*Vous êtes assis à nos places*,' Paul reiterated, his tone getting edgier. '*Vous devriez en chercher d'autres.*'

Again, nothing.

'*S'il vous plaît*,' Paul added.

The two guys exchanged a cool, amused glance and continued to say nothing.

At this point the other young guy, who'd been singing along to his iPod, turned around and said something in Arabic to the two toughs. One of them shot back a short verbal response – which, from its menacing vehemence, was clearly a warning to stay out of this. The young guy remained cool in the wake of this exchange. He just quietly shook his head, then popped his earphones back on his head.

Meanwhile the elderly man suddenly erupted in an angry flow of Arabic. So angry that all eyes in the bus were on us: the two foreigners standing in the aisle. The same guy who had hissed at our friend with the headphones now said something to the elderly man that was so unpleasant that several people nearby – including a large woman, her face completely baffled by a burqa – began to shout back at the pair. Again they sat there silently, refusing to budge, refusing to listen to reason, determined to play out this scenario to some sort of unpleasant conclusion.

'I'm getting the driver,' Paul said to me.

But the driver – a harassed, constricted man with sunken eyes and a pencil-thin moustache – was already on his way, looking less than pleased. He walked into a sea of raised voices, as the elderly man, the woman with the burqa and three others began to tell him what had just transpired. The driver asked Paul something in fast French. Paul responded rapidly, indicating that he had politely asked these two boys (they couldn't have been more than seventeen) to vacate the seats which we'd had since Casablanca.

The driver started yelling at them, staring into their menacing black sunglasses. But as before, they refused to respond. The driver's voice now ticked up another angry octave. As he put his face close to them, the more verbal of the pair did something startling: he spat at the driver, catching him directly in one eye.

The driver looked beyond stunned. To his credit he didn't lash out, didn't explode into understandable fury. Rather, with immense quiet dignity, he pulled a handkerchief from his pocket, wiped the spittle from his eye, then hurried away down the aisle, leaving the bus and heading into the depot.

The young dude with the headphones stood up. Gently touching my shoulder, he motioned that I should take his seat.

'*Ce n'est pas necessaire*,' I said, trying out my French.

'*J'insiste*,' he said. The man seated next to him – a quiet businessman-type in his forties, bespectacled, wearing a light blue striped suit – also slid out of his seat.

'*J'insiste*.'

Paul thanked them as he gently directed me towards the window seat, then positioned himself next to me, ensuring that I was out of range of the aisle should anything violent happen.

'You OK?' Paul whispered as I reached for his hand.

'What's this about?'

'Macho bullshit. Showing they can stand up to a Western woman.'

'But I said nothing to them.'

'Doesn't matter. They're idiots. Fortunately everyone else around us thinks that too.'

At that moment two policemen entered the bus, both looking as hot as the rest of us. The driver was right behind them. Seeing us now seated he explained something to the officers in rapid-fire Arabic. One of the officers turned and actually saluted us. The elderly man began to get angry, pointing an accusatory finger at the two toughs, expressing his outrage at what had transpired with the driver. The second officer now picked up the nastier of the pair by his shirt, whipped off the kid's sunglasses and threw them to the floor, stamping on them with his foot. With his eyes exposed

31

the boy's gangster image suddenly vanished. He was just a sallow adolescent. The other officer did likewise with his cohort. Only this time, when the dark glasses were pulled from his face, all I could see was sheer fear.

Within moments they were both being frogmarched down the aisle and out of the bus. As soon as they were clear of the front door, the driver was back in his seat, revving the engine, wanting to put immediate distance between himself and all the events that had just transpired. Paul and I stood up, offering to move back to our previous seats. But the businessman and the young headphone dude insisted we stay put. I glanced out the window and regretted doing so. I saw the tougher of the tough guys trying to break free of the grasp of one of the officers. Immediately the cop had his baton out and slammed it directly in the boy's face. He fell to his knees and the cop responded with a direct blow to the head. The other tough began to cry out, but was slapped across the mouth with an open hand by the officer holding him. The bus picked up speed, shrouding this brutal tableau in a cloud of dust. Behind me the young headphones dude began to sing his toneless song again. I buried my face in Paul's shoulder, feeling profound guilt, as if my presence here had caused all this. Sensing my distress, Paul tightened his arm around me.

'It's all in the past now,' he said.

And the bus sped off into the future.

Five

THE CAT LOOKED as though she was trying to figure out: *What am I doing here?* She was dusty, grubby, world-weary; a cat who lived on the streets and had no human home to which to retreat. And tonight – for reasons only she must have understood – she was hanging off a wall. The way that her claws were dug into the chalky texture of the brickwork meant that she appeared to have been glued into place, her back in perfect parallel with the wall. There was something spectral and unsettling about the way she seemed to be frozen. I was reminded of images I'd once seen of wildlife that had been caught in a volcanic lava flow and had fossilised into place; their final steps as sentient creatures frozen in time. I must have spent a good minute looking at the cat and the place in which she now found herself. How was she able to sustain this absurd, improbable position? And what fear or apprehension had forced her to take refuge on a crumbling bit of whitewashed stone down a dark alleyway within the labyrinthine confines of a walled city?

What was she doing here?

And what was I doing down this black passageway in the middle of the night?

To jump back around fifteen hours . . .

The bus deposited us at its terminus – the depot at Essaouira – in the early afternoon. As we staggered off that motorised steam bath, the headphones dude – still singing that ludicrous tune (was that the only song on his iPod?) – gave us an amused wave goodbye. The bus driver, smoking what was evidently a much-needed cigarette, also nodded farewell as we grabbed our luggage and fended off several touts who were trying to convince us to take up their offer of cheap accommodation.

'You want room . . . very clean . . . good price.'

'*Nous avons déjà une chambre,*' Paul replied, steering me towards a line of beat-up taxis nearby.

'But I have better room . . . you come with me, I show you everything in Essaouira . . .'

Paul waved him away. Just as I had to sidestep several women holding up woven shirts, multi-coloured shawls and cheap beaded necklaces. The afternoon sun was still punishing. This concrete plaza was thick with gas fumes and dust. I grabbed my scrunched-up field hat out of my shoulder bag, then pulled it down so squarely over my head that it shielded my eyes. The crowd of hawkers followed us as we moved towards the taxis. They were relentless in their need to hound us. They wouldn't take no for an answer.

'Just keep walking,' Paul told me. 'They're a nuisance, but harmless.'

The first cab we approached – a cream-coloured Peugeot which appeared to have been in a demolition derby – was driven by a man who looked like he'd last slept in 2010. He had a cellphone to his ear, into which he was shouting. Paul approached him and gave him the name of our hotel.

'Two hundred dirhams,' he said in English, even though Paul addressed him in French.

'But the hotel is maybe ten minutes' walk from here.'

The cabbie put down the phone for a moment, taking in all our luggage.

'That's the price. You don't like it, walk.'

'*Charmant.*'

The cabbie just shrugged. Paul, shaking his head, led us to the car behind this unpleasant fellow. When the first cabbie saw us approaching the next driver he was immediately out of his taxi, shouting. The new cabbie – a rather stubby man with a look of fatigued resignation on his face – ignored the protestations of Mr Charm.

'*Vous allez où?*' he asked Paul.

'*Vous connaissez l'hôtel Les Deux Chameaux?*'

'*Bien sûr. Ça vous coûtera environ trente dirhams.*'

Thirty dirhams. An honest man.

'*D'accord,*' Paul agreed and we loaded our bags into his trunk.

As we drove off we ran into a small flotilla of geese and chickens, herded by a man in a white djellaba and skullcap alongside the city walls. The driver honked his horn in a short nonchalant manner, indicating that the shepherd should get his livestock out of the way. A shepherd guiding barnyard animals by city walls. Nearby was a man wheeling a barrel filled with unrefined cotton. And – now this was hallucinatory – a fellow sitting in front of a basket, intoning a tune on a reedy instrument as a python ascended upwards from the straw hoop.

Paul could see me taking this all in. The taxi followed a route along the walls of Essaouira; walls that looked like fortifications from some medieval bulwark.

'It gets even stranger,' he said, clearly at home amidst all this vivid chaos.

We hugged the road adjacent to the wall for another minute, then turned in through a narrow archway and down a back alley with blue walls and tiny lanes branching off it. At the end of the alley was a latticed doorway, also painted a deep blue. This was the entrance to our hotel. *Les Deux Chameaux.* The Two Camels. Inside, the lobby was dark, shadowy, austere. An elderly man was asleep behind the reception desk. He was dressed for a day out at the races: a flowery shirt, a gold chain with the Moroccan star which heaved up and down with his snores, gold rings on his fingers, heavy dark sunglasses hiding his eyes.

I looked around. Old Moroccan furnishings – all heavy wood. Once-luxuriant brushed velvet upholstery – now dust-ridden and showing serious signs of neglect. There was a loud 1920s railway-station clock hanging next to the reception area: a clock which counted off each passing second with an ominous click. And there was a half-starved cat on top of the reception counter, eyeing us warily: intruders, outsiders, here to disturb the soporific order of things.

As we approached the counter where the old man was asleep, Paul took the initiative, whispering '*Monsieur*', then raising his voice several decibels with each additional rendition of '*Monsieur*'. When this proved pointless I tapped the hotel bell near the open guest register. Its loud clang jolted him back to life, the shock on his face coupled with bemusement, as if he didn't know where he was. As he tried to adjust his gaze Paul said:

'Sorry to have woken you so abruptly. But we did try . . .'

'You have a reservation?'

'Yes.'

'Name?'

Paul gave him this information. The man stood up and, using the index finger on each hand, spun the register around towards him. He peered at today's page, then rifled back through several more, shaking his head, muttering to himself.

'You have no reservation,' he finally said.

'But I made one,' Paul said.

'You received confirmation from us?'

'Of course. I made it on the Internet.'

'You have a copy of the confirmation?'

Paul looked sheepish. 'Forgot to print it,' he whispered to me.

'Surely if you went online,' I said, 'you'd find it.'

'I think I deleted it.'

I stopped myself from saying: 'Not again.' Paul was always clearing out old mail and frequently removed essential correspondences.

'But you still have rooms?' I asked the guy behind the desk.

'Yes and no.'

He now picked up an ancient house phone – of the sort that seemed to belong in some movie set during the German occupation – and started speaking Arabic in a loud, fractious voice. This was something I was beginning to notice: how Arabic was often a language declaimed in a stentorian manner, making it seem aggressive, swaggering, bordering on the hostile. It reminded me that I should really resuscitate my still-reasonable, if rusty, French while here; something I'd been promising myself to do ever since leaving Montreal behind.

The desk clerk finished his conversation. Turning back to us he said:

'My colleague, he gets the owner now.'

We had to wait ten minutes for the arrival of the man in charge. His name was Monsieur Picard. He was French, in his mid-fifties, short, fit, dressed in a crisp white shirt and tan trousers, formal, chilly; his face reflecting, I sensed, a lifetime of enforced diffidence and the dodging of emotion.

'There seems to be a problem?' he asked, his tone borderline supercilious.

'We booked a room, but you don't seem to have a record of it,' Paul said.

'Do you have the confirmation?' Monsieur Picard asked.

Paul shook his head.

'Nor do we. So a reservation mustn't have been made.'

'But I made the reservation . . .' Paul said.

'Clearly not.'

'Well, you do have rooms, yes?' I asked.

'Has not Ahmed here told you that we have just one room free?'

'And how much does that cost?'

'It is a room with a balcony and a sea view. And you will need it for how long?'

'A month,' Paul said. 'That's what we booked it for.'

Monsieur Picard pursed his lips, then turned to Ahmed. He directed him in French to scan the ledger. Ahmed thumbed through its many pages, glancing down, clucking his tongue against the roof of his mouth, seeing if they could house us for all that time. I began to wonder: did Paul actually make the reservation, or was this one of his many 'little oversights' (as he called them) that seemed to decorate our lives? Now I was starting to feel angry with myself for not checking up on the reservation before departure. Another part of me was castigating myself for questioning him; that given the sliminess of the hotel owner and the sleep-walking style of his desk clerk, who's to say they didn't lose the reservation or were playing games to get a better price from us?

This latter scenario began to seem more plausible after the next exchange. Ahmed turned to the owner, nodding his head, saying something that sounded positive. The owner now spoke to us.

'I have good news. We do have that room available for the entire period you desire. The other good news is that it is the best room in the house – a mini-suite with a balcony that faces the Atlantic. The price is seven hundred dirhams per night.'

Paul's face fell. Immediately the adding machine in my brain was whirring away: 700 dirhams was about $80, double the price Paul told me he had negotiated.

'But the room I booked cost three-fifty,' Paul said.

'You have no record of this offer, do you?' Monsieur Picard said. 'As we too have no record of this reservation and are trying to accommodate you . . .'

'I booked a room for a month at three hundred and fifty dirhams,' Paul said, angry, stressed.

'*Monsieur*, if there is no proof, all we have is words. And words—'

'What are you, a fucking philosopher?' Paul hissed.

I put a stabilising hand on my husband's left forearm.

'He didn't mean that,' I told Monsieur Picard. 'We are both exhausted and—'

'I did fucking mean that. This guy is playing with us.'

Monsieur Picard smiled thinly.

'You act as if you are doing me a service by staying here. By all means find another hotel – and one of this quality and cleanliness that can offer you a suite of this size for a month. The door is there. *Bonne chance*.'

He turned and started heading up the stairs.

'Could we see the suite, please?' I shouted after him.

'As you wish.'

I started following him upstairs. Paul lingered by the reception desk, fuming, sullen.

'You coming up?' I asked.

'Looks like you're the one in charge now.'

'Fine.'

I continued up the stairs. As we reached the first landing Monsieur Picard turned to me and said:

'Your husband does not seem to be a happy man.'

'And what business is that of yours?' I asked.

The sharpness of my tone startled him.

'I meant no offence,' he said.

'Yes, you did.'

The upstairs corridors were narrow, but reasonably well painted, with ceramic blue tiles surrounding the door frames. We walked up a set of stairs barely wide enough to accommodate a modest-sized person.

'Splendid isolation,' Picard said as we reached a wooden door carved with lattices. He opened it.

'*Après vous, madame.*'

I walked inside. Picard turned on a light on a side table. My first thought was: *Oh God, this is small.* We were in a narrow sitting area with carved wooden tables, a heavily brocaded red sofa and a small armchair. The entire area couldn't have been more than around ten square feet. Tiny slits of light from the blue wooden shutters caught the dust in the air. Sensing my disappointment, Picard said:

'It gets better.'

He opened a connecting door and we were now in a high-vaulted room, augmented by wooden beams, the centrepiece of which was a king-sized bed with huge round cushions propping up the carved wooden headboard, upholstered in faded red velvet. Everything here was heavy dark wood and maroon: the bedspread, the large desk with a matching carved chair, the large chest of drawers, the sultan-like armchair with a matching footrest. Stone walls. The bathroom was acceptable and clean, with a shower stall enhanced by an intricate painted design. I turned on the knobs and discovered there was reasonable water pressure. When I returned to the bedroom area I was taken aback. Picard had opened all the shutters, allowing light to flood in. This darkened enclave was suddenly awash with crystalline sun. I followed onto the balcony; out into a day that was still white hot, incandescent.

The balcony itself wasn't substantial, perhaps ten feet long by three feet wide, but its prospect was ravishing. Turn right and you peered directly over the walled fortress that was Essaouira. The absolute wild originality of the place – its medieval bunkers, its spindly laneways, its visual and human density – was laid out in front of me with a near-cartographic clarity from this haughty outlook.

Then, when you turned left, the entire spread of the Atlantic enveloped the eye.

Is there anything more balming than the sight of water? Especially this body of water, linking us to home?

There were two folded deck chairs on the balcony and a small table. I quickly envisaged Paul here, his sketchbooks and pencils and charcoals spread out in front of him, engaged with the sky, the sea, the jagged rooftops, the strange scenic concoction laid out directly beneath us. I would be in the next chair, hunched over a French grammar book, fresh from a language lesson I'd had that morning, working my way through the complexities of the subjunctive case.

'Not bad, is it?' Picard said, his voice more diplomatic since I'd tackled him a few minutes earlier.

'It will do.'

I stepped back inside. Never negotiate a price when facing a peerless view. Picard joined me.

'I saw the email that my husband received from you,' I said.

'He never received anything directly from me.'

'From your reservations person then.'

'Madame, we have no record—'

'But I saw it. I know that you agreed a price of three hundred and fifty dirhams for a room with a balcony and a sea view.'

'It was not this suite. And as this suite is the only room we have left—'

'Be smart here.'

'You think I am stupid?' he asked, the tone shifting back into superciliousness.

'I'm beginning to think that I should contact the person running my accounting firm back in the States and get her to find the email and send it over. Then I can find the local tourism authority and report you for price gouging.'

'Now I must ask you to leave.'

'A pity. Not a bad room – and you could have had us here for a month. But your call, sir.'

With that I turned and headed for the door. When I was halfway out he said:

'I can accept six hundred per day.'

Without looking back at him I said: 'Four hundred.'

'Five fifty.'

'Five hundred – breakfast and laundry included.'

'You expect us to wash your clothes every day?'

'Twice a week. We have little in the way of clothes.'

Silence. His thumb was rubbing up against his forefinger, always a surefire sign of anxiety.

'And you will be here for the entire month?' he asked.

'I can show you our return tickets.'

'For this price I will need payment in full in advance.'

Now it was my turn to feel as if the tables had turned a bit. But looking around the suite, the hard radiant blue of that North African sky clarifying everything, I decided that a decision was in order. Throw in breakfast and laundry and the reduction of 200 dirhams per night, and I had saved us $1,000 overall. I also sensed that Picard would be relatively civilised from this moment on.

'All right, sir,' I said. 'You have a deal . . . but I want written confirmation of our agreed price before I hand over my credit card.'

A small, tight pursing of his lips.

'*Très bien, madame.*'

'By the way, you wouldn't know anybody who might want to give me a daily French lesson? I've decided I'd like to improve my fluency in your language.'

'I'm certain I can find someone.'

We filed back downstairs. Picard went behind the desk. On a piece of hotel stationary he scribbled the length of our stay and the 500-dirhams-per-night rate. Signing it he handed it to me. I turned over my Visa card, and watched him process the agreed payment. Business done, we shook hands. Then I found Paul, sitting at a table near the hotel entrance, sipping mint tea, staring out at the alley beyond the picture window.

'Can you please have our bags sent upstairs?' I asked Picard.

'*Très bien, madame.*'

He signalled to the man at the front desk to take up our luggage. Paul was now on his feet, incredulous.

'Don't tell me we're staying,' he said.

'Come see the suite.'

Then I turned and headed back upstairs. After a moment Paul was right behind me. We reached the next floor, then walked down the narrow corridor and up the final set of tiny stairs. When we reached the suite I walked straight through the two rooms and out onto the balcony. Standing outside, the sun full frontal on my face, the blue contours of the rooftops mirroring the bleached azure of the sky, the choppy waters of the Atlantic luminous with reflected light, I wanted to marvel at this exceptional vista. Marvel that I was here on the eastern lip of North Africa, high above a medieval enclave, about to spend a full month immersed in such an alien, but (I could tell already) strangely compelling corner of this planet. What a privilege to escape the humdrum and be here. I owed all this to the man in the other room; a man with whom I so wanted things to go right.

I felt Paul's hands on my shoulders.

'This view is wondrous,' he whispered.

'And the suite?'

'Couldn't be better.'

'So you're staying?'

He spun me around and kissed me deeply. Feeling his body so close to mine, his hands sliding up my T-shirt and caressing my back, his penis thickening against my thigh, I had a strong charge of desire; of wanting to obliterate the fatigue, the anger, the doubt, through the wonder of losing myself in him.

So I pulled him closer. And reached down and felt him grow even harder as my hand covered his crotch. Looking briefly over his shoulder to ensure that the door was closed and our bags now in the room, I walked him backwards to the bed. The two of us fell on top of it. And then we were pulling off each other's clothes. I was already so wet, so in need of him, that I pulled him immediately inside me. I threw my legs around him to take him even

42

deeper. My desire was immediate, all encompassing, and I came twice within moments. That only seemed to embolden Paul even more; his thrusts became deeper, slower, bringing me again to the edge of a certain crazed abyss, over which I tumbled again, every nerve ending electrified. I could feel, as always, the slow, relentless build-up within Paul of his own release – and how, like the extraordinary lover that he was, he held back the moment of climax, wanting us to remain fused, deranged, hungry for each other. When the build-up became unbearable, and his moans grew louder, I could feel his loins tensing wildly and his penis within me becoming even more rigid, more penetrating. Suddenly he burst forth, letting out a cry followed by shudders, and I whispered: 'Love of my life, love of my life,' feeling that to be the truth right now. Hoping against hope that, this time, a baby would come of it all.

Paul rolled off me. After over thirty hours of travel – and all the inherent tension accompanying that long, difficult journey – a siesta was desperately needed. So I reached down and pulled the white sheet over us, the ceiling fan circling overhead at a speed reasonable enough to generate a bit of chilled air against the heat. Putting my arms around my already passed-out husband, I shut my eyes.

Then it was pitch dark. Drifting back into consciousness I had absolutely no idea where I was for several strange moments, the clip-clip rotor movement of the ceiling fan overhead intermingling with a voice of incantation from a loudspeaker. I opened my eyes. The windows were still open, no curtains pulled against the stars shining with astonishing clarity in the night sky. And then that voice started again – a loudspeaker crackle, then 'Allahhhhhhhhhhhhh', the last 'h' held as a long intoned note, wafting through the darkness. Reality began to reassemble itself. Morocco. Essaouira. The hotel. The suite where we would be spending the next month. My husband, now curled up in a corner of the bed, still closed down and unconscious. And me holding the dial of my watch close to my face and discovering from the glowing hour and minute hands that we had been asleep for almost twelve hours. I had an urgent need to pee. I got to my feet, my balance just a little askew after such a deep sleep. The fan overhead kept up its percussive rattle as my bare feet touched the cool stone of the floor. The middle of the Moroccan night was temperate; an antidote to the immense heat through which we had travelled yesterday. I reached the bathroom, tiled in a shade of ultramarine that called to mind the sky above, the Essaouira rooftops below. The ceramic floor was also an intriguing blue and white, and like everything else about the suite it was clean. Monsieur Picard might be a bit of an oily customer, but there was something raffishly stylish about his hotel.

I was feeling very awake. Twelve hours of sleep does that. Having last washed almost two days ago in Buffalo I was also rank. I dug out my toiletries and made a beeline for the shower. There was proper hot water and it remained hot throughout the twenty minutes I stayed under its spray. When I got out, wrapping my hair in a towel and using the other spare towel around my body, I caught sight of myself in the mirror and shuddered. Not because I looked wretched and aged and beaten up by life. All that sleep had actually restored some vitality to a face that had been capped with dark, exhausted rings. What the mirror told me this morning was: I too am fighting the inevitable forward momentum of time.

When finding yourself grappling with uncertainties, there is only one solution: organise. I opened my bag and got dressed: loose linen pants, a blue linen shirt. Then I opened the wardrobe and spent the next fifteen minutes hanging up and arranging all my clothes before turning to Paul's bag. I hesitated for a moment, but I knew how grateful he was whenever I took charge of the domestic details of our lives, so I unzipped it. I found chaos. Shirts, underwear, jeans, socks, pairs of shorts all in an unwashed, beyond disordered state. Dumping them into the room's wicker laundry basket I put on a pair of sandals. Then, hoisting the basket, I let myself out and down the two flights of darkened stairs to the reception. A different man was asleep behind the counter: thin, brown teeth, dressed in a djellaba, mid-forties, a lit cigarette still fuming away between two fingers, his mouth open wide. I put the wicker basket down beside him and reached for a notepad and pen on the counter to write a note, asking him to get our clothes washed. But suddenly he mumbled something in his sleep, then snapped awake, squinting at me.

'Sorry, sorry,' I whispered. Then, pointing to the basket, I said: '*Linge.*'

The man's watery eyes began to come into focus. He glanced at the clock on the wall. It was now four-twenty-eight.

'*Maintenant?*' he asked. '*On est au beau milieu de la nuit.*'

Before I could tell him the laundry could wait he disappeared through a back doorway, returning a few minutes later with a shy young girl – I guessed she was around fourteen – in a simple gingham dress, her hair covered by a headscarf. She looked half-awake.

'There was no need to have gotten her now,' I said.

He just shrugged, then spoke in rapid-fire Arabic to the young girl while pointing to the basket. She answered back, her voice hesitant, demure. The man asked me:

'*Laver et repasser?*'

'Yes, yes,' I said. 'And I need them this morning.'

More Arabic to the little girl. Again she looked shy about speaking in front of these two adults – especially one who was so far outside her language. Nonetheless she answered him back. The man turned to me and said:

'You will have to wait for the sun to dry your clothes.'

'I can't argue with that,' I said, smiling at the young girl. She smiled back.

'*Shukran,*' I said, Arabic for '*thank you*' and just one of a small handful of words I knew in that language. I pressed a 50-dirham note in her hand; an apology for her being woken so early.

'*Afwan,*' she replied, all smiles. *You're welcome.*

And she disappeared with the laundry basket.

'I have one last favour to ask,' I said to the man. 'Since all my husband's clothes are being washed, do you have a robe or something he could wear?'

'*Une djellaba pour votre mari?*'

'*Oui, oui.*'

'*Attendez là.*' Then he disappeared through the door behind him.

At that precise moment, that voice began to incant again over the loudspeaker. *Allahhhhhhhhhhhhhh.* The 'h' was held so long and in such a haunting, mellifluous way that I felt compelled to step outside and see if I could find where it was coming from.

Leaving the blue carved archway of the hotel I looked down the back alleyway, which was unpaved, narrow enough for one vehicle but little else. The amplified voice started chanting again. I moved away from the doorway. Just ten or so paces from the hotel and I was enshrouded in darkness: hostile doorways, shuttered shops, tiny laneways filtering off this constricted street. I knew I shouldn't be here. It was like falling into a blackened maze. But the voice kept beckoning me forward, inviting me deeper into the shadows, making me fearless.

Then I saw the cat. Hanging off a wall directly in front of me as if she had been glued onto its crumbling stone surface. So emaciated, so grubby, so spooked. Had something truly terrifying thrown her against that wall? She was clinging to it, perpendicularly paralysed. Catching sight of her threw me. The impossibility of her position – as if all four paws had been hammered into the wall – was so unnerving that I felt as if an ice-cold hand had been placed on one of my bare shoulders.

Then an ice-cold hand was placed on one of my shoulders.

I found myself surrounded by three men. They had come out of nowhere. A guy in his fifties with a grizzled half-shaven face, three teeth, wild eyes. A plump kid – he couldn't have been more than eighteen – wearing a T-shirt that failed to cover his hairy stomach, his face oleaginous, his eyes darting up and down my body, a goofy smile on his lips. The hand belonged to a hunched young man, sallow skinned, his countenance glassy, disturbed. The touch of his fingers made me jump. I shrugged him off, spun around, saw him gazing at me with loon-like eyes. The plump kid whispered: '*Bonjour, madame,*' the grizzled old guy puffed on a stub of a cigarette, a half-smile on his face. Immediately the hand reattached itself to my shoulder. Immediately I shrugged it off again.

'Leave me alone,' I hissed.

'No problem, no problem,' the plump kid said, his face even more greasy as he came right up to me. 'We're friends.'

I tried to move forward, but the hunched guy had his bony fingers around my arm. Not in a restraining way, more as if he just wanted to touch me. My mind was racing. I figured the plump kid would make a grab for me, though at the moment he was simply hovering behind me, laughing a low laugh. And the old guy, though now in close, was just watching, clearly enjoying my fear.

'We like you,' the plump kid said with another unnerving laugh. The hunched guy's hand was tightening around my right forearm. I took a deep steadying breath, quickly calculating that I was close enough to catch him squarely, cripplingly, in the groin. I began to count to myself: one, two . . .

Then all hell broke loose. A man came running towards us, a stick in his hand, shouting one word over and over again:

'*Imshi, imshi, imshi.*'

It was the night man from the hotel, brandishing the cane over his head, ready to lash out. All three men scattered, leaving me there, frozen to the spot, terrified.

As soon as he reached me the night man took me by the arm the way a father would reach for a child who had gotten herself into deep trouble, pulling me along the alley and out of danger.

When we reached the hotel he all but pushed me inside. He had to sit down for a moment and compose himself. I too slumped in a chair, shocked, benumbed, feeling beyond stupid.

The night man reached for his cigarettes, his hands shaking as he lit one. After taking a steadying drag he spoke two words:

'*Jamais plus.*'
Never again.

47

Six

JAMAIS PLUS. JAMAIS plus. Jamais plus.

I sat on the balcony of our room, watching light break through the night sky, still reeling from that incident in the alleyway.

Jamais plus. Jamais plus. Jamais plus.

But my 'never again' exhortations had less to do with the behaviour of those men and more to do with my arrogance and inanity. What was I thinking? Why did I even dream of following the loudspeaker voice out into the shadows? The accountant in me was trying to separate the menace and dread of the scene from the hard cold facts of what I'd walked into. Would they have actually attacked me, tried to rape me? Or was I just an object of curiosity for them?

My hero from the front desk served me mint tea, deftly entering the room and placing it on the balcony table without waking Paul. He was still collapsed flat out in the bed, oblivious to all that had just transpired. Sitting there, looking out at constellations diminishing with the emerging dawn, I came to the conclusion that, though deeply creepy and offensive, this encounter hadn't had a serious sexual threat behind it. But there had been, without question, some sort of recklessness on my part that sent me out into the shadows. And I wouldn't forgive myself for such impetuousness until I fathomed what had pulled me towards trouble.

'Well, hello there.'

Paul was standing in the doorway of the balcony, dressed in the white djellaba that the night man had brought up along with the mint tea.

'You really slept,' I said.

'And you?'

'Oh, I was out almost as long as you.'

'And I see that I have no clothes.'

'They're being washed as we speak. That djellaba suits you.'

'The French have a word for an ageing hippy still dressing as if he's just come off an ashram – a *"baba-cool"*. Even during my year here I never wore a djellaba.'

'But it now suits your ageing-hippy look.'

He leaned down and kissed me on the lips.

'I walked into that, didn't I?' he said.

'Indeed you did.'

Now it was my turn to lean over and kiss my husband.

'Tea?'

'Please.'

I poured out two glasses. We clinked them.

'*À nous*,' he said.

'To us,' I repeated.

He threaded his hand in mine. We both stared up at the emerging daylight.

'Do you know what this time of day is called?'

'You mean, besides "dawn"?'

'Yes, besides "dawn" or "the break of day".'

'The last one's poetic.'

'So is "the blue hour".'

There was a pause while I let the phrase resonate for a moment or so. Then I tried it out myself:

'The blue hour.'

'It's rather lovely, isn't it?'

'Indeed. Neither darkness nor light.'

'The hour when nothing is as it seems – when we are caught between the perceived and the imagined.'

'Clarity and blur?'

'The pellucid and the obscure? Simplicity masking enigma?'

'Nice image,' I said.

He leaned over again and kissed me deeply. And said:

'*J'ai envie de toi.*'

And I wanted him so much too. Especially right now after all that restorative sleep. After that business in the alley. With the blue hour enveloping us.

He lifted me right out of my chair, his hands under my T-shirt. I pulled him towards me, feeling his hardness against me. Then he was steering us towards the bed. Some time later, as I bit into his shoulder, I came again and again. And then he let out a cry and shot into me.

We lay there, arms around each other, bewildered and, yes, happy.

'Our adventure begins now,' I said.

'In the blue hour.'

But in the world beyond our bedroom window, emerging sunlight had already eradicated the dawn.

'The blue hour has passed,' I said.

'Until sunset this evening.'

'The beginning of a day is always more mysterious than the onset of night.'

'Because you don't know what lies ahead?'

'At sunset you are more than halfway through the day's narrative,' I said. 'At dawn you have no idea what will transpire.'

'Which is perhaps why the blue is always bluer at dawn. And why a sunset is always more wistful. The entry into night, the sense of another day of life spinning towards its end.'

Paul leaned over and kissed me on the lips.

'As the Irish would say: "There's a pair of us in it."'

'How do you know that expression?'

'An Irish friend told it to me.'

'What Irish friend?'

'Someone long ago.'

'A woman?'

'Perhaps.'

'Perhaps? You mean, you're not certain if a certain Irish woman told you that?'

'OK, since you asked, her name was Siobhán Parsons. She was a professor of art at University College Dublin and not a bad painter. At the university in Buffalo for a year. Unmarried. As mad as a lamp, to use another of her favourite expressions. It lasted between us maybe three months. It was all around twelve years ago, when neither you nor I were aware of each other's existence.'

Paul kept so much about his life before me in a room marked

'Off Limits'. And there was a part of me that was jealous about his past. Jealous about the fact that there were women who had known him intimately before me. No man had ever pleasured me the way he had, so I didn't like to think there were others who'd felt what I'd felt when he was inside me. Yet thinking all this here, now, I couldn't help but feel ridiculous. *Stupid. Stupid. Stupid.* As stupid as wandering off down that murky alleyway.

'I'm sorry,' I whispered.

'Don't be sorry. Just try to be happy.'

'I am happy.'

'That's good to hear,' he said, kissing me.

'Hungry?' I asked.

'Famished.'

'Me too.'

'There's no way I'm going downstairs dressed like this.'

'But the outside world beckons. And do you really think anyone will care that you've gone native?'

'I'll care.'

'I won't,' I said. 'And that must count for something.'

'It does – but I am still waiting for my clothes.'

'Isn't there a movie where someone says: "Come with me to the casbah"?'

'Charles Boyer to Hedy Lamarr in *Algiers*.'

'Impressive,' I said. 'So come with me to the casbah.'

'They don't call it the casbah here. They call it the souk.'

'What's the difference between a casbah and a souk?'

'Mystery,' he said.

Seven

THE SOUK AT midday. The sky cloudless, a hard cobalt blue. A pitiless sun overhead, pushing the mercury to steam-bath levels. But down here, in Essaouira, everyone bar us seemed to be oblivious to the punishing heat. A heat so intense that the unpaved ground beneath our feet felt near-molten.

The souk at midday. A back-street labyrinth of stalls and shops and hidden alleyways containing more back streets, more spindly precincts where every sort of merchant was plying his trade. The sense of human density was extraordinary. So too was the prismatic concentration of colour. An entire alleyway with piles of auburn, maroon, crimson, scarlet, chestnut, sorrel, even chartreuse spices, displayed side by side, fashioned into minaret-style anthills. The contrasting aquamarine, ultramarine, turquoise and lapis lazuli of the intricately designed tiles on display by a vendor who had created a mosaic on the ground, which the passing crowd seemed effortlessly to dodge. The searing reds of the butcher meats; all hanging limbs and fatty flanks, dripping blood, around which flies congregated in mercenary clusters. The burnt yellows, sea-green, ochre, jet-white, electric-pink, salmon-pink bales of fabrics. The stalls selling beautifully patterned leather goods, shaded in every synonym for brown, tan, khaki. Then there was the melding of aromas, some enticing, some extreme. Fetid sewage interplaying with the redolence of the spice market; the pungent tang of the salted sea overhanging the flower stalls; the brewing mint tea at every kerbside stand we passed.

Add to this the souk's crazed acoustics. Loudspeakers blaring French and Moroccan pop music. Hawkers shouting everywhere. Merchants beckoning us forward, blurting out: '*Venez, venez!*' At least two competing muezzins – Paul told me the actual Arabic name for these distended voices – intoning high-noon prayers from a pair of strategically located minarets. The lawnmower chop of motorbikes and scooters, their drivers beeping manically as they

52

negotiated the dirt-surfaced, potholed terrain, dodging stands piled high with Van-Gogh-ish oranges and mangoes, and vegetable stalls where the tomatoes were primary in their redness. And here was a man trying to reach for my hand and pull me over to a corner of the souk where soaps in many hues – ivory, copper, scorched cream, ebony – formed a geometric sculpture several feet high.

Even with the Atlantic nearby the air was still so parched, so arid, that after twenty minutes of exploring the souk's early byways, my loose-fitting T-shirt and linen pants were sodden. So too were the T-shirt and shorts which Paul had pulled on when our laundry was delivered to our room later that morning (he held firm to the 'no djellaba outside' rule). By that time we'd had a large breakfast on our terrace. Then we set up what he called his 'outdoor studio' – Paul getting me to help him move the desk from the outer room to a corner of the balcony shaded by an overhanging roof, from where he had a direct view of the rooftops. He excused himself for a moment, returning ten minutes later with a brightly striped parasol he said he'd bought at a local shop. Positioning its plastic stand to ensure that his desk was fully shielded, he began to ready himself for work. A sketchpad was opened. Eight pencils were laid out with great formality on the varnished wood surface of the desk. Pulling his khaki safari hat onto his head, he sat down, peered out at the rooftops in the immediate distance, and then began his intricate, architectural rendering of them. I stood inside, watching him for a good ten minutes, marvelling at the precision and intensity of his vision, the amazing sense of line that he maintained, the way he seemed oblivious to everything but the work at hand, the ferocious discipline that rose up within him as he drew. All I could feel was a strange rush of love for this very talented, off-kilter man.

I drifted back inside and set up my own little workspace: my laptop, a very nice Moleskine journal bought before my departure and an old Sheaffer fountain pen which belonged to my dad. It was red with the sort of chrome trim that recalled the fins on a vintage Chevy. Dad always kept it filled with red ink, a source of dry amusement to my mother. 'Your whole damn life is about the accumulation of red ink,' she said on more than one occasion. But Dad once explained to me that he loved that colour for the richness of its imprint:

'It really does look like you've been writing in blood.'

Before I was able to make the first crimson entry in my notebook, the phone by the bed jumped into life. I answered it to hear the guy at the front desk telling me:

'Your French professor is downstairs.'

Monsieur Picard clearly worked fast, as I'd only asked him to find me a teacher yesterday.

Before I went downstairs to meet her, Paul said:

'Whoever is going to be giving you the lessons will need the work. Don't let her charge you any more than seventy-five dirhams an hour.'

'But that's only nine dollars.'

'It's great money here, trust me.'

When I entered the lobby I saw a demure young woman waiting by the reception desk. Though she was wearing the hijab, a headscarf that allowed her full face to be seen, she was nonetheless dressed in blue jeans and a floral blouse that – while it completely hid her décolletage – wouldn't have been out of place in a 1960s commune. A touch of retro hippy chic. You could tell immediately that this was a young woman who was very much caught between disparate worlds.

When she accepted my outstretched hand the softness of her grip and the dampness of her palm hinted that she was anxious about this meeting. I tried to put her at her ease, motioning to two dusty armchairs in a corner of the lobby where we could talk undisturbed and asking the guy behind the desk to bring us two mint teas. She was intensely shy and seemed keen to please. Her name was Soraya. She was a Berber from the extreme south of the country, deep within the Sahara. Soraya was just twenty-nine and a teacher at a local school. Through gentle probing I discovered that she'd studied at the university in Marrakesh and even did a year in France. When she couldn't get her visa extended she had to return home. Languages were her passion. In addition to her

54

native Arabic and French she had mastered English and was working on Spanish now.

'But the Moroccan passport makes it difficult to actually live or work anywhere else,' she told me.

'So you've never lived in England or the States?' I said, completely amazed by her English which we occasionally slipped into, despite agreeing on an 'all-French rule' at the outset.

'That's my dream – to find my way to New York or London,' she said with a shy smile. 'But with the exception of France, I've never been out of Morocco.'

'Then how on earth did you get so good at my language?'

'I studied it at university. I watched all the American and British films and television shows that I could. I read many novels . . .'

'What's your favourite American novel?'

'I really liked *The Catcher in the Rye* . . . Holden Caulfield was my hero when I was fifteen.'

I told her about having first learned French in Canada, and how I was here with my artist husband this summer, very determined to rejuvenate my French in four weeks.

'But you speak it well already,' she said.

'You're being far too kind.'

'I'm being accurate – though a foreign language is one you must continue to work at, otherwise it does fade from memory.'

She asked me how I'd found my way to Essaouira. She was interested to know about Paul's time in Morocco over thirty years ago, and where we lived in the States, and might Buffalo be a place that she would like?

'Buffalo is not what one would call a particularly cosmopolitan or elegant city.'

'But you live there.'

Now it was my turn to blush.

'Where you end up may not be where you want to live,' I said.

Shutting her eyes for a moment she bowed her head and nodded agreement.

'So if I wanted to regain fluency in French in a month, how many hours a week would I need?' I asked.

'That depends on your schedule.'

'I have no schedule here. No obligations, no commitments, no pressing engagements. And you?'

'I teach at what you would call "lower school". Children between the ages of six and nine. But I am free from five o'clock onwards every afternoon.'

'If I was to suggest two hours a day . . .'

'Could you afford three hours?' she asked.

'What would you charge?'

Now she turned an even greater shade of crimson.

'You don't have to be shy about this,' I said. 'It's just money – and it's best to get these things settled at the beginning.'

God, how American I sounded. Cards on the table. Name your price and let's talk.

After a moment or two she said:

'Would seventy-five dirhams per hour be too much?'

Seventy-five dirhams was a little under nine dollars. Immediately I said:

'I think that's too little.'

'But I don't want to ask for more.'

'But I want to offer more. Would you accept one hundred and five dirhams per hour?'

She looked shocked.

'That's a huge amount per week.'

'Trust me, if it was not affordable for me I would tell you.'

'OK then,' she said, looking away but now with a small smile on her face. 'Where shall we do the lessons?'

'I have a suite upstairs. I'll have to check with my husband – but I think that should be fine.'

'And if I may ask . . . what do you do professionally?'

'Nothing very interesting.' When I told her about my work as an accountant I could see her maintaining a neutral pose about it. I could also sense that she was wondering if I had children, and where were they right now? Or was this just me projecting my own concerns and insecurities onto this shy but observant young woman?

'I'm sure your work is very interesting,' she said.

'When it comes to money, you do get to know a great deal about how other people function. Anyway . . . can you start tomorrow?'

'I see no problem with that.'

'Brilliant – and can you get me all the books I'll need?'

I handed her 300 dirhams, telling her that if they cost more, I'd reimburse her after our first lesson.

'Three hundred dirhams will buy them all,' she said. 'I'll bring them tomorrow.'

'Do you want payment every day or once a week?'

Again she looked away.

'Whatever is easier for you. If you pay me on Friday the bank here is open until nine in the evening so I can deposit most of it then.'

Ah, a saver.

'Payment every Friday it is then. One last thing – how do you know Monsieur Picard?'

'My mother is a cleaner here.'

I considered my response for a moment before saying:

'I'm certain she's very proud of you.'

She averted her gaze as she nodded acknowledgement. I told Soraya how much I looked forward to being her student and that I would see her tomorrow. Then I went upstairs. Paul was still on the balcony under the umbrella, a good half-dozen drawings strewn across the table. His face was swathed with sweat; his shell-shocked eyes indicating the onset of heat exhaustion. I grabbed the litre bottle of water that was by the bed and insisted that he drink it. He drained half of it in moments, staggered inside and collapsed onto the bed.

'Are you insane, courting disaster like that?' I asked.

'Inspiration trumped perspiration.'

'But you, of all people, know what the sun is like here.'

'Can you rescue the drawings before they get bleached by the light?'

I went outside and gathered up the six drawings exposed to

the sun, bringing them inside. As I shuffled through them one by one, I felt myself sucking in my breath. What I saw floored me. They were a half-dozen variations on the same visual theme: the immediate rooftops in the direct vicinity of our balcony. What made these depictions so remarkable was the way that, in each drawing, Paul had re-envisaged the minarets and water towers and crumbling roofs and dangling laundry and satellite dishes that defined the Essaouira skyline. I glanced up at one point and stared out at the actual panorama on which Paul had based this sequence of intricately sketched compositions. Then I returned to his highly detailed draw-ings, marvelling not just at the sheer refined technique, but also the fact that, seen as a totality, they reminded me that there is no such thing as a correct vision of the state of things; that none of us ever see the same objects, landscape, vision of life, the same way. As such, everything is, by its very nature, an interpretation.

'These are extraordinary,' I told him.

'Now it's you who's suffering sunstroke. They're a couple of sketches I knocked off in a few hours.'

'Didn't Mozart often write a piano sonata in a morning?'

'He was Mozart.'

'You are incredibly gifted.'

'I wish I could share your fulsome opinion of me.'

'I wish that too. But in my humble opinion I think that these mark an entire new direction for you.'

'You're biased.'

'Take the compliment. They're brilliant.'

But Paul just turned away, unable to accept such praise. I quickly changed the subject.

'I start French lessons tomorrow,' I said, then told him all about Soraya.

'How much is she charging per hour?' he asked.

'She asked for seventy-five, I'm paying her one five.'

'You're a soft touch.'

'Only when it's the right thing to do.'

'Even seventy-five dirhams an hour is a huge amount of money for her.'

'And not that much money for me. So what's the big deal?'

'None whatsoever. Your generosity is admirable.'

'So too is your concern about our finances.'

'Do I hear a tone?' he asked.

'Can we drop this?'

'Of course we can,' he said, getting up and heading into the bathroom. A moment or so later I heard the shower being turned on. When he came out ten minutes later, a towel wrapped around his midriff, he informed me:

'I really wish we could get beyond these "exchanges".'

'So do I.'

'Let's try to steer clear of all stupidity.'

'It gets corrosive, doesn't it?' I said. 'Kindness is the better option.'

He considered this for a moment.

'That just might be a solution.'

He came over and put his arms around me.

'A fresh start, OK?'

'Fine by me,' I said, kissing him lightly on the lips while simultaneously wondering if I would be replaying this dialogue a day or two from now? Maybe I simply need to accept that this is how our marriage operates; that this is our weather system as a couple, and one in which the moments of inclemency do get supplanted by periods of genuine tranquillity and, indeed, the adventure that is love.

Adventure. Now there's a word I've been grappling with recently. The next day, during my first lesson with Soraya, I asked her whether it had multiple meanings in French. She blushed slightly, noting:

'Yes, "*une aventure*" is the word for "adventure". But also it's a very French expression for a love affair. "*J'ai eu une aventure avec Jacques . . . seulement une aventure, rien de bien sérieux.*"'

She didn't need to translate. *Une aventure* was just that: a fling that wasn't love. When I asked about the semantical difference between adventure and love, Soraya said:

'In French if someone says – as they often do – "*C'est l'amour*", it indicates its profound seriousness, for the moment anyway. When I lived in Lyon I had several French friends who always seemed to be exclaiming the fact that they had fallen in love after seeing a man for two or three weeks. Then when it ended a few months later the next fellow they got involved with . . . "*Oh, c'est l'amour*" after the fourth night. The way I heard it used so frequently made me think that to exclaim "I'm in love" is to express immediate emotions that haven't been allowed to deepen. It's also to admit to being in love with the idea of being in love.'

'And in Morocco?'

Now her shoulders tightened.

'We need to return to other things,' she said, tapping the textbooks. This time I didn't protest, because I realised that I had mistakenly crossed an invisible boundary, one which Soraya was going to maintain.

So back we went to the pluperfect subjunctive.

We sat together on the sofa in the small living area of the suite, the French books she'd brought along spread out across the little coffee table. Paul was at work on the balcony, shaded by the big umbrella and his wide-brimmed hat, the sun still at high wattage at five-thirty in the afternoon. He had come out to say hello when Soraya earlier knocked on the door of our suite. I could see that she was taking in his lankiness, his long grey hair, the age difference between us. Just as she was also (I could tell) impressed by his French and by the drawings that I had placed around the room.

'Your husband did all these?' she asked.

'You approve?'

'They capture Essaouira so well.'

'Or, at least, the rooftops of Essaouira.'

'Will he start doing street scenes as well?'

'You'll have to ask him.'

'Imagine being married to such a talented man. Your children . . .?'

'We have none.'

Now Soraya looked as if she wished the floor could open and swallow her whole. I quickly added:

'None yet.'

Her relief was immense.

'I'm so sorry,' she said. 'I should never have pried like that.'

'That was hardly prying.'

'But it was an inappropriate question. Even though I know that, in the West, having children is not obligatory for married couples.'

'That's true. My first husband didn't want any.'

Soraya seemed thrown by my directness.

'Is that the reason you left him?'

'One of the many reasons.'

'I see . . .'

'But Paul definitely does want children.'

Soraya seemed to approve of this.

'He's had none before now?' she asked, but then added: 'If that isn't another inappropriate question on my part.'

'Not inappropriate at all,' I said.

'In Morocco, marriage is so much about having children.'

'Is that how you see it?'

She considered this for a moment.

'How I "see it" and how things are . . . those are two very different things entirely.'

Over the first ten days of my lessons with Soraya the non-French-grammar conversations were an intriguing game of verbal ping-pong, in which her innate caution and cultural reticence were frequently undercut by her immense curiosity not just about my life but about the way a woman like me functioned in modern America. A rapid sense of trust developed between us, though it was not until the second week of our lessons that some of the more private aspects of her life began to be revealed. I sensed very quickly that her time in France had completely altered her way of thinking, and that her return to Morocco had been a reluctant one.

'So when you went to university you actually lived on the campus itself?' she asked in wonder when I started telling her about leaving home for the University of Minnesota.

'Isn't that the usual way in France or here?' I asked.

'In Morocco, if you go to another city for university, it is arranged that you will live with family there.'

'And when you were in Lyon?'

Her lips tightened.

'The only reason I was allowed to go to Lyon was because my paternal uncle Mustapha was there. He and his wife have lived there for thirty years. He has a rather successful taxicab business and she is a teacher in a *lycée* – so they are both, on a certain level, quite assimilated. Except when it comes to their responsibilities as guardians of their niece from Essaouira. The entire year was a power struggle. Especially when they discovered I was not wearing the hijab when I went off to class, and was even using a friend's place to change my clothes. When it came to staying out late, which I started to do when Fabien came into my life . . .'

'Who was Fabien?' I asked. But at that very moment Paul came in off the balcony, en route to the bathroom. The subject was abruptly dropped.

Later that night, in a little back-street restaurant that had quickly become a favourite, I told Paul how Soraya had mentioned the name of a Frenchman whom I sensed she was involved with during her year in Lyon.

'That's what most educated Moroccan women dream of,' he said. 'Meeting a Westerner who can get them out of here.'

'So speaks the voice of experience.'

'Was I indicating that I had any experience of that whatsoever?'

'Surely there must have been a Moroccan woman or two in your life back then.'

'What makes you say that?'

'Because you are a most attractive man now, which means you must have been even more so in your twenties. And you were probably hanging out with fellow artists, the Casablanca bohemian circle, right? Wasn't there some abstract painter cutie who . . .'

'What's the point of this?'

'The point is that I want you right now.'

An hour later, we were back in bed in our hotel room, his body entwined with mine, the two of us sharing the most extraordinary metronomic symmetry; when he whispered to me just how much he loved me, promising wondrous times ahead, free of the shadowy recesses of the past, what else could I do but also proclaim my love for him? As actual and true a love as I had ever known.

Afterwards, as we lay close next to each other, our arms interlocked, I said:

'Maybe we did it this time.'

Because it was right in the middle of my cycle. And because, tonight, our normal level of passion hit an even more dizzying summit.

Paul kissed me lightly on the lips.

'I'm sure it happened this time. We're blessed, after all.'

Outside, the muezzin sang praises to his Almighty. '*Allahu akbar! Allahu akbar!*'

To which I could only think:

Your timing, sir, is impeccable.

Eight

THE NEXT TWO weeks were supremely happy ones. Happiness has always struck me as a fleeting event – a moment here or there when the dreck of life washes away for a few precious hours. You're free of all the fears and pathologies that seem to act as a subtext to everything you are trying to do in life. The problem when you are a couple is that you are also in thrall to your partner's fears and pathologies. So if there is a period when you are both outside the reach of all the historic dark stuff you both cart around with you . . . well, that is one of those rare, sublime junctures when you can truly think: *We are blessed.*

Those first fourteen days in Essaouira were magic. Paul got into a serious, high-end creative groove when it came to his work, spending close to six hours a day on his line drawings, moving from the panoramic eyrie that was our balcony to a café table right in the heart of the souk. There he became something of a local celebrity. Its manager – a young guy in his mid-twenties named Fouad – saw the quality of the work that Paul was producing and made it his business to keep him free of unnecessary distraction, especially from hawkers and tourist touts. Paul, in turn, paid Fouad's protective decency back by drawing him a small postcard image every day. This came at the end of his three to four hours at the café where he was at work on a larger line drawing – always capturing some essence of souk life in a manner that was both representational and simultaneously skewed. He caught the kinetic madness of the life screaming around him, as the souk was never in respite. Yet his artistry was to delineate it all in a manner that made it both tangible and oblique.

Fouad was a shrewd, cool customer. His *patron* was his father, who owned the café but spent much of the time in Marrakesh – where, as his son once intimated to Paul, he had a mistress. Fouad had studied in France – at a school of Beaux Arts in Marseille where he'd fallen in love with a fellow painter. She was from Toulon and she wasn't a Muslim. Fouad's father – though willing to pay for his son's three-year adventure on the other side of the Mediterranean – pressed the paternal guilt button and insisted, at the end of his course, that he drop all hopes of a life of art and love with the Frenchwoman. He had to return home to Morocco and learn the family business.

So now Fouad managed this café and a small hotel in the souk for his largely absent father. The café was located right at a corner of the medina where spice and fruit merchants plied their trade next to butchers with animal carcasses bleaching in the midday sun. It gave Paul a ringside seat on all the manic, chromatic action, which he captured in edgy black pencil and charcoal on off-white card. Fouad – clearly in need of an older brother (especially one who was a fellow artist) – insisted on settling Paul at a shaded corner table which became his office, and on keeping him supplied with mint tea throughout the hours he worked there. He also provided lunch for us both. He refused to take any payment, which is when my husband began to pay with a daily original postcard. Paul told me that he was borrowing a trick from Picasso, who paid for his hotel and bar bills in the French seaside town of Collioure by leaving a sketch with the patron every few days . . . in the process making him the possessor of a very lucrative art collection.

'I doubt Fouad will be able to retire to the Côte d'Azur on the proceeds of my scribbles,' Paul noted one afternoon when we had retreated to the hotel to make love and have a nap.

'Don't underestimate your market value just yet. This new sequence of drawings you're doing is such a breakthrough.'

I was making progress myself. My classes with Soraya were rigorous. Most of the mornings I would spend hunched over my textbooks, forcing myself to learn ten new verbs and twenty new words per day. I also read local newspapers in French and bought a small radio so I could hear RFI – France's version of the BBC World Service.

'You really are committed,' Soraya said when, around ten days into our lessons, I surprised her by asking all sorts of questions about the uses of '*soutenu*' French – the most elevated and formal version of the language.

'Bravo for your diligence,' she said. 'To be able to speak *un français soutenu* is the key to so much. If you can master it, the French will be most impressed.'

'If I ever get to France.'

Soraya looked at me quizzically. 'Why do you think you won't get to France?'

'I've never travelled much before.'

'But you're travelling now.'

'It depends on certain things happening in my life.'

'Of course it does.'

'Still,' I said, '*les enfants sont portables*.' *Children are portable.*

'You used the word "*portable*" incorrectly here. *Un portable* is a cellphone or a laptop computer. The verb to use here is "*transporter*". So try rephrasing it.'

There was one central reason why I was obsessed about getting my French back in working order: the sense of accomplishment. I wanted to use my time here in a positive, beneficial way. Watching Paul so focused on his own work made me push myself even harder, as I told him when he complimented me on my progress.

Essaouira became a home for us. I figured out, by and large, the maze-like geography of the old city and was able to find my way unencumbered through the souk. I also learned how to deflect attention from the occasional tout or young guy playing macho. But though I began to feel as if I had a true handle on Essaouira's exuberantly twisted realities, the city after dark was a place I never ventured alone. This precaution did not dim my appreciation of the place. Or the fact that, as I discovered, its residents were supremely welcoming and pleased to see that you had decided to spend time among them.

I became a beach walker, setting off most afternoons after our siesta along the endless strip of sand that fronted the Atlantic. Once past the bathers, there would be the women in hijabs lifting up their all-covering djellabas to wade in the water. Nearby, the camel guides were touting a half-hour on top of one of their haunted beasts for a negotiable fee. Another two kilometres further south all traces of habitation fell away. I was alone. The beach stretched into infinity, the Atlantic mirroring the declining summer sun, its horizon boundless. How I always wanted to live on a strip of beach, with little hint of the twenty-first century in sight, walking it daily, revelling in the way that the rhythmic pounding of the surf always seemed to smooth out, for a time, all the stress and doubt and anxiety that we haul around with us. We're a bit like Bedouins when it comes to the trappings of our lives. No matter where we roam, or how far we venture away from our place of birth, we still haul so much of the past with us.

On an empty beach – especially *this* empty beach – you could almost convince yourself that it might just be possible to detach yourself from your history and all its weight.

Given what a productive place Paul found himself in right now – and how free of shadows he also seemed to be – when I got back from my daily two-hour hike he'd greet me with a smile and a kiss and the suggestion that, after my lesson with Soraya, we watch the sunset from the rooftop of a very elegant hotel just inside the city walls. It was called L'Heure Bleue (of all things); very much an old-style travellers' hotel of the 1920s, redone in subdued, five-star chic style. Totally out of our league, budget-wise, but one glass of Kir at the open-air roof bar wouldn't break the bank. And it did provide the most ravishing panorama of the red globular sun slowly liquidising into a tranquil ocean.

'Interesting, isn't it, how the Atlantic is so becalmed here,' Paul noted one evening as we sipped our drinks, both fixated on the wide-screen sunset.

'Especially when compared to Maine.'

'We'll be there in a couple of weeks.'

'I know,' I said.

'You sound less than enthusiastic about that prospect.'

'You know how much I love Maine. It's just . . . well, it's home, right?'

'My thoughts entirely. So why don't we extend here for another two weeks?'

'But that means losing Maine – and our deposit for the fourteen days there. Our plane tickets are non-exchangeable and non-refundable . . . and, yes, I know I'm sounding like an accountant.'

'You're right to do so, especially given my behaviour in that department.'

I reached out and took his hand.

'That's all behind us now,' I said.

'Because you forced me to grow up.'

'It wasn't about you "growing up". It was about just exercising a bit of restraint.'

'I know I have this compulsion to spend,' he said. 'And I know that the compulsion is rooted in the fact that I allowed life to turn out in a way I never wanted. Until, that is, I met you. You saved me from myself.'

'Happy to be of service,' I said, kissing him lightly on the lips.

Just beyond us the sun had been rendered fluid; thawed orange coalescing like spilled paint on the surface of the Atlantic. I shut my eyes and felt tears. Because I sensed a real breaking down of a barrier here; an honesty and complicity between us that had been overshadowed by manifold demons.

The next morning was pitch perfect. An aquamarine sky, cloud-free, faultless. We awoke from a late carnal sleep to a knock at the door. Glancing at the bedside clock I noticed it was High Noon. Damn, damn, damn. Soraya had asked if she could organise the lesson earlier today (it was a Friday – the Sabbath day in Morocco), and if it could only last one hour. She was catching a two p.m. bus to Marrakesh and a weekend with a friend from university.

'I had to have my friend's mother phone my mother and vouch that she would keep an eye on me over the weekend. I am twenty-nine years old and am still having to check in like an adolescent,' she told me in a low, confessional whisper.

I had agreed to that midday Friday lesson. And now it was . . . two minutes past twelve. Soraya was always punctual. Damn. Damn. Damn.

As I jumped out of bed and scrambled for some clothes, Paul groaned awake.

'What time is it?' he asked, half-asleep. When I told him he smiled and said:

'I'm glad you're succumbing to my bohemian ways.'

Actually it was the first time we'd overslept since arriving here; Paul always wanted to get to the café by eleven to capture the souk at its most manic.

'That's Soraya,' I said. 'I'll do the lesson downstairs.'

'No need. Do it in the front room and I'll slip out in around twenty minutes.'

So I quickly dressed and let Soraya in, apologising for the slight delay. As she set up her books and pens and papers in the small living area I went running downstairs and asked for coffee and bread and preserves to be brought upstairs. When I returned to the room I could hear the shower going in the adjacent bathroom – and Soraya looking just a little uncomfortable with the notion of a naked man in the immediate proximity.

'Sorry, sorry,' I said. 'I should have suggested we go elsewhere.'

'No problem.' She was clearly relieved to have me back in the room. 'Shall we start?'

We began by discussing the verb '*vouloir*' – to want – and variations of its usage. Especially in the conditional. *Would like*. The great aspirational hope. I began to recite:

'*Je voudrais un café . . . voudrais-tu un café aussi? . . . il voudrait réussir . . . nous voudrions un enfant . . .*'

At which point the bedroom door swung open and Paul emerged, dressed, his hair still wet from the shower. He greeted us with a big smile.

'*Tout à fait, nous voudrions un enfant,*' he said, coming over and kissing me on the lips. *We would definitely like a child.*

Then greeting Soraya, he asked her in French:

'And how is my wife progressing?'

'She's doing fantastically. Really gifted with the language. And she works so hard.'

'That she does.'

'You think too highly of me,' I said.

'She doesn't think well enough of herself,' Paul said. 'Maybe you can help her in that department, Soraya.'

I told him that breakfast would be here in a minute, but saw that he had his satchel over his shoulder, stuffed with his sketch-books and pencils.

'I'll let Fouad provide that for me. Come find me after the lesson. *Je t'adore.*'

With another kiss on the lips he was gone.

Once the door was closed behind him Soraya looked away as she said:

'*Je voudrais un homme comme votre mari.*'

'*Mais plus jeune?*' I added.

'*L'âge importe moins que la qualité.*'

I would like a man like your husband.

But younger?

The age is less important than the quality.

'I am sure you will find someone of quality,' I told her.

'I'm not,' she said in a near-whisper.

And then:

'All right, *essayer* in the subjunctive. Give me an example in first person singular.'

I considered this for a moment, then said:

'*Il faut que je voudrais d'être heureux.*'

Soraya did not look professorially pleased by my answer.

'I must would like happiness,' she said, translating my sentence into her excellent English. 'You can do better than that.'

'Sorry. The problem is the use of the subjunctive with "would like". As you noted you can't "must would like" something.'

'So if you were to talk about wanting happiness . . .'

'*Je voudrais le bonheur.*'

'Fine. And in the subjunctive?'

'I would sidestep *vouloir* and use *essayer*. To try. As in: "*Il faut que je essaie d'etre heureux.*" *I must try to be happy.*'

Soraya then had another one of her thoughtful pauses.

'It is all about "trying", isn't it?' she said.

Breakfast arrived and she shared the coffee with me. We worked on until one p.m. Then I paid her for the week and wished her well in Marrakesh.

'*Entre nous* there is a man – French – whom my classmate wants me to meet. A banker working at Société Générale. My parents would half-approve – the banker, not the French part. But I am getting ahead of myself here, aren't I?'

Then, telling me she'd see me on Monday at the usual time, she headed off for her weekend and her meeting with the Frenchman who might, or might not, become a conduit into a new life. Travelling hopefully is the key to so much.

When Soraya was gone, I took a long shower and changed into fresh clothes, then checked my watch and thought that, if I moved quickly, I could still join Paul for a late lunch at Chez Fouad. But as Friday was the one day when I read my email I decided to quickly scan this week's dispatches before heading out to the souk.

The first email I saw had been sent just twenty minutes earlier from my ever-scrupulous book-keeper Morton. It read:

> *Now that we have your husband's audit problems with the IRS out of the way I've been doing his books in an attempt to bring them up to date so we are not in a 'beat the clock' bind at tax time next year. You know how he throws all his receipts and invoices and credit card statements into that box file you gave him. Well, I started working through it on Wednesday and came across this invoice this morning. I debated about whether I should send it to you now or wait until you got back in a few weeks. But I decided that – as this was something of an ethical/moral call – I should err on the side of immediate transparency.*

I clicked on the attached file and found myself staring at an invoice from a Dr Brian Boyards, MD, Urologist. The invoice was for a patient named Leuen, Paul Edward. His date of birth – 04-11-56 – was the same as my husband's. So too was the home address. And the Blue Cross/Blue Shield health insurance policy that he used to defray 80 per cent of the $2,031.78 charges for the procedure listed on the invoice.

Outpatient Non-Scalpel Deferentectomy.

What is a deferentectomy?

I switched over to Google and typed in that exact word.

And discovered that a deferentectomy is the clinical term for a very common bit of urological surgery . . . also known as a vasectomy.

And the date on which this Outpatient Non-Scalpel Deferentectomy was performed on my husband? September 7th of last year. Around the same time that we both agreed we should start trying for a child.

Nine

I SAT IN front of my computer screen, trying to convince myself that what I had just read was somehow false. A fabrication; an invention dispatched by a malevolent individual who wanted to see my marriage thrown completely off course.

The problem with hard-and-fast evidence – and an invoice from a doctor in the wake of a surgical procedure is about as irrefutable as it comes – is that you can't negotiate with its black-and-white veracity. It's a bit like a client of mine who had run up around $10k of Internet porn charges on his MasterCard one year. All the transactions were marked Fantasy Promotions Inc., and the time codes showed they were all late in the evening. His wife had seen the MasterCard statements and was just a little appalled. My client entreated me to provide him with an alibi for these purchases. As I told him at the time: 'How do you explain over one hundred and fifty dealings after midnight with an online company called Fantasy Promotions Inc.? There's no wiggle room here. It's the smoking gun.'

Strange how that client – who was divorced with extreme prejudice by his wife thereafter – popped into my head as I found myself staring at the document from Dr Brian Boyards, MD, Urologist. All the facts in front of me. Facts which I must have reread a dozen times, trying to find a way of reinterpreting the irrefutable:

Patient: Leuen, Paul Edward.
Date of birth: 04-11-56
Home Address: 5165 Albany Avenue, Buffalo, NY 10699
Insurance: Blue Cross/Blue Shield A566902566
Procedure: Outpatient Non-Scalpel Deferentectomy
Date of Procedure: 09-07-14

The seventh of September last year. Around ten months ago. A few days after the Labor Day weekend, which we spent in a friend's cottage in the woods fronting Lake Placid. My husband and I making love twice a day. And me, after a candlelit dinner at some nearby inn, stating that, after two years together, and with my fortieth birthday looming, I wanted to come off the pill . . . though it would be, as my gynaecologist told me, at least two weeks until I would be moving into a fertile cycle.

Paul did not blanch or talk about joining the merchant marine when I brought this up. On the contrary, he told me that having a child together was 'the essential bonding of a couple in love' or some such rhapsodic line. Back in Buffalo a few days later he returned from the gym one evening limping slightly, telling me how he'd pulled a muscle in his groin and was worried that he'd given himself a hernia. With my complete understanding, he absented himself from sex for several days, saying that he'd be going to the university infirmary the next day to get himself a medical opinion. Then when he got back that night he informed me that, though it was only 'lightly herniated' – I remember his exact words – he was advised not to exacerbate it and to refrain from sex for another week. Which we dutifully did.

Now, here I was, all these absurd months later, on the website of Dr Brian Boyards, MD, reading all about this seemingly simple, no-fault surgical procedure:

> *Over 500,000 vasectomy procedures are done each year in the United States.*
>
> *Vasectomy is a simple, safe surgical procedure for permanent male fertility control. The tube (called a 'vas') which leads from the testicle is cut and sealed in order to stop sperm from leaving.*
>
> *The procedure usually takes about 10 to 20 minutes.*
>
> *Since the procedure simply interrupts the delivery of sperm it does not change hormonal function – leaving sexual drive and potency unaffected.*
>
> *The No-Scalpel vasectomy is a technique used to do the vasectomy through one single puncture. The puncture is made in the scrotum and requires no suturing or stitches.*

The primary difference compared to the conventional vasectomy is that the vas deferens is controlled and grasped by the surgeon in a less traumatic manner. This results in less pain and fewer postoperative complications.

This procedure is done with the aid of a local anaesthetic called 'Xylocaine' (similar to 'Novocain').

The actual interruption of the vas which is done with the No-Scalpel technique is identical to the interruption used with conventional techniques.

The No-Scalpel technique is simply a more elegant and less traumatic way for the surgeon to control the vas and proceed with its interruption.

So my husband murdered my chance at motherhood with him by opting for 'elegant and less traumatic' surgery. The child I so wanted.

I snapped my eyes shut, caught somewhere between desolation and pure unalloyed rage.

'Tout à fait, nous voudrions un enfant.'

The bastard actually said that at midday today. Just as, for months, he'd kept reassuring me that it was only a matter of time before I got pregnant . . .

I slammed down the lid of my computer and began to sob. I was in free-fall. Beyond stunned. Stupefied. As if this new life we'd built together was nothing more than a house of cards. Built on the lies of a man I had been dumb enough to trust. How could I – Ms Forensic, Ms Extra-Scrupulous, Ms Exhaustively Thorough – not have sniffed out the con behind all his declarations of intimate commitment?

I knew the answer to that question.

We only see what we want to see.

I understood from the outset that Paul Leuen was, on certain fundamental levels, incapable of proper adult responsibility. But I chose to sidestep such realisations and embrace the bohemian lure, the romantic effluence, the hallucinogenic sex. I was so desperate for love that I shoved all doubt into that mental basement room and plunged right into the delusion of domestic bliss and child-rearing with a man who . . .

Who? Who?

Can I even define him now? If he had betrayed me in such a fundamental way, if he had deliberately had himself fixed while assuring me passionately that he wanted a child with me . . .

I went to the bathroom. I threw cold water on my face, avoiding the mirror. I didn't want to cast a cold eye on myself right now. I returned to the room and went out onto the balcony, staring out at the North African world below. *This could have waited until our return, Morton.* But decent rabbinical Morton had, no doubt, done a considerable amount of soul searching before deciding to send me the urologist's invoice. And he had finally decided: cards on the table. But leave it to my disorganised husband to have thrown the doctor's invoice into his box of financial paperwork, forgetting that I would eventually see it – because I was still his accountant.

I clutched the balcony railings, steadying myself, rage trumping sorrow; a certain clinical clarity asserting itself. I returned inside to my laptop. I opened it and wrote a fast email to Morton:

Knowledge, they say, is power. But it's also often a sorrow beyond dreams. Can you please look around his MasterCard statements for September 2014 and see if there is an insurance excess payment for $400 to Dr Brian Boyards. Then scan it to me. I sense I will be back in Buffalo in a matter of days. Alone.

As I awaited a reply I dug out our plane tickets and discovered (through some further searching on the Net) that Royal Air Maroc would change my flight before the return date for a charge of 3,000 dirhams – around $350. Yes, I had paid for the entire month at the hotel, but we were already into the third week. Paul could stay behind and finish his drawings and remind himself what it was like to be alone once more. I was pretty certain that this was the outcome he privately desired. When he'd had his secret vasectomy part of him must have known that all would eventually be revealed. Surely he had to figure that after, say, a year of trying with no success, I'd insist that we go to a fertility clinic for tests. At which point . . .

Bing. An email from Morton.

Found it. Attached as a scan. I am here for you. Anything I can do, just ask. Courage . . .

I started crying again, and was then interrupted by a light knocking at the door.

'Go fuck off,' I immediately yelled, certain it was Paul. But why would he knock when he had a key? Instantly I was on my feet heading into the other room and opening the main door to the suite. Outside stood the young girl who cleaned our room and did our washing. She looked ashen and cowed.

'*Mes excuses, mes excuses,*' I said, taking her hands. '*Je suis . . . dévastée.*'

I broke away and went inside, attempting to keep down the new sob that was trying to escape from the back of my throat. Don't break down, don't break down. The young girl was gone from view, no doubt running down the stairs, unnerved and fearful by the sight of this crazy woman in the throes of a nervous collapse.

Back to the bathroom. More water on my face. My eyes were red. So I returned to my desk, fastened my sunglasses on my nose, grabbed my passport, a pad and paper, the printout of my plane ticket, my wallet and credit cards. I stuffed it all into my shoulder bag and headed out the door. On my way downstairs I dug out a 100-dirham note. The young girl was hovering at the bottom of the stairs, clearly uncertain at my approaching presence, wondering what I might pull next.

'I am so sorry,' I said, thrusting the note into her hand. 'I received some difficult news today. Please forgive me.'

Her eyes went wide when she saw the sum involved – what Soraya told me was two days' wages – and she whispered:

'*C'est trop . . . Ce n'est pas nécessaire . . .*'

'*Si, c'est nécessaire . . . Et merci pour ta gentillesse.*'

'J'espère que tout ira bien, madame.'

'On verra,' I said. We'll see.

And I headed out into the blazing early afternoon.

There was an Internet café two alleyways from the hotel. I walked in and asked the bored-looking guy – mid-twenties, cigarette screwed in one side of his mouth, scatting along to some local pop song – if he had a printer.

The guy pointed to a beat-up machine.

'Two dirhams per page, ten dirhams for an hour on the computer. You can pay me afterwards.'

The hotel had a printer and computer for guests which I could have used. But I was concerned that, somehow, the documents I'd be printing would be seen or duplicated. I sat down. I went online and printed the medical invoice, the scan of Paul's credit card statement, and all the details from Dr Boyards' website about the non-scalpel vasectomy. Then I crossed over to the Royal Air Maroc website. Using my credit card, I booked myself on the 12 noon direct flight tomorrow from Casablanca to New York. It arrived at 2.55 p.m. (with a five-hour time change). I switched over to the Jet Blue website and found a seat from JFK to Buffalo. There was a final email to Morton:

Arriving tomorrow at 9 p.m. If you could pick me up and get me home that would be a mitzvah. And if you know the name of a good divorce lawyer . . . But more on all that when we meet.

Three minutes later . . . *bing* . . . his reply:

I'll be there and will bring you to E. B. Green's for a sirloin and several needed martinis. Hang tough.

Not only was Morton a great friend; he was also one of the few Jewish accountants I knew who liked to drink. He always liked taking on the role of older brother to me, yet never played the 'I told you so' card when it came to Paul. I knew, from the outset, that he didn't approve of him, once telling me: 'As long as you know you're about to marry Vincent van Gogh, my blessings upon you.' But after this single admonition he never said another questioning word about my husband again. Morton knew how desperate I was to have a child. And Paul had promised . . .

I was getting shaky again. Shutting my eyes I willed myself back to an appearance of normality. Standing up and collecting all the documents I had printed, I settled the bill with the pleasantly spacey guy at the desk, watching him take in my distraught state.

'*Ça va, madame?*' he asked me.

I just shrugged and said:

'*La vie.*'

I checked my watch. Paul would have been expecting me at Chez Fouad for lunch. Steering myself away from the alleys that passed through the centre of the souk, I took a byway that led to a narrow unpaved thoroughfare and out the main gates. I was bracing myself for the usual vulture-like swoop of the touts who descend on any unsuspecting foreigner (especially a woman alone). But today when one such guy – sweaty, overweight, the usual smarmy ingratiating smile on his face – approached me and said: 'A camel ride for the beautiful lady?' I simply put up my hand like a traffic cop and barked the one Arabic word: '*Imshi.*' *Get lost.* The man looked startled. I felt like an asshole. I raised my sunglasses, showing him my red-from-crying eyes.

'*Mes excuses, madame,*' he said.

'*Je m'excuse aussi,*' I said, hurrying off to the bus depot, dodging the women hawking embroidered linen, the little kids selling strings of cheap candy, and a twelve year old on a moped who kept yelling: 'Lady, lady . . .' Reaching the bus depot, I stood in line for around twenty minutes – everyone seemed to be having an extended conversation with the guy in the ticket window. I finally got my chance to speak with him, and discovered that there was a bus early tomorrow morning for Casablanca airport, non-stop, leaving at 6 a.m., arriving there at 9.45. I bought a one-way ticket for 50 dirhams, and was told that I should be here no later than 5.30 a.m.

'*Entendu,*' I said. *Understood.*

Actually, nothing was now understood, comprehensible. I felt myself getting shaky again. I glanced at my watch. It was now 2.18 p.m. Paul would be wondering where I was and might come back to the room looking for me. Or maybe he'd simply decide that I had drifted off elsewhere, as I sometimes did. I was hoping that time was on my side. I would get back, pack my bags, leave him the corroborating evidence, a short note, head off for a long walk on the beach. And then . . .

Part of me wanted to simply jump a cab from the hotel to the bus depot, change my ticket and hop the next coach to Casablanca. But this expedient part of me was being held back by the need to confront Paul with everything, to demand some sort of explanation, to let him see just how decimated I was, how he had destroyed so much.

Where would that bring us? Me recriminating, screaming. Him playing the little boy and begging me to give him another chance.

Why is it that we always want some sort of payback, reprisal, a long tearful aria of apology, even when we know it won't change anything? The damage is so comprehensive that there's no way the two of you will ever recover from this. Why even confront the guy? Just leave.

I got back to the room ten minutes later, handing 10 dirhams to an elderly woman out front who wore the full burqa, and had the most haunted pair of eyes beaming out from the narrow black slit.

'*Je vous en supplie . . . je vous en supplie,*' she hissed at me. *I beg you, I beg you.* I thrust the money in her hand.

'*Bonne chance!*' she whispered. And even though she was wishing me luck, the way she sibilated it made it sound like a curse.

At the hotel I ran into the cleaning girl in the corridor.

'*Tout va bien, madame?*' she asked me, eyeing me carefully, fearful that I might explode again.

'*Ça va mieux,*' I lied. *All is better.*

'*La chambre est prête, madame.*' *The room is ready.*

I went upstairs. I walked into the room and stared long and

hard at the bed in which we had made love every day; passionate, deranged love, always with the hope that . . .

I had been wavering for the past ten minutes about what tack I should take. The sight of the bed made me adopt a different strategy. After packing all my bags, I laid out on the newly made bed all the documents I had just printed, beginning with the invoice, continuing with his credit card statement showing the excess amount he paid for the procedure, then his doctor's mission statement about the non-scalpel deferentectomy. I wanted Paul to understand that he'd been well and truly found out. Leaving him alone with the evidence of his betrayal would sufficiently unnerve him to make him . . .

Make him what? What do you think he'll do? Fall on his knees and beg forgiveness? Even if that does happen, then what?

Let him cry himself to sleep. Alone. Let him reflect on what life without me will mean for him.

I reached for a notepad. I scribbled:

You have killed everything and I hate you. You don't deserve to live.

Then I scrawled my name and placed the note at the end of the documents I had left fanned across the bed. Grabbing my sun hat and my bag, I headed out. I rushed past the reception desk. Ahmed must have sensed my disquiet, as he said:

'Is there a problem, *madame*?'

'Ask my husband,' I shouted.

I stormed my way to the beach. Keeping my head down. Walking ferociously down the sand, sidestepping the camel drivers and the elderly men selling roasted corn, keeping on the move until I reached that point where all signs of the external world disappeared. I sat down. I stared out at the ocean over which I would travel tomorrow, fleeing the worst sort of heartbreak and knowing full well that, even after I'd run back home, the anguish would cling to me like a metastasising cancer. I could only begin to imagine the emotional blowback ahead. For the second time, I was about to deal with the debris of a collapsed marriage. Only this time the sense of failure and betrayal would be beyond agonising. Because I had bought into a lie.

I let go, crying wildly for around ten minutes. There was no one around to watch in disconcerted unease; here my grief was drowned out by the surf. When I had subsided I found myself thinking: *Now what? I go home. I go back to work. I try to pick up the proverbial pieces. I face into the most crippling sort of loneliness.* As much as I now hated Paul, another part of me was convulsed at the thought of losing him. How can you feel that way about someone who has violated your trust? Why was I needy of Paul at the very moment that I wanted to leave him for ever? How could I be so torn?

Guilt began to inveigle its way into my psyche, even though I knew I had no cause to feel any; that it was me who had been wronged. It was me who had to grapple with the agony of an act of intimate treason. And it was me who was sitting here, alone on a North African beach, beginning to wonder if I'd been too extreme in the note scribbled in fury.

The problem with ongoing guilt – especially the sort that has been clogging up your psyche since childhood – is that you simply cannot rationalise your way out of its choke-hold.

The light above was beginning to fade. I checked my watch. It was edging toward five p.m. Had I been out here all this time? Was one of the reasons that I had stayed so long on the beach the vain hope that Paul – having discovered my packed bags along with the documentary evidence left for him – would have rushed here to find me, knowing that I walked these sands every afternoon.

But I must have hiked for over an hour to reach this empty spot. Maybe he only got back to the hotel from his lunch and working afternoon at Chez Fouad just a few minutes ago . . . perhaps he was heading this way?

And there you go again, wanting some sort of Hollywood moment: 'I have made the mistake of my life. The vasectomy is reversible. I've made an appointment with the urologist. I will fly back tomorrow with you and be unfixed by the weekend.'

But the beach was empty. Paul usually returned home from Fouad's by three for a siesta. It was now almost five. Not a sign of anyone on the horizon. I was totally alone. His non-show on the beach was proof – if it was truly needed – that we were kaput.

The walk back to the hotel seemed to take an inordinately long time. When I reached the front desk Ahmed appeared unnerved by my arrival.

'Is something wrong?' I asked him.

'*Le patron, Monsieur Picard* . . . he needs to speak to you.'

Not *wants* to speak with you. *Needs to.*

'What's happened? Where's my husband?'

'You wait here, please.'

Ahmed ducked into the back office. I shut my eyes, wondering: *What fresh hell is this?*

Monsieur Picard emerged a few moments later, looking as grim-faced and bleak as an oncologist about to articulate bad news.

'We've been looking everywhere for you, *madame*. We were deeply worried.'

'What's happened? Where's my husband?'

'Your husband has . . . vanished.'

I blanched, but perhaps in a way that indicated I was not surprised, as Picard said:

'You were expecting this?'

'No, not at all.'

'But you left him documents and a note—'

'You've been in our room?' I shouted, suddenly angry. 'Who gave you the right to—?'

'What gave me the right was the fact that the cleaners heard your husband screaming in the room. Screams that followed loud thumps.'

Immediately I was dashing up the stairs, Picard calling after me, telling me I shouldn't go in there; that it was a potential crime scene, and the police were . . .

But I raced ahead, throwing open the door when I reached it. When I stepped inside what I saw was . . .

Chaos.

It did look like a crime scene – in which robbery and violence were part of the perpetration. Clothes strewn everywhere. Every drawer pulled out, contents dumped. Two of his sketchbooks torn apart, the ripped, decimated paper littering the room like deranged confetti. And on the stone wall in front of our bed, a cascade of blood in the process of drying.

Next to the documents and the note I had left for Paul was a piece of paper. On which was scrawled – in his characteristic cramped calligraphy – five words:

You're right. I should die.

Ten

'DON'T TOUCH THE documents,' Picard warned me when I reached for Paul's scrawled note.

'But they belong to me,' I said.

'The police might think otherwise.'

'The police?'

'Your husband was last heard screaming in this room. Then there was silence. Ahmed reported all this to me when I returned to the hotel just ten minutes ago. He said he didn't want to disturb Monsieur Paul, as there had been no further screaming since his initial outburst. I told him to go upstairs and check. What Ahmed discovered was that your husband had vanished, but blood was covering the walls. Of course we called the police, as I was initially concerned that it might be your blood. Until I saw the letter you left him. Where were you when all this was going on?'

'I was out hiking along the beach.'

'I see.'

The tone of that last comment unsettled me. It sounded studiously neutral – as if he was hinting that he didn't believe me.

'I was back here briefly around two-thirty p.m. and then went out for my usual walk—'

Picard cut me off.

'There's no need to explain this to me. It is the police who will be asking the questions.'

'Questions about what? I should be out looking for my husband.'

'They will be here shortly. I had them standing by, waiting for your return.'

The cops did arrive two minutes later. A corpulent officer sweating in his blue uniform, and a narrow-shouldered detective in a cheap suit, a white shirt yellowed from over-washing, and a thin paisley tie. He was around forty with a pencil moustache and slicked-back hair. They both saluted me, simultaneously eyeing me with professional interest. Ahmed showed up in the doorway as well. The detective and Monsieur Picard spoke to each other in fast Arabic, then the detective questioned Ahmed who half-gestured towards me several times. Meanwhile the uniformed officer was inspecting the bed, the documents and the two scrawled notes that we had left for each other, the disarray of the room, the bloodied stonework. He said something to the detective who came over to inspect the blood, pulling out a small handkerchief to daub in it, studying it intently. He asked a question of Ahmed who replied in a torrent of Arabic, again gesturing at me throughout. Then the detective introduced himself to me in French as Inspector Moufad.

'When did you last see your husband?' he asked.

'Around twelve-fifteen. We'd slept in late. My French teacher, Soraya, woke us up . . .'

'What's her full name and address?'

Picard supplied these immediately, which the officer dutifully wrote down. Moufad continued:

'So you slept late, your teacher arrived, and then . . .?'

'I had my lesson. Soraya saw my husband leave our room. He was heading off to have lunch and work at Chez Fouad.'

'Your husband was working at the café?' the inspector asked, finding this just a little strange.

'He's an artist . . . and a professor at a university back in the States. He was working on a series of line drawings about life in the souk.'

'Where are these drawings?'

I pointed to the cascade of torn paper everywhere, tears coming to my eyes as I took in the debris around me. His exquisite, extraordinary drawings. The best work he'd ever done; the new turning point in his creative career. And now . . . shredded beyond redemption.

'Who tore up these drawings?' Moufad asked.

'I presume it was Paul.'

'Do you have your husband's passport?'

'Of course not.'

'Why do you think he tore up his artwork?'

'You'd have to ask him that.'

'But he's not here, is he, *madame*? Monsieur Picard reports that one of his cleaners heard a commotion in the room around four p.m. Monsieur Ahmed went upstairs to check – but found the room empty, turned upside down, this fresh blood everywhere.'

He brandished his handkerchief with the still-wet sample blotting into its cotton fibres.

'Was someone here with him?' I asked.

'Was that someone you, *madame*?' Moufad countered.

'I was taking a walk on the beach – as I do almost every afternoon.'

'Did anyone see you take that walk?'

'No, I was on my own, as always.'

'So you weren't with anybody then?'

'I just told you I was on my own.'

'How do I have proof of that?'

'What you have proof of is an incident in our room when my husband was here and I was out walking the beach. Look at the state of this place. My husband's been robbed and clearly injured.'

'But where is your husband now if he was so injured? If it was a robbery, why didn't they take either of your laptops?' he asked, pointing to the pair of laptops side by side on the desk. 'And there is that very expensive Canon camera by the bed.'

The uniformed cop now picked up a mug from the desk, looked inside and said something to Moufad. When it was handed to him the inspector pulled out a small wad of dirhams.

'A thief would definitely have taken all this cash that you unwisely left out.'

Picard seemed offended by this remark.

'In the twenty-three years I have run Les Deux Chameaux,' he said, 'we have never once had a robbery.'

'There's always a first time,' I said. Picard and Moufad exchanged a knowing glance.

'Even if your husband had surprised the thieves,' Moufad said, 'even if they had slammed his head against the wall, they would have left with the cash and the electronic goods. They would have grabbed what was valuable and in plain sight – as all these items were. So the fact that the laptops, the camera, the cash were left behind . . . a little strange for thieves. Then there is the matter of the whereabouts of your husband. Why would thieves smash his head against a wall and then drag him away with them, while leaving all the valuable booty behind? It simply doesn't make sense.'

'But surely someone saw my husband leave the hotel.'

'One of the young cleaners – Mira – heard the commotion in the room,' Picard said. 'She came downstairs to the reception and raised the alarm. Ahmed then heard more screaming, raced upstairs, found the room in its current state of disorder, and found me. We searched the hotel. No sign of your husband.'

'Might he have headed out while Ahmed was upstairs?'

'That is a possibility,' Moufad said. 'Another possibility is that you and your husband had an altercation.'

'We didn't have an altercation.'

'There was an angry exchange of notes, wasn't there? I don't read English – but Monsieur Picard, when he called us, translated them for me.'

Inspector Moufad reached into the breast pocket of his jacket and pulled out a small black vinyl notebook. He thumbed through it until he found the page he wanted.

'One note – I presume it was yours – reads: "*You have killed everything and I hate you. You don't deserve to live.*" You did write this, yes?'

I hung my head, then quietly said: 'I wrote that.'

'And his reply: "*You're right. I should die.*" If, that is, he actually wrote that.'

'Who else could have done that?' I asked, sounding angry now.

'Someone who might have wanted to harm him.'

'Let me get this straight, Inspector. Are you actually thinking that I had an altercation with my husband that saw me – a woman around half his physical size – slam his head against the wall, smuggle his unconscious body out when nobody was looking, but before doing that, write a note in his handwriting, indicating that he was planning to kill himself?'

The inspector thought this one through for a few moments, then said:

'Who's to say that you haven't hidden the body somewhere in the hotel?'

'But I wasn't here.'

'Nobody saw you leave for your alleged beach walk.'

'I did no harm whatsoever to my husband,' I said, the anger again flashing. 'After he headed out to Chez Fouad I didn't see him again.'

'But you nonetheless left all these documents behind for him to discover, along with a note wishing him dead. Monsieur Picard translated all the medical transcripts for me. They too make interesting reading. A record of your husband having undergone a vasectomy.'

Silence. I could see the three men quietly relishing my immense discomfort at discovering that they knew everything about this grubby business. I motioned to a chair, indicating that I would like to sit down. Moufad gave me his OK. I positioned myself in the armchair, trying to figure a way out of this, eventually deciding the only way forward was to tell the truth.

'I am an accountant back in the States. My firm also does my husband's accounts. One of my associates contacted me today with the information you discovered on the bed. Information that my husband, having agreed with me that we would try for a child – and knowing full well that, with my fortieth birthday only weeks away, I no longer had time on my side – had gone and got himself . . . sterilised. As you can imagine the discovery of this . . . betrayal . . . well, it was shattering. My husband was out at Chez Fouad when these documents arrived. I printed them up and left them on our bed with an angry note in an attempt to prick his conscience. Then I left for my beach walk – and returned to find all this.'

Silence. A quick glance between the inspector and Picard. The inspector then approached me.

'As sympathetic as I am to what has befallen you, *madame*, you have left out a key part of your story – the fact that, earlier this

89

afternoon, you booked a flight back to the States tomorrow at twelve noon from Casablanca.'

I felt myself tense.

'You work fast, *monsieur*.'

'My job,' he said.

'But the decision to fly back tomorrow . . . that was my determination to leave him there and then. In the wake of what I had discovered, it was over.'

'And you left him a note saying he should die for what he did.'

'That was anger. Pure rage. I certainly wouldn't want any harm to come to my husband.'

'Even though there is written evidence that you wanted him dead. Perhaps with good reason – as he did something so cunning, so calculated, so treacherous.'

Moufad had me locked in his line of vision – I was beginning to feel my hands go clammy and beads of sweat were cascading down my face. As far as he was concerned I was the person of interest in this case.

'*Monsieur*,' I said, trying to calm myself, 'why would I leave a note like that if I was planning to do my husband harm? Why would he leave me his reply if he didn't feel horrendous about being caught out in this terrible lie?'

A little shrug from the inspector.

'Perhaps you wrote his note yourself.'

I stood up and walked over to the desk where Paul kept the large black hardcover Moleskine notebook that was his journal – and which I never touched, as I believe that privacy is sacrosanct. The uniformed officer tried to stop me, but the inspector said something that made him back off. I opened the journal and found page after page of Paul's spindly handwriting. Followed by pages of sketches, doodles. And several bulky items in the inside pocket on the back cover. I came over and placed a page of his journal next to the note he had left on the bed. Even if you weren't a trained forensic graphologist it was blindingly obvious that the writing belonged to the same person. Moufad, the uniformed officer and Picard all took turns staring down at the comparative scrawls. The inspector pursed his lips.

'And who's to say this isn't your journal?' he asked.

I stormed back over to the desk and picked up my own diary, flinging it down on the bed next to the enraged note that had landed me in such deep trouble.

'This is my journal – and, as you will note, the handwriting matches my own.'

Another shrug.

'I will need to take all this evidence with me, along with your passport.'

'Are you charging me with a crime?'

'Not yet. But there is clear evidence here that—'

'What?' I said, now emboldened and angry. 'The way I see it, my husband saw that I had found out about his lie and that I was planning to leave him, and went berserk. Tearing up his drawings, slamming his head against the wall. We have to find him. *Now*.'

My delivery of this statement was so vehement that it rendered Moufad and Picard wide-eyed. Moufad finally replied:

'I am still taking the journals, the documents, the notes and your passport as—'

'You will do no such thing,' I said, 'unless you want to formally charge me with my husband's disappearance . . . if, that is, he has disappeared.'

'*Madame*, you do not know the law here.'

'I know that the United States has an embassy in Rabat and a consulate in Casablanca. If you try to seize my passport or any of my possessions – and that includes my husband's effects – I will make a phone call. You will then have to deal with the consequences.'

Just to prove that I meant business I started to reach for my journal. The uniformed officer instinctively reached out and grabbed me roughly by the arm. I broke away and screamed at him:

'*Comment osez-vous? Je connais mes droits!*'

The officer backed off immediately.

'There is no need for drama, *madame*,' said Moufad.

'Yes, there is. My husband is in distress, perhaps terribly injured. And probably wandering around Essaouira, bleeding and disorientated. We are wasting precious time here. I suggest that we all go to Chez Fouad to see if he's gone back there, or if Fouad has got him to a doctor's.'

Silence. I could see that the inspector was calculating his next move.

'OK,' he said. 'We will go to Chez Fouad. But everything remains here.'

'No way. Because we'll get back from Fouad's and find that your men have cleared the place out.'

'You will have my word, *madame*.'

'With respect . . . that's not enough, *monsieur*.'

Another silence. Then an idea dropped into my head.

'I will, however, allow you to photograph everything – just as it is now. Before we leave. But the documents, the notebooks, remain with me.'

Moufad bit on his lower lip, not completely disliking this idea . . . but not at all pleased with the way I was setting the agenda.

'I will agree to that – on two conditions. The suite is sealed after we photograph it. I am certain Monsieur Picard can find you another room for the night. And I will assign one of my men to watch guard over you . . .'

'That is not at all necessary.'

'Yes, *madame*, it is. Though you have not been charged with any crime so far there is the fact that some sort of potentially criminal activity took place in this room. Perhaps you are right. Perhaps your husband has indeed attempted to harm himself, burdened by guilt and the realisation that he has lost you – that you are leaving him. Which, no doubt, must be something very hard to bear. But who's to say he might not come back and try to harm you? We must rest assured that you are safe here tonight. Would you not agree?'

I felt myself about to flinch again.

'I am certain that Paul will not do me any harm.'

'But if he's left blood on the walls from self-inflicted wounds, and has ripped up his precious artwork . . .'

I knew I didn't have a retort to that so I said nothing. The inspector asked Picard if there was any access from the roof or a back door into the hotel. Picard informed him that only a cat could find a way from the roof into one of the rooms, and that the rear entrance was always padlocked from the inside.

'There is no way for a guest to leave the hotel except by the front door.'

'Then I will, with your permission, have one of my men stationed in front of the hotel all night to ensure that no harm comes to *Madame* . . .'

'If I choose to go for a walk?' I asked.

'The officer will accompany you. By the way, I will be approaching a judge tomorrow morning to obtain a warrant to seize the evidence we've photographed, and to force you to turn your passport over to us until the investigation into your husband's disappearance has been concluded.'

'Then I will be contacting my embassy first thing tomorrow morning as well.'

'That is your prerogative, *madame*.'

He turned to Picard.

'With your permission I will have several of my men search your hotel to see if *Madame*'s husband might still be here, hidden away somewhere.'

Picard nodded his assent. But then I said:

'Surely my husband could have gone out when someone wasn't watching the front door?'

Now all eyes were on Ahmed. He looked uneasy at the attention.

'I was at the desk all afternoon – and never saw Monsieur Paul leave,' he said.

'So he must still be here,' the inspector noted.

'But surely if Monsieur Ahmed had to pick up the phone, or deal with a guest, or answer a call to nature, my husband could have slipped by undetected.'

Again all eyes were on Ahmed. He just shrugged and said:

'Of course the nature of my job means that I am not at the front desk one hundred per cent of the time.'

'So he could easily have gone out,' I said.

'Someone would have seen him,' Picard interjected. 'We have a man out front most of the time too. Karim. He is our informal security person during the day – always outside, sweeping, tending to the plants, ensuring no one loiters near the entrance. We have another man there at night – as *Madame* knows, since he rescued her on her first night when she made the dangerous mistake of wandering off on her own.'

Trumped again. I could see the inspector, in the wake of this little tale, deciding: *This woman is trouble.*

Just to twist the knife deeper, Picard added:

'I spoke to Karim after we heard the commotion in your room. He was out front all afternoon and never saw your husband go out.'

'But I didn't see Karim when I left for my walk,' I said.

Picard narrowed me in his sights.

'Yet he saw you leave – and he told me you had murder in your eyes.'

'That's not true.' Though of course I knew that I had stormed off, looking frenzied. But that line about Karim seeing me . . .

'Does it matter if he thought I looked angry?' I said. 'The fact that he saw me leave the hotel before my husband got back—'

'He never saw your husband come back,' Picard retorted. 'Nor did he see him leave. Neither did Ahmed. Isn't that right, Ahmed?'

Ahmed nodded his head several times. Who wants to bite the hand that pays him? Especially when the hand belongs to such a cold, calculating operator as Picard, who wants to keep the police on his side and will happily see me framed for this if it wins him credit. I've no doubt that, in a place like this, having the police in your corner is a serious necessity.

'I will say this once more. My husband left the hotel around twelve-fifteen. I left around two p.m. I came back a half-hour later, then went and took a walk on the beach. In my absence something happened in our room which left blood on the wall and my husband . . .'

I felt myself welling up, but I held down the sob and managed to say:

'He's somewhere out there, injured, in desperate need of help. So can we please get out of here and over to Chez Fouad?'

The inspector studied his fingernails for several moments, then said:

'We will leave for Chez Fouad when we have photographed everything in the room and when we have searched the hotel and are satisfied that your husband's body hasn't been secreted here. And no, you may not go to Fouad's alone. I may not as yet be able to take your passport away from you, but I can have you escorted and followed everywhere in Essaouira. Which is exactly what I am planning to do.'

Eleven

IT TOOK THEM over two hours to search the hotel. Every room was opened – and several guests disturbed – as the police, all led by Inspector Moufad, looked under every bed and in every bathtub and insisted on opening every wardrobe. All storage closets were inspected on each of the four floors. The meat locker and the big freezer in the kitchen. The extra-large garbage bins in the rear alley. The staff bedrooms in the basement.

On and on the inspection went, despite my entreaties to let me go to Fouad's accompanied by an officer. The inspector was letting me know that, from this point on, we'd be playing by his rules. He insisted on sending for 'the official police photographer' to take detailed pictures of the two telltale notes, the two journals, the shredded drawings, the broken chest of drawers, the crimson splatter on the stonework. At one juncture the young cleaner, Mira, came in with a tray of mint tea for the policemen (but Ahmed, accompanying her, insisted on pouring it himself). I could tell immediately that Mira was finding the sight of the destroyed room more than a little unnerving. She was also looking at me with silent trepidation, as if she wanted to tell me something but couldn't with all the officialdom around. I caught her eye and motioned that we could talk in the corridor but she shook her head and hurried off. When the inspector came back into the room I said:

'We could have spent all this time searching for my husband. Instead we—'

'Are you telling me how to run this investigation, *madame*?'

'I just want to find Paul. I'm scared, *monsieur*. Scared for him.'

'You will be pleased to hear that I've had two of my men scouring the beach. They had our four-by-four, so they were able to drive around ten kilometres down the sands. No sign of your husband . . . unless, of course, he decided to go into the water. Or was pushed.'

I could see the inspector again studying me, trying to fathom how I was dealing with that less-than-veiled accusation, or the thought that perhaps Paul threw himself into the Atlantic with his head haemorrhaging blood. Again I felt the anguish welling up. But I managed to push it away as I met his accusing stare straight on and said:

'*Vous êtes un homme très sympathique. Très classe.*'

I could see him flinch. Just as I could also see him quickly recover and shoot back:

'*Vous allez regretter cette parole.*' You will regret that word.

A moment later the same uniformed officer who'd arrived with the inspector showed up to inform him that the hotel search was complete and nothing had been found.

'Can we now go to Fouad's?' I demanded.

'We first need to make an inventory of all the goods you are taking with you.'

This process took another half-hour. Every object I was moving into the new room that Picard found for me down the corridor had to be registered in a police log. After the journals, the papers and notes, the laptop computers, our respective clothes and toiletries had been documented, I was allowed to put the crucial items in a backpack. Picard called Mira back and told her that she should pack up all our clothes and move them with our suitcases to Room 212, and also deal with anything left in the bathroom or elsewhere. Again I sensed that she wanted to make contact with me. Again the presence of others thwarted her.

'All right, we will now go to Chez Fouad,' Moufad announced.

I hoisted the backpack onto my shoulders.

'Surely you should leave that behind in your new room,' Picard said.

'And discover it all not here, but with the police when I return?'

'I appreciate your confidence, *madame*.'

As we were leaving, Picard asked to speak to me for a moment.

'I will have to charge you for the new room in which I am putting you until the police allow me to redecorate the one that you and your husband have destroyed.'

'I had nothing to do with—'

'I must inform you that, in addition to the five hundred dirhams per night for the new room, I estimate that, to replace the chest of drawers, repaint and repair everything in your old suite . . . it will be around eight thousand dirhams.'

8,000 dirhams was $900. Absurd. Especially as just two of the drawers were smashed, and the hand-painted chest itself remained undamaged. There were only three long blotches of blood on the wall, most of which would come off with soap and hot water. But I was too stressed to argue with this oily little man. So I said:

'I will pay for the extra room tonight. We have paid the entire month for the suite in advance. Your lawyer can speak to my lawyer about the cost of the alleged damages.'

'That is not satisfactory, *madame.*'

'Nor is your attempt to gouge me for money at a time like this.'

I walked off down the stairs to the foyer, the hefty backpack strapped across my shoulders.

When I reached the front desk part of me wanted to make a break for it; to dash out into the dark alleys and byways of Essaouira and run to Fouad's and find my husband sitting there, his head bandaged, nursing a glass of red wine, sketching mournfully, a sad smile crossing his face; me rushing into his arms, so relieved to find him alive, willing for the next few days to push aside the terrible things that had caused all this madness, and simply be happy that he was out of danger. Even though the other part of me seriously doubted I could stay in this marriage. And that gut feeling was overshadowed by the guilt I felt about springing the trap on him, which I'd known would send him into a downward spiral. That was the worst part of all this. Had I simply confronted him, face to face, with the urologist's bill, at least we could have yelled at each other and worked out some sort of resolution, even if it meant the end of us as a couple. But instead I took the cruel option. Leaving those documents out, accompanied by my note suggesting he should die . . . that was vindictive. Like most attempts at revenge the blowback had now badly singed me.

A tap on the shoulder. The inspector was by my side.

'OK, we can go now,' he said.

'If it turns out he isn't there . . .'

'Then he isn't there.'

I checked my watch: nearly half-past nine. Hours since he fled the room, unseen by anyone. As we began to walk down the back lanes towards the souk my gaze was fixed on everyone who came towards us, who lurked in a doorway or was slumped against a wall. This must be how the parents of a missing child feel: the desperate horror of knowing that the centre of their lives has disappeared, and hoping against hope that he or she will suddenly stumble out in front of them, ending the nightmare from which there is no other release.

It took less than ten minutes to reach Chez Fouad. The six tables on the little veranda out front were all packed. Fouad was taking an order when he caught sight of me. From the way he tensed – and then tried quickly to mask his distress – I sensed that he must know something about Paul's whereabouts. But when the inspector approached him – flashing his badge, giving him the suspicious once-over – Fouad played dumb.

'Of course I know Monsieur Paul,' he said. 'One of my best customers. Always sits at the corner table over there. We have a collection of his drawings behind the bar.'

'And the last time you saw him here?' Moufad asked.

'When he left at four o'clock.'

'You're certain he didn't return?' I asked.

'*Madame*, it's me who poses the questions,' Moufad said.

'And it's my husband who's missing. I also know Fouad, so . . .'

'When Monsieur Paul said goodbye to me at four that was the last time I saw him today.'

'Surely someone has seen him since then,' I said.

'I've been on duty here since three. Had Monsieur Paul shown up again I would have seen him.'

'Could you ask any of the other waiters?'

'I am the waiter, as you well know, *madame*. Had he been here I would tell you.'

As he said this I glanced down and saw him rubbing his right thumb manically against his forefinger. The inspector was glancing elsewhere. When he informed Fouad that he wanted to 'look around the kitchen and any storage room', Fouad said he had carte blanche to search wherever he wanted. As soon as Moufad had gone inside the café I turned to Fouad and said:

'I know you know where Paul is. You need to tell me – is he all right?'

'Can you come back later?'

'Not easily. They have a cop positioned at the door of the hotel, under orders to follow me everywhere. They think I hurt Paul.'

'Find a way of getting back here before midnight.'

'Please, please, let me know if my husband is OK.'

But the inspector emerged from inside, asking Fouad to come with him.

'Be back before midnight,' Fouad whispered, then disappeared. I was momentarily free of my police escort, but knew if I vanished now it would just raise more suspicion. But how would I be able to get out of the hotel later and find my way here?

There was a moment when I thought I could dash off into the night now, hide somewhere for an hour, then creep back and learn the truth from Fouad. But as soon as I took a few steps away from the café, a uniformed police officer emerged from the shadows. Saluting me he said:

'*Madame*, I have been instructed to ensure that you don't leave this immediate area. So please return to your table and await the inspector.'

I had no choice but to do as ordered. When Moufad returned a few minutes later with Fouad he told me that he had searched the entire inside of the café, and there was no sign whatsoever of my husband's presence.

'I will now have you escorted back to the hotel. I will be sending my men to the bus station and the taxi rank to see if he tried to leave town. We have our contacts there, so if he did board a bus or arrange a car to take him elsewhere we will know.'

'And if I want to go out again?'

'Then one of my men will accompany you.'

The officer who'd stopped me from leaving the café took me back to Les Deux Chameaux. When I walked past the front desk Ahmed informed me that Mira had moved all our clothes and personal effects to the new room, and that Monsieur Picard was demanding 500 dirhams now before I would be allowed to go upstairs. I handed over the cash, telling Ahmed:

'Please inform Monsieur Picard that I consider him to be nothing less than *un connard*.'

I could see that Ahmed was both shocked by my choice of insult and struggling not to grin in agreement. He insisted on carrying the heavy backpack upstairs and I followed him to Room 212. It was tiny – a small cell with a narrow single bed, a sink, a view of the wall in a nearby alleyway, an elderly bathroom with peeling paint.

'Couldn't you find me something else?'

'Monsieur Picard told me that you have to sleep here tonight. When the boss returns tomorrow—'

'I will call him "*un connard*" to his face. Could you please ask Mira to bring me some mint tea.'

'*Très bien, madame.*'

As soon as he closed the door, I sat down on the bed, threw open the backpack and dumped out its contents. I reached immediately for Paul's journal. Its rear pocket revealed a shock: my husband's passport. On one level this was a relief, as it indicated that he wasn't planning to leave town or country. But like me, Paul went nowhere in Essaouira without this important piece of documentation. Why had he dashed off without it? Unless, in the anguish of discovering that I had learned his nasty little secret, he simply ran out, not knowing what to do next. Which increased my sense of guilt tenfold.

Then another discovery in the same pocket hit me like a donkey kick. A small three-by-five photograph of a young woman, no more than early twenties. Moroccan, yet with certain features that hinted she might be of mixed parentage. A rather beautiful young woman with a cascade of jet-black curls. Slim, perfect skin, lightly rouged lips, stylish: a tight black T-shirt and jeans that managed to highlight her long-leggedness. Moroccan-French I decided – and one who could easily be labelled a heartbreaker.

I stared at the photo in quiet shock for several moments. This deepened further when I turned it over and saw the following inscription:

From your Samira
Absence always makes the heart grow fonder.
With all my love
S xxx

She now had a name. Samira. A young woman – almost four decades his junior – who had sent a photograph of herself to my husband, expressing her love for him.

'*L'absence rend le coeur plus affectueux.*'

Not just her love for Paul, but a statement that being apart from him was causing her to yearn.

Samira. *La belle Samira.* Whose handwriting was highly calligraphic – as if she'd used a special italics pen to write this declaration, signing it with a little heart next to her name. I tossed the photograph onto the bed, away from me, my head reeling.

I grabbed his journal. Page after page of his tortured penmanship. With Mira arriving any moment bringing tea I didn't have time to decipher it. Instead I whisked through the entire journal, looking for some sort of indicator of where this Samira might be found.

A stroke of good luck. On a page creased in half, and partially decorated with sketches of . . . oh God, this was too hard to bear . . . her face . . . I opened the fold to read:

I have to find a way of getting Samira back in my life. Robin will freak – to put it mildly. But she has to know the truth sometime . . . though if she found out all the truth I would lose her for ever.

So there it was: the second secret he'd been harbouring for some time now. The other woman. How could I have been so naive?

How did I not see this life in parallel that he was having? And how did he meet this Moroccan beauty . . . whom he was desperate to get back into his life?

The other woman. The stuff of cliché.

And a younger woman who lives at: *2350 rue Taha Hussein, Casablanca 4e*.

No phone number. Damn. No email. I flipped open Paul's computer. The strangest feeling hit me, of unease about violating his privacy; yet another part of me simultaneously castigated myself for even allowing guilt to enter the current equation. I didn't know Paul's password for his computer – and it was very much locked. I tried several combinations of possible passwords – I knew that our joint bank account was robinpaultogether. That was his suggestion. Simply typing it made me well up again.

A knock at the door had me scrambling to put everything away, ensuring that the photograph of Paul's beloved was slipped back into the inside pocket of his journal. When I opened the door I found Mira there, holding a tray of mint tea, looking as though she wanted to be anywhere but here. I ushered her inside. As soon as I shut the door she asked where I would like the tea. I pointed to the chest of drawers.

'You know something, don't you?' I asked.

She looked at me, wide-eyed, as if I had caught her in the act of theft, and shook her head several times. I saw that her eyes were brimming with tears.

'It's all right, it's all right,' I said.

That's when a shudder ran through her body. Reaching into the pocket of her djellaba she pulled out a $100 bill.

'I'm sorry, I'm so sorry. I should have never taken this . . .'

'Did my husband give this to you?' I asked.

More tears.

'I told him I didn't want it. But he pushed it into my hand. "This is what I make in two weeks," I told him. He just shrugged and said it was a little thank-you if he could . . .'

She seemed on the verge of breaking down.

'You didn't do anything wrong.'

'Yes, I did. Because I took his money in exchange for showing him a way out of here that avoided going by the front desk.'

'Did he say why he wanted to sneak off without anyone knowing?'

'Of course not. He just said that he needed to "vanish without a trace" – his exact words. He gave me all this money after asking me if I knew a hidden passage out of the hotel.'

'And do you?'

Mira now looked even more perturbed by this question.

'I should never have helped him.'

'Did he say he was running off?'

'All he said was: "Can you find a way for me to disappear without being seen by anyone? And can you keep a secret and not tell anyone that I left?"'

'So why are you telling me now?'

'Because you're not anyone. You're his wife. He's done something bad, hasn't he?'

'Nothing criminal – just hurtful.'

'I let him escape.'

'All he was doing was running away from himself.'

Silence. I could see that thought lodging in her consciousness, and leading to more confusion.

'Did my husband say where he was going?'

She shook her head, then added:

'I insisted on bandaging his head before he left.'

'What had he done to himself?'

Pointing to the bed – and asking my permission to sit down – she positioned herself on the edge of the thin mattress, grasping onto it as if it was keeping her afloat.

'I heard a lot of noise before I came into the room. It sounded like he was throwing himself against the wall. Deliberately smashing his head. When I opened the door I saw him run towards the wall and take the entire blow against his head. The room was madness, as if it had been torn apart. When he collapsed on the ground and I started running out the door to get help, he shouted at me not to. Then he apologised for yelling, and

104

asked if I could find a bandage for his head, again begging me not to mention this to Ahmed or anyone else. So I ran and found a bandage and some hot water. When I got back Monsieur Paul was sitting on the bed, looking as if he might pass out. I cleaned up the wound and wrapped his head in a bandage, as there was a lot of blood. I told him that he had a very large lump on his forehead – already blue-black in colour – and that he should really see a doctor, in case he had a concussion. They can be dangerous, *n'est-ce pas?*'

'Yes, they can be dangerous. What happened next?'

'He asked me if there was a way out of the building that would avoid the front desk.'

'Did he say why he wanted to sneak out?'

'No.'

'I suppose he didn't want anyone to see what he'd done to himself.'

'I wouldn't know. He seemed very . . . unstable. I was worried that, after injuring himself, it mightn't be a good idea for him to go out. But he said he had to see a friend.'

'Did he tell you the name of the friend?'

'The man who runs the café. He asked me again if I knew a way out the back of the hotel. When I told him I didn't want to get into any trouble he gave me this . . .'

She brought out the crumpled $100 bill.

'I was shocked when he insisted on giving me so much. I told him I didn't want his money and that Monsieur Picard would be furious if he discovered that I had helped him sneak away . . . especially with the state of the room. But he told me that Monsieur Picard would get money from you to pay for it – and the one hundred dollars was a gift to me for helping him out and not saying anything. But I really can't keep it.'

She proffered the creased bill, making me wonder if Paul had a stash of American dollars he hadn't told me about.

'Of course you must keep the money. I will give you an additional three hundred dirhams if you show me the back way out of here.'

'But the police . . . they will get very angry with me . . .

maybe get me into trouble if they find out that I have helped you.'

'They didn't know you helped Paul. They won't know that you helped me. Anyway, I will be back in an hour or so. What did he take with him?'

'Take with him? Nothing. Once I had bandaged his head he stood up and said he could walk, and gave me the money. I asked him to wait in the room, then returned when I was certain it was safe for him to go.'

'Where's that secret way out of here? Will I be able to get back in by myself?'

'Please, *madame*, if they catch me aiding you . . .'

'I will take the blame.' I reached into my pocket for the cash and thrust it upon her.

'You and *Monsieur* are being too generous.'

No, what we are being is very American: thinking that money can buy our way out of everything. Mira looked at the cash. I could see her hesitating.

'I will come back in twenty minutes,' she said at last. 'Ahmed will be on a break then. We won't have much in the way of time, because he only gets fifteen minutes off. But as long as you are ready when I return . . .'

'I'll be ready.'

Mira nodded and left. I went over and poured out a glass of the 'Moroccan whisky', but the mint tea was balming nothing tonight. I quickly repacked the backpack with things I didn't want left behind in the room: my laptop, my passport and journal, Paul's diary. I counted all the remaining cash that I had hidden away in a sleeve at the back of my journal; money that I had secreted just in case emergency funds were ever needed. There was close to 8,000 dirhams – around $900. My great hope was that, once I got over to Chez Fouad, I would discover that Paul had hidden himself in some room within the café which the inspector hadn't found. With some coaxing and kindness (and putting aside my maimed pride for a day or so) I could get us back to the States and Paul into the hands of a good shrink – who would help him negotiate the aftermath of my leaving him.

I finished the tea. Resisting the temptation to look further through Paul's diary, I tried to keep the hurt and anxiety that were coursing through me under control.

A light knock on the door. When I opened it Mira put her finger to her lips and motioned for me to follow her. I hoisted the backpack. We both scanned the corridor. It was clear. We crept along like cats. At the end of the hallway was a small door – I had to take off my backpack to squeeze through it – and after that a narrow stairway, the steps crumbling, the walls reeking of damp. Down and down we went, entering some subterranean warren. We reached another door. When Mira opened it the stench of sewage hit my nostrils: vile, overpowering. Reaching into her apron pocket she brought out a candle and a disposable lighter. Holding a flame to the wick she whispered:

'Don't say a word, don't make any unnecessary noise.'

We were in a low tunnel, with wet muddy walls and a damp dirt floor. The height couldn't have been more than six feet. Paul must have been forced to painfully crouch down all the way along its moist, odorous passageway – further pain after the self-inflicted wound. I sucked in my breath, put my hand over my mouth and used my thumb and forefinger to pinch my nostrils shut. I followed the candle held by Mira. It took us a very long and unsettling five minutes to reach its far end. The walls seemed to be sweating, as trickles of liquefied dirt mingled with insects, worms, and . . . oh God, no . . . a rat that ran right out in front of us and made me gasp. Mira – completely unfazed by the sudden emergence of this filthy rodent – put her finger to her lips. I kept wondering if one wrong move, an accidental bump into its delicate substructure, would cause the entire tunnel to collapse, burying us alive. My horror at being in this tiny passage was magnified many times over by the thought that I had endangered a young girl, no older than fourteen, by insisting she take me along the same escape route as my husband.

We reached a metal door. Mira tried to open it but it wouldn't budge so she rapped on it harshly with her tiny knuckles. After a moment it creaked open. A small hand reached in and pulled Mira through. Then the same hand reappeared. I took it and was hoisted around the door's rusted frame and found myself face to face with the owner of the hand: a kid around fifteen, with a sly, challenging look on his face. He said something to Mira in Arabic. She answered back in a way that made it clear to him that she wasn't impressed with his wise-assed comment. Switching to French she told me:

'This is Mohammed. He thinks he is my boyfriend. He is not. He wants one hundred dirhams for opening the door and guiding you up to the street. I have told him thirty dirhams. We've agreed fifty. You pay him half now, half when you return.'

Then she barked something at Mohammed, which made him tense for a moment before that flirtatious look returned to his face. Mira saw this and rolled her eyes – and then raised her finger close to his face and said something that, from its tone, sounded half like a warning, half a threat.

'I've told him if he plays any games with you – like asking for more money – he will have to answer to me,' Mira said. 'Now I have to go back. Mohammed will wait for you on the street above here. He will guide you back through the tunnel, and get you to the doorway into the hotel. From there you climb three flights and then you will be on the corridor where your room is located. You must assure me that if anyone finds out you disappeared for a few hours . . .'

'I will never tell them of your involvement in my disappearance. That is a promise.'

'*Merci, madame*,' she said formally.

'I can't thank you enough.'

'There is no need to thank me, *madame*. You and your husband paid me well for my silence.'

With a nod – and a last withering glance at Mohammed – she pulled open the rusted door and disappeared back into the underworld.

Mohammed motioned for me to follow him. We were in some basement, above which was loud music and the sound of rhythmic chopping. When I looked quizzical at this noise, he said in a very rudimentary French:

'*Mon père est boucher.*'

My father is a butcher.

His establishment was evidently right above us. And he was dismembering something as Mohammed held out his hand for the first instalment of his fee. The 25 dirhams turned over to him, Mohammed then guided me through a basement that looked like a makeshift abattoir. Garbage pails and industrial-sized dumpsters filled with the remains of carcasses. Dried congealed blood on the concrete floor. All the associated stenches that accompany the left-behinds of dead animals. Mohammed smiled when he saw the effect that the aroma of his father's basement had on me. I clamped my hand over my face as we went up the stone steps into the back of the shop. When I emerged from behind the counter, Mohammed's dad – a man around forty with a hangdog face and bad teeth, a bloody hatchet in one hand – looked bemused to see me coming up from the lower depths. He nodded a polite hello, then barked something at Mohammed. When Mohammed barked back – and also rubbed his thumb and forefinger together – his father seemed placated. He even offered me mint tea.

'*Mille mercis, mais j'ai un rendez-vous,*' I said. But where was I now? Though I knew the souk well after several weeks here, the fact remained that it was so densely structured, so labyrinthine in design, you inevitably found yourself down a dark laneway not encountered before. Just like the alley I was ushered out into. It was full of ominous shadows and no markings to tell me where I might be. Mohammed pointed to his father's shop and said.

'*Je reste ici.*'

'*Mais où suis-je?*'

'*Essaouira.*'

'*Mais où?*'

'*Vous cherchez où?*'

I told him that I was trying to find a café owned by a man named Fouad. Mohammed looked at me blankly.

'*Vous ne connaissez pas Chez Fouad?*' I asked.

Mohammed gave me another bemused shrug.

'*Aidez-moi*,' I asked, getting worried that Fouad might think I wasn't returning and would vanish before the midnight deadline he'd set.

Mohammed held out his hand again. I decided not to argue with this – and started reaching into my pocket for another 10 dirhams. But before I could hand the money to him his father emerged from his shop, running towards him with one of those mallets (soaked in blood) that is used to tenderise meat, shouting loudly, clearly terrifying his son who ducked behind me. When his dad reached us he grabbed his son by the shoulder and began to shake him furiously, castigating him in a free flow of Arabic. I sensed he had caught sight of his son demanding further money from me – and had taken offence. I tried to intervene on Mohammed's behalf, explaining that I had asked him for directions to a certain café, that it was me who offered to pay for his services as a guide. Mohammed, who was now sobbing, translated my words into Arabic. Though it took a few very tense moments for his father's anger to subside, he seemed to buy into this story, shaking Mohammed once more and telling him something that Mohammed then translated into broken French.

'My father he says . . . you lie to protect me.'

'Tell him I'm not lying.'

And then, all but acting out my words, I pointed to myself as I explained:

'I asked your son to bring me –' I gestured to the laneway ahead – 'to a café owned by a man named Fouad.' I mimicked handing him money. 'I offered to pay him for his services. Your son never asked me for money –' Again I gesticulated between myself and Mohammed and pointed to my pocket and back to him, shaking my head to emphasise he never insisted on payment . . .

It was quite a pantomime performance. But the butcher finally believed me. Gripping his son by the shoulder he pointed to the geographic far distance and barked another order. Mohammed translated.

'My father tells me to bring you to Fouad's café.'

'But where is the café?'

Mohammed posed that question to his dad. Another angry torrent of Arabic poured forth – but halfway through this tirade I realised that this was Poppa's way of giving directions. At the end of his rant – replete with gesticulations indicating right and left turns – the butcher looked at me and became instantly polite, touching his heart with his right hand, executing a little bow, and (from what I could glean by his countenance) begging apology for his son's behaviour.

I shook my head and touched Mohammed on his right shoulder in a manner that was both maternal and protective, then asked him to tell his father:

'Your son was most respectful and courteous. A great credit to you, *monsieur*.'

That seemed to finally placate the butcher. He bowed gravely to me, then swiped his hand forward to indicate that Mohammed should get a move on.

We headed down the darkened laneway. As soon as we turned a corner Mohammed stopped and began to start crying. The cocky kid was reduced to a sad unloved little boy with an unforgiving dictator of a father. I tentatively put my arm around him, wanting to comfort him, but thinking he might just push me away. To my surprise he buried his face in my shoulder and sobbed. How I wished that I could lift him out of his life and bring him to a happier and less threatening place. How I wished I could lift myself out of my own life.

When Mohammed subsided he said one word: '*Merci*.' Then he led me down several other byways until we reached Chez Fouad. I knew full well that I would not be able to find my way back without his help, so I handed Mohammed 50 dirhams and asked if he could wait here until I was finished.

'*Mon père sera fâché*.'

My father will be angry.

'*Je vais parler avec ton papa. Je vais tout régler*.'

I will talk with your dad. I will make everything all right.

Mohammed nodded and found a stone step on which to sit as

I approached the café. When I looked back in his direction he was perched on this stoop, looking forlorn, not knowing what to do with his time. I could not help but think of all those men I'd seen everywhere in Essaouira, sitting on brick walls or by carts stuffed with goods, quietly despondent, inert in the midst of life's chaotic flow. I always felt compassion for these idle men – and the blank look that creased their faces which seemed to be posing that supremely thorny question: *Is this all there is to my life?* How I didn't want Mohammed to end up like one of those men. How I sensed he was facing a future in his father's butcher shop and a lifetime of animal carcasses in the basement.

As I walked onto the terrace of the café Fouad looked at me as if Typhoid Mary had just come a-calling. But with a grimace of resignation he motioned for me to take a table in the far corner. Then he disappeared inside for several minutes, returning with a plastic shopping bag in one hand. Mint tea arrived. Fouad poured us two glasses. We sat there in silence for several moments. It was clear that he was expecting me to initiate the conversation . . . or, more to the point, the questioning.

'Do you know where my husband is?'

'Perhaps.'

Fouad was not going to be immediately forthcoming. I chose my next words with care.

'I am concerned – not just because my husband has gone missing, but also because he has injured himself.'

'He told me you did that to him.'

'He what?' I yelled. Immediately all eyes in the café were on us. This displeased Fouad even more. He raised his finger to his lips.

'You do not want to draw attention to yourself,' he whispered.

'I did not hurt my husband.'

'That is your story.'

'That, *monsieur*, is the truth. My husband is in a very unstable state, and one of the maids at the hotel saw him slam his head against the wall—'

'Which you made him do.'

112

Oh God, I was lost now.

'I did not force him to hurt himself.'

'He said you rejected him.'

'I caught him out in a lie. A terrible lie.'

'Then you left him a note, telling him to kill himself. Which is what he tried to do.'

Silence.

'I was angry,' I said. 'Desperately angry.'

'He took you at your word. And now . . . why should I help you?'

'Because he needs my help. Because he is fragile and in a bad place.'

Fouad looked away.

'I am begging you . . . just tell me where he is.'

Another shrug.

I reached into the backpack and pulled out Paul's journal. I opened it and showed him the photograph of the young woman named Samira.

'Do you know her?' I asked.

Silence.

'Do you know if he was heading to Casablanca to see her?'

Silence.

'You have to help me, Fouad.'

'No, I do not.'

'I will give you one hundred dirhams if you tell me.'

'Five hundred.'

'Two-fifty,' I said.

'Three hundred.'

I nodded my assent. He motioned for me to hand over the money and I did as demanded. He counted out the small pile of dirhams I had given him before saying:

'Yes, Monsieur Paul has gone to see this woman.'

'Did he explain why he's been seeing her? Why he has her photograph in his journal?'

'You have to ask him.'

'But how am I going to do that?'

'Go to Casablanca.'

'He met her at the university where he teaches,' I heard myself saying, articulating a scenario that had become clearer to me since I'd made the discovery of her photograph. She was one of his students, and he'd become intoxicated with her during the course of their affair over the past year. When she said she was going back to Morocco for the summer he felt the compulsion to follow her across the Atlantic to North Africa. But as he couldn't disappear without me, he convinced me to join him. However, he was always looking for that decisive moment when he could run off into her arms. Did he use the head-butting incident to give him an excuse to vanish – and to land me with the guilt of believing I had tipped him over the edge? Did the discovery that I had found him out make him play the self-destructive card, then realise that the only future now open to him was with her in Casablanca?

'Tell me, please,' I said, 'did he meet her back in Buffalo?'

Another of his infuriating shrugs. Then:

'Ask him yourself.'

I held open a page of Paul's notebook and pointed to the place where he'd marked down her address.

'Here's where she lives. Can you get me there?'

'What would the police think?'

'I can make it worth your while.'

'If I take you to Casablanca there will be questions, many questions, from the inspector. He might even consider closing my café down. So . . .'

'Then find somebody else to drive me.'

'Ten thousand dirhams.'

Nearly $1,100.

'That's absurd.'

'That's the price. You don't like it, take the bus. There is one that leaves at midnight. Of course, the police always have men stationed there to see who is coming or going out of town. We are a police state, Morocco. A very polite police state. But everyone is, in some way, under surveillance.'

'So how did Paul get away undetected?'

'He had help.'

'Now I am asking for your help.'

'And I have given you a price.'

'All I can give you is four thousand dirhams cash.'

Pause. He stood up.

'You wait here,' he said, and disappeared into the interior of the café. I glanced over in the direction of Mohammed. He gave me a shy wave. I waved back, wondering simultaneously if Fouad was going to return with the police, telling them how I had snuck out of the hotel and was trying to bribe him to get me out of town.

But after a minute or so, Fouad returned alone.

'OK,' he whispered. 'Four thousand dirhams one way to Casablanca. You pay me in advance.'

'When do we leave?'

'Now.'

THE CAR WAS an ancient Peugeot with bad suspension and a tendency to emit an automotive burp every few minutes. We'd be driving along at 80 kilometres an hour and, out of nowhere, there would be a loud glottal belch from the engine that was evidently on the verge of cardiac arrest. These ominous internal combustion noises didn't seem to faze the driver, a man named Simo: wiry, edgy, around fifty, with a pronounced hacking cough courtesy of a ferocious cigarette habit. In the four hours it took us to reach Casablanca, he always had a butt on the go. When one was almost burnt down to the filter, he reached for the packet on the seat next to him and lit a fresh one off the cigarette that was about to expire.

Simo insisted that I sit in the back seat, where I had both windows wide open to rid the car of his incessant cloud of smoke, and to provide some ventilation on a torpid night in which the humidity made the air seem as glutinous as maple syrup. Simo also made it very clear that, apart from driving me, he wanted absolutely nothing to do with me. When I asked him if he knew the address that Fouad had given him – having written it out in Arabic – he nodded. In answer to my question about the chances of encountering police checkpoints en route, he just shrugged.

Fouad had warned me while we were still in the café that Simo was the wrong side of taciturn. Before we got up to leave and meet him I went over to where Mohammed was sitting. I told him that I was having to head off somewhere, and asked him to not say a word about this to anyone.

'But Mira might be concerned if you don't come back.'

'You can tell Mira I had to go find my husband. She won't tell anybody. She assured me of that. Please say that you will keep this secret.'

I then brought out two 100-dirham notes and pressed them into his hand. His eyes grew wide.

'*Shukran, shukran,*' he said.

'That money is for you, not your father. Do you think he'll wonder where I've gone?'

'I will give him the fifty dirhams you gave me. That will keep him quiet.'

'I wish you well, Mohammed.'

'Bless you, *madame.*'

Then I hurried back to the café. Fouad escorted me through the kitchen – a small, cramped, hellishly steamy place where two men in stained and sodden white T-shirts were frying falafels and scooping hummus onto plates. They glanced up at me. Fouad favoured them with a scowl and their eyes returned to the task at hand.

Within a moment we were in the back alley, into which the ancient Peugeot had been squeezed. A man was standing in the shadows, smoking a cigarette. Fouad introduced us and explained that Simo would be driving me to Casablanca. He then asked me for the address. I opened Paul's notebook and showed him the spot where it had been written. He, in turn, took out a small crumpled notebook from his back pocket, pulled a pencil from behind his ear, licked the lead and transcribed it into Arabic. Handing the address to the driver he barked several instructions, then motioned with his hand for Simo to get lost for a few moments. The man walked deeper into the shadows.

'I didn't want him to see you handing over the money,' Fouad explained. 'I will pay him later. I chose him because, although he doesn't say much, he's not the sort who will try to hit on you for money. He knows that he'll have to answer to me should anything go wrong, or if he tries anything – which he won't.'

I reached into my pocket and counted out 4,000 dirhams. My crazed hope was that, on arrival in Casablanca, I would find Paul at the apartment of his mistress, verify that he was all right, give him the chance to get on that midday flight with me to New York and, at worst, have the door slammed in my face, ending a marriage that was, in my mind, already finished.

Fouad counted his way through the money. When he was

satisfied that he had the complete amount he called the driver over and spoke to him in a low, firm voice, once again showing him the address in Arabic, gesticulating towards me several times, then making a point of writing out a series of numbers on another scrap of notebook – licking the lead of the pencil yet again. This page he tore along its perforated edge and handed to me.

'If there is any problem, you phone me on this number. But there should be no problem whatsoever. Simo . . . he is OK.'

Then he handed me the plastic bag.

'Your husband left this behind when he showed up late this afternoon. I'm not saying he wanted you to have it, but I'd rather that you keep it safe for him.'

'You still won't tell me where your other driver dropped him?'

'I cannot . . . because I gave him my word I would not.'

'Can you at least tell me if I am right to be going to this address?'

Fouad considered his response for a moment, then answered with one word:

'*Insha'Allah.*'

Allah willing.

Five minutes out of Essaouira I discovered that the reading light in the back of the car was not functioning. When I asked Simo if there was a problem with it he just shrugged. Then I asked if he could pull over and fix it, as I was completely in the dark and very much wanted to see what was in the shopping bag that Fouad had given me. Just as I wanted to use the four or so hours on the road to read through Paul's journal, even though the prospect of delving into the inner sanctum of his mind made me uneasy. Maybe the blown light was a hint that I shouldn't even begin to pry. But the very fact that I was in this beaten-up car, fleeing our hotel in search of this lost man . . .

'*J'ai besoin de lire, monsieur,*' I told Simo when he reported that he could do nothing about the busted light. He responded by reaching into his pocket and tossing a disposable lighter into the back seat.

'*Ce n'est pas suffisant. Vous n'auriez pas une lampe-torche?*'

He shook his head and accelerated, causing the first of many belches from the exhaust pipe. I sank back into the seat, conscious of springs sticking up through the vinyl upholstery. Then I reached into the plastic bag. I felt something close to massive relief when I pulled out one of Paul's large sketchbooks. Flicking on the lighter – its flame meagre – I opened the hard black cover and felt myself tearing up as I looked at page after page of his Essaouira line drawings. Whatever agony or fury or self-destructive rage made him rip up several of his notebooks back in our room, some sliver of self-preservation had clearly kicked in, for this was the book containing his best work by far. Over fifty drawings, so innovative and daring in his use of line, in his mingling of the abstract and the representational, in the heat and dust authenticity that Paul brought to the souk, underscored by his absolute need to draw these scenes in such an original way. At one point I had to shut the album and sit silently in the dark, absorbing the sense of loss that was careening through me like a fast-acting toxin. I looked out at the scrubby landscape, the clouded sky that blocked out all celestial light. The sheer immense stress of the past few hours, the fear and anguish of what (if anything) I would find in Casablanca . . . all of it suddenly sideswiped me. I found myself overcome by the realisation that the terrain of my entire life had changed. And the hope of a child . . .

I began to cry. Weeping in the dark of this shabby car, being watched in the rear-view mirror by a silent man, uncomfortable with this show of emotion. He lit another cigarette. When I subsided he reached into a bag on the front seat and handed me several cubes of baklava wrapped in paper.

'My wife . . . she makes these,' he said in basic French. 'You eat them.'

'*Shukran.*'

He nodded acknowledgement. Not another word passed between us until we reached Casablanca.

I closed my eyes, hoping sleep might overtake me. It didn't – so I snapped them open again. Then, thinking what a bad idea this was, I reached into my backpack and pulled out Paul's journal. Holding the lighter so close to its pages I was afraid that a bump might set it all aflame, I began to go through it page by page. Most of them were taken up with quick sketches, doodles, visual improvisations on the life he was incessantly observing. Interspersed with these were jottings, musings, confessions – never more than a line or two at most. The flame from the plastic lighter threw strange, spectral shadows as I read page after page of my husband's frequently epigrammatic confessions. The fact that they were all undated . . . that was so Paul, wasn't it? Numbers, deadlines – he eschewed them all. There was no definitive chronology to this cavalcade of self-doubt and self-reproach and . . .

Robin looked so shocked and disappointed when I told her, on arrival in Casa, that I wanted to run back home. I don't blame her for being disappointed. She married a man who shouldn't be married and who knows that his wife is far too good for such a two-faced loser like himself.

Then, a few pages later, a sketch of me nude in our hotel bed.

Amazing sex, as always. My ambivalence to her, to all this, ebbs away when I am deep inside her.

I snapped my eyes shut. This is why you should never trespass into your loved one's journal.

Robin sometimes looks at me like I am a five-year-old who has just thrown all his toys out of the crib. Which is not far from the truth.

Close the book now.

She overpraised the new drawings today. I felt humbled by her kudos. Why does her reassurance about my alleged talent make me feel so small?

120

There was another fast-rendered sketch of me, standing on the balcony of our room, staring out into the great distance.

She'll leave me when she finds out. She'd be an idiot to stay. I will mourn her. Then I'll turn the page. And tell myself it's better this way. Because I don't deserve happiness. I can't even begin to fathom what it would mean to be responsible for a new life.

So he knew that, by having the vasectomy in secret, he'd loaded a gun that was eventually going to go off in his face.

I can't ever say what I want. No, the real problem is: I can't say what I don't want.

Like assuring me he wanted a child when he clearly didn't want a child.

This place is full of too many shadows for me. And reminders of all that promise squandered. I must get Samira back in my life. Can Romain B. H. aid my cause?

Who is Romain B. H.? I had an answer to that question a few moments later when I came across a page with the name *Romain Ben Hassan* scrawled across the bottom, followed by an address also in Casablanca 4e. I searched my memory, trying to remember where I had heard that name before. Then the penny dropped. Ben Hassan had been his fellow artist friend during Paul's Casablanca year; French-Moroccan, and something of a louche character who kept Paul endlessly amused and frequently drunk. Luck was on my side: there was a phone number below the address. He lived in the same district of Casablanca as Samira. Was there some sort of connection between them? Didn't Paul tell me that he had fallen out of contact with Ben Hassan when his name came up a few weeks ago? One more lie to join all the other falsehoods he had been feeding me.

Something still puzzled me. Why did Paul take his last remaining sketchbook, but vanish without his passport or any clothes or personal effects whatsoever? The fact that he left without even his all-crucial pencils and charcoals unnerved me. Paul never went anywhere without a notebook and his beloved French pencils, which he meticulously curated from several key art-supply stores in Manhattan. The trauma of all that self-harm . . . perhaps the fact that he was concussed or, at the very least, disorientated after slamming his head against the wall – was that the reason he left the hotel carrying nothing but the sketchbook? Or did he already have clothes and toiletries at his girlfriend's house? How would he have gotten them there? Unless he gave her a suitcase to bring back to Casablanca when they were having their assignations in Buffalo, and he was just looking for an excuse to stalk out of the marriage, which I certainly gave him today.

Will you listen to yourself, engaging in crazed speculation . . .

But how otherwise could he have gotten involved with this woman? In the three years we'd been together he'd never travelled anywhere without me bar three quick two-day trips to his gallery in New York. We'd spent a few days in Montreal when he was in a group show there at the Musée des Beaux-Arts. Beyond that we'd never been outside the country either alone or together. So he couldn't have met his mistress anywhere but Buffalo. Which must mean that he got to know her at the university where he taught. The photograph in the journal showed that she was only in her early twenties. Did he get the vasectomy to ensure that she didn't get pregnant as well?

Stop, stop, stop. This is getting you nowhere.

But the problem with discovering a lie – especially when you cannot yet confront the liar – is that it leads into even greater hypothetical scenarios.

I lied earlier when I said that Simo didn't address another word to me all the way to Casablanca. Actually he said one word:

'Police.'

Up ahead there was a roadblock and two cops were standing in the middle of the road, one of them using a powerful flashlight to indicate that we should pull over. *Oh God, they've found out somehow that I've fled the hotel and am on the run. I'm going to be brought back to Essaouira and made to face Inspector Moufad whose suspicions about me have trebled since I disobeyed his order and fled town. Now he's going to have someone guarding my door until he gets a judge to sign an order allowing him to relieve me of my passport. I am definitely going to be his prime suspect. And he will argue in court that only a guilty person would have tried to run.*

But another part of me thought that Mira wouldn't have betrayed me like that. Because she would simultaneously land herself in immense trouble. And also because she was, I could tell, someone who believed in keeping her word.

Still, here we were, being pulled over. I could see Simo's lips tighten. He sucked hard on his cigarette and his back and shoulders noticeably stiffened. The beam from the powerful police flashlight filled the windshield of the car, semi-blinding both of us and forcing Simo to slow right down.

He pulled up in front of the parked police vehicle, stubbing out the cigarette in the brimming dashboard ashtray. The window was already down and I could hear the static of a police radio nearby. As the flashlight beamed around the car I could see two youngish policemen in ill-fitting uniforms, the lateness of this night shift in the middle of nowhere augmented by their immediate curiosity on discovering a woman – a Western woman – in the back seat. There was a lot of talk in Arabic and Simo handed over his identity papers and driver's licence. One of the officers disappeared for a long five minutes, then returned and talked at length with his colleague. This officer turned his attention to me, saying: '*Vos papiers, madame.*' I had my passport ready and handed it over. The two cops spent far too long studying it, going through it page by page. There was so much blank space on those pages, evidence of how little I knew of the world outside of my own country. I saw them reach the page on which my Moroccan entry visa had been stamped. They studied this intently and talked among themselves. Then the more senior of the two asked me if I spoke French. I nodded affirmation. He asked:

'The driver says you hired him as a taxi to take you to Casablanca. Is this true?'

'Yes, I have paid him to do exactly that.'

'Why are you travelling in the middle of the night?'

I had already reasoned that this was a question they just might ask. I had an answer already prepared.

'My husband is arriving in Casablanca off an early flight tomorrow – and I am meeting him at the airport.'

They then disappeared with my passport. I watched as they walked over to their vehicle, lighting up cigarettes, passing my travel document back and forth. Meanwhile Simo had lit up again – and I could see that he was sweating over the outcome of their deliberations as much as I was. I knew if one of them reached for a phone – or the handset attached to the crackling police radio in their car – to verify my identity I would be screwed. A good five minutes passed. The older of the cops opened the door of their vehicle. Here it comes – the beginning of the end. But then he pulled out a bottle of water. More talk between them. Then he approached us and knocked on the back window. I rolled it down again.

'*Donc, madame . . .*'

He handed me back my passport.

'*Bon voyage à Casa . . .*'

With a nod to Simo, he saluted us as we drove off into the night.

Two minutes after we'd passed the roadblock Simo let out a pronounced sigh. Did he sense that I was on the run? The stress of those past few minutes hit me sideways. So too the lateness of the hour, the immense strain of the day. Stretching myself along the back seat, again manipulating my body so as to avoid the protruding springs, I passed out. Though the lack of suspension in the car, and the roughness of the road, jolted me awake several times, my exhaustion was such that I vanished instantly again into the underworld. Until there was a massive lurch, followed by the loud braying of an animal and the even louder braying of a car horn. We were on a city street, tall apartment blocks defining the horizon, no traffic except a cart with a donkey parked right in front of us.

A man in a djellaba was attempting to move the donkey, but the animal was refusing to budge and was blocking the road. Its driver was using a whip to get it to move, but the beast was obstinate even in the face of pain. Simo – who could not get around the donkey and cart, given the narrowness of the street – was blasting his horn. Jerked back into consciousness, but still foggy, I glanced at my watch. It was just a few minutes before six. Light was beginning to claw back the night sky. It took me a moment to work out that we were in Casablanca.

'*Arrêtez, s'il vous plait,*' I told Simo, indicating that honking the horn was doing no good. His reply was to point to a building across the street, a semi-crumbling apartment block, art deco in style, with an all-purpose neighbourhood shop on the ground floor that was already open. Directly opposite was a café with a terrace. I also took in an optician's and a boutique displaying white and maroon leather jackets in its window, along with stonewashed jeans and paisley silk shirts. A cavalcade of expensive bad taste, playing visual games with me after a night of brief, fitful sleep in the back seat of a rusted car. The donkey-cart driver finally got his beast moving, clearing the road. Simo pulled the car over, pointing again to the building across the way.

'*Votre adresse,*' he said, motioning for me to leave. I reached into my pocket and dug out a 100-dirham note. When I proffered it to him he just shrugged and accepted it with a fast nod. As I slid off the back seat, he uttered two final words:

'*Bonne chance.*'

When I and my backpack were on the street and the car door shut, the engine belched one last time before disappearing into the already congealing traffic. I checked my watch again and wondered if I could go up to Samira's apartment now, bang on the door and confront her, force my husband to leave her bed and come with me.

But all my instincts told me to walk away now. Cut my losses. Accept the sad finality of it all. Try not to save him – as much as I still wanted to. However frightened and worried I was that my husband was heading towards some point of no return.

125

I knew I was negotiating with myself, talking myself into some sort of compromised position from which nothing good would come.

Go to the café. Order a coffee. Ask them to call you a cab. Immediately. Get to the airport. Get on the plane. Hit the portal marked: 'I'm out of here . . . permanently.'

Instead I hoisted my backpack and crossed the street to her building. I scanned the list of names accompanying the apartment numbers and buzzers that were banked on a wall to the left of the entranceway. They all listed the tenants by last name, with no Samira or even an S in sight. Damn . . . I considered going inside the shop next door and showing the picture of Samira, asking the man behind the counter if he knew her. Then I reasoned that, as she lived upstairs, she was a regular here. Which would probably mean that if some sleep-starved, stressed middle-aged American woman held up her snapshot and demanded to know her last name and apartment number, the guy in the shop would undoubtedly ring to warn her of some crazy lady lurking below. He might also call the cops. Best to be prudent and wait.

What I discovered inside the shop surprised me. It was well stocked with upscale prepared food, largely French in origin. It did have a considerable amount of local produce – hummus, tahini, couscous, assorted Moroccan pastries. But it also sold teas from Hédiard in Paris. And Nespresso coffee capsules. And Belgian chocolate. And Italian extra-virgin olive oil. This was the sort of local deli that would fit into any cosmopolitan city, and clearly catered to an educated clientele. There was also a rack of foreign newspapers in French, English, German, Spanish, Italian – all that day's editions. I grabbed a copy each of the *International New York Times* and the *Financial Times*, paid for them, then crossed back across the street and found a table on the terrace with a direct view of the entrance to the apartment building. A waiter arrived at the table. I ordered breakfast, realising that, in addition to dealing with virtually no sleep, I hadn't eaten anything except a single baklava since my late breakfast the previous day, fear and stress supplanting hunger. I started to take in my surroundings. The buildings here all were largely art deco, with a few new structures dotting what was otherwise a fairly intact architectural quarter. The café I was in wouldn't have been out of place in Paris. There was an interesting-looking bookshop next to one of those places that specialises in exquisitely packaged soaps and bath oils. Advertisement posters showed young, vibrant, professional couples looking dreamily at each other while holding the latest in mobile phones. There was a high-tech electronics store, stocking the latest in laptops and cellular communications. A woman in tight track pants came jogging by. There were a considerable number of high-end Audis and Mercedes and Porsches parked on the road. There was not a burqa in sight. I was in a Morocco completely divorced from the realm behind the walls in Essaouira; a world familiar, yet utterly foreign.

Two more men with donkey carts came trudging down the road. One of the animals stopped to pee, simultaneously splashing the fender of a Mercedes SUV. Its owner – a portly business type in a black suit and white shirt, with a cigarette and a cellphone in either hand – rose from his café table and came waddling over, shouting reproaches and abuse. The donkey driver tried to ameliorate the situation by rubbing the fender with a corner of his djellaba. This infuriated the owner even more. My orange juice and croissants arrived just as a policeman showed up, telling the businessman to calm down and also instructing the driver to stop rubbing more donkey urine into the Mercedes paintwork.

I bit into my croissant, relieved to be eating something. I stared down at the *International New York Times*, thinking that during our time in Essaouira never once had I thought about buying a newspaper. Now I was learning about a Wall Street downturn, and another wave of bombings in Beirut, and the death of a one-time dictator in the Caucasus, and . . .

The yelling across the street rose in volume. The businessman was now so frustrated with the donkey driver's mild-mannered reaction to the bestial baptism of his car that he actually pushed him, causing the policeman to restrain him. Then, in a moment beyond stupid, the businessman shoved the cop so hard that he tumbled into the street. Regaining his balance the officer dodged an oncoming car. It braked wildly, front-ending the Mercedes.

Chaos ensued as the businessman became near-deranged, yanking open the door of the car that had just flattened the front of his own, clawing at the driver. The donkey, a little distressed, began to bray. His cries of confusion made me look directly across the street at a crucial moment – just when the door to the apartment building opened and a young woman with long, richly curled black hair walked out. She was exceptionally tall – over six foot, long-legged, absurdly thin, dressed in tight blue jeans, chic sandals and a loose white linen shirt. I had Paul's notebook on the table and I pulled out the photo of Samira. It must have been taken a few years ago, as the woman before me was more mature, but still unbearably beautiful. I threw some money down on the table and raced over. She was standing not far away from the scuffle still in progress – the businessman now being handcuffed – watching the drama unfold. I approached her.

'Are you Samira?' I asked.

She seemed thrown by the question, but still asked me in flawless English:

'Who wants to know?'

'Paul's wife.'

Her face tightened.

'I have nothing to say to you.'

She turned and started walking off. I followed her, calling out:

'Please, I need to know—'

'Did you just hear what I said to you?'

She kept walking, me alongside her.

'Is he here, with you?' I asked.

'I am not talking to you.'

'You have to.'

As I said this I made the mistake of touching her on her arm. She shrugged me off, hissing:

'You put a hand on me again . . .'

She stalked off. But I kept pace with her.

'You know where he is,' I said.

'No idea. Now leave me.'

'Don't lie to me.'

Now she stopped and turned on me:

'Lie? Lie? You dare—'

'Tell me where he is.'

'Let him tell you that.'

'So he's upstairs? In your place?'

'I wouldn't let him through the front door.'

'So he came here?'

'I am getting into my car now.'

'You have to help me,' I pleaded.

'No, I don't . . .'

She reached into her bag, pulled out a set of keys and clicked open a small Citroën parked on the street. As she went to open the driver's door I blocked her path.

'I know who you are. I know that you're involved with him. And if you want him, that's actually fine by me. But I just need to know—'

I was all but yelling. But her voice became louder than mine.

'Involved with him? I *want* him? Do you know who I am?'

'Yes, I do . . .'

'Do you really?' she said, suddenly very cold and quiet. 'Because if you did know, you wouldn't dare make accusations like that.'

'Who are you then?' I demanded.

She met my gaze with a look of ferocious contempt and said:

'I'm his daughter.'

Thirteen

I STOOD ON the kerb for a long time after she had pulled away in the car. I was so stunned by the revelation just delivered that I stopped dead in my tracks as she brushed me aside. When I glanced up I caught sight of her face, staring back at me with hardened contempt. Yet her eyes also radiated the saddest sort of despair.

Then she accelerated and the car shot off down the street.

I remained motionless for several moments, not knowing what to do next. Eventually I retreated to the café. The waiter was keeping an eye on my table: my newspapers, my croissants, my orange juice. As I approached he handed me the 100-dirham note I had thrown down before I got up to pursue Samira.

'You left all this behind, *madame*.'

'I had to speak to someone.'

A small nod of acknowledgement. Had he watched that scene unfold? Did he put two and two together and reason that it was a wife confronting the woman she thought was her husband's mistress? If only he knew the truth. If only I knew the truth.

I sat back down and shut my eyes, exhausted and confused and flattened by a disclosure that I simply never saw coming.

He has a child. He has a child who is at least thirty years old. Maybe older. A daughter. A beautiful daughter. Evidently conceived with a Moroccan woman. Judging by her age, the point of conception was decades ago – and the photo Paul kept of her in his notebook must have been ten years old. A secret he kept from me always. A secret that made his other great deceit – promising me a child and then having a vasectomy – even more heartbreaking.

'Would you like your coffee now, *madame*?'

It was the waiter. I indicated that would be fine. Hunger forced me to eat the croissants, drink the very good orange juice. I tried reading one of the newspapers. The words swam in front of me and I pushed it away. The businessman was now being forcibly pushed into the back of a police car, struggling against the cuffs that were restraining his hands behind his back. He was going to be arrested for assaulting a police officer and would have to spend serious money on a lawyer. We really are the architects of our own miseries, aren't we? Just as I saw the hatred and the hurt in Samira's eyes and knew that her father had deeply wounded her in some way.

Her father.

Who was her mother? Where was she now?

I checked my watch. Six-forty-three a.m. My midday flight was not far off. I drank my coffee. Having been turned away by his daughter, seeking refuge in the city he once called home, Paul would surely turn to friends. Or more specifically: a friend. Someone whose name he dropped both in conversation and in the pages of his journal. Opening it I found the entry I was looking for. The entry where he wrote about wanting to re-establish contact with Samira.

Can Romain B. H. aid my cause?

Romain Ben Hassan. Whose address was written just below.

I called the waiter over, showed him the scrawled address and asked where it might be.

'Two streets from here,' he said, then insisted on drawing me a map on the back of a bar coaster, explaining that I could make it to the man's front door in around five minutes.

A manic plan began to form in my head. I would walk over to Ben Hassan's place – where, no doubt, my husband was sleeping off the events of last night, which must have involved some sort of confrontation with his daughter. Knowing Paul, the last thing he would have done was find a hotel and recuperate alone. Which is why I was pretty sure that he had taken refuge at his friend's apartment. The idea of crossing the Atlantic now, uncertain of his whereabouts or his injuries, would be impossible for me. If he was at Ben Hassan's I could, at least, make sure that he was in one physical piece (whatever his mental state), and have a direct face-to-face with him. Then hit the street. Jump a cab to the airport. And fly out of all this sadness.

131

The coffee arrived. I drank it quickly, the caffeine giving me a fast antidote to my fatigue, and I ordered a second. I threw it back and settled the bill, counting my remaining dirhams. I asked the waiter how much a taxi would cost from here to the airport.

'You will need to negotiate, but don't pay more than two hundred dirhams. Make sure you agree the price before he starts driving.'

I thanked him for his kindness and his advice, as well as his impromptu map which I now used to guide me to 3450 rue Hafid Ibrahim. Though I was too preoccupied to take in much in the way of my immediate surroundings I did note that this quartier – which the waiter told me was known as Gauthier, after the French architect who designed the layout and many of the 1920s apartment buildings that decorated the area – was still very jazz era, albeit in a slightly crumbling way.

Number 3450 rue Hafid Ibrahim was a building that had seen a happier past. Chipped masonry. A broken sequence of pavements in front of its main entrance. A huge water stain above its front doorway. Electrical wires dangling down from a broken entrance light. I scanned the list of names by the front door and spied 'Ben Hassan, R., 3eme étage, gauche'. To hell with the fact that it was still so early in the morning. I had to see my husband. But I knew that to ring the bell would be to alert both Ben Hassan and Paul of my arrival. So I loitered with intent until a woman around fifty – dressed in a black business suit and big Chanel sunglasses – came out. She looked at me askance when I walked in past her, holding the door for her as she exited. I was about to invent some excuse – 'I forgot the door code' – but thought better of it. I simply headed to the staircase – probably once grand and marbled, now showing signs of the same water damage that marked the ceiling, with wooden banisters that bent when I grabbed hold of them.

The spiral staircase tilted upwards at a dangerous angle, and – as I noticed when I reached the first and second landings – the space between the apartment doorways and the deteriorating banister was minimal. A misstep or two and over you could go. The lack of sleep, the pressing sense of anxiety, the thought: *What am I doing here?* and the sheer dizzy incline all conspired to make me hug the wall on the way up, terrified of losing my balance and encountering what would certainly be a downward plunge.

I reached the third floor and turned left. The door in front of me was painted a crazed shade of purple, its outer frame gloss black. The choice of colour immediately threw me. Too hallucinatory, too out there. I rang the bell. No answer. I waited thirty seconds and rang it again. No answer. Everybody inside – my husband included – must be asleep.

I leaned on the bell, holding it down for a good thirty seconds. Eventually the door cracked open. I was facing a very short man in his early thirties, with a bald head and immaculate skin. He looked like he'd just gotten out of bed. He stared at me with tired, leery eyes.

'I need to speak with Monsieur Ben Hassan,' I said in French.

'He's sleeping.' The man's voice defined tonelessness.

'It's urgent.'

'Come back later.'

He started to close the door, but I inched my foot into its path.

'I can't come back later. I must see him now.'

'Not now.'

Again he tried to close the door, but my foot stopped him.

'You see him some other time,' he said.

'No, I am seeing Monsieur Ben Hassan now.'

I barked that last word. I could see the man's eyes grow wide. I grabbed the knob and pushed my left knee up against the door just as he tried to force it closed.

'You go away,' he now hissed.

'I am Monsieur Paul's wife. I know he's inside. I have to talk to him.'

Then shoving against the door I began to shout:

'Paul? Paul? You have to see me . . .'

Suddenly the door swung open and I found myself face to face with a man who must have weighed three hundred pounds. He was in his early sixties, with thin hair that he brushed leftwards across his great bowling ball of a head. His face, besides being corpulent and treble-chinned, was also oleaginous. His eyes – vampire blue – hinted that my entreaties had just roused him into consciousness. But it was his girth that threw me. Encased in a sweaty white kaftan, he had the appearance of a monumental block of Camembert cheese that had been left out in the sun and was now oozing. He studied me through squinting, tired eyes.

'Your husband is not here.'

I was thrown by this comment.

'You know who I am.'

A shrug. 'Of course I know who you are, Robin. I am Ben Hassan. And, alas, your husband is gone.'

'Gone where?'

As I said this I felt my equilibrium giving way. I leaned against the wall for support. Putting my right hand over my face I wondered if I was about to pass out. I heard Monsieur Ben Hassan say something to his friend in Arabic. That's when he put his hand on my arm. I flinched, pulling away.

'Omar simply wants to help you inside – before you faint.'

Wooziness was now overtaking me.

'He's gone where?' I asked.

Ben Hassan looked directly at me. And said:

'He's gone to see his wife.'

Now I was in free-fall.

'His wife?' I heard myself saying. 'I'm his wife.'

That's when I felt myself pitch forward. Omar caught me. I remember mumbling something about needing to sit down. What happened next? I remember little, except being led into a large room that also appeared to be painted purple and furnished with a surfeit of heavily embroidered velvet cushions. I was guided to what seemed to be a mattress on the floor covered by some sort of velvet blanket. Words were being spoken to me in French. They wafted over me, garbled. I kept telling myself: 'Get up, you have a plane to catch.' Just as that declaration *He's gone to see his wife* kept ricocheting around my head. Surely I hadn't heard that correctly.

And then, having been settled by Omar on the mattress, I promptly blacked out.

When I woke again I was in a world of shadows. It took a moment or two to work out where I was. Just as it took another nanosecond for me to descend into panic as I glanced at my watch and saw that it was four-twelve. That's when I jolted upright and found myself in a state of panic. Four-twelve in the afternoon. I had been asleep for hours. I had missed my flight.

I was in a large living room with dark purple walls. Floorboards painted black gloss, heavy red velvet drapes. Red velvet cushions. The red sheet covering the mattress on which I'd crashed for the last . . . had I been asleep almost nine hours? Strange, inferior abstract art on the walls; boxes within boxes, or gyrating circles that seemed to spin inwards and had been painted in blooded tones against a black background.

I had a terrifying thought: *Where is my backpack, with my laptop, the printout of my plane ticket, my wallet with all my credit cards and, most crucially, my passport?* I was on my feet, scrambling around the room in search of its whereabouts. When there was no sign of it in this velvet whorehouse of a room I started shouting: '*Monsieur, monsieur, monsieur,*' and running down a corridor, throwing open doors. The first one led into a room that was bare except for several wooden folding tables, on which were piles of passports in a variety of official colours, a photocopier, assorted embossing stamps, and a machine that, on closer inspection, seemed to provide a plastic covering for documents.

What the hell was this all about? Why did Paul know this guy?

I charged down the hall, entering a kitchen that had several days of dirty dishes and brimming ashtrays scattered everywhere, not to mention a stench that I associated with rotting vegetables. I kept shouting: '*Monsieur, monsieur.*' Again no answer. Another charge down the long corridor. Another door thrown open. Only this time I found myself staring in at a huge carved bed, on which Omar and Monsieur Ben Hassan were sleeping naked. They were on separate corners of the expansive mattress, Omar looking so diminutive and compact compared to the fleshy enormity of Ben Hassan. As soon as I threw open the door Omar snapped awake. Seeing me he scrambled for a sheet to cover himself, then started hissing at me in Arabic. At which point Ben Hassan opened his eyes slowly, took me in, and said:

'You interrupted our siesta.'

'I can't find my backpack.'

'And you immediately thought that the dirty Moroccans had stolen it.'

'You let me sleep through my flight. Where have you put my bag?'

'In the cupboard by the front door. You will find that nothing has been touched. If you need the bathroom it's the door next to the cupboard. There is a shower there as well. Fresh towels have been laid out for you. Please excuse the state of the kitchen. We have been working flat out on a project for several days, and housekeeping, alas, has taken a back seat. But we'll eat out tonight.'

'I need to get going.'

'Get going where?'

'To find Paul. You know where he's gone, don't you?'

'Go and have a shower. I will ask Omar to make some tea, and then we will discuss your husband and his whereabouts.'

'I left Essaouira in a hurry yesterday when I learned that Paul had come to Casablanca. So I have nothing to change into, no toiletries.'

'I can supply you with a toothbrush, but I sense we are in two different worlds when it comes to clothing size or taste. However, there is a big French clothing shop a five-minute walk from here. Omar would be happy to guide you.'

'I'll think about it. Could I use a phone, please?'

'Are you wanting to call Royal Air Maroc?'

'Perhaps.'

'I've taken care of that for you.'

'You what?'

'When you passed out I tried waking you many times. When you wouldn't stir I took the liberty of looking in your bag and finding your travel documents. I saw that your flight was at midday today. Given your exhaustion I knew you simply wouldn't be making the flight. So I called a friend who runs everything at

Royal Air Maroc and you are booked on the same flight at midday tomorrow. May I now extend the invitation for you to take advantage of our guest bed tonight and allow me to take you out for dinner?'

I found myself just a little bemused by all this.

'If you will give us ten minutes to wash and dress . . .' he said.

I nodded accord and headed down the corridor. In the closet near the front door there, indeed, was my bag. My passport was in place. So too my laptop. And my wallet with assorted credit cards. And a fresh printout of the changed reservation with the old one stapled behind it. The new printout also showed that the flight change had been made without cost to me.

I reproached myself for assuming that my host and his assistant/lover had robbed me. I was having that knee-jerk Western reaction to things North African: a belief that, with few exceptions, no one here was to be trusted. But if the past few weeks had proven anything it was that, outside of a few hassled moments, I had been treated with considerable respect and propriety. And Monsieur Ben Hassan, rather than turning me away from his door, had taken me in, allowed me to pass out and sleep undisturbed for much of the day, changed my flight reservation to the following day, and was now offering me the chance to stay here tonight. I owed him thanks for that. Just as I was also still a little dubious about him going through my bag to see if I had a plane ticket in need of changing. Wasn't there some hidden motive? The man was up to something in what I presumed was the false-passports department. Just as I kept wondering what he might have on Paul in the way of information that my husband might not want shared with others. Then there was the way that, like a ruthlessly cool bridge player, he had trumped me with that little bombshell: '*He's seeing his wife.*' A revelation that landed like a kick to the head.

Still, I couldn't fault his hospitality to date, though I could certainly fault my hyper-anxiety and paranoia for coming across as wildly suspicious and distrustful. I returned to the living room and began making up the bed in which I had slept.

'There is no need to assuage your guilt by tidying up.'

I turned around and saw that he was in a white djellaba, already marked with sweat, as the ceiling fans did little to temper the heat of the late afternoon.

'But I do feel guilty – especially for the way I immediately assumed—'

'We all have our prejudices – even when we tell ourselves that we are not prejudiced.'

'I apologise.'

'*Ego te absolvo.*'

I smiled back. 'You're Catholic?'

'My mother was. My father kicked with the Muslim foot. *Moi* . . . I am somewhere in between. But the Catholic in me likes the instant redemption of confession. There is no need to be apologetic about before. You will join me for dinner tonight?'

'That is most generous of you. But I need to find some clothes first. I left Essaouira with nothing at all.'

'Being on the run from the police usually means urgent departures.'

'How did you know I was running away from the cops?'

'I have my sources. But fear not, none of them know you are here. I am *completement discret*. But bravo for eluding them the way you did. Of course they think that you beat up Paul with some heavy object. Perhaps he deserved your wrath. A brilliantly talented man, Paul. One of the most gifted artists I've encountered, yet someone who cannot face any sort of grounded reality. Instead of simply saying what he does not want, he plays the game of agreeing to something that he knows he cannot follow through on, and then uses these lies as the beginning of an exit strategy.'

I looked at Monsieur Ben Hassan with even greater respect. Never before had I heard someone nail Paul's manifold psychological complexities. Of course, when you are in the midst of a crisis with somebody else, you are more than receptive to anyone who confirms your own dark thoughts. I sensed that if I hung around today and accepted Mr Ben Hassan's hospitality, I would learn much more about the man I once thought I knew and understood, but whose outer shell was a veneer behind which multiple contradictory versions of the same person lived.

'If you can put up with me for another few hours,' I told Ben Hassan, 'I'd very much like to stay.'

'I think I can put up with you,' he said.

Fourteen

THERE WAS, INDEED, a large chain department store just a five-minute walk from Monsieur Ben Hassan's apartment. I took what few worldly goods I had with me, knowing that a passport is something you never leave anywhere in Morocco – especially with a man who dealt in travel documents of an illegal variety.

'Do you want a shower before you depart?' he asked.

'I'll get one when I return with clean clothes.'

'Omar can show you the way.'

'Just tell me.'

Ben Hassan explained how to find this store, and how there was a café next door – the Parisian – that had Wi-Fi.

Ten minutes later I found myself back in a monocultural world of consumerist goods and fashion; of air-conditioned environments and a low hum of poppy muzak which, some marketing guru no doubt reasoned, provides the right sonic smoothness to encourage you to buy more. As I filled my basket with several pairs of underwear, T-shirts, a pair of tan cotton pants, khaki shorts, two white linen shirts, a pair of sandals, I felt another stab of desperate sadness. A comment Paul made just days earlier refilled my ears. Standing out on the balcony of our room, the sun declining into the Atlantic, a glass of wine in hand, still intoxicated with the love we had just made inside, the heat of the day diminishing, the light bathing the cityscape in a cognac glow, my husband turned to me with a near-beatific smile. And said:

'There is so much to be said for slamming the door on consumerism. Because we're all slaves to it. But here we are free from all that . . . for a spell.'

Then we talked excitedly about how we should consider a new way of dealing with that world. How, perhaps, in four or five more years, Paul could take early retirement from the university; how I could sell my accounting firm; how our house in Buffalo would be paid off, and could be sold and exchanged for a smaller house on the Maine coast, with a barn we could transform into a studio for Paul, and maybe with a large attic which we could convert into an office for me. An office where I could finally try to pound out the novel that had been gestating within me for years (but which, given my creative self-doubt, I'd never gotten around to starting): the story of my dad's life, and the sadness inherent at the heart of the American success ethos.

'You'll be able to write and I'll be able to draw without encumbrance,' he said. 'If I manage to shift a few drawings a year, we can easily afford a couple of months here in Essaouira, or maybe somewhere in the South of France where I've heard you can rent cottages in the Pyrenees for three hundred euros a month . . .'

'A life of ongoing adventure.'

'That will be us,' he said. 'It's all there for the asking. Even when we have our son or daughter with us.'

I felt myself going rigid with fury again. Hurt and rage and . . .

He has a daughter – and he has a wife.

Another wife.

'*Madame*, are you all right?'

It was one of the shop assistants – a very pretty young woman, no more than twenty-one, her hand on my arm, trying to steady me. Did I need steadying? Did I look as if I was about to tip forward into . . .?

'Fine, fine,' I heard myself saying, even though I knew that was anything but the truth.

'My apologies. I shouldn't have intruded. Can I help you find anything?'

'Toiletries. I need toiletries.'

'And make-up?'

'Do I need make-up?'

'*Madame*, I am not trying to interfere. My apologies again.'

'No, it's me who's sorry,' I said. This kind young woman informed me that the toiletries were on the second floor, near the café. I thanked her and went upstairs and bought deodorant and talcum powder and shampoo and conditioner and a hairbrush and a toothbrush and toothpaste and a facial cream that ludicrously promised to reduce all noticeable wrinkles in two weeks. I paid for all my purchases and asked the woman behind the register where I could find the nearest post office. She said there was one right opposite a café called the Parisian. Now there was a bit of synchronicity. It was the café that Ben Hassan had told me had reasonable Wi-Fi. Leaving the department store I walked the block to the local outpost of Poste Maroc. I bought an extra-large padded envelope, then reached into my backpack and withdrew Paul's one intact sketchbook, containing over fifty of his Essaouira drawings. I resisted the temptation to look through them again, certain that the sight of his artwork would toss me into further tumult. I sealed the book into the envelope, wrote the name and address of my accounting firm on the front, then had it airmailed by registered post back to the States. I wanted to get Paul's recent work home right away. I figured that, whatever was to become of us, he would be relieved to know that not all his drawings had been lost in the vortex into which he had thrown himself.

I adjourned to the café across the street.

The Parisian was very much a facsimile of one of those big brasseries in Paris – like La Coupole or the Terminus Nord – which I had read about in guidebooks, and which I vowed to loiter in someday. I found a table. I ordered *un express* and asked the waiter if he could find me some bread and jam. I was ravenous. Seeing my laptop he told me the name of the network and the password that I needed to get online.

I hadn't checked my email since yesterday, so there were over forty messages awaiting me. Mostly spam or commercial mail shots. A few professional matters to do with clients, all of which I answered while simultaneously forwarding them on to Morton.

The coffee and sliced baguette arrived. I thanked the waiter and layered the bread with strawberry jam, eating it quickly, hunger and disorientation making me feel light-headed. I drained the coffee in one go, then asked for another, along with *un citron pressé*.

'*Le petit dej' est à dix-sept heures,*' he said with a smile. *Breakfast at five p.m.* I managed to smile back.

I switched over to a new screen, calling up the joint MasterCard account that Paul and I shared; a credit card with a severely enforced credit limit, over which neither of us could spend. I checked the balance and was horrified (but not surprised) to see that the $3,000 limit had been exceeded earlier today – whereas when I last looked at its balance only three days ago, it had just $300 worth of eating out and small incidentals in Essaouira. But since yesterday, there had been two large cash withdrawals of 10,000 dirhams apiece, a plane ticket on Royal Air Maroc this morning to Ouarzazate, and a 1,600-dirham charge to a hotel named the Oasis in that same city. I googled the hotel and was directed to its website, where I discovered it was a two-star establishment with rooms at this low-season time of year costing 400 dirhams a night. Which meant that he must have booked himself in for at least four nights. I wanted to call and find out if he was indeed in residence there right now, to confront him on the phone, to demand . . .

His 'wife' – his other wife – must live in Ouarzazate. So why did he drag us to Essaouira instead of going to that city where he could have snuck between the two of us? Why run here – to Casablanca – to see his daughter after I had exposed his deceptions? Why did his daughter slam the door in his face, and why did he feel the need to run off to his wife? And how did he get on a plane without some piece of identification . . . like the passport he left behind, and which I was now carrying?

Ouarzazate. I googled its name and discovered that it was a city of around sixty thousand people in the south-east of the country; that it was considered 'the gateway to the Sahara'; that it had a film studio and was often used by foreign film companies as a location for anything with a desert setting; that it prided itself on 'its modern infrastructure and historic Saharan architecture'; that it was home to an international airport with daily flights to Casablanca and Marrakesh, and three-times-weekly direct service to Paris Orly.

It was now five-twelve in coastal North Africa. Twelve-twelve in Buffalo. I found the printout of my changed Royal Air Maroc reservation. I went to their website and tapped in my reference number. I switched over to the Jet Blue website and changed my internal JFK-to-Buffalo flight to the same time tomorrow. The *citron pressé* arrived. I added a small half-teaspoon of sugar and a dribble of water to the freshly squeezed lemon, then downed it in one go. *Citron pressé*: such a simple drink; the soothing and beneficial within a very sour fruit.

I felt improved by this late-afternoon breakfast. I paid the waiter. On my way back to Ben Hassan's I passed a florist and purchased a gift for my host: twelve long-stemmed lilies. Yes, I smelled my host's deviousness, but he was also being hospitable and I needed that right now. And my mother would have climbed out of her grave to haunt me if I hadn't followed one of her key social directives: always bring a gift.

'Lilies!' Ben Hassan said when I returned to his apartment. 'How did you know I love this flower?'

'Just a guess.'

'Perhaps you think me death-obsessed?'

'Are you?' I asked.

'When you weigh two hundred kilos and cannot walk more than two blocks without chest pains, yes, lilies do remind you that the River Styx is just a few streets away. But thank you for the gesture.'

'Speaking of death wishes . . . I know that my husband is now in Ouarzazate. That's where she lives, isn't it?'

Ben Hassan pursed his lips.

'Paul told me that you were a dangerously thorough woman, as befits your profession. We will talk more over dinner. The guest bathroom, as you may remember, is two doors down on the right. If you throw your clothes out into the corridor, Omar will have them washed and ironed by the time we return tonight. We don't want to send you back to the United States with dirty laundry, now do we?'

'Don't we all have dirty laundry, *monsieur*?' I asked.

'Ah, an accountant with soul.'

The bathroom was cramped; the shower a tiny stall with a hand-held hose. But the water pressure was reasonable, the temperature

144

hot. And it was good to strip out of clothes in which I had travelled and slept for the past twenty-four hours. I did indeed crack open the door to toss them into the corridor.

Getting dressed in the new clothes I had bought I caught sight of myself in the mirror. The eight-hour snooze had lightened the dark circles beneath my eyes. The seismic disturbances within had hardly dissipated. But the upending of a life – *my life* – is so much better handled after a proper sleep and a very hot shower.

'Don't you look radiant,' Ben Hassan said when I wandered down the corridor and found him and Omar at work in the office in which multi-coloured passports were stacked high.

'I thank you for all your kindnesses.'

'You deserve nothing less than that, *madame*. Especially with all that you have discovered in the past few hours. Not that Paul himself would ever stare directly into the wrecked ship that is his life. Who on earth wants to do that?'

A pause, as Ben Hassan let that last comment hang between us. Then he whispered something in Arabic to Omar who got up from the laminating press at which he was at work on a Belgian passport. He brushed by me.

'Time for a Kir,' Ben Hassan said, 'if that is agreeable with you.'

'Yes, I could use a drink.'

'Glad to hear it. I am a good Muslim who believes in Allah and the inevitable gates of paradise from which I can finally cast off this corpulent worldly shell and spend the rest of eternity floating in the celestial vapours. But I am also a bad Muslim who believes that it is very hard to get through the day without having a drink, or two, or three. In fact I am rather suspicious of anyone who doesn't drink. Paul doesn't overindulge . . . unless the world is crowding in on him.'

'So he was drinking heavily when he was here last night?'

'Of course. Especially after his daughter slammed the door in his face. But more on that anon. May I ask how you figured out that he went to Ouarzazate?'

I explained how we shared the same credit card and could track all purchases online.

'You really are Big Brother.'

'Hardly. Had I been watching him closely I would have known long ago about his secret.'

'You mean, his *secrets*.'

'Yes, I have discovered they are plural. But let me ask you something – as Paul ran off without his passport, how did he get onto that Royal Air Maroc flight?'

Ben Hassan smiled wryly, then fanned his hand out to indicate our immediate surroundings.

'Surely you know the answer to that question already.'

'So he's now travelling on what passport?'

'British.'

'How much did you charge him?'

'My usual price is ten thousand dirhams.'

'Which is why he withdrew that sum yesterday.'

'Your powers of deduction are exceptional. But ten thousand dirhams is, I should point out, my "friends and family" price. If you are someone in need of false documents owing to problems with the authorities – or must vanish thoroughly – the price does head considerably northwards.'

'You were benevolent towards your old friend.'

'That's one way of looking at it.'

'Did Paul tell you why he showed up in Casablanca, without papers and in what I gather was an extreme mental state?'

'The business with his daughter, of course – but how much exactly do you know of all that?'

'Only that he has a daughter named Samira and a wife named . . .'

'Faiza.'

'What does Faiza do?'

'She teaches English language and French literature in a *lycée* in Ouarzazate.'

'How long were they married?'

The drinks arrived.

'We'll get to that matter – and many others – over dinner. Meanwhile . . .'

Omar handed me a glass of cassis-coloured wine.

'The basis of this Kir is a white from the Meknes region, which is the Moroccan Bordeaux when it comes to our *vignobles*,' Ben Hassan explained, also accepting a glass from Omar. 'Your very good health, Robin – and a good flight tomorrow out of all this unfortunate mess.'

We clinked glasses. Ben Hassan whispered something again to Omar, who withdrew from the room, closing the door behind him. Once he was out of earshot Ben Hassan said:

'It was rather unfortunate, attacking poor Paul with a bottle.'

'I never did that.' I was stunned by this accusation.

'So you say.'

'I'm telling the truth. Paul threw himself against the wall of our hotel room after—'

I cut myself off, not wanting to go further.

'After what?'

I chose my next words with care.

'After I caught him out in an enormous lie.'

'But if you caught him deceiving you – I presume it was another woman . . .'

'It wasn't another woman.'

'Then what was it?'

'That's my business.'

'And it's also your business why you attacked him with a bottle.'

'Why won't you believe me?'

'Why should I? Paul is my friend. Paul arrived on my doorstep last night in a state of emotional disarray, telling me that he fled Essaouira when his wife attacked him with a bottle, and showing all the physical side effects of this attack. Had the person I shared my bed with attacked me with a bottle . . .'

Ben Hassan maintained a light, almost jovial tone throughout this banter – as if this was all a rather amusing turn of events.

'Why did Samira turn him away?' I asked.

'Because he was a very bad father who hadn't bothered to show any interest in his daughter until just a few months ago.'

'How do you know this?'

'Samira considers me to be her surrogate father.'

He looked straight at me as he said this.

'Where was her mother?' I asked.

'Here in Casablanca until her daughter entered university – and they began to have all sorts of problems. Then Faiza, who was also having a variety of professional difficulties, lost her job. And lost her home, owing to manifold debts and a man in her life who was not honourable, let alone honest.'

'Not Paul?'

'No – Paul cut complete contact with his wife and his daughter when he left for the States some months before Samira's birth.'

'Then why did he feel the need to reconnect if he hadn't been in contact for decades?'

'You would have to ask Paul that.'

He raised his glass again, downing it all in one long draught. After a small but indiscreet belch, he raised his eyebrows and said:

'Of course the fact that he discovered he was a grandfather might have had something to do with it.'

'Samira has a child?'

'Yes, an eighteen-month-old son named Claude. The father is a French lawyer from Marseille. Married. Highly intelligent. Highly complex. But Samira has always liked her men intelligent and complex. Which is why she was always intrigued from afar by her absentee father – and also desperately hurt that he refused all contact. But it's the strangest damn thing. Not a word to Faiza or Samira for decades. And he never once sent them anything in the way of money. He'd vanished across the Atlantic, out of sight, clearly uninterested. Then, a few months ago, he suddenly gets in touch with me, asking for news of his daughter. Not just news, but recent photographs and her email address. And he began to write to her, wanting to know everything about her life. Samira came to me, upset and confused.'

'Why would he contact her after all this time?' I asked. 'Why now?'

'I told Samira she should ask that question of Paul in an email. His response was: "I have just discovered that I cannot have children with my new wife."'

I was so thrown by this statement that my glass of wine fell to the floor.

'He wrote that?' I whispered. 'He *actually* wrote that?'

Ben Hassan pursed his lips, suppressing a smile.

'Yes, he wrote that he could not have children with you . . . that you were not fertile.'

'That is beyond a lie,' I said, starting to sob. 'And the reason he came fleeing up here to Casablanca is because I found out that he'd had a vasectomy behind my back.'

Ben Hassan received this information with a momentary shocked stare – quickly morphed into what I had begun to discern was his default wry passivity.

'That is quite an accusation.'

I was now digging into my backpack, searching for the clutch of documents I had brought with me.

'It's not an accusation,' I cried. 'It's the truth.'

I slammed the documents down on the work table in front of Ben Hassan.

'There it is, in black and white.'

In a hurried, manic stream of words I told how the invoice for the surgery had found its way to me, and everything that had happened from that point onwards, leading to me being here now. Ben Hassan listened in silence. When I was finished he picked up a small bell near to where he sat and rang it twice. Omar was back in the room within seconds. An interchange in Arabic. Omar disappeared and returned immediately with a new glass of Kir for me. He also began to pick up the shards of glass that were scattered everywhere on the floor. When I tried to apologise for my angry clumsiness Ben Hassan held up his hand and told me to go easy on myself.

'You have been subject to far too many shocks in the past twenty-four hours. Happily the glass in question is not Rosenthal crystal, just *un verre ordinaire*, so no damage done.'

More whispered words to Omar, who dumped the broken glass into a nearby trash can and left us alone again. As soon as the door was closed, Ben Hassan reached for the surgery invoice and held it up.

'Here is the proverbial smoking gun – further proof that you did attack him with a bottle upon discovering the nature of his treachery.'

I snapped my eyes shut. I should never have uttered a word of this to the crafty operator seated opposite me. I finally said:

'You need to know that I am telling you the absolute truth when it comes to Paul's head injury. And that I am desperately worried about him. I have to find him.'

Ben Hassan fell silent for a moment, sipping his wine. Then he said:

'I hope you will take solace in the fact that your husband has worked very hard at making amends with his daughter.'

'By which you mean . . .?'

'He helped buy her an apartment.'

Now I really was lost.

'He what?'

'He helped buy Samira the apartment she lives in now – the apartment in front of which you verbally attacked her this morning.'

'I was not verbally attacking her. I was simply—'

'Letting it be known that you believed she was your husband's other woman. Samira called me while you were asleep, just a little aggrieved at such an accusation and the way you accosted her in public.'

'I did not accost her.'

'As before, *madame*, you are, I know, telling the truth.'

'Paul couldn't have bought her an apartment.'

'He only paid for half of it. The other half came from her French lover.'

'How much did my husband give his daughter?'

'One million dirhams.'

Ben Hassan watched me absorb that little detail.

'I can't believe that,' I said.

'Why can't you?'

'Because that's what? . . . Eight point eight dirhams to one US dollar . . . something in the neighbourhood of one hundred and twenty-two thousand dollars.'

'You are the human abacus, *madame*.'

'There is no way he could have borrowed that money in the States without me knowing about it.'

'Which is why Paul borrowed the money here in Casablanca.'

'But he has no credit rating here, no equity that he could have put up as collateral against a loan of that size.'

'Again you have hit the bull's eye. Which is why your husband didn't turn to a bank or any other financial institution.'

The penny (actually an ocean of pennies) dropped.

'Are you telling me he turned to a loan shark?'

'"Loan shark" is rather pejorative, is it not? A "financial facilitator" is a far more elegant turn of phrase and not as derogatory.'

'Do you think I care about verbal niceties right now, Monsieur Ben Hassan? He borrowed money from a loan shark, which means he's in even more trouble than I had imagined. I suppose you know the name of the gangster to whom he's now probably paying three times the sum borrowed?'

'The man is no gangster. He's just a businessman.'

'And his name is . . .?'

A long pause as my host drained his glass, belching loudly and pointedly. Finally he said:

'His name is . . . Monsieur Romain Ben Hassan.'

Fifteen

WE MOVED ON to a local restaurant. And by the time the first bottle of wine was empty, Ben Hassan was trying to insist that he was my new best friend.

At the start of the meal, however, he was oozing neither bonhomie nor easy camaraderie. On the contrary, he was showing me his more menacing hand.

'When Paul heard from me that Samira might talk with him again if he helped her buy an apartment for herself and her son, his immediate response was: "Get her the money." I told him that, if he was actually serious about borrowing one million dirhams from me, he would have to take the consequences if he did not meet his monthly payments.'

'What sort of consequences might these be?'

'Unpleasant ones.'

'Surely you weren't planning to send somebody over to Buffalo to rough him up . . . or worse?'

'Had that become necessary, of course there were ways and means – contacts, so to speak, in that corner of the world, who could have been called upon to intervene on my behalf. For a price, *naturellement*. A price which would have been tagged onto the monthly repayment.'

'I think the actual term in loan-shark speak is "vig". The monthly "vig" – which you have to meet or else contend with grievous bodily harm.'

'I presume you picked that term up from some sort of crime novel, *un polar*, yes?'

'In my business you occasionally run into a client who has made the mistake of borrowing money from a thug like you.'

Ben Hassan put his fingers together in front of his face, as if creating his very own cathedral into which he now stared. I could see his lips twitch. Was he trying to contain his anger, his disdain? Had I crossed the line of no return? If my husband had signed something quasi-legal and binding, had he fled to Ouarzazate because he simply could not pay the 'vig', leaving me behind to clean up his financial mess as usual? Only the sum involved – one million dirhams – was a vertiginous one. I certainly didn't have that sort of cash in a bank account, let alone my back pocket.

Ben Hassan stopped looking through the lattice of his thick sausage-like fingers. Then, favouring me with a paternal smile, he said:

'There's no need to hold onto your bag, as if I am going to snatch it away. I know you still don't trust me. But you have my word that I would not dream of harming you in any way.'

'My husband, on the other hand . . .'

'He will hopefully work out a way to honour our little arrangement.'

'You know he doesn't have that kind of money.'

Ben Hassan covered my hand with his own – actually burying it under his soft mound of flesh.

'Let us discuss such matters later on . . .'

With that he insisted on ordering dinner for us. The waiter was immediately at our table, treating Ben Hassan like some godfatherly pasha, telling him that the *patron* wanted him to have a bottle of the best cuvée on the house, and informing him that the chef had prepared a lamb tagine with preserved lemons 'especially for Monsieur Ben Hassan and his lovely guest'.

Part of me wanted to ask my host whether they owed him money as well, and as if anticipating my question he said:

'I made a small investment in this establishment some years ago – and the management remain exceptionally grateful for my aid at a moment when they sorely needed assistance.'

'You are quite the businessman, *monsieur*.'

'Such flattery,' he said. 'But I find myself a less-than-interesting subject. Especially when seated opposite such a lovely, fascinating woman.'

He got me speaking about myself and I gave him the abbreviated version of my life, sidestepping much in the way of any telling detail about my father, my first marriage, how I fled a journalistic career for the surer waters of accounting. But Ben Hassan turned out to be a master of subtext, immediately deducing much and using it to make me feel even more uneasy. The man was ruthlessly clever when it came to taking an inference ('Dad never could really settle down') and turning it into a psychological revelation ('So you have always been attracted to unstable, unsound men'). I quickly cottoned on to his game. Instead of getting defensive, I started asking him about his own background, discovering that his French father had run a vineyard in the Meknes region, had married a Moroccan woman from a bourgeois Rabat family, but abandoned her and his young son when an opportunity arose for him to return to Bourgogne; how his father refused to see his son thereafter, 'excising me from his life as if I was a nasty boil'; how Ben Hassan had studied commerce in Paris and tried repeatedly to maintain contact with his father; how 'my attempts to enter the world of international business in Paris came a little unstuck'; how 'I returned to Casablanca and began to make my fortune here'; how . . .

'Did you get into some sort of trouble in France?' I asked, the exceptional food and wine emboldening me.

'Why do you immediately assume that the discrimination I encountered in France was due to some sort of scandal?' he demanded.

'Aren't there plenty of North Africans who have successfully integrated into French society?'

'It is still the country of *Le Front National*. I couldn't stay there.'

'But you must have a French passport, thanks to your French father. When were you last there?'

'My girth has militated against my ability to travel.'

The second bottle of wine arrived. The waiter opened it and, with great ceremony, placed two fresh glasses on the table and delicately poured a fingerful for Ben Hassan. My host again made great theatre of sampling it, swirling it around the glass, sniffing in with such great force that I feared he might just inhale it, then taking a sizeable sip and rolling it around his mouth like a gargle before gulping it straight down and nodding his approval. The waiter poured out two glasses, then left. As soon as he was out of earshot I posed a question that I had been wanting to raise for several hours:

'How serious was Paul's relationship with Faiza?'

Ben Hassan ran his finger several times around the top of his wineglass. The man loved creating a sense of drama before making a statement. Finally he spoke:

'We were all part of a bohemian circle in Casablanca – writers, poets, visual artists. I may have studied commerce in Paris, but that was to please my mother. As I sense you know, you can never please your mother. Still, before Paris, after Paris, abstract painting was my métier. I even had a gallery here in Casablanca that sold my work. Was I considered a serious painter? Quasi-serious. But not a major artist like your husband. And Faiza – well, she was teaching in a *lycée* here and trying to write the Great Moroccan Feminist Novel, seeing herself as a sort of North African Simone de Beauvoir. Truth be told, she had little in the way of actual literary talent. But she was rather fetching all those years ago, before disappointment and cigarettes began to work their toxic magic. Paul back then was the young American bohemian of every artistic girl's dreams. Faiza comes from a good family in Rabat. Her father worked for the Moroccan Central Bank as an economist, and they were hardly rigorous Muslims. But even if you are a secular Muslim – as so many Moroccans still are – you are also the byproduct of a conservative society, especially when it comes to sex. Paul was Faiza's first lover. They were quite the handsome couple. She wanted him to whisk her off to New York, make her his wife and fund her writing while he became the famous artist.

'We all have a flaw when it comes to matters intimate. Faiza's was her need to control at all costs. Within two months of their involvement she was already starting to make demands, to criticise Paul's lack of order, to argue with him over just about everything. Frequently Paul told me that he was finding it all *de trop*. I advised him to cut his losses and get out. But on the two or so occasions that he suggested ending things, Faiza turned all tearful and apologetic, saying: "You are the man of my life." From what I also ascertained, though she was not experienced in the world of sex, she'd become a very fast learner. And Paul, being a man who likes sex—'

'You think I'm not aware of that?'

'I've spoken out of turn.'

'I was just making a point. An exceedingly defensive point.'

'I like a woman who can laugh at herself.'

'Now . . . let me guess. Paul being Paul, he couldn't deal with her emotional meltdowns in the face of him trying to leave her, and was too cowardly to walk away. Given the way she was making him feel like a sex god, he trusted her when it came to little matters like contraception.'

Ben Hassan emitted a curious giggle, reminiscent of a little boy who'd just heard something 'naughty'.

'It's you who should be telling this story,' he said. 'Yes, Paul believed Faiza when she told him she was on the pill. So when she announced: "*Mon chéri, j'ai une grande nouvelle à t'annoncer. Je suis enceinte*" . . . well, Paul was stunned by the news that she was pregnant. When he didn't exactly sweep her up in his arms and proclaim that she was the love of his life and, that, *bien sûr*, a child together would be the ultimate expression of their *amour éternel*, she began to hector him, insisting that they get married. When he hesitated she told her family. Her father showed up with her two somewhat virulent brothers at the École des Beaux-Arts just a kilometre or so from here, threatening to castrate Paul if he didn't marry Faiza. They also raised so much stink with the head of the college that Paul was suspended on the spot, but told by our enlightened principal that he could have his job back if he made an honest woman of her. For around twenty-four hours the two brothers actually had Paul trapped in his flat. Then their father showed up with Faiza, an imam and a lawyer. They insisted on being let in, Faiza crying wildly, telling Paul that she was going to die if he didn't marry her. Paul panicked and let them in. He went through with the shotgun service there and then. Said the vows, signed the legal document, and tried to kiss the bride who shouted insults at him and stormed off with her father, saying

156

she'd see him tomorrow when her brothers returned to move him into their new home in Rabat. "I have found you a job teaching English there," his new father-in-law announced to him. The brothers informed Paul that they would be downstairs, guarding the front and back doors – so there was no way he was going to be able to do a run for the airport. As soon as they were gone, Paul phoned me in a total panic. I told him he'd been insane to go through the marriage, but that I would find him a way out of this nightmare. Which is what I did. Around three hours later I called Paul back and told him to get his passport and a small bag and head to the roof of the building at precisely midnight. I put on a djellaba with a hood. I didn't know if Faiza had alerted her brothers to Paul's fat gay artist friend who might try to rescue him, but I was taking no chances. Dressed in my djellaba – my face hidden by the hood – I drove down to his *quartier*. He lived in an area where the buildings were so packed together that it was only a one-metre jump from one roof to the next. But you had to do the jump right, as it was a ten-storey fall if you didn't. I bribed the superintendent of the adjoining building to give me access to the roof. It cost seven hundred dirhams – a small fortune back then, but I had just sold a painting and I knew that if I didn't get Paul out of the country he would be throwing his future away on a woman who, for all her bohemian, "second sex" cant, was a future harridan in waiting.

'Faiza's brothers were not stupid. I discovered that they had hired some stooge to guard the rear of the apartment building where Paul lived. That rear entrance was located next to the building onto which he was going to jump. Anyway, I left, returning around quarter to midnight. One of Faiza's brothers was positioned outside Paul's building. When I entered the adjoining building – still wearing the djellaba with its hood tied close across my face – the superintendent told me that their stooge was still guarding the back door. Up I went to the roof. Even thirty years ago, walking up ten flights was torture for me. There was Paul on the other roof, looking down with fear at the gap between the two buildings, terrified of making the jump, rooted to the spot. I had to signal him with a cigarette lighter. When he wouldn't move, I remember hissing at him:

"It's just one metre. If you don't jump you are sentencing yourself to a lifetime of marital servitude with a woman who will grind your talent, your gift, into the ground. Stand still and die. Or jump and live."

'Of course he jumped – and managed to twist his ankle on landing, which made things just a little complicated when it came to getting him down ten floors. But we eventually made it. The superintendent brought us through a series of corridors to the rear exit. Before Paul set foot outside he changed into the hooded djellaba I'd brought for him. He hobbled out the back door, leaning on my shoulder for support, walking right past the stooge who'd been posted by the brothers to look out for their sister's fleeing American lover. When the guy saw Paul limping he actually took his other arm and helped him to where I'd parked the beat-up Peugeot I drove back then. To his credit, despite being in terrible pain, Paul kept his mouth shut. And he'd tied the djellaba so tightly across his face that his very Caucasian identity remained hidden from view. The stooge was asking me why Paul was limping. I informed him that he was deaf and dumb and had been set upon by bandits. Fortunately for us the man was so stupid, with a shred of kindness for a cripple, that he never once questioned the absurdity of the story I was spinning. He even wished us both luck as we drove off.

'I knew that Faiza's father – having connections, owing to his position at the Moroccan Central Bank – was probably having the airport watched, or at least had made certain that Paul wouldn't be able to board a flight back to the States. Which is why I drove him the six hours – no *autoroutes* in those days – up to Tangier, and got him on the six a.m. ferry to Malaga. I even gave him enough pesetas to get himself a doctor for his ankle, a hotel room for the night, and a train ticket up to Madrid. And then . . .'

Ben Hassan snapped his fingers.

'Whoosh. Paul Leuen vanished from my life.'

'Surely he contacted you when he got back to the States?' I asked.

Ben Hassan shook his head.

'Did he ever repay you?'

Ben Hassan shook his head.

'What happened when the baby was born?'

'What happened? Faiza endured the shame of being a single mother. She wasn't allowed to work at the *lycée* for several years, and struggled to make ends meet through tutoring and even cleaning other people's apartments, as her family largely disowned her.'

'Surely she tried to contact Paul.'

'She tried. She failed. She went to the US Embassy with her father, demanding some sort of action, see if they could get him extradited back to Morocco to play house with her. The US consul said that, outside of finding an American lawyer who could chase Mr Leuen for child support, there was nothing they could do to get him back here. Though Faiza wrote to him several times, enclosing pictures of their baby daughter, he maintained his veil of silence. Even when I wrote him after . . .'

He reached for his glass of wine, draining it in one go and pouring himself another substantial slug.

'After what?' I asked.

Ben Hassan hesitated before speaking.

'Faiza's father was furious to discover that Paul had managed to slip out of the building undetected. He vented his rage on his sons who, in turn, beat up the sad little stooge who'd been guarding the back door. Beat him up so badly that he was hospitalised for months. Then, on their father's orders, they strong-armed the superintendent of the building next door and found out who had whisked their brother-in-law away. The superintendent gave them my name. They cornered me leaving the École des Beaux-Arts that evening. They dragged me into an alley and, using a hammer, they smashed all my fingers.'

'You're serious?' I asked, my voice a stunned whisper. 'They did that?'

He held up his hand.

'Every finger. Smashed to a pulp. All bones broken. The pain was so overwhelming I passed out. I was found hours later by a street cleaner. Thank God he ran into the École and found two of my colleagues still on duty, teaching night classes. They called the police and the *pompiers*, and both came with me to the hospital. Thank God they were there, as the doctor on duty was so appalled by the catastrophic state of my fingers that he wanted to have them amputated. My colleagues – both artists – insisted that he do nothing so rash. But the fingers were so pulverised that I was in a pair of casts for over a year. I was lucky. There was a French orthopaedic surgeon who had decided on a change of scene and was on a three-year secondment to the big hospital here in Casablanca. He took an interest in my case and convinced me to undergo a series of experimental bone-reconstruction operations. Ten in total, followed by around three years of physiotherapy. It took just two or three minutes for those pathetic men to destroy my hands, and over thirty-six months of agonising surgery and reconstruction for me to be able to hold a pen again.'

I truly didn't know what to say. Except:

'Was Paul aware of the price you paid for helping him escape?'

'I wrote to him. Correction – I dictated a letter to him, as it was around two months after the attack. I explained what had befallen me in the wake of driving him to Tangiers. I didn't ask for any money or recompense. I just wanted him to know what had happened, what those bastards did to me.'

'What was Paul's reply?'

As Ben Hassan reached for his wine, I noticed for the first time just how much work it took him to grasp the stem of his glass, and how his large fingers were more misshapen than corpulent.

He took another long sip of wine, and I could see that he was steadying himself, tamping down some of the anger within.

'Paul's reply was . . . silence. Even when I wrote to him again another eight weeks after my first letter, even when several of our fellow colleagues at the school tried to contact him about what happened, even when Faiza – who, to her credit, disowned her

160

father and two brothers after this "incident" – tried once more to contact him, begging him to at least write me . . . nothing but silence.'

'Were the brothers and father ever prosecuted for what they did?'

'Yes, the police did arrest the three of them. But Papa had connections. And the two boys said in court – there was a hearing in front of a judge – that they had attacked me after I attempted to come on to one of them. This being the 1980s they accepted gay bashing as a defence. They reached an out-of-court settlement with me for one hundred thousand dirhams—'

'But that's only just over eleven thousand dollars.'

'Back then it was enough to buy an apartment – which is what I did with the money. The apartment in which you will be staying tonight.'

'What about your hands?'

'The French surgeon was a miracle worker. He did reconstruct the bones, and he did reconnect certain nerve endings so I could have some feeling in them. But not an exceptional amount. Even today . . .'

He reached into his jacket pocket and brought out a disposable lighter. Igniting the flame he held it directly under his left pinky – and didn't flinch once as the flame came into direct contact with his flesh.

'As you can see,' he said, 'there is considerable permanent numbness. And my ability to hold a paintbrush, even after the ten operations and all that physiotherapy . . . well, to be blunt about it, my career as a painter was decimated. Those paintings you see in my apartment . . . *à la recherche du temps perdu*. Ancient history.'

'I don't know what to say. It is such a terrible story.'

'That it is. Still, in Chinese calligraphy, the symbol for "crisis" has two meanings – danger and opportunity. My opportunity in the wake of the attack on my hands was to become – how shall I put this? – a facilitator. Someone who could pull strings, grease palms, work wonders with travel documents, settle scores.'

There was a question I wanted to ask, but didn't dare bring up. Ben Hassan did it for me.

'I sense you want to know what happened to Faiza's father and brothers, after they bought me my apartment. Faiza, as I mentioned, wouldn't have anything to do with them again, while regularly visiting me in hospital and also insisting on bringing in friends to do the initial decorative work on the apartment. I can't say that we were ever friends. She's quite the bitter, disappointed woman. She truly never got over losing Paul, especially as the next man in her life was a stockbroker who was, in my opinion, Prince Not So Bright, though I gather he could play a decent round of golf. Her attempt to act the role of the bourgeois wife to a stupid man – even though he did make good money. By the time Samira was an adolescent their mother-daughter relationship was like something out of a bad Joan Crawford film – all gay men, even in North Africa, love Joan Crawford. Then the stockbroker lost everything, including the home they called their own. Samira lived in my guest room for several months, then went to France for a spell, but didn't have a *carte de séjour* so she couldn't find work. Even though she could have got an American passport through her father, the fact that he never claimed paternity and refused to answer the letters from Samira asking if they could meet, or at least tell the US authorities that, yes, she was her daughter . . . that made it administratively difficult for her. And her bitterness just grew.

'Faiza, meanwhile, managed to alienate the director of the *lycée* where she taught. But then, at a cocktail thing here in town, she met a man named Hamsad who was the director of the film studios in Ouarzazate. Within months she was living down there on the edge of the Sahara – a place which, though somewhat picturesque, has always struck me as a recipe for despair after seventy-two hours. Still, with her daughter estranged from her, with another relatively well-heeled man willing to look out for her, and even a job opening at a language school there . . . off she went to the desert. That was five years ago. The relationship fell apart after around eighteen months. Hamsad showed her the door.

I gather that she's still teaching at the language institute, and she was supportive of Samira when she fell pregnant and her foreign lover returned to France.'

'So history repeated itself.'

'Except that in this instance, the gentleman – whose name is Philippe – acted reasonably. He's paying close to the equivalent of five hundred euros a month in child support, and also offering to part-finance an apartment for Samira and her child.'

'With my husband paying the other half.'

'As I said earlier, when Paul contacted me out of the blue last autumn – clearly in the wake of his little surgical procedure to secretly deny his new wife a child – I was flabbergasted. When I heard him sounding sad and guilty about being such a bad father to Samira – well, how can I put this? I saw an opportunity . . .'

'For revenge?'

'For payback.'

'By which you mean?'

'We communicated for several weeks by email and spoke twice on the phone. He actually sounded increasingly unstable and just a little haunted. Especially as he'd written twice to Samira who informed him by return email that she wanted absolutely nothing to do with him, that he couldn't simply drop back into her life after thirty years and think there was any chance whatsoever of a relationship. That's when Paul asked me directly if there was anything he could do for his daughter. At which point a plan fell into my head.'

My mind was racing. As someone who had spent much of her accounting career second-guessing malevolent tax inspectors and certain fraudulent clients, I did have an intuitive nose for a scam, a subterfuge, an ambush.

'You decided to set him a trap.'

'I decided to give the man what he wanted – which, on a certain existential level, might be interpreted as being what Monsieur Paul also subconsciously thought he deserved. Payback for abandoning his daughter, and for not once offering assistance or even basic compassion for his great friend whose life was, on a certain level, ruined. Not least by his thoughtlessness and callous disregard. I told him that his daughter needed an additional one million dirhams to buy her apartment and that she couldn't afford a mortgage of that magnitude.'

'Was that the truth?'

'Put it this way – she wasn't asking for the money and her lover had given her enough to put down a deposit on a small two-bedroom apartment in this *quartier*.'

'Did you lead him to believe that, having given her essentially half of the apartment, he could repair his relationship with her?'

'Perhaps.'

'And let me guess – you also told him that in order to borrow the money from you he would have to come back to Morocco to sign the papers and give you the first payment?'

He laced his fingers together again, staring through the cathedral-like structure.

'Absolutely.'

'So since he never spent any time away from me while here, where did you meet him?'

'I had Omar drive me to Essaouira. We had a very pleasant lunch at Chez Fouad while you were off improving your French and walking the beach, if my memory serves me right. He signed the papers, and he handed over the first month's repayment. Since you strike me as somewhat legally minded, I took the liberty of bringing along the loan agreement – drawn up by a local notary whom I arranged to meet us there.'

He reached into his jacket pocket and brought out a three-page document in French and Arabic. I scanned it briefly, turning to the back page to see my husband's cramped signature located right next to a notary's seal and corroborating signature. On page two I found the piece of information I also needed (and could understand *en français*): the terms of the loan. I could see that the 1 million dirhams would be paid back over ten years, at an annual rate of 160,000 dirhams, in monthly instalments of 13,333 dirhams – around $1,500, or close to $18,000 per annum. As Paul only earned $100k gross from the university and maybe another $15k tops for his artwork, by the time he'd finished paying tax, social security and his share of the mortgage he had around $40k to cover his car costs, pay his share of utilities, his cellphone, his health club, buy food, contribute to the month away on the Maine coast we allowed ourselves every summer. That gave him very little left over from the $500 a week he had to meet all these not extravagant expenses. For him to then take on a loan that was going to cost him $1,500 every month . . . it was madness.

I tossed the document back in front of Ben Hassan.

'You are certainly getting your revenge on your friend. And you will be making a considerable profit from this little loan.'

'Madame, I am not Société Générale or Chase Manhattan Bank. I am a businessman, and one who had to dig into his resources to finance his friend.'

'Now I know why Paul was so insistent that we spend these weeks in Morocco. You wouldn't give him the money unless he was in the country. Because that would mean you'd have him here, potentially ensnared. I bet you didn't even tell Samira that her father gave her the one million dirhams . . .'

'She just closed on the apartment last week, and won't move in for another month. Perhaps it was an oversight on my part not to mention that Paul had helped her . . .'

He was barely containing a smile as he said this.

'Bullshit. You wanted him to confront her on her doorstep and let her slam the door in his face.'

'Perhaps. But do remember, *madame*, that the only reason he came running up to Casablanca was because you caught him out in his little lie.'

'And then he probably called you in a panic, asking you to smooth the way for him to see Samira. You gave him her address, and didn't warn her that he'd be showing up, knowing what her reaction would be.'

'Revenge is a dish best eaten cold.'

'How did you revenge yourself on Faiza's father and brothers?'

'That's for you to find out. But, again, Madame Robin, I must say that I am most impressed by you. And my advice to you is very straightforward – cut your losses. Get up tomorrow, head for the airport, leave your husband to whatever destiny brings his way.'

'And if Paul doesn't pay you the monthly vig . . .?'

Ben Hassan unlocked his fingers and stared directly at me; a stare as arctic as it was menacing.

'What will happen to your dear husband if he doesn't meet his legally binding commitment to me? I will have the great pleasure of watching Omar use a hammer to smash every one of his fingers.'

166

As SOON AS he uttered his threat the temptation arose to toss the contents of my wineglass in Ben Hassan's face. For several edgy moments I had to keep the glass fixed to the table. He worked out what I was stopping myself from doing and raised a finger upwards, saying:

'If you create havoc here – and shame me in public – there will be ramifications.'

'You're a gangster.'

'That is an interpretation. But so is the fact that I am your only friend here.'

'A "friend" who tricked my husband into—'

'Your husband is the architect of his own maelstrom. He approached me. He begged for a way back to his daughter. I gave it to him.'

'While achieving payback at the same time.'

'He knew how much I would be charging him for the money. He accepted the sum. He knew that he would have to return to Morocco to sign the papers – and yes, now you know the real reason why you came to Morocco this summer. He accepted that too. I did warn him that finding a way back into Samira's heart would be challenging, that she grew up haunted by the absence of her father and the way he never once contacted her. She herself must have written to Paul at least once a year until she was twenty-five. Even after she had that terrible rupture with her mother she still held onto the naive hope that, somehow, he was going to be the good father and rescue her from her immense loneliness. In short, he was fully aware that, by trying to re-engage with his exceptionally messy past, he was walking right back into a compromised and precarious situation. But he still chose to head across the Atlantic and into my open arms. And you, innocent you, who knows all about absentee fathers and men in endless negotiation with their various conflicted selves – you should stop cloaking

167

Paul in maternal protectiveness and let him play the adult for a change. But you can't do that, can you? Which is why you want to dash that glass in my face – and, in doing so, earn my displeasure. Which, as I think you can sense by now, is not a wise thing to do.'

'Because you might smash my fingers? Or maybe I'll suffer the same fate meted out to Faiza's father and brothers?'

'I don't remember alluding to any fate being "meted out" to them.'

'But they are no longer with us, right?'

'I never said that.'

'Because I didn't ask it before. But I'm asking it now.'

'Why don't you ask Faiza about all that? Because that's where you're heading now, isn't it? In fact, let me expedite matters for you and give you her address in Ouarzazate.'

'You're a mind reader now, are you?'

'Actually I am. I know you are someone who can't simply walk away, even if it means following the man who betrayed you into the vortex.'

He pulled out a notebook and an elegant silver pen, then scribbled for a few moments before tearing the page out and handing it to me.

'Here is Madame Faiza's phone number and address. You already know the name of the hotel where Paul is staying.'

'Why haven't you dispatched Omar there to drag him back?'

'Because the next payment isn't due yet. Of course, if you prefer to pay it now . . .'

'I don't have it on me in cash.'

'And I don't accept credit cards. Anyway, he has ten days' grace. Meanwhile, you are still more than welcome to avail yourself of our extra bed tonight.'

'You can't be serious.'

'Just trying to be generous. The other option is an all-night bus that leaves the Central Station at eleven p.m. I know this because that is the bus which Paul boarded last night. It is a monstrous journey, via Marrakesh, of around ten hours. Or there is a flight at six-fifty tomorrow morning. Royal Air Maroc. But a last-minute ticket is somewhat on the expensive side. Around five thousand dirhams one way. The bus, on the other hand, is one hundred and fifty dirhams. Your call, *madame*.'

'You're going to call Faiza as soon as I've left the restaurant, warn her I'm on my way.'

'Actually, you're wrong there. I'm going to make no such call. I'm going to let the element of surprise guide things from now on. Like the look on Monsieur Paul's face when you surprise him at his hotel room. Or perhaps find him in Madame Faiza's bed.'

'Whatever I discover I am ready for it.'

'I love a forward-thinker. But before you dash off into the night, surely you will want to try one of the celebrated desserts they make here. The baklava is especially sublime. And the *patron* will no doubt offer us a very good *digestif* to accompany *le thé à la menthe*. You still have almost forty-five minutes before the bus leaves. It is a mere ten minutes by taxi from here to—'

I stood, hoisting the backpack, uncertain what my next move should be.

'Going so soon?' he asked. 'A pity.'

'Are you going to keep your word about not contacting anybody in Ouarzazate?'

'*Madame*, if I give my word I always keep it. Which is why, when I lend money, I always remind the client that they have my word that all will run smoothly as long as the money is paid back on time. If you do catch up with your husband, tell him I will expect to see him in ten days. Without fail. And if you think you can spirit him out of the country and somehow elude me . . . do please think again.'

Then, slowly pushing back his chair and slowly elevating the mountain that was himself to his feet, he executed a small, very formal bow and uttered two words:

'*Bon voyage*.'

I stared at him long and hard, trying to communicate the fact that he didn't frighten me. Truth be told he terrified me.

'Until next time.'

Out on the street I didn't know what to do next. I needed to think clearly, logically. Checking my watch I considered the fact that I had forty minutes to make the bus. Finding a taxi seemed to be no problem. There were plenty around here. But the thought of ten hours on a bus heading south over the Atlas Mountains – and an all-night bus at that – filled me with dread. My budget needed to be managed with care, however, so I decided to hurry back to the Café Parisian, go online and find out whether a flight was available tomorrow at dawn and whether there was a way of ensuring that it wouldn't break the bank.

The café was a three-minute walk. I ordered a mint tea and told the waiter that I might have to leave within ten minutes. Then I opened up my laptop and, using assorted travel sites, discovered that, yes, the actual price of the ticket was 5,400 dirhams, but one last-minute site was offering it for 2,600 dirhams – just under $300. Not a bargain, but still cheaper than the official price. I booked myself onto it. The tea arrived. I informed the waiter I was no longer in a rush. I drank the Moroccan whisky, allowing its soothing properties to act as an antidote to all the food consumed, and to momentarily balm my considerable distress.

Another search engine led me to a hotel – the Select – located just three streets away from here. One star, very basic, but the photos of the spartan rooms indicated a degree of cleanliness, and it was cheap. They didn't have an online booking service, but I asked the waiter if I could borrow a phone. He offered his own, and turned down my offer of 10 dirhams for its use: 'As long as you are calling locally.' I assured him that I was, and quickly punched in the hotel's number. I explained that I needed a room just until four o'clock in the morning.

'No problem.'

Five minutes later I was at the reception desk of the hotel. Why are so many dives called the Select? There was an elderly man in a shiny suit behind the counter. I paid cash and told him I needed a wake-up call at four a.m. and a taxi here promptly at four-thirty.

'I'll handle it,' he said.

'And please, I am counting on you to bang on my door loudly at four.'

The room was Early Nothing. Basic drab furniture. A hard double bed with stiff, much-laundered sheets and a floral bedspread. A sink, a toilet, a tiny shower stall with a meagre hose. I undressed and brushed my teeth, then rubbed on some of the miracle face cream. I noted that I would be having to get up again in five hours and cursed myself for not having found a bookshop this afternoon and choosing something in the English-language section.

Then my mind began to race. How would Paul react to my arrival in Ouarzazate? How would he deal with the realisation that I knew all about Ben Hassan, and that we were going to have to find some way of getting out of Morocco undetected? Didn't I read somewhere that the border with Algeria had been closed by the Moroccan authorities since that very bloody and frightening civil war in the 1990s? Could we get into Mauritania on US passports without a visa? Would Ben Hassan have people watching for us at the port at Tangier?

But these logistical questions were overshadowed by a flash-back of my father. I was eighteen and had just arrived at the University of Minnesota. My second day there Dad called from Las Vegas (of course) to tell me that the professional windfall he'd been waiting for had finally landed.

'Here's the thing, kiddo,' he said. 'Just had this big interview for a senior job in casino management out here. A VP for Human Resources at Caesar's Palace. The guy who interviewed me today told me I was head and shoulders above all the other candidates. So looks like me and your mom will be singing "Viva Las Vegas" before too long. And as soon as my John Hancock is on that employment contract I am organising that big Christmas trip to Hawaii I've been promising you and your mom for years.'

'No rush, Dad. I mean, Hawaii has never been on my list of priorities.'

'Well, if you want to transfer next semester to Columbia . . .'

'Minnesota offered me the full scholarship, Dad.'

'You're being too nice here, Robin. My little girl gets admitted to an Ivy League university and has to go to State U because her deadbeat father can't afford to pay the tuition.'

'Don't think that. You're a wonderful dad.'

'I don't deserve such kindness.'

Then the line went dead. As this conversation took place in 1993, before the cellphone era, I had no way of knowing the number from which he had been calling me. Nor did he call me back – though I waited by the phone in my dorm for an hour, hoping Dad and I might finish the conversation.

But no call ever came.

Until six o'clock the next morning. Only the person on the phone was my mother. And her voice was so hushed that she could hardly get out the words:

'Your father died last night.'

I remember the world going so quiet that all peripheral noise seemed to have been smothered.

'He had a heart attack after losing five thousand at the craps table.'

She'd heard this from the cops in Vegas. He'd been winning all night, then put all his chips on one throw of the dice. Which didn't go his way. This time he didn't weather the impact of another act of self-sabotage. This time it proved overwhelming to his psyche, and the cardiac incident that followed killed him. How I've assembled and reassembled this scene in my mind since then – and all based on those few terse details supplied by my angry mother. Part of the overwhelming grief that followed – the sense that I was now very much alone in a difficult world – was racked with the incessant reproach which rang in my ears for months, years afterwards; a lament that, truth be told, has never faded away: *You should have been able to save him.*

Is that what was at work now? Is that what I was chasing here: a chance at redemption? Was I somehow convincing myself that – despite the desperate betrayal, despite the realisation that I had been truly shammed – I still needed to rescue my husband from harm as a way of appeasing the guilt about my tragically affectionate wreck of a father; a man who gave me the only love I'd ever encountered until Paul Leuen walked into my life? Might I claw back a little final peace if I could do what I was too young and too unschooled in life's harsh contours to do at the time: get him off that path marked 'the Abyss'? Is that why I was sitting alone in this sad, cheap hotel room, my brain on overdrive, desperate to find Paul and bring some resolution to all this?

I can fix this. I must fix this. I will fix this.

Heaviness clouded my eyes. Then came darkness and several hours of mental void before the loud knock on the door. I had a fast shower and was in the taxi to the airport at the agreed time of four-thirty. Casablanca in the middle of the night was still the strange, faceless metropolis I'd briefly passed through, in which the sense of ugly modern sprawl was omnipresent.

At the airport I picked up my boarding pass and then proceeded to the Royal Air Maroc ticket counter where I was told that, if I didn't fly to New York today on the scheduled flight onto which I had been re-booked, I would lose the ticket.

'But I changed it once already,' I said. 'Can't I please change it again?'

'That was an exceptional change, clearly made by someone in authority,' the clerk told me. 'If you can get back in touch with him before your flight departs at midday, then perhaps he can make a second exceptional change. But I cannot do anything, *madame*. My apologies.'

The flight south was on a small turbo-prop with just thirty seats. The sun was ascending as we took off. As we were flying low the view was more than intriguing. Especially when we passed over Marrakesh after twenty minutes and the Atlas Mountains came into crisp silhouette. These were proper stern alpine peaks: craggy, with frequent switchback roads clearly defined. There were dazzling valleys and impossibly positioned villages clinging to the mountainsides. There was even a hint of snow on one summit.

Then, out of nowhere, the sand began. It was as if someone had flipped a topological switch, transporting us out of high rugged terrain and into a world of endless aridity. Sand that was not white, but actually bathed in a bleached red ochre. Sand that was full of strange undulations and irregularities. Sand in dunes; crimson in the emerging sunlight. Sand that stretched into an absolute infinity. Sand that could bury you with ruthless disinterest. Sand on a scale and a dimension that I had never glimpsed before; a realm so well known by mythic repute, yet unseen by most of the planet's inhabitants. That ultimate empty quarter. The Sahara.

We were coming in to land, passing buildings that had 1930s French Foreign Legion atmospherics. The sand was just beyond; the encroaching reality abutting the city's frontiers. As apprehensive and tense as I was – as much as I dreaded the confrontation that was ahead of me – there was still something extraordinary about my first sighting of the Sahara.

The airport was hot and fly-blown, its style post-war military. Inside the arrivals hall was an information desk, manned by a young woman in a hijab. I told her the name of my hotel. She knew it immediately and said it was a short taxi ride from here. I also showed her the scrap of paper on which Ben Hassan had scribbled Faiza's address. She got out a map of Ouarzazate and marked the location of the hotel, then used a yellow highlighter to trace a route to Faiza's front door. It was, she said, five minutes by foot.

'Don't pay the taxi driver more than thirty dirhams,' she said. 'If he says no, tell him that you are going to report him to me – Fatima. He'll know me. They all do.'

Actually the cabbie accepted the offer of 30 dirhams without the usual bartering. And indeed the Oasis Hotel was very close, just off the very wide main drag that, so early in the morning, still seemed half-awake. I took in the desert deco architecture, the languid men loitering in cafés, the blast-furnace heat. The cab had no air conditioning and according to the gauge on the dashboard the temperature was forty-three degrees Celsius. By the time we reached the hotel – all two minutes later – my lightweight clothes were sodden.

The Oasis was, at first glance, a slightly shabbier version of our hotel in Essaouira. At least the lobby was air conditioned – and the heavyset woman behind the desk was welcoming. When

I explained that I was Paul Leuen's wife I could see her lips tighten.

'Monsieur Leuen has just gone out for a walk,' she said.

'Really?'

'You seem surprised.'

'It's a bit early for a walk, that's all.'

'Monsieur Leuen . . . he was out walking until three a.m., so my night man told me. And he came in very intoxicated. I am sorry to report this, *madame*.'

'I'm sorry to hear it.'

'He was also shouting in his room late last night. The night man had to go up and tell him to be quiet. He found Monsieur Leuen in a very bad place. Drinking wine and crying. He got very apologetic when he was told he was waking the other guests.'

I shut my eyes, trying to keep my emotions in check. I was furious at Paul. But I was also terrified for him – and the crazed trajectory down which he was travelling.

'Do you have any idea where he headed to just now?' I asked.

'None at all. But Ouarzazate is not a big place. And he left only five minutes ago. Try the cafés on the Avenue Mohamed V.'

'I apologise for all the trouble he's caused you.'

'I am simply happy to see you here, *madame*. If you can assure me that he will be quiet tonight I will let you both stay here. Had you not arrived I would have shown him the door.'

I wanted to go upstairs and drop my bag and have a shower before facing the heat again. But part of me also knew that time was of the essence; that I needed to find Paul now.

'A question, *madame*,' I said. 'Besides the flights to Casablanca, isn't there a direct service from Ouarzazate to Paris?'

'Every Monday, Friday and Sunday at five p.m. So yes, as it is Sunday today . . .'

'Could you please find out if there are any seats on this afternoon's flight while I go look for my husband?'

'With pleasure, *madame*. If you would like to leave your bag here I will make certain it is kept safe for you.'

'Thank you for your kindness and decency.'

'I wish you luck, *madame*.'

I wished myself that too.

Before I left I dug out Paul's passport from my bag, and slipped it into the button-down pocket on my pants.

I headed out into the back street, turning up a dusty alleyway in which a young boy – he couldn't have been more than seven – was milking a goat, the white liquid spraying into an empty tin can. He looked up and smiled at me, saying:

'Fresh milk – just ten dirhams.'

I smiled back and moved on, dodging two elderly women on canes, their faces hidden by black burqas. They moved so slowly in the maniacal sun. How could they cope with the hefty black Islamic garb in this inferno? One of them held out a hand. I stopped, reached into my pocket, found a 5-dirham coin and placed it in her palm. Out of nowhere her fingers closed against mine. In a croaky whisper she uttered:

'*Faites attention, madame*.'

Be careful.

What did she know that I didn't?

I turned down another spindly street before reaching the city's main drag, Avenue Mohamed V. Adobe-shaded sandstone in a colonial fortress style defined the architecture. The sun was, after just two minutes outside, beginning to play games with my equilibrium. So I stopped at a small stall and bought a replacement green khaki field hat and a litre of bottled water, drinking almost half of it in one go. Then, over the next twenty minutes, I went from café to café, scanning all the terraces and interiors for any sign of my husband. I approached every waiter I saw, Paul's passport in hand, showing them his photograph, asking them if they'd perhaps seen this man in the past few minutes, indicating that finding him was an urgent matter. All the waiters were polite. All said that, alas, they hadn't seen him.

One man at a café – mid-fifties, a little portly, but still relatively well preserved and dressed in Moroccan merchant casual (cream slacks, a grey polo shirt, Italianate loafers) – overheard me enquiring about Paul and stood up.

'Perhaps I can help you,' he said in excellent English, motioning me over to his table. He introduced himself as Mr Rashid and offered me a coffee.

'You think you've seen this man?' I asked, holding up the passport photo.

'Indeed I have. But you first need something to drink, I think.'

'Where did you see him exactly?'

'On this street a few minutes ago.'

'Can you tell me exactly where?'

'I'd love to know your name first.'

I told him.

'Well, Robin, let me offer you a *citron pressé* and then we can get into my car – I have a very large and comfortable Mercedes – and start looking for him. And if we don't find him, maybe you can have lunch with me.'

I stood up.

'Thank you for wasting several valuable minutes of my time.'

The man looked shocked at this rebuff.

'There's no need to talk to me that way.'

'You never saw him, did you? You were just hoping to take advantage of a woman in distress.'

'Are you always so aggressive?'

'Are you always so oily?'

'Now I know why your husband went missing.'

He said this with a smirk on his face, then added something in Arabic to the men who were seated nearby, watching this scene with amusement. That's when I lost it.

'What the fuck did you say?' I hissed.

He was taken aback by my use of that expletive.

'*Madame* has an ugly way with words.'

'Only when being hustled by a little man with a small penis.'

Now he looked as if I had kicked him directly in the crotch.

'Go on, translate what I just said to your friends,' I said, hurrying off down the street, trying to contain my considerable fury.

But then I suddenly stopped dead in my tracks.

There, on the far side of the street, was my husband.

He was wearing the same white shirt and shorts he'd left the hotel room in two days ago. He was seriously unshaven, his long grey hair askew across his head. Even in the white light of the Saharan morning I could see that he was exhausted, lost.

'Paul! Paul!' I yelled. But as soon as those words were out of my mouth a vast truck – the length of a city block – came rattling down the Avenue Mohamed V. Paul didn't seem to hear my cries, or maybe they were drowned out by the approaching lorry. Not thinking, I tried to dash across the street, but was thrown backwards by the deafening blast of the truck's horn, the driver gesticulating wildly. I found myself now almost in the path of a Renault van coming in the opposite direction. The driver slammed on the brakes and started shouting things at me through his rolled-down window, while men in the nearby cafés stood up to watch the spectacle, caused by a deranged American woman trying to get to her missing husband who now stood just feet away.

When the lorry pulled away fifteen seconds later, I prepared to rush over and take my husband in my arms and assure him that, despite everything, I still loved him; that we would be out of this craziness and in Paris tonight.

But when the lorry pulled away . . .

Paul was no longer there.

It took me a dazed moment to register this fact. He had vanished.

I hurried across to where I'd seen him standing. I looked north. I looked south. I ran into the little patisserie directly in front of which he had been momentarily rooted. There were only two people in the shop, along with the baker behind the counter.

'Anyone seen an American?' I shouted. 'Very tall, long grey hair?'

They all looked startled by my outburst. When the baker shook his head I ran back into the street, scanning all corners of the immediate horizon, certain he was there somewhere. There were two cafés nearby and I charged up the street towards them. No Paul. A fast trot back to the exact place I'd seen him, thinking maybe there was a rear laneway directly behind this spot into which he had disappeared. No laneway. No Paul. Up the street I hurried, turning left into the first side street I could find. It was open and spacious, with blocks of modern apartments on either side. No Paul. And no shops or restaurants or cafés into which he could have ducked. Back to the Avenue Mohamed V, now getting increasingly stricken by all this running about in one-hundred-degree heat. No Paul. Again I stood in the spot where I'd seen him less than three minutes ago, beyond perplexed as to how I could have lost him moments after finding him.

I still had the half-litre of water in hand. Standing under the shade of the patisserie's awning I leaned against the wall and downed it in moments, wooziness overtaking me. Suddenly I felt a hand on my shoulder. Paul!

But no, it was the baker, who'd come out with a small folding stool, a pastry and a bottle of lemonade. He insisted on helping me onto the stool. After ensuring that I was eating and getting some necessary sugar into my bloodstream, he went back inside and returned with a linen cloth soaked in cold water. He put this around my neck – evidently a fast desert remedy for anyone suffering from dehydration. It worked. I felt a bit better within a few minutes. Refusing my offer of money he asked in French again if I was certain that I was all right; that he could get one of his assistants to help me back to my hotel. I thanked him repeatedly, telling him how truly touched I was by his kindness.

'I wish you luck, *madame*.'

Could he too read the despair in my eyes?

I stood up, testing my legs. Their present status was somewhere between rubbery and resilient. I headed out across the boulevard, intending to go back to the hotel and see if Paul had returned in my absence, and suddenly cursing myself for forgetting to tell the woman at reception not to mention that I'd been looking for him. But as I made it to the other side of the Avenue Mohamed V and cut down the same narrow laneway where I saw the boy milking the goat, a figure maybe fifteen feet in front of me veered to the right, taking an even narrower by-path. The man's height and free-flowing grey hair left me in no doubt that it was Paul. When I shouted his name he seemed oblivious to my voice. I started to sprint, determined to catch up with him. But when I reached the laneway – a tiny passage, no more than four feet wide – no Paul. There were no immediate doorways into which he could have disappeared. Even when, after around a hundred feet, I reached an archway, all I saw inside were two elderly men brewing tea on a little gas stove. Again I showed the passport photo. Their reaction was bemusement. I returned to the lane – so narrow and confined – trying to figure into what nook he could have vanished. Or did he clear out of this byway further on? I hurried to the end of the lane, only to discover it was a dead end. The wall had some rusted barbed wire on it, which made the idea of getting over it just a little daunting. When I touched it I discovered that it had the density and grip of damp chalk. There was no way whatsoever that even a particularly adept cat could have scaled that wall.

I shut my eyes, wanting to be anywhere but here and also knowing that I had to get out of this blind alley now. So back I went, retracing my steps until I found the main alleyway again, glancing frantically everywhere as I made my way back to the hotel.

The woman who'd greeted me earlier was at the front desk.

'No luck?' she asked.

I shook my head.

'Maybe he'll come back soon. If you want to go upstairs . . .'

'I would like that.'

'Housekeeping hasn't been in to clean the room yet.'

'I'm sure it will be fine. Just one small request – when my husband does come back, please don't tell him I'm upstairs. He's in a delicate place and might run off if he finds out I'm here. My hope is that, when he does come upstairs, I will be able to talk him into leaving this afternoon.'

'I have good news on that front. There are still seven seats open on the Paris flight. They are expensive, being last-minute – five thousand two hundred dirhams apiece. Still, if you want them you should let me know no later than one o'clock. *D'accord?*'

'*D'accord.*'

The room was air conditioned. And reasonably spacious, though given the narrowness of these back streets its balcony only afforded a view of a wall some ten feet away. But was what immediately

180

distressing was the chaotic state of the place. Twisted sheets with streaked bloodstains on the pillows – was his head wound still bleeding? Crumpled paper everywhere. An ashtray brimming with cigarette butts (he gave up nicotine around the same time we got together). The remnants of two bottles of wine. And in the bathroom – no, this was too grim – an unflushed toilet.

I pulled the cistern chain. I picked up the house phone and rang downstairs, asking if the maid could be sent up now. I then returned and dumped the contents of the ashtray into the toilet and flushed it all away. I found a box of matches and lit two of them, walking between the bathroom and the bedroom in an attempt to mask the faecal smell and the lingering aroma of sweaty sheets which permeated these two rooms. I emptied the remnants of the wine bottles. I began to uncrumple the many pieces of paper that had been balled up and tossed everywhere. Tortured line drawings of a lone man in an empty space that seemed to be a desert. The drawings were half-finished. In each one of them it was evident that Paul was having trouble finishing the figure's face; a figure so tall that he seemed to be towering over a sand dune. But this self-portraiture was underscored by a face that had turned grotesque. Drawing after drawing showed this representation of Paul with his face half-melting away, or being scorched beyond recognition by the sun. Amidst these discarded, unhinged sketches, there were several half-started letters. *My love . . . Dearest Robin . . . You have married a catastrophe . . .* Most chillingly, there were two notes, already partially burnt, with the same word repeated on both scraps of paper:

Finished.

The second of these notes unnerved me – because the word appeared to have been scratched on the page with blood.

The maid knocked on the door. I told her to give me a minute and quickly finished dumping all the paper into a bin, pulling off the bloodied pillowcase, gathering up the soiled towels so she wouldn't be exposed to such extremity. Yet again I was cleaning up after my husband – and even slipped the very young cheery maid 30 dirhams, apologising for the state of the room.

'*Mon mari est bordélique*,' I told her. *My husband is all over the place.*

The maid seemed nonplussed by the state of things.

'I've seen worse,' she said.

She told me to come back in a half-hour: 'Everything will be all fine again.' Would that a magic wand could be waved.

All I could think of now was that one word – *finished* – interspersed with those wildly destructive self-portraits. And my fear that unless rescued . . .

No, don't enter that terrain. He's still here in Ouarzazate. It's only a matter of time before he shows up back at the hotel. I glanced at my watch. It was just a little after nine a.m. As long as he returned within four hours we could secure those seats on the Paris flight and be out of all this.

But first . . . I went down to the lobby. The woman behind the desk asked if she could get me anything. She also told me her name was Yasmina. I suddenly needed to confide in someone – not about the grubbier aspects of the story, but about the fact that my husband had suffered a breakdown, had disappeared from our hotel in Essaouira and, through the wonders of the Internet, I had traced him here.

'Anything you can do to help me find him – or, at the very least, hold him here and get us on that plane to Paris . . .'

'I don't have a pair of handcuffs,' she said with a half-smile. 'But I do have a man who runs things here at night. His name is Yusuf, and he usually sleeps until eleven a.m. But if you would agree to give him, say, three hundred dirhams, I think he wouldn't object to me ringing him now and getting him out of bed to search Ouarzazate for your husband. He knows every corner of this town. He knows everybody here. If he can't find him then he is lost to the sand.'

I handed over the 300 dirhams, thinking this was a small price to pay for someone who might be able to root out Paul.

The maid came downstairs to tell me that the room was clean, and that she had lit a jasmine incense stick to 'purify' the place. She actually used that word. Again I thanked her and Yasmina for their benevolence.

'If you leave your clothes outside the door we'll have them washed and dried in less than two hours.'

I felt absurdly tired – the short night, the adjustment to the ferocious Saharan heat, the fruitless hundred-yard dashes all morning in search of Paul . . . all I could think of now was a cool shower and then a spell in clean sheets. I headed back upstairs. Once inside I stripped everything off and dropped it outside the door. Then I stood in the shower for a good ten minutes. Before climbing into the freshly laundered bed, I called downstairs and asked Yasmina to give me a wake-up call at one o'clock . . . unless Paul arrived before then.

I fell asleep instantly. Then, out of nowhere, the phone rang. The little alarm clock on the bedside table glowed in the shuttered room: 13:02. And here I was, alone. No sign of Paul. I reached for the phone.

'Your wake-up call, *madame*,' Yasmina intoned.

'And my husband?'

'No sighting of him so far. But Yusuf is still out looking, and he is phoning in regularly. Alas, not a trace.'

'I'll be down in a few minutes. Might you be able to call me a taxi?'

'But the Paris flight isn't until five o'clock.'

'I'm not going to Paris. I'm going to . . .'

Reaching over to a pile of paper I'd dug out of my pocket before tossing my dirty clothes outside the door, I found the scrap on which Ben Hassan had written Faiza's address. I read the details into the phone. Yasmina told me that it was a five-minute drive – and that my clean clothes were now on the way upstairs with the maid.

A quarter of an hour later I was in a taxi headed to an apartment complex not far from the entrance to the Atlas Film Studios. The complex was semi-modern, semi-brutalist in a 1970s reinforced-concrete style. There were three separate blocks, all no more than seven or eight floors tall. I asked the driver to drop me in front of Block B. I paid him and headed up four concrete flights of stairs to Apartment 402. I took a long steadying breath before pressing the doorbell, expecting either no answer or an angry woman refusing to see me and telling me to go away and never come back.

But on the third ring the door opened. There stood a woman who was surprisingly tall and stylish, albeit wildly thin, with a face once beautiful, now cracked and leathery. She had a lit cigarette in one hand, a glass of pink wine in the other. When she spoke her voice sounded nicotine cured.

'So,' she said, 'you finally got here.'

'You know who I am?' I asked.

'Of course I do. You're the other wife.'

Seventeen

'I PRESUME YOU drink a bit,' Faiza said.

'A bit, yes,' I said.

'I drink a lot.'

She motioned for me to seat myself on a brown corduroy sofa. I was in a modest one-bedroom apartment. Concrete walls painted white. A bentwood rocking chair. Splatter-paint abstract canvases. An elderly rug. A few framed photographs of Samira at varying stages of life. An air conditioner that, though effective, emitted a low wheeze. A couple of old lamps that, like the rest of the decor, seemed around twenty years out of date. A balcony which overlooked the encroaching desert.

Seeing me take everything in, noting numerous empty wineglasses and brimming ashtrays and the general dustiness, she coughed like a true smoker and said:

'I didn't invite you here, so I'm not going to apologise for this place. Except to say that I had a change of personal circumstances in April and had to find a new apartment in a hurry. Life, sometimes, is a series of let-downs. Especially when it comes to men, wouldn't you agree?'

She then began to cough again wildly.

'Are you all right?' I asked.

'Of course not.'

She was as thin as a stalk of celery, dressed in black linen pants and a black linen shirt, with around nine gold and copper bangles on her spindly wrists. Her hair – long, very straight – was still jet black. But her skin was leathery, and her teeth were tobacco-stained.

She disappeared into the kitchen for a moment, returning with a chilled bottle of rosé and a second glass.

'It's Moroccan, but good.'

'Like most of the wines I've had here.'

'So Little Boy Paul married himself a much younger woman,' she said, lighting up another cigarette.

'I'm not that young.'

'But you are at least twenty years younger than me . . . which, in my book, makes you a kid. More to the point you are his wife.'

'So are you.'

'Actually, the marriage only lasted about ten minutes . . . and then was annulled.'

'Annulled? Really?'

'You seem surprised.'

'I'd been told that you were still his wife.'

'Whoever told you that – and I have my suspicions – simply wanted to play head games with you. I am *definitely* Paul's ex-wife.'

She splashed some wine into a glass and handed it to me. When I raised it she just nodded curtly.

'No need to get friendly,' she said. 'Anyway, I have a class to teach – conversational English – in around forty minutes. So though speaking conversational English with you might have its professional benefits, it doesn't please me having you here.'

I apologised for showing up on her doorstep unannounced and uninvited. 'But I am genuinely worried about Paul.'

'Poor you for being so involved with that fool. Because that is what he is – a fool. And one who has to shoot himself in the foot with a Kalashnikov, pausing twice to reload.'

Faiza was suddenly hit with another horrendous coughing fit. When she had brought it under control she used some wine to clear her throat, then said:

'Well, they always told me smoking was a stupid habit. But without it life would be even more intolerable. Not that you've probably ever smoked a cigarette in your life. I bet you're one of those Americans who work out six days a week.'

'I know Paul came here to see you,' I said, refusing to take the bait.

'Paul came here to plead with me. To ask me to intervene with our daughter and get her to have some contact with him. Of course I refused to do any such thing.'

I took another sip of wine, choosing my next words with care.

'I can understand why you turned him away. Especially as he

186

has spent the last few decades denying your existence and that of his daughter. Please understand – until yesterday I didn't know that you and Samira existed. Nevertheless, Paul has had a major breakdown and he has gone missing.'

'Perhaps this time the disappearance will be a permanent one. I can handle self-destruction. It's a personal choice. Like me smoking forty cigarettes a day. The difference is – mine harms only myself. Paul is someone whose self-destructiveness ends up destroying everyone else in his immediate path. When I kicked him out last night I told him to do the world a favour and kill himself.'

Pause. Then I said:

'Your capacity for hate is impressive.'

'And who are you – Mother Teresa?'

'I am probably going to divorce Paul as soon as I get him back to the States. But first I am going to get him home. And away from Ben Hassan.'

'That fat fuck – he can be your best friend and your worst nightmare.'

'Are you still in contact with him?'

'You mean, considering that he might have killed my father and two brothers . . . not that I entirely blame him for that.'

'They're all dead?'

'Well, they are all planted in the earth now. So that should answer your question. Was Ben Hassan behind all this? That's the great question.'

She splashed some more wine into our glasses and continued.

'I wouldn't blame Ben Hassan for killing them. After he helped Paul escape his shotgun marriage to me – that's the term you use, isn't it? – they destroyed his hands, his future as a painter. The police and the judiciary let them off with a small cash payment. But Ben Hassan was never able to hold a paintbrush again. I was so disgusted with my father for acting like a thug that I broke with him and my brothers – two not very bright stooges who did everything their father told them to. Like crushing the fingers of a man whose great sin was that he helped his friend.'

'Didn't you feel guilty about that too? According to the story Ben Hassan told me last night, you were pounding on Paul's door, telling him you'd be killed if he didn't marry you . . .'

Faiza stabbed her cigarette into the ashtray.

'Do you have any idea whatsoever what it means to be a woman in this culture? There was no possibility of negotiating with my family once I found out I was pregnant. Did I deliberately get pregnant? Put it this way – we were careless. And no, I wasn't on the pill. And yes, it was my hope that Paul would marry me and get me out of Morocco and to the States. So I was being completely mercenary. But Paul and I loved each other back then . . . for a while anyway. I even said to him: "Marry me, get me my green card, and once we're in the States I'll make my own way." But when he baulked I made a fatal error and told my father that I was pregnant. From that moment on we were doomed. Because Papa could never do anything subtly or cleverly. He always had to bring out the heavy artillery. He had to get his way, and punish anyone who tried to stop him – which was poor Ben Hassan's fate.'

'And did he eventually kill your father and brothers?'

'As I said before, that is still the ongoing question. My father died in a car accident, driving alone between Casablanca and Marrakesh. According to the police report, the brakes of his Mercedes failed. They couldn't establish if they had been tampered with or not, but there was a school of thought that someone had so significantly stripped back the brake pads that when a motorcycle swerved in front of him and my father braked, the result was catastrophic. He lost control of the car. It flipped over three times and then ignited. The chassis was so badly burnt that they couldn't really establish if there had been foul play. Of course the driver of the motorbike was nowhere to be found. The fact that it happened late at night on an otherwise empty road . . . it all seemed to me and many others to have been carefully planned. So carefully planned that the police couldn't even justify an investigation.

'Then around seven years later, my brother Abdullah was found hanged at his condominium on the Costa del Sol. Abdullah had done very well in the wall-to-wall carpet and linoleum game. He'd married a very beautiful, very stupid woman quite late in life – he was over forty – and had two little girls whom he doted over whenever he was at home, which wasn't very often. He'd expanded his business into Spain, bought a *petit bourgeois* seaside condominium – the man had no taste whatsoever – and was showing no signs of depression or any other signs of psychological instability. It was his mistress, a local bar girl, who found him. She was the prime suspect for a while. The thing was, Abdullah had grown almost as large as Ben Hassan. So it was very unlikely that she could have strung him up herself. The fact that he seemed to have taken three too many sleeping pills that evening raised all sorts of suspicions. She was held with her actual boyfriend under suspicion of conspiracy to murder for many months. But I was always convinced that the hand of Ben Hassan was behind it all.'

'Why didn't you alert the authorities?'

'To what? To the fact that, fifteen years previously, my father had ordered his two sons to carry out an appalling act of violence on a man who, in the intervening years, had become, in his own ingratiatingly corrupt way, a sort of Mr Fixit in Casa and Rabat, and had so many connections in so many echelons of the establishment here? Not that anyone high up in government administration or the world of finance would ever admit to calling a sleaze like Ben Hassan a friend. He knew this too. It didn't bother him. He still had "connections". Tainted, blemished connections, but it kept him and whatever young man he was sodomising that month in a level of modest comfort. Yes, I am getting nasty. Talking too much. But after kicking our husband out of here last night, I found myself unable to sleep. As I had two classes to teach this morning I popped a Dexedrine to keep myself up. I took another one just fifteen minutes before you turned up. The wine works wonders with its speedy properties. A sort of yin-yang effect.'

Silence. I put down my glass of wine, suddenly too buzzed from the alcohol and the desert afternoon which the wheezing, consumptive air conditioner was just about keeping at bay.

'You didn't tell me about your other brother?' I finally said.

'Driss? A bigger fool even than Abdullah. Never married. Never succeeded at much. Worked for his brother running inventory in Casa. After Abdullah was "suicided" – I know that's what happened – the man who bought up the company sacked Driss. As there wasn't much in the way of family money – and what little Driss had inherited he spent at the roulette table and on prostitutes – he ended up as a limousine driver for a company ferrying people from the airport to one of Casablanca's five-star hotels. Every summer he had a week off down in Agadir, our dreadful package-holiday resort. He went swimming one evening, maybe fifty metres from the shoreline. A speedboat ran over him. Split his skull in two. Being a speedboat it sped away. Not a trace of who was commandeering it, or even a glimpse of its registration. The thing is, Driss loved swimming at night – and it was his fifth night in Agadir, so I am pretty certain that someone had been watching him, working out his habits.'

A shrug. Another slug of wine. Another cigarette.

'I don't think I like your silence,' she finally said. 'It feels very fucking judgemental.'

'Your English is impressive.'

'So is your sense of irony.'

'I'm hardly being ironic. I'm just trying to figure out your story.'

'What's to figure out? I have never asked Ben Hassan directly if he was behind everything that happened to my family. Because he has been, on one level, a very good friend to myself and my daughter. When Samira pushed me away over a decade ago – after I moved down here, but also as a result of a lot of anguish about so many things – he acted as a surrogate parent for her in Casa, and also gradually brought her around to establishing some sort of detente with her mother, for which I will always be grateful. You know she got pregnant by a French businessman. But Ben Hassan negotiated with him on Samira's behalf. He might have headed back to his wife and children, but he does give her three hundred euros a month—'

'Ben Hassan told me it was five hundred.'

'Maybe he pays Ben Hassan five and he gives her three. Who cares?'

'But that means Ben Hassan is pocketing twenty-four hundred euros a year.'

'Yes, Little Boy Paul did tell me you were an accountant. What was a highly rational, competent woman like yourself thinking when you hooked up with such a disaster?'

I met her gaze straight on.

'I was thinking about the sex – which was pretty spectacular. I was thinking about the sexiness of being with an actual artist – and one with real talent. I was thinking how wonderful it would be for our child to have an artist for a father.'

As I spoke these words I felt myself slipping into a haze, my boldness succumbing to fatigue. Perhaps it was the wine, or the absolute despair of the bitter woman sitting opposite me, or my naive wish to connect with someone else who once wanted everything with Paul and, like me, was betrayed by him. I took a deep steadying breath before continuing.

'With Paul I thought I could have adventure and culture and freedom. Freedom from all the trappings of modern American life. But Paul wanted all those trappings – the nice home, the gym membership, the summers in Maine, good food, fine wine – even as he bemoaned our materialist culture. And he knew I would deliver all that to him, because I had what he lacked – which was a sense of responsibility. And a real belief in *us*. Our life, our future together. Of course I also made that pathetic mistake of thinking I could change him. So, yes, you're right. I hooked up with a disaster. Guilty on all charges. Despite all that, though, despite everything he's done, I still don't want to see Paul come to harm.'

Silence. She reached for what must have been her fifth cigarette.

'Do you want me to congratulate you on your directness, your openness?'

'I just want to know two things.'

'Go on.'

'Did you know about Ben Hassan talking Paul into taking out this loan for your daughter's apartment?'

'What loan?'

'Ben Hassan told me that Philippe gave Samira one million dirhams towards an apartment in Casablanca.'

'Oh, please. The Frenchie has been reasonable about giving her a degree of child support. But one million dirhams? That is beyond absurd. Samira lives in a fifty-square-metre apartment that she rents for two thousand dirhams a month – which is quite a bargain for the Gauthier area of Casa. You know she is a professor of literature at the university there, specialising in Romantic Melancholy. How apt. She got her doctorate in France, at Aix-en-Provence. Her thesis was even published. So yes, I am very proud of her. And I love being a grandmother to her wonderful son. But the idea that her Frenchman gave her a million dirhams for an apartment . . .'

I felt myself getting hyper-stressed, because I was beginning to figure out the game that Ben Hassan was playing. I said:

'But Ben Hassan also told me that when Paul contacted him, begging to be put in touch with Samira, he said that a quick way back into her life was by matching the one million dirhams for the apartment she was buying.'

'And Paul agreed?'

'I'm afraid so. Ben Hassan showed me the loan agreement he signed. He's repaying one-point-six million on a one-million dirham loan.'

'The first I've heard of it. If he'd given that money to Samira – or went and bought an apartment for her . . . well, Samira and I are reasonably close now, so she would have told me. I mean, one million dirhams would buy her close to a hundred square metres in the Gauthier district. She'd be over the moon. So . . . it is clear that your husband allowed himself to be scammed.'

I picked up the glass of wine I'd put aside. I took a long sip, trying to absorb what I had just heard.

'So Paul going missing . . .' I said.

'That's largely down to you. I heard all about the secret vasectomy.'

'Paul told you that?'

'Hardly. It was Ben Hassan.'

'That bastard. And let me guess – he also called you last night or this morning, telling you I was on my way to Ouarzazate.'

'Indeed he did. I'm sure he promised that he wouldn't phone me. Just as I'm certain you regret letting him in on that little betrayal that Paul perpetrated on you. Again I'm amazed by how a bright woman like you—'

'Yes, I was naive. Naive because I was also so hopeful. Never a good combination, apparently. Just as I now know that Ben Hassan has deceived Paul. Lending him money on the basis of giving it to your daughter, and then not passing it on to her. Isn't that known as embezzlement?'

'That's a matter of conjecture. Did you read the loan agreement? Did Paul? I doubt it. Do you know what I think – having heard about Ben Hassan's newest game? Even though this is all speculation, I bet that after Samira gave birth to my grandson Ben Hassan got in touch with Paul, telling him that he was a grandfather and that Samira desperately needed his help. He probably played up the fact that, because he never answered any of her letters or emails over the years, Samira had written him off as a terrible man, a non-existent father. But Ben Hassan told Paul that, if he could find her the money needed for her apartment, he would be able to re-establish his relationship with her and play a role in his grandson's life – and that he would also right the wrong that he perpetrated on Ben Hassan all those years ago. Of course Ben Hassan being Ben Hassan he probably sent that email as a way of seeing if he could play on Paul's guilt after all these years. Knowing my fat "friend" as I do I'm certain he felt the account wouldn't be closed until he'd found a way of ensnaring Paul. What he couldn't have known – until you told him last night – was that his email arrived right after Paul promised you a baby and had himself fixed in secret – an act that Paul knew, when revealed, would destroy everything between you. Ben Hassan's email allowed Paul to think that here was his chance to right past wrongs, here was a chance to reconnect with the only child he would now ever have.

'So maybe that's why Paul showed up on Samira's doorstep two days ago, expecting her to greet him as the man who'd finally redeemed himself in her eyes. Instead she rebuffed him. Which had him running back to Ben Hassan – who comforted him and put it into his head that maybe if he headed south to Ouarzazate, I would be able to help him find a way back to Samira.'

'Ben Hassan did all this to break him. He got your father, your brothers. Now Paul. He was the last member of the quartet who cost him his career. And he has certainly avenged himself.'

'But he is still an obese man with a sad life. And someone who was denied his life's dream – to become a great painter. How does revenge fix that?'

I drained my glass. Faiza glanced at her watch.

'I really don't feel like talking much more,' she said. 'And I have a class to teach – not that I want to do that either. Still, it's my work. And my work, as minor and inconsequential as it is, tucked away in the mouth of the Sahara, does give some form and shape to the day. So I'd like you to leave now.'

'I just need to know one last thing . . .'

'Which is what?'

'Did Paul give you any indication that he was suicidal?'

'Or would follow my advice and kill himself? Put it this way – I told him that he had ruined my life, that he had ruined his daughter's life, that he had ruined Ben Hassan's life. Then I told that I knew all about how he tricked you into believing he wanted a child with you. That really sent him into a spin.'

'And he said what?'

'"I've fucked everything up." Then I said he had to leave. He started to cry, begging for my forgiveness. I told him I was kicking him out, just as he'd kicked me out of his life years ago.'

'So you had your revenge too. Has it changed anything?'

She lit another cigarette.

'It's changed nothing. Nothing at all.'

She walked to the front door and opened it.

'Leave,' she said.

'I'm sorry you're so bitter.'

'And you're not?'

I left.

Outside I found myself frantically searching for a taxi, the mid-afternoon heat now even more frightening in its intensity. My brain was spinning like the wheels on a slot machine – and turning up zip in the way of solutions. Except the absolute need to find Paul immediately – and to alleviate at least one of his fears by telling him he owed Ben Hassan nothing.

Had he kept a copy of the loan agreement? Was there a lawyer in Casa I could hire to break the contract and sue Ben Hassan for fraud, while also pursuing the authorities to prosecute him for embezzlement?

Absurd thoughts. If, as Faiza said, Ben Hassan really had all those high-up connections, I knew the best I could hope for was that, once Paul was back home, he never came near us.

A taxi passed by and halted when the driver saw my frantic waving. I was back at the hotel in five minutes, scanning every passing corner along the way for a sighting of Paul. When I walked in Yasmina stared at me wide-eyed.

'Why aren't you with Monsieur Paul?'

'Paul! You found him?'

'He came back to the hotel.'

'He what?'

'He came back. Maybe three or four minutes ago. Left this here for you.'

She handed me an envelope with the letter R in his characteristic calligraphy.

'Surely you saw him as you were pulling up in the taxi.'

'If he'd been there I would have seen him.'

'But he just wandered out a minute ago. Maybe even less than that. Heading to the bus station. With no bags, but saying he was going south. You can't have missed him.'

'But I did.' I was frantic now. 'Was he on foot?'

She nodded.

I turned around. My taxi had pulled away.

'How do I get there?' I cried.

'It's a five-minute walk. Head to the main street, turn left, keep going until you see the station. It is opposite the Q8 petrol station. But hurry – the bus he's taking, I think it leaves very soon.'

Envelope in hand I charged down the maze of alleyways, then bounded along the Avenue Mohamed V, oblivious to the scorching afternoon, the pavements burning through my sandals, certain that up ahead I could see Paul's six-foot-four frame, his long grey hair bobbing with his bouncing gait. Running faster than I have ever run, my eyes suddenly going foggy, the bus station up ahead, the bus there, me pushing myself against a heat so dense, so viscous, my equilibrium going sideways, but, oh God no . . . there he is getting on the bus, and I'm starting to scream: 'Wait, wait, wait,' and no, this cannot be, the door closing and the bus pulling away, and I am seeing people on the street in nearby cafés, hearing me scream, signalling to the driver to stop, and the bus now turning out of the depot and down the main drag of Ouarzazate, and me just reaching the bus station around thirty seconds later, and falling into the dirt, and blacking out for a moment, and people rushing over, and two men helping me to a nearby café table, one of them rushing inside while the other keeps my head between my legs. The second man returned with a sodden cloth that he put around my neck. As he helped me back into an upright position, a flash flood of sweat rolled down my face. I was handed a chilled bottle of water which I drained in moments.

The men kept asking if I was all right, if they could get anyone to help me, why was I running like that?

I still had the envelope in my left hand. I asked for more water and opened the letter. Though my eyes were still having trouble focusing I was able to make out the following lines in Paul's tortured scrawl:

I have hit the wall. I am heading to the end of the line. Don't pursue me. Let me do what I have to do.

I am beyond sorry. But forgiveness is not deserved in this instance. Which is why I am disappearing. Permanently.

You were the love of my life. I only see that now.

Farewell.

P.

I looked up from the letter and into the faces of the men huddled around me, their concern about my mental and physical state evident.

'Where was that bus heading?' I asked.

'Tata.'

'What's Tata?'

'A town six hours south of here.'

I shut my eyes and made an instant decision.

'What time is the next bus to Tata?'

Eighteen

ONE OF THE men who came to my aid was a taxi driver. He insisted on bringing me back to the hotel and refused my offer of a fare. When I reached the front door, Yasmina came racing out and helped me into the lobby. She found me more water. She sent one of the cleaners for another wet cloth to put around my neck, then told me I should go upstairs and lie down. She would check on the flight to Paris, as there was still time to catch it.

'He left on the bus to Tata,' I said. 'The next bus to Tata leaves in ninety minutes. I'm getting on it.'

'But Tata is a six-hour journey from here. And it is absolutely in the middle of nowhere.'

'He's threatening to kill himself,' I said, brandishing the letter. 'If I get there tonight there is a good chance I can find him before—'

'*Madame*, one simple call from me to the *gendarmes* will see the bus stopped somewhere between here and Tata, and your husband taken into protective custody.'

What she said made sense. But I was operating according to a different sort of logic, in which I had convinced myself that if he fell into the hands of the authorities Ben Hassan was certain to be contacted. Given that he was still set on revenge who's to know what horror he would instruct them to concoct for Paul. Two days in a Moroccan jail would break him. No. Two hours would be enough to upend what little equilibrium he had left. Especially given Ben Hassan's ability to pull all sorts of evil strings. The stories about Faiza's father and brothers were still fresh in my mind. I could easily see Paul being 'suicided' while in protective custody – and the officials (along with everyone else, from Ben Hassan to Samira to Faiza to the very kind woman behind this hotel desk) all corroborating the fact that he was mentally troubled in the days leading up to his death by hanging in his padded cell; a suicide that Ben Hassan could easily arrange for 5,000 dirhams tops.

'I'm getting on that bus,' I told Yasmina. 'Because it's me and me alone who can get him out of trouble.'

'I beg you—'

'No discussion! None!'

I could see Yasmina recoil at the way I snapped at her.

'I'm sorry,' I whispered.

She put a restraining hand on my arm.

'I implore you. Go to your room, have a shower, lie down, let me call the *gendarmes*.'

'My decision is made. And I am going to say this – if, when I get to Tata, I find that he has been taken off the bus by the police . . .'

'You have my word. I will not make that call. But as you have a little time I ask that you go upstairs and stand under the shower and drink at least another litre of water. You are in danger of dehydrating.'

I did as ordered, asking her to have a taxi here in just under an hour.

After my shower I got dressed again, constantly pushing out of my head any conflicting thoughts about the wisdom of chasing Paul to Tata. *There is no choice*, I told myself. *I told Paul he was better off dead. He may have betrayed me, but my initial fury set this entire nightmare in motion. And now he seems determined to kill himself. I know I am beyond panicked, beyond confused. But the only end to this is to get to him before he falls off the edge.*

Downstairs I offered Yasmina money for letting me stay in the room long after the check-out hour. She refused.

'You have been too kind to me,' I said.

'I wish I could convince you to stay.'

'I have to see this through.'

Her reply was a look that said: *No, you don't . . . and you know that*. Then she handed me the hotel card with her cellphone number on the back of it.

'If I can help you in any way, you know where to find me.'

Half an hour later I was on the bus heading south. It looked like a relic of the 1980s, with half-stripped paintwork, chewed-up seats, grimy windows, no air conditioning, no ventilation.

Thankfully there were only ten of us boarding at Ouarzazate, which meant that I had two seats to myself all the way. The other passengers were four elderly women in full burqas, three men of equally advanced years, a young mother with two babies, and a shy adolescent girl who glanced back at me on several occasions, clearly curious as to why I was on this bus. I managed to smile back, but drifted into my preoccupied reverie. Outside, the terrain was part oasis – trees, patches of arable land – and part encroaching sand. There was the occasional change in the topography – a vista in which stern mountains could be seen on the horizon; a densely populated village, its souk in full late-afternoon swing; the tents of Bedouin families pitched alongside the road; the sense that, with every kilometre, we were travelling deeper into a void. Didn't I read online yesterday that, in Berber Arabic, Ouarzazate means 'without noise, without confusion'? Gazing out at the darkening landscape – the sand turning copperish in the declining sun – I could understand just why, when compared to the noisy jumble that was other Moroccan cities, Ouarzazate wasn't simply the doorway to the desert, but also to the immense silence into which I was now venturing. When you stared at the ever-expanding Sahara, you could understand why it was something akin to a blank canvas, divorced from the disarray and chaos of life beyond. But I began to wonder if that too was an illusion. You look at a sea of empty sand, two Bedouin parents crossing this terrain with their children, and marvel at the timeless simplicity of it all. The truth is more complex: the need to find water, to find money for food and other essentials. The daily ordeal of survival in a harsh, unforgiving universe.

Without noise . . . without confusion.

Life is noise, confusion. We can run to the ends of the earth, and it will still impinge on us. Because the demons within us never vanish – even in a landscape as hushed as the Sahara.

The bus stopped in a tiny village next to a small stream. I bought a cup of mint tea from a sad-faced man. There was a toilet in a nearby shed: a hole in the ground over which had been constructed a wooden box with a makeshift seat. The smell was overpowering. I emerged, choking, desperate for fresh air. But even at sunset, the heat stifled everything.

I boarded the bus again. I attempted to nap. But the bus's lack of suspension and my own preoccupations hindered sleep. Tata couldn't be that big a place. A handful of hotels at best. I'd stop in each one until I found Paul. I'd soothe and comfort him. Then I'd call Yasmina in Ouarzazate and get her to book us tickets on the next flight to Paris. I'd get us back to her hotel by midday tomorrow. I'd . . .

Make plans, as usual. In the hope of imposing reason on someone for whom reason was more than a stretch. Faiza – as angry and vindictive as she was – did get one thing right: Paul brought chaos into everybody's life. But there was a difference between the Paul I met three years ago – who feigned obliviousness to the mess he engendered – and the man who left me what was clearly a suicide note. He could no longer run from himself. But he could run into the Sahara.

The hours on the bus went by slowly, the vanished sun lowering the temperature somewhat, but not acting as a palliative against the grubbiness of the journey. I nodded off for a spell, waking with a jolt when the bus screeched to a halt, the horn was honked, and the driver shouted:

'Tata.'

We were in a parking area outside a walled town. I had been sleeping against my backpack. Getting off the bus I was immediately confronted by two young men – both in their early twenties, both trying to grow beards with not much luck, both wearing baseball caps, both looking me over.

'Hello, pretty lady,' one of them said in French.

'You need some help to guide you around?' the second one asked.

I held up the photo page of Paul's passport.

'I'm looking for this man – my husband.'

'I know where he is,' the first guy said.

'You do?' I asked. 'Honestly?'

'You come with us, we show you . . .' the second one said, but he was interrupted by the bus driver, who began to shout at them in Arabic, telling them several times to '*imshi*'. These two operators were not intimidated, however, and began to sass him back, until another man – in his late fifties, wearing a dark suit – also weighed in on the argument. The two guys were clearly enjoying the confrontation. The older was being bold and arrogant, eyeing me up and down, making flip comments ('Don't you want a date with me?' . . . 'I love American women' . . . 'You don't need your husband, you need a younger man') amidst this heated interchange with my two protectors. Eventually the older man, who was tall and heavily lined, a cigarette clutched between his teeth, ash dropping on his brown suit jacket, mentioned the word 'police' and the two operators backed off, but not before Mr Arrogant winked at me and said: 'Maybe some other time.'

Once they were gone the older man handed me a card and explained in French that he worked for a small hotel within the walls, and he could offer me a very clean, safe room for 300 dirhams . . . discounted from the usual 500. If I was hungry he could persuade the cook to stay on and make dinner for me. I pulled out Paul's passport and showed him the photograph, asking if he knew where I might find my husband.

'When did he arrive?'

'On the bus before mine.'

'That's impossible.'

'Why? I saw him leave on the earlier bus.'

'I met that bus – as I meet all buses here. And there was only one Westerner on it – a German of around seventy, travelling alone.'

'Couldn't he have gotten off when you weren't looking?'

'*Madame*, I promise you, I see everyone who arrives by bus in Tata. You can check the other hotels, if you wish.'

I was suddenly in free-fall again.

'I'll give you fifty dirhams if you take me to every hotel in town.'

'But I assure you—'

'One hundred dirhams.'

The man shrugged, then nodded for me to follow him.

We went through the archway that led into the centre of Tata. The town was something of a maze. Dark, twisting streets. Little in the way of street light. We stopped by a true dive of a place, which from the outside looked like a flophouse. A man with a haunted face – his eyes sunken, forlorn – came out from behind the desk and greeted my escort. They embraced. Words were exchanged. I was asked to show Paul's passport. The desk clerk shook his head, pointing out into the darkness of the night. I asked him to study the photo again to make absolutely certain that he hadn't seen him. Again he shook his head.

Ten minutes and three hotels later we had come to the end of the line, apart from the place to which I was now being brought to spend the night. At each of these establishments it was the same routine: the passport photo, the question about whether this man was staying there, the shake of the head.

As we left the last hotel I asked my escort his name.

'It's Naguib, *madame*.'

'What time is the first bus back to Ouarzazate?'

'There's one at five a.m.'

'So I should leave my hotel when?'

'Four-forty-five will be fine. It's all downhill and just a ten-minute walk.'

From the shadows a voice began to chant: 'Downhill, downhill,' the tone mocking, amused.

Out stepped those two young tough guys who had harassed me just half an hour earlier upon my arrival. They lit up cigarettes and the flirtatious one even tipped his baseball cap in mock salute. When Naguib snapped at them – hissing something angry in their direction – Mr Arrogant said to me in French:

'We were not trying to be disrespectful, *madame*.'

Then they disappeared back into the shadows.

'Do you know them?' I asked.

'I'm afraid so. They come from Marrakesh. They work on the crew that is resurfacing part of the road near here. They've been here for two weeks and think they're big men from the big city. They're stupid, but harmless. Shall we head to my hotel now?'

We began to ascend the narrow pathway that led up a Babel-like hill. It was a steep climb, but the moon was full tonight, so we weren't stumbling in the dark. When we reached the summit I was panting and feeling parched. It had been quite an ascent. Immediately an elderly woman in a hijab insisted that I sit down and found me a bottle of water. Naguib took my passport and 300 dirhams, saying he would fill in all the necessary registration forms. The woman asked if I liked lamb couscous. I indicated that would be just fine, as I had hardly eaten all day and was now famished. Naguib returned and led me through an extraordinary structure: castellated, with great open spaces and an outside walkway that looked down on the village below. The sky was dominated by the very full, spectral moon.

My room was under the eaves: simple, well-furnished, clean. There was a double bed and a decent shower. I handed Naguib 100 dirhams and thanked him.

'I am back on duty here at six-thirty tomorrow morning,' he said. 'You don't have to take the five a.m. bus, as there is one that leaves at eight. You could sleep in a bit and have breakfast and still be back in Ouarzazate by two o'clock.'

'Is there any chance whatsoever that my husband could have gotten off somewhere between Ouarzazate and here?'

'The bus can stop at assorted villages – but only if a passenger requests it. So, yes, he could have possibly done that – but these places have little in the way of hotels or restaurants.'

'Might the driver of the earlier bus be here now?'

'No – because he returned as a passenger on the evening bus back to Ouarzazate. He won't be back until tomorrow and I have no way of contacting him. You could wait until he returns tomorrow, and we could ask him together.'

'I think I'm going to head back on the early bus,' I said.

'As you wish, *madame*. But here's my phone number if you need me.'

Taking a notebook and a pen from his pocket he wrote it down and handed it to me.

'Thank you so much, Naguib.'

'How long will you need before dinner?'

'Fifteen minutes at most. I just want to shower and freshen up.'

'I'll tell the cook to expect you shortly.'

A quarter of an hour later, I arrived at the outdoor terrace that served as a dining room. It was a wonderful open area with six or seven tables. There was only one other guest in situ – a lean grey-haired man, with round wire-rimmed spectacles, a blue short-sleeved shirt, tan shorts, orthopaedic sandals on his feet. There was a book propped up against his wine bottle: *Der Zauberberg* by Thomas Mann. This must be the German who arrived on the earlier bus. The same bus as Paul! Someone who can confirm his whereabouts. Immediately I approached his table. He looked up, his face somewhat lined but still strong, with deep blue eyes that seemed to be harbouring some quiet sadness . . . or was that just me projecting my own sadness on everyone?

'I'm sorry,' I said in English, 'but I don't speak German.'

He smiled at me. I continued:

'But I am very competent in English and not bad in French . . . My apologies for interrupting your dinner.'

'My dinner is finished,' he said, also in English, pointing to his empty plates. 'But if you are about to eat and would like company . . .'

He indicated the empty seat opposite his own.

'That's really kind of you. But before I sit down I have a rather urgent question.'

'By all means.'

'Were you on the bus that left Ouarzazate at two o'clock this afternoon?'

'Indeed I was.'

'Did you see this man?'

I reached into my pants pocket and pulled out Paul's passport, flipping it open to the photo page. The gentleman studied it carefully for several moments.

'I'm afraid there was no one at all like this individual on the bus.'

'Are you absolutely certain of that?'

'When I got on in Ouarzazate I took a seat right at the back, so I walked by everyone who had already boarded.'

'But he got on right when the bus was leaving.'

'I remember looking up when the last person got on, but that was the driver.'

'Sir, please, I saw him get on the bus.'

'Who's "him"?' he asked, pointing to the photo.

'My husband.'

That got his attention.

'Sit, sit,' he said, motioning to the empty chair. 'My name is Dietrich.'

I told him my own. We shook hands. I changed the subject.

'Germany is one of around fifty countries that I keep telling myself I should visit,' I said.

'If you come, besides Berlin and Hamburg and Munich, you should drive along the *Romantische Strasse* – and stop at Rothenburg ob der Tauber. A medieval city between Würtzburg and Nürnberg. Completely restored after much bombing in the war. *Sehr gemütlich*, as we say. A very quiet, beautiful town – and the place I've called home for thirty years. I had a very faithful congregation in Rothenburg until I stepped down last year.'

'You're a priest?'

'A pastor. Lutheran. And recently retired.'

'If I may ask – what brings you to the Sahara in midsummer?' I asked.

He paused for a moment, collecting his thoughts.

'I remember once reading in an English novel about a man traversing this corner of the world after suffering a terrible grief, and the writer noted: "He crossed North Africa, trying to empty his mind." I came here, at an absurd time in the calendar, trying to empty my mind.'

'Because of a terrible grief?'

He nodded, again gathering his thoughts.

'My wife of forty-four years died at Christmas.'

'Oh God, that is awful. Was it sudden?'

'Completely out of nowhere. A brain aneurysm. She got up

from the dinner table at home to fetch something from the fridge. Suddenly she looked startled, then in terrible pain, then she fell to the floor. When I raced over to her she was no more. You know that line, "In the midst of life we are in death."'

Immediately I heard myself saying:

'"Earth to earth, ashes to ashes, dust to dust." It's from the Book of Common Prayer. One of the side benefits of being raised an Episcopalian.'

'And it was also a Latin antiphon: *Media Vita In Morte Sumus*. And it has appeared often in poetry. Rilke used it in a poem once . . . and now I am showing off.'

'Hardly. It's most impressive. And it is good to be speaking with you.'

'Were you hoping to be speaking with your husband?'

'Of course,' I said, the tears welling up again.

'I apologise for intruding.'

'You're hardly intruding.'

'Would you like a glass of wine?' he said.

'I think I'd like that very much.'

He reached for the still-full bottle and poured me a glass. At that moment the lamb couscous arrived. I thanked the diminutive woman for bringing it, apologising for keeping her up so late.

'*Pas de problème*,' she said in a near whisper, disappearing back into the kitchen.

To his infinite credit Dietrich steered us into more neutral waters, asking me about my work, about how I shifted from journalism to accounting, noting that I must know much intriguing detail about my clients through their financial affairs. I asked him about his student years at Heidelberg, and learned that he had two sons, a lawyer and a tax inspector ('We'd have much to talk about'), living in Nürnberg and Munich respectively.

Then the couscous was finished. Having drunk a second glass of wine I was feeling considerably less shaky. But I now had a desperate need to talk; to sit and speak calmly about my life with Paul – beginning with my doubts and concerns about him before we were married, ending with the discovery of his appalling betrayal and all the crazed uproar since then.

'Truth be told,' I said at the end of this monologue, 'I cannot say for certain that it was Paul whom I saw on the Avenue Mohamed V today. I kept thinking I saw him everywhere before that. But when I shouted at him in the streets of Ouarzazate he never turned around, even though we were only a few feet away. And I'm haunted by the letter he left for me – a letter which let it be known that he was considering taking his own life. In my darkest moments, I cannot help but wonder if I was seeing a ghost.'

'There is no reason to think he is dead. You told me the woman at the hotel confirmed that he'd left just before you arrived back from seeing his ex-wife.'

I nodded. Dietrich sipped his wine, cogitating.

'I'd like to posit two thoughts here,' he finally said. 'The first is that one of the reasons why his former wife, and his rather dangerous friend, Ben Hassan, were so furious with him was that, on a certain level, he behaved just like an old-fashioned colonialist. He came into a fragile country. He took advantage of many of the people he encountered. He wreaked a degree of havoc. Then he packed up and left, accepting no responsibility at all for the mess he left behind.

'But the other thing that strikes me about this story is your desperate sense of guilt. He betrayed you terribly. All you did was confront him with his betrayal. That story you told – about his assurances that he wanted a baby with you, and then doing what he did – is nothing less than horrible. I think that you leaving him evidence of his crime – and I do think what he did was emotionally criminal – was an elegant approach. It speaks volumes about your maturity. The fact that you have been desperately trying to track him down since his disappearance from Essaouira, the fact that you are here in the middle of a great sandy nowhere, on your own, still trying to save him from himself . . . Robin, you have my admiration.'

I felt my eyes welling up. I lowered my head, fighting back tears. Dietrich reached over and took my hand, squeezing it in a way that implied one word: courage.

'You will get through this,' he said. 'Think of it as a maze, a labyrinth. But you haven't lost your ability to negotiate your way out of its ensnaring contours. The biggest devastation, in my experience, is the loss of hope – and the revelation that there is so much you just didn't see.'

'Oh, I saw a great deal about him . . . but I chose to ignore all the early-warning signs; all the telltale indications that he truly couldn't handle the responsibility implicit in building a life with another person.'

'Sometimes the need for hope blinds us to other more evident verities. What else can we do but keep trying to see things a little more clearly?'

'As you do.'

'Don't be certain of that. I have my limitations and flaws like everyone else. Just as my marriage was hardly perfect.'

'It did last forty-four years.'

'That it did. But we separated for six years, during which time we both had relationships with other people. It was my initial weakness – an involvement with a woman who also happened to be a parishioner – that sparked the separation. It caused many problems and hindered my clerical career. Finding our way back to each other . . . that was a remarkable journey. Not facile. And not without considerable pain. But the result was twenty more extraordinary years together. Then, out of nowhere, she died. Herta was only sixty-eight. As I used to tell parishioners who had suffered a tragedy, we never can completely fathom God's plan for us.'

'But do you truly believe that it was His hand which "smote" your wife down?'

Dietrich smiled.

'I appreciate your use of Old Testament language. I have no answer as to whether He is an all-seeing, all-controlling God who decides our fate. God for me is a more complex idea. You know it was Montaigne who stated that the unknowingness of life is something that we all must embrace.'

'I do believe you can have religious faith and be thinking at the same time.'

'But you yourself have never been able to embrace the idea of faith?' he asked.

'Oh, I have plenty of faith . . . in the need to fight forward. And though I would, on a certain level, like to fall on my knees right now and beg Him to somehow deliver my husband to me, I sense I would be talking to myself.'

'I will nonetheless pray for you tonight . . . and for your lonely journey into this *Niemandsland*. A no-man's land. Like the terrain beyond Tata. Last week, in another corner of the Sahara, I spent two days out on the dunes. I drove myself – which was very risky, as once you leave the road you are driving directly on the sand. I had to rent a four-by-four – and the owner of the hotel wanted me to hire a driver, a guide. But I had to do it alone. Solo.'

'What were you trying to prove by heading out on unpaved Saharan tracks, alone? Was it about communicating with God?'

He pulled off his glasses and rubbed his eyes.

'It was about confronting my loneliness.'

'Loneliness in the face of grief?'

'Of course. But also loneliness in the face of God. And the fact that I finally know now that He cannot provide me with the answers I need.'

'Yet you still believe?'

'Indeed I do. I do so not out of habit or the need for ritual – though I do love so much about ecclesiastic ritual. I think I also still believe because I need to allow myself to be open to the inherent enigma of life. What is real to us? What is a mirage? Why do we spend a lifetime trying to somehow discern between the two? And when we die, when this corporeal self is no more, if it is simply the end of consciousness . . . then what?'

'That is the great mystery,' I said.

He glanced at his watch.

'I promised my son Horst that I would Skype him late tonight. He is going through a divorce now. He's just thirty-two with a little daughter – my granddaughter – and he is devastated, even though he's been unhappy in the marriage for years. But he is choosing immense sadness at the moment. I can appreciate that. I chose that myself at certain difficult junctures in life.'

'You're a very good father, calling him so late.'

'Being a parent – it is a lifetime job. They are always your children. And you are always engaged with their vulnerability and their own struggles to try to carve out something happy . . . or not.'

'Being a parent . . . that dream is dead for me.'

'Don't say that.'

'I turned forty last October.'

'The way medicine works today you still have time.'

'I wish I could believe that.'

'I must say this was not a conversation I was expecting to have in Tata,' he said. 'The man of faith in me might even posit the idea that we were brought together tonight for a reason. Even when you are stricken by the most desperate solitariness or doubt, someone can come along and remind you that no one is alone.'

'Beautifully said. One final question. Did God speak to you when you were all alone – and so severely vulnerable – in the Sahara?'

'Of course He did.'

'May I ask – what did He tell you?'

'He told me to get back to a place of safety.'

'Good advice.'

He stood up.

'I will be taking the eight a.m. bus tomorrow – so if you'd like a travel companion back to Ouarzazate . . .'

'I need to take the five a.m. bus.'

'You'll have no sleep.'

'True – but there's an afternoon direct flight to Paris. I am going to see if I can get a place on it. And the early bus will get me back to Ouarzazate in time.'

Now it was my turn to stand up. As I took Dietrich's hand he executed a small, almost formal bow – a hint of old-world courtesy in the midst of the desert.

Five minutes later, back in my room, the air conditioner cranked up, I couldn't help reflecting on that sage piece of advice that Dietrich received from the Almighty while facing the void of the Sahara.

Get back to a place of safety.

I dug out my laptop. I went online, found a travel website and booked myself on three flights tomorrow: Ouarzazate to Paris, Paris to Boston, Boston to Buffalo, arriving at 9.45 p.m. local time. The cost of this last-minute ticket was absurd: $1,700 in economy. But it was also just money. I needed to finally call time on this madness and return home.

After paying for the ticket with my credit card I sent an urgent email to Morton:

> *I hope you have your BlackBerry in hand, as I know you are due to meet me at Buffalo airport tonight at 9 p.m. I am still in Morocco, so don't bother. I will explain all when I see you at the office in two days. I fly tomorrow and arrive late. And yes, I have a story or two to tell.*

I hit the 'send' button, then set the little alarm clock for four-fifteen a.m. It had been, on every level, a vast, difficult day – and I had to remind myself that this time last night I was having a short sleep in a Casablanca hotel. The narrative of one's life can become so skewed in such a short space of time.

Now, in a less frantic, more reflective moment – and after that interesting dinner with the German man of God – I saw that the 'essential' clarification of the last frenzied few days was my decision to abandon ship and head back to the States. I had made a crucial decision. I could now surrender to sleep without hesitation – for just four hours.

When I was jolted awake at 04.15 I forced myself into the shower. I dressed, loaded up my small backpack with everything I had taken out for the night and left the hotel.

Outside it was still moonlit and I had to watch my step on the descent down into the main town. The bus depot was just a minute beyond the city walls and checking my watch I saw I'd arrive there with ten minutes to spare before the bus left town.

When I reached the end of the descending pathway I spied two figures leaning against a wall, smoking. As I came into their field of vision, they tossed away their cigarettes. Suddenly I noticed the two matching baseball caps and realised these were the two guys who'd flirted with me the previous night.

'Hello there, pretty lady,' the talkative, arrogant one said. They were now positioned directly in front of me, and a red warning light went off in my brain.

'You're up early,' I said, trying to keep my tone light while simultaneously glancing frantically from side to side, desperate to find a way to squeeze by them. But this was a narrow pathway and they had comprehensively blocked the way forward.

'We wanted to say goodbye,' Mr Arrogant said.

'Goodbye then,' I replied.

I attempted to dash past the other guy, who was holding a jar of some liquid and a rag. As I made a break for it Mr Arrogant caught me by the arms and pinned them behind me. I tried to scream but his friend had the rag over my nose and mouth within a nanosecond. It was sodden in a liquid that gave off a high chemical aroma. Kicking out with my feet, connecting with nothing, I tried not to inhale its toxic fumes, but he pushed it down on my face with such force, while simultaneously yanking my hair backwards, that I could no longer hold my breath.

When I exhaled the chemicals hit me like a sucker-punch to the head. *This is not happening, this is not happening.*

And then the world went black.

Nineteen

WHEN THE WORLD came back into focus I wanted to jump back into the darkness again. Because to be conscious meant facing my imminent death.

I was nowhere. I was being bounced up and down. Tossed from side to side. My head felt as if it had been split in two. Nausea was consuming me. But I fought it back, as a rag had been tied tightly around my mouth. To vomit would be to risk suffocation. My hands had been bound to my feet. Movement was impossible.

I had been thrown into the back of an open truck. It was still night, though a small hint of dawn was beginning to cleave the sky. I forced myself upright for a moment and spied nothing but emptiness around me. Then another bump in the terrain slammed me back down against the floor of the truck.

I was being driven into the Sahara. Once they had me at a place far away from any hint of civilisation I knew what they would do with me. I also knew that once they had raped me, they would kill me. And bury my body deep within the desert. Then return to their job on the road gang by sunrise and act as if nothing had happened. When my absence was eventually reported, what trace would there be of me? I saw my backpack out of a corner of my eye. It had been thrown into the truck bed, near a plastic jerrycan which had slid down and was bumping against my face. From the fumes issuing from its cap I could tell that it was filled with spare fuel.

They are going to rape me and strangle me. Then they'll use the gas to burn my body and bury its charred remains deep in the drifting sand.

I began to scream. I screamed through the gag. I screamed like a lunatic. I screamed in the desperate absurd hope that someone would hear me. I screamed with rage and fury and disbelief. I screamed with hatred. I screamed with terror.

I tugged at the ropes that were binding me. My hands had been so fiercely tied to my feet, the knot pulled so tight, that there was absolutely no way of loosening it, certainly not undoing it without a knife. I pulled and yanked and desperately tried to get my fingers – gone numb owing to the pressure on my wrists – to deal with the knot. But it was impossible. Every time I tried the ropes seemed to apply more pressure, increasing the numbness, making me wonder if the lack of circulation would . . .

This is not happening . . . this is not happening.

But this was definitely happening. With the sky beginning to lighten, I was pretty certain it was going to happen very soon. That would be their logic: fuck and strangle her before sun-up. Cremate the body, bury the remains, be back on the road with the new day dawning, and . . .

I struggled and struggled and struggled. My muffled screams turned into hysterical crying as I began to realise that there was no way out of this. *I am going to die. Before that happens I am going to suffer the worst sort of degradation imaginable, followed by a monstrous death by strangulation.* There was nothing I could do to stop them.

The truck began to slow down before coming to a halt. The motor was cut. I heard both front doors being opened and slammed shut. Footsteps. Then a voice.

'Sleep well, pretty lady?'

He climbed into the back of the truck and began to stroke my hair. When I started struggling he slapped me hard across the left ear, a ferocious pain coupled with a profound echo effect. I screamed in agony, and was rewarded this time with a fist to my cheekbone. I blacked out for a moment. When I came to again, it felt as if my cheekbone had been fractured. The little shit was now brandishing a knife in front of my eyes and yanking my hair at the same time.

'You fight me again I will cut you,' he hissed. 'Cut off your tits, maybe gouge your eyes. You want that, cunt?'

I shook my head many times, fear making me whimper. Now his fury turned into a broad frightening smile.

'You fight me, you will get hurt. You no fight me, everything will be very nice. Understand?'

To emphasise that last word he yanked back hard on my hair. I whimpered again, nodding several times.

'Good girl,' he said, stroking my cheek. Then he shouted something in Arabic and his accomplice came over, a knife in hand.

'My friend is about to cut off the ropes, remove the gag,' the little shit said. 'You going to struggle?'

I shook my head many times.

'Good girl.'

More shouts back and forth in Arabic as the cords were cut, the gag pulled down from my mouth. Immediately the restoration of blood flow to my hands made me shudder. A hard clip across the ear was the punishment for that involuntary movement.

'I fucking told you – no movement.'

'Sorry, sorry,' I whispered.

'Tell me you want this,' he whispered.

I tensed and was hit again, crying out.

'Tell me you want this,' he repeated.

'I want this.'

'You move, you get cut.'

He threw my untied hands behind me and, with his accomplice helping him, cut the remaining rope off my ankles, then proceeded to lift my buttocks up and unzip my pants, pulling them down with my panties at the same time. As he did so my free right hand darted around the immediate vicinity, trying to find something I could use as a weapon. I knew I only had seconds but nothing came to hand. Until my fingers connected with the jerrycan. I managed to get my fingers around its cap when I felt my legs being spread wide and I looked up and saw the little shit above me, his pants pulled down, his penis erect.

'You going to fight me?' he asked as he climbed on top of me.

I shook my head, seeing out of the corner of my eye his goon standing on the ground, folding up his knife, lighting a cigarette with a Zippo he kept clicking open and shut, clearly frightened but also waiting his turn. With my right hand still on the cap of the jerrycan I reached over with my left and touched my assailant's arm, actually stroking it in a come-on way. A huge smile lit up his face.

'You want me, yes?'

I nodded. Another big smile from him. The head of his penis was rubbing against me, trying to gain entrance but defeated by the absolute dryness within.

'Open wider,' he ordered, and he spat into his hand before rubbing it against the lips of my vagina and forcing his way in. I felt as if I was being ripped apart; an agony beyond agony. He began to thrust wildly within me, his eyes now snapped shut. My left hand tightened around his arm, and I deliberately began to match his thrusts with my own as a way of letting him think I was into it. Meanwhile, my right fingers were manically unscrewing the cap of the jerrycan. As I could hear his moans rising, and his penis beginning to stiffen even further as ejaculation approached, the cap finally loosened enough for a small trickle of fuel to spill out. That's when I reached up with my free hand and stroked his face. He opened his eyes and I dug my nails directly into them, digging down, blood spurting forth, his screams deafening. I let go with the jerrycan, drenching him with the fuel. He jumped back, falling to the ground with his face in his hands, blood now pouring from his eye sockets. In a nanosecond I jumped off the truck, grabbed the Zippo from the hand of his startled accomplice, set it aflame and tossed it directly at my rapist. All this took maybe three seconds. There was a huge conflagrating whoosh. The lighter ignited the gas. The little shit burst into flames.

His cries of agony were mirrored by a scream from his accomplice, for whom I was now gunning with my claws. But as I sideswiped his cheeks, he caught me with a punch to the face and I fell to my knees. He kicked me with full force in the head.

And the world went black again.

Twenty

THE HEAT BROUGHT me back to life. Then it threatened to finish the job and kill me.

As I came back into murky consciousness the pain was ferocious. My head was battered, my cheekbone fractured, my lips split; there was a reverberating echo in one ear and the throbbing in my skull was unbearable.

I'd collapsed face down in the sand. I knew this because when my eyes finally opened sand cascaded into them, making me jump upright and then nearly fall over again as the pain hit. I held my head for several moments, eyes tight shut, as I became aware of the boiler-room heat. And the fact that I had no pants on. The entire exposed lower half of my body felt as if it was charred.

I tried to stand up but failed. I sank to my knees, but the sand was so fiery that it forced me somehow to become vertical. That's when I doubled over. Because that's when I saw him – or what was left of him. Still on his knees. Charred all over. Most of his features burnt beyond recognition, but his face still partially intact.

I turned away. I was sick, the vomit disgorging from me with a ferocity and a vehemence that had me collapsing again. Until the scorching sand forced me up onto my feet again.

It all came flooding back now. Every appalling detail from the moment they'd grabbed me. Everything they had done. Everything I had done – evidence of which was right there in front of me. And the punch in the face and the kick to the head that had blacked out my world. Blacked out everything until now.

The vomiting left me with a voracious thirst and I was already severely parched from all the time unconscious under that pitiless sun. How long had I been left here? Instinctively I glanced at my wrist, thinking they must have snatched my watch. But my father's

Rolex was still there. So too were my engagement and wedding rings. The watch told me it was 8.23 a.m., the hands on the dial blurring before me – my vision felt as if it had been knocked out of kilter with that final boot to the head. The intensity of the sun blanched the landscape. As I tried a step forward my foot felt something soft. I stared down, almost crumbling again. The blurriness in my vision was alarming. But I could discern tan pants in front of me. My tan pants and underwear, stripped off me by the little shit before he forced his way inside me. Before I set him ablaze.

It took considerable effort to reach down and pick up these discarded garments. Trying to put them on was torture. When I finally got the underwear and the pants back on, and also located the pair of sandals pulled off my feet, I noticed the tyre track right by me. A tyre track which continued forward for a few feet before turning into a circle and then . . .

He'd driven off. After kicking me in the head the punk had clearly jumped into the truck and driven off into the dawn. Leaving his accomplice on fire and his victim unconscious in the sand, exposed to the monstrous elements that would kill her in a manner that might have made strangulation preferable. Because as I looked up from the encircling tyre track what I saw was . . .

Nothing.

Nothing but sand.

It stretched to infinity. Burnt beige in colour. Lunar-like, with craters and fossilised dunes. A boundless, evaporated void on the far side of the moon.

And nothing hinting at human life in any direction.

Nothing but the tyre track. When that punk raced off in the truck he took with him everything that gave me an identity and a means of contacting the outside world. My passport, my credit cards, what cash I had left, my plane reservation, my laptop. He also took the few spare clothes I had, including a hat to shield my head. I was alone in the Sahara with nothing. No water. No protection from the fireball above. No papers indicating who I was.

I glanced back at the blackened corpse of my attacker. This would be my fate. I would not last more than a few hours out here. I would fall over somewhere, succumbing to sunstroke, dehydration, raging thirst. I would slowly die. If I was ever found – and that was unlikely, given that they had brought me to a place few dared to venture – my body would be so burnt by the sun that . . .

No, no, don't think that. You can't think that. You must somehow try to find help. Or a water hole. Or . . .

I scanned all corners of the horizon again. Nothing. Not even a speck in the distance of any outpost of civilisation. Nothing but the tyre tracks.

The punk did a U-turn and headed back. Just follow his tyre tracks and you will eventually . . .

Die. For you are miles and miles away from anything resembling life.

I stared down at the tracks. I started following them, my gait hesitant, unstable. My head was throbbing, my vision obscured, my need for water desperate. I could feel the sun smouldering the top of my head.

But I forced myself to walk, to let the tracks be my guide. I had no choice. To stand still was to accept death.

My sense of balance began to leave me. I must have been walking a good quarter of an hour, each step a small agony, my mouth desiccated with dried vomit, my saliva in increasingly short supply, the back of my throat beginning to tighten. Is this how death by thirst begins? The oesophagus slowly contracting due to the lack of hydration, eventually strangling you?

My death.

I felt myself beginning to stumble.

My death.

Who would notice my passing? Who would care that I was no longer walking the planet? Would Paul – were he still alive – feel some sort of guilt? And beyond him, who? A few friends and work colleagues might mourn my absence. Otherwise . . . my forty years on this planet wiped clean. My footprint on life as insubstantial and impermanent as the marks that my sandals were now making in this Saharan sand.

I stumbled, collapsing onto one knee. The sand singed it but I didn't have the strength to lift myself up. I wanted to ask for some sort of celestial help; for God to save me. But how could I call out to an Almighty whose existence I still doubted? How could I cry out: *Don't forsake me . . . show me a way out of this wilderness, this hell.*

My other knee sank into the sand. I tried to swallow. I shut my eyes. My head felt near to implosion. This was it. Endgame. The final moments of my sorry little life. Throwing my head back I reopened my eyes and looked straight up at that fiery object that was about to kill me.

Thy kingdom come.

The sun burnt right into me.

Thy will be done.

I pitched forward. Gone from this world.

No white light greeted me. No heavenly way station. No cognisance of anything. Just blackness. I remained there until . . .

Until I felt a hand touching me. And whispering in a language foreign to me. The whispering became louder, as if the voice was now right up against my ear.

'*Salaam, salaam . . . es-hy, es-hy . . .*'

I opened one eye. My vision was clouded, indistinct.

'*Es-hy . . . es-hy.*'

I tried to open my mouth but it was seared closed. I had no energy, no will to do anything, let alone to respond to the hand shoving my shoulder, her little voice louder:

'*Salaam, salaam . . . es-hy, es-hy . . .*'

Her little voice.

What I could discern from my one befogged eye was a small figure, in a robe, her face obscured by a flowing headscarf that covered everything but her eyes and mouth. From the sound of the voice emitting those words, and the lack of force behind the hand trying to rouse me, there was a young girl crouched beside me.

Was she some intermediary figure sent to guide me to the afterlife?

But why was she speaking to me in Arabic?

'*Salaam, salaam . . . es-hy, es-hy . . .*'

Hello, hello.

And I knew what '*es-hy*' meant because one of the cleaners in Essaouira used it when trying to rouse the man always asleep behind the hotel front desk.

Wake up, wake up.

But I couldn't do anything beyond half-open that one eye. And wish myself back in the darkness again.

Suddenly I felt liquid against my lips.

The little voice intoned:

'*Ma'a . . . ma'a . . . shreb.*'

More liquid against my lips. I opened my mouth wide and let her pour in . . .

'*Ma'a . . . ma'a.*'

Water.

Within moments my throat opened again.

Water.

With it came the knowledge that I was still here. Prostrated in the Sahara. Alive, albeit barely. But still here. With water flowing into my mouth. And the little voice then saying:

'*Bellati . . . bellati.*'

Then I felt a cloth being put over my face.

And I was alone again.

Within moments, the darkness enveloped me once more.

Until I heard the little voice yet again. Accompanied by two other voices. Older. Male. Shouting to each other. Then to me.

'*Shreb . . . shreb.*'

Now someone pulled the cloth off my face and was holding up my head, while someone else was filling my mouth with water. At first I gagged it up. The man supporting my head gripped me tightly as I heaved, used something to clean my mouth, then gently pushed the bottle back between my lips. This time I could hold it down. And drank and drank and drank, the water surging through me. At another point I started choking on it again. The man cleaned me off, then made me drink more. He was not going to stop feeding me water until he was certain I was somewhat hydrated again. I have no idea how long this process took. What I do know is that the water brought back enough consciousness for me to see two men – both with hard, wizened faces – engaged in the act of saving my life. I also heard the one who seemed to be doing all the talking shouting orders. Then I was lifted and put on a mattress. The smell of animal dung nearby. Then someone climbing in beside me. Opening one eye I saw the young girl who had found me now seated beside me, smiling shyly before covering my head again with a cloth, then taking my hand and holding it. I felt some movement in front of us, and the slope on which I had been placed righting itself, and heard the crack of a whip and the bray of a donkey, and I passed out again as the cart upon which I was travelling began its slow trudge along the desert track.

I have no idea how long I descended back into the darkness. When I awoke I was in a very different place. As my eyes opened, I saw candles and two gas lanterns lighting what seemed to be the walls of a tent. The fact that I could open both eyes was surprising. So too was the fact that there was an elderly woman – her face like a bas-relief, with only four or five teeth – gazing down at me, and exclaiming as I stared up at her:

'*Allahu akbar!*'

I tried to sit up. I was too weak to do so. The elderly woman spoke quietly to me, gently pressing my head down on what seemed to be a cot of some sort. Another woman came over: much younger, pretty, all smiles.

'*Hamdilli-la!*'

She touched my face with her fingers. I flinched. Even the light pressure she'd placed on my cheek set off wild nerve endings of pain. She was immediately contrite, especially as the elderly woman shouted at her to do something. Moments later, some sort of balming oil was being lightly rubbed into my face. It was at this juncture that I realised I was virtually naked from the waist down.

Lain out on this bier-like cot, my legs and thighs covered with assorted cloths; my crotch encased in a white bandage that was covered in dried blood.

As soon as I saw the blood I was back in that truck, my assailant thrusting into me, tearing me apart.

I began to shudder. Immediately the young woman was holding me, whispering to me in Arabic, calming me, once even gesticulating to the bloodied bandage, then spouting out a long array of reassuring words, as if to say: *I know what happened, and it is terrible. But you will be better.*

Meanwhile the elderly woman approached us holding a mug of something steaming and strangely aromatic. She motioned for the young woman to help me up, and then encouraged me to drink this highly herbal, bittersweet brew. It had an immediate soporific effect. Within moments I was elsewhere again.

When I woke it was daylight. I still felt desperately weak, concussed, with a ringing in my ears that wouldn't go away. I also urgently needed to pee. But as soon as I tried to sit up I lost my equilibrium, and fell back against the cot. At which point I saw the young girl who'd found me scramble up from a mattress in the corner of the tent and hurry over. Though still half-awake she smiled broadly at me. I managed a fogged smile back.

'*Parlez-vous français?*' I asked.

She shook her head, then raised her finger telling me to wait and ran outside. I could hear her shouting to someone. Within a few minutes she returned with the very pretty young woman whom I'd seen – when? – was it yesterday? How much time had evaporated around me from the moment I had found myself dying in the desert to the place and moment I found myself now? I only knew it was that same young woman when she removed her burqa.

'*Salaam alaikum,*' she said to me. The little girl was by her side, holding onto her djellaba.

'*Mema,*' she said.

'Your mother?' I asked. A baffled look from them both. I tried a more phonetic word: 'Mama?'

That worked. They both smiled and nodded.

I asked the young woman if she spoke French. She seemed a little embarrassed by this and shook her head.

'No problem,' I said, trying to smile back, but suddenly feeling woozy. The young woman told her daughter to run outside. My need to pee was now immense. From my French lessons with Soraya I remembered that she would occasionally drop Arabic words into our conversation to help me negotiate the Essaouira streets. She taught me a few phrases. Such as:

'Aynal hammam?'

Where is the toilet?

The fact that I had asked this question in Arabic had her beaming. She answered back in a stream of words, none of which I managed to follow. But she did indicate to me that I should wait a moment as she raced over to the far side of the tent and returned with a long black djellaba. As she started helping me into it the elderly woman returned, shouting orders to the young woman, who in turn explained that I needed the toilet (or, at least, I heard the word *al-hammam* in her onslaught of words).

With the elderly woman in charge of things, I was helped into the djellaba. The weakness I'd felt lying down on the cot was exacerbated when I tried to stand up. But the elderly woman had hands as rough and reinforced as a vice. She forced me up vertically. When I attempted to look down at the condition of my crotch and legs she held her hand under my chin and moved my gaze, while the young woman and her daughter removed all the bandages and dressings. Then they helped me slowly into the djellaba, keeping me upright throughout. The elderly woman held up a burqa and started explaining – with a lot of hand gestures – that I needed to put it on, as she pointed to the flap in the tent, letting me know that the *al-hammam* was outside. I nodded agreement. With the help of the young woman, she organised the burqa around my face. Within moments I felt like a blinkered horse. All peripheral vision had been cut off and I was looking at the world from a narrow horizontal slit. I was very conscious that my legs felt raw. Just as my face seemed somewhat out of place. Walking was an arduous business. All three women had to support me as I took my first tentative steps forward.

Once outside the tent the heat and the harshness of the light made me snap my eyes shut. From what I could take in, we were in some sort of encampment – several tents, shaded by a few sparse trees. Was this an oasis? The burqa cut off any view to either side. All I could see were the meagre trees, the tents, the sand beyond.

The women led me to a small tent. As the little girl opened the flap, the elderly woman told the others to halt for a moment. Disappearing inside she returned moments later, tucking a mirror into the folds of her djellaba. That got my attention and heightened my sense of fear. She didn't want me to see myself.

When I motioned to the mirror the elderly woman became very maternal, shaking her finger vehemently at me as if I was a child who had been caught seeing something she shouldn't. Then she motioned for the mother and daughter to bring me inside, giving instructions along the way.

The toilet was a bucket, with a pail of water nearby. The young girl pulled up my djellaba. But when I attempted to inspect what I suspected was severe sun damage to my legs, her mother repeated the same procedure as the elderly woman. She placed her hand under my chin to keep my gaze upwards.

They settled me on the bucket, and I let go. The stinging that accompanied the urination was frightful. The young woman gripped my shoulder, helping me through the pain. When I was finished the little girl went over to the pail, dipped a rag into the water, and handed it to me. When I touched myself it was agony. The mother saw this and gripped my shoulder again, her hand gestures indicating that I needed to be patient, not to be afraid, to give it time.

They got me back to the tent. The elderly woman helped me off with the burqa and the djellaba. Once I was naked they lay me down again on the cot, the little girl keeping my gaze upwards by standing over me and touching my chin with her index finger any time I looked away. I felt oils being rubbed into my legs; then some sort of balm was applied to my cheekbones and the areas around my eyes. I smelled that strange herbal beverage being brewed again – one which ensured that I fell into a deep slumber. They were knocking me out again. The elderly woman raised my head, putting the mug between my lips. I drank down the scalding brew in several gulps. Moments later, as the darkness recaptured me, I wondered: *Will I ever leave this place . . . and do I even care?*

Twenty-one

I SLOWLY BECAME aware of minutes, hours, days – whenever I was awake. Which wasn't very often, as my rehabilitation involved drinking that herbal concoction twice a day and sleeping almost nine hours each time.

The curious thing about this 'tisane' was that it was ferociously potent, but also left me feeling peculiarly clear-headed when I re-emerged into the world.

Not that I was in any way clear-headed. On the contrary, the battering that my head and eardrum had received meant that I was suffering from some sort of serious concussion and inner-ear damage. Only some time later did I realise why the elderly woman who took charge of my recovery had insisted on having me knocked out. This was her way of keeping me sedated and allowing the brain to heal.

The elderly woman was named Maika. Her daughter – the beautiful young woman who had been at my side throughout – was called Titrit. And the little girl who came upon me and saved my life was Naima.

I discovered their names on the day that Maika decided I was ready to come off the eighteen-hour sleep cure. Before then the herbal medicine had kept me so drugged that only the basic sort of information seeped through. But on the morning when Maika did not give me another dose of the tisane, a certain fog had lifted by the early afternoon. Gesturing to myself I explained that my name was Robin.

'And your names?'

It was Naima who understood immediately and pointed to her grandmother and mother, informing me of their names before pointing to herself and saying, in a wonderfully bold and forthright voice: 'Naima!'

Her grandmother rolled her eyes, as if to indicate that such exuberance would be tolerated only for a certain number of years. But when I gave Naima the thumbs-up she mimicked the gesture, delighting in it, showing her mother and grandmother with amused pride how well she could do it. Though Titrit encouraged her, clapping and laughing as her daughter marched around, Maika called time on this little escapade when she gestured for me to stand up, indicating that I should walk towards her unaided. For the first time since Naima had found me in the desert I was being permitted to take steps without the three women to help me. I was uncertain at first, wondering if I could actually make it across the floor of the tent – which wasn't more than six feet – without stumbling. When I tried to rush it at first Maika held up her hands and indicated that slowness was key here. I followed her advice, carefully putting one foot in front of the other, testing my balance, acutely conscious of my fragile state. But I did actually make it over to the far side of the tent, and was rewarded with applause from Titrit and Naima and a curt nod from Maika.

The tent. There was the cot on which I had spent so much time sleeping. There was a dirt floor. There was a gas lamp. Two buckets: one for washing, one for drinking water. There were two stools for guests to sit on, and a single mattress on the floor. That had been my world for at least a week, maybe ten days, perhaps longer.

When I reached the other side I had to sit down on one of the little stools for a few moments, as I had started to feel woozy. Maika touched my head, made a flapping gesture with one hand, then held both up. I took this to mean: *You are still not completely well in there. The head injury is going to leave you rather shaky, and we will take things slowly.* Then she got me to stand up and ordered Titrit and Naima to help me out of the simple white nightgown which Titrit had brought several nights before and in which I had recently been sleeping. My legs and thighs were still wrapped in white cloths, prepared with oils that gave off a herbal, medicinal aroma. The bloodied bandage wrapped between my legs had been changed daily, but though the bleeding had long since stopped, Maika had insisted on using what seemed to be a salve on the lips of my vulva and deep inside, administering this on a twice-daily basis in a matter-of-fact way.

Maika had now decided the moment had arrived for me to inspect the damage done to me . . . or perhaps to see how its recovery was progressing. As they began to undress me, and to remove the cloths from my legs, I instinctively looked away. Whereas earlier on I had wanted to see how bad it all was, now that I was finding my way back to some sort of skewed norm the last thing I wanted to contemplate was how badly disfigured I might be. That would begin to raise the question of my life beyond this tent – and whether I could ever get back to it. Or, if the injuries were so severe, whether I would ever want to.

Maika – shrewd old bird that she was – worked out my fear on the spot. Being someone who clearly did not believe in the art of mollycoddling, she disappeared outside for a moment as Titrit and Naima undressed me, returning with a mirror in hand. Now that I was naked she started to remove all the cloth bandages around my legs. As I had been left for dead, half-naked in the sun, my lower extremities had been exposed unprotected for several hours. So too my face. When the bandages were finally off – and I refused to look – she gently but firmly forced my head downwards. My thighs had long red welts on them, some truly virulent, others already starting to fade. My lower legs also displayed several nasty burnt blotches. But what was most alarming were the clusters of tiny off-white and red welts everywhere, up and down both legs and concentrated around my right thigh.

'What are these?' I said, pointing to these dozens of micro-blisters, very alarmed.

Maika began to lecture me in a reassuring way, explaining (by tapping her thumb rapidly against her middle finger and then diving with it against my thigh) that while unconscious I had been attacked by some sort of insect. She even tried out a word of French:

'*Des puces.*'

Fleas. Sand fleas. Which I had read about in one of the many Moroccan guides I'd devoured prior to my trip. They were prevalent in the desert. They came out at sunrise, merciless whenever any sort of human or animal flesh was in their immediate vicinity.

The density of bites was shocking. Maika saw my distress. Through the usual elaborate pantomime of hand gestures, she indicated that, in time, they would diminish.

'And the burns,' I said, pointing to the deep red welts, some still blistering. Maika motioned downwards with her hands, as if to say: *They will lessen.* Then she touched my shoulder in a firm but comforting way, and said one word:

'*Shaja'a.*'

When I looked baffled as to its meaning she tapped my heart, my head, and then forced my chin up with her index finger. The penny dropped.

'*Courage?*' I asked, trying to give it a French pronunciation. Titrit immediately nodded her head several times, saying something to Maika who concurred. Waving her finger in my face like a corrective Mother Superior, she repeated that word again:

'*Shaja'a.*'

Immediately Naima was imitating her grandmother, wagging her finger at me, saying several times over: '*Shaja'a, shaja'a, shaja'a,*' even causing her usually grim-faced grandmother to smile for a moment or so.

Maika now moved the mirror directly in front of my vulva, making me see that the lips were largely healed. She asked Titrit to bring over the tin of homemade salve with which she had been treating my ripped insides. Then, indicating that I should spread my legs a bit, she dipped her fingers into the salve and began to explore within me. Again I wasn't just struck by the matter-of-fact way she examined me, but also the fact that Naima wasn't shooed away as this internal inspection took place. On the contrary she came close up to her grandmother, fascinated. The way these women treated what is euphemistically called 'female matters' in such a utilitarian, non-prudish way was both surprising and necessary for my still-fragile state of mind. The fact that they were involving the young girl in all this – without, I'm certain, going into the reasons why I had been injured – struck me as canny and demystifying. Here, Naima watched while her grand-mother prodded and probed within me. That I wasn't frantic with pain – just a small amount of discomfort – I took to be a positive sign. Withdrawing her fingers Maika put her thumb up (she too had adopted this gesture after seeing me show Naima how to do it). She made assorted hand movements to indicate that, in her expert opinion, all was repaired within.

Now it was time for the revelation I was most dreading: the state of my face. What's that old line about it being the mirror of the soul? If that was the truth then my soul was a still-battered and scarred one. As Maika presented me with the mirror I could see her daughter looking distinctly uneasy, as if expecting me to fall apart at first glimpse of the lingering impairments. I closed my eyes, took a deep steadying breath, and opened them.

What I first noticed were the sunburnt red patches on my forehead and cheeks, and a plethora of small bites. All those hours with my face in the sand had allowed the fleas to run riot. Again Maika signalled that, in time, they would diminish. So too the blistering welt that covered my chin. But what shocked me even more was the deeply discoloured bruise that covered my left cheek, spreading upwards to the blackened ring beneath my eye. My left ear was slightly cauliflowered from the punch that the little shit had landed on me; a punch which left me with an ongoing echo. And my lips were still severely chapped, almost fractured.

I lowered the mirror. I tried to stifle a sob. I failed. I was a disfigured freak show. Seeing my battered self brought back the monstrosity wreaked on me – and the insanity of my pursuit of a man whom I should have cast aside as soon as the nature of his treachery became clear.

When I started to break down Titrit put her arms around me, letting me bury my head in her shoulder. But Maika wouldn't stand for such a show of self-pity. Literally pulling me away from her daughter she bore down on me with that bony, exclamation point of a finger of hers, almost shouting at me as she gave me a fast and furious lecture in a language completely beyond my comprehension, but which, by this point, I could somehow understand. Following her broad gestures I understood the central gist of her sermon:

Don't you dare feel sorry for yourself. What has happened has happened. You have survived. You are not dead. You will be able to walk. You will be able to have babies. Your face will heal. So too your legs. There may be scars, but they will not be disfiguring ones. We all have scars. But now your duty to yourself is to get back to your life when you are ready. But no more self-pity. That is not allowed here. I will not accept it – because I know you are better than that. Understand?

Maika's vehemence was so forthright (and loud) that Naima hid in her mother's skirts. I stood there with my head lowered, fighting back tears, feeling like a censured child, while also knowing that everything she was saying made complete sense; that I had no choice but to somehow get beyond the horror of it all.

But Maika also made it clear that there was no way I could travel yet. She held up ten fingers, then four, indicating that she might consider letting me go in two weeks. That's when I had – courtesy of my hand gestures – the conversation that I had for some time been dreading; when I explained that the men who had raped me had also robbed me. I had no money, nothing. Maika shrugged as if to say: *Why do you need money here? You are our guest.* I acted out and said at the same time:

'But I feel bad about taking your hospitality and giving you nothing for it.'

Maika understood immediately what I was saying and got even more vehement, telling me (or, at least, this is what I was thinking she was telling me):

There is absolutely no need to consider money. You are our guest. We will look after you. We will continue to help you get better. When you are ready we will figure out a way for you to get home.

I thanked her profusely. She held up her hand, as if to indicate: *You're welcome . . . now stop.* Then she ordered me back on the cot, and got Titrit and Naima to begin re-administering the cold compresses and the oils and balms to my injuries and scars.

The next ten days marked a time when, on so many levels, a certain clarity descended upon me. I was still being given the soporific tisane every evening around eight p.m. Though she was no longer knocking me out twice a day Maika had upped this nightly dose so that I was sleeping twelve hours. I understood that this was her ongoing cure for head injuries. I was largely restricted to my little tent and had nothing in the way of reading material or writing paper and pen to fill my waking hours, let alone any of those modern distractions – the Internet, television, even a humble radio – with which we all seem to pass the time. For the most part I was being kept separate from the life of this encampment. So I found myself very much thrown back on my own thoughts, my own reflections. As the concussive fog began to lift, as I became mobile again, as the terrible shock in which I had been living transformed into a functional numbness, I found myself alone for nine hours a day with little to do except try to sort through the inventory of my life.

Maika – having taken charge of my recovery – was also insisting that I begin to eat normally again, as I had lost (I could tell) a shocking amount of weight since the attack. One day I tried on the tan pants which I'd been wearing when the two men grabbed me, and which Titrit had laundered for me. I wasn't more than 120 pounds when I arrived in Morocco. Even trying to tie the drawstring as tightly as possible the pants still all but fell off me. All that time in a semi-comatose state, existing on small amounts of bread and couscous and vegetables, had resulted in me losing so many pounds that Titrit – who was quite wide-hipped and clearly liked her food – indicated that I needed to be fattened up.

The heat outside was maniacal. I was finally able to leave my tent on my own to use the toilet. I was also invited to join the family for group meals. Maika made it clear that, as their guest, I needed to abide by their customs. Wearing the burqa when outside the tent was obligatory and I was certainly not going to express my feminist distaste for this practice. These people had saved my life. They had taken me in. They had nursed me back to health. They were not asking a penny for all the immense kindness and generosity shown to me. How could I question their request that I cover my face when outside?

Once inside, however, I was allowed to be as unmasked as all the other women in this little village.

I was, I came to understand, among Berbers. It was Idir – Titrit's husband, Naima's father – who explained a bit about the Berbers to me. Idir was one of the men who'd returned with Naima to rescue me. I wanted to ask her what she'd been doing out in the desert alone. I could only surmise that she was allowed to roam the Sahara, and that I hadn't seen the oasis – which, I came to discover, was behind a stone wall that, when seen from the desert, blended in with the dusty horizon. You would only know of the little world existing behind that wall if you could find the wall – which was so camouflaged that it was impossible to spot from any distance. Idir was somewhat older than Titrit – his heavily grooved face and bad teeth made him look as though he was in his early fifties, though I sensed that the harshness of life in this great sandy nowhere aged everyone considerably. From the freshness of her outlook and the flawlessness of her skin I guessed that Titrit was, at most, in her early thirties. Idir wasn't a great conversationalist – but it turned out he did speak a smattering of French, enough for the two of us to understand each other. He explained that the Berbers weren't a tribe but a people; that there were Berbers in Algeria, Tunisia, even Egypt, with the greatest concentration here in Morocco, specifically south of Ouarzazate.

'Here you are in our country,' he explained. 'We may be officially governed by Rabat, by the King . . . but we see this as our own kingdom.'

The other man in this encampment was Immeldine. He was Maika's husband and, like his wife, showed the wear and tear of a life lived under a fierce Saharan sun. He was a compulsive smoker – he always had a cigarette on the go. In the two weeks during which I ate with the family nightly he spoke very little and I often wondered if he considered me an imposition. I discovered that he and Idir farmed a bit in the oasis, growing herbs and a few vegetables that they sold at a market once a month in Tata. They also raised a few goats for milk. The women had a loom on which they made simple rugs of traditional design. They also made small lace items and knitted skullcaps of the type worn by Idir and Immeldine.

'They do very good work,' Idir told me in his basic French. 'Every month we have a friend, Aatif – he drives a lorry to Marrakesh. He takes everything our women make and sells them to a dealer. Last month he returned with two thousand dirhams for us! Most money ever! A fortune!'

I thought of my husband, spending the equivalent $230 on a bottle of wine he could hardly afford. Or how I took a potential corporate client out to dinner a few weeks before leaving for Morocco and insisted on picking up the $300 tab at Buffalo's best steakhouse. And how 2,000 dirhams (at best) was keeping these five people alive for a month. From what Idir had indicated, this was more than twice what they were used to. I could see Titrit and Naima beaming as he said this – because, with Maika, they were the labour force at the loom.

It was exactly that – an old-style loom, located beneath a sheet of canvas that had been attached to four poles embedded in the ground. I wandered over one morning to see the women at work. Wearing a burqa and djellaba was like being encased in a sauna. But the three women didn't seem at all fazed by the crazy heat. Watching Maika work the loom, barking orders, stitching with fiendish precision, I couldn't help but wonder how she managed this in the long garment and severe mask that hid all but her eyes. Titrit favoured lighter materials in cream or off-white – but she too was imprisoned in fabrics that covered every inch of her body. Only Naima – still too young to wear the burqa – got away with a headscarf and djellaba. Like her mother and grandmother she never seemed to succumb to the ocean of perspiration that overtook me every time I stepped outside, hidden from worldly view, my eyes and hands the only parts of my anatomy visible.

When I offered to help at the loom, Maika tried to teach me some basic techniques. But the heat overcame me after a few minutes and I was ordered inside.

Water was an issue out here. There was, I discovered, a small water hole within the oasis – and an old-style pump garnered this essential fluid up from the ground. It was rationed by Maika. I was handed an old plastic litre bottle four times a day – and had to make do with that. Which also meant that spending much time outdoors before nightfall was tricky. I was given a large pail of water twice a day for washing. There was a bucket and a rag in the toilet tent to clean myself.

Titrit was home-schooling Naima. Every afternoon they spent several hours on reading and writing and basic mathematics. One morning, Naima came into my tent hugely excited as her father and grandfather had returned from selling their produce at the market and Papa had brought her back a large book. *Tintin*. In Arabic. She showed me its large glossy cover, a little battered in places. I too had read Hergé's books when I was Naima's age, and tried to explain to her that, yes, I knew all about the intrepid Belgian journalist Tintin and his faithful wire-haired terrier Snowy. I asked Naima to read me some of the text. She actually climbed up on my lap to do so, and proceeded to read me the entire book, even sometimes acting out the voices of Tintin, his dog, and the highly egotistical Captain Haddock. Having Naima on my lap, listening to her wondrous singsong voice, feeling the way she snuggled in against me, my longing for a child was immense. So too was my sadness that this would now never be.

I was so engrossed in listening to Naima read to me that I didn't notice Titrit enter the tent, watching us with a smile. When I caught sight of her I was just a little thrown, thinking that she might not like me having her daughter in my lap. Seeing my concern she indicated that this was hardly a problem – and in fact said something to Naima that made her return to her reading.

Later that day, when she returned alone to change my bandages, she touched the engagement and wedding rings on my finger and made a hugging gesture, followed by a touch to her head. It was her way of posing the question: *Where is your husband?* In reply I made an outward flapping motion with my hands, saying: 'He's gone.' She looked at me with great pity. Then touching my stomach and making a curving motion with her hand, she indicated pregnancy. I shook my head. And said:

237

'I want a baby. But . . .'

Even though she might not have understood English she certainly grasped what I was saying. Her reply was:

'*Insha'Allah.*'

Allah willing.

The days passed slowly. As I was still unsteady both physically and psychologically, the languidness of my current existence didn't bother me. Apart from the nightly meals with the family, the arrival of breakfast and lunch in the tent, and Maika and Titrit spending a good hour on my wounds, the highlight of the day was the hour or so I had every late afternoon with Naima. After a morning spent helping her mother and grandmother on the loom, and several hours of tutoring by her mother, she would race over to my tent to spend time with me. Early on, Naima said one word to me while pointing to her mouth:

'English.'

In reply I said one word while pointing to mine:

'*Arabie.*' Which I knew from Essaouira was the word for Arabic.

We spent the next ten days or so teaching each other words, expressions, numbers. I learned how to count to ten in Arabic. Naima got very proficient at English pronouns: I, me, you, he, she, it. I picked up phrases like: '*Shukran min fadocik*' (*Thank you for dinner*), or '*Min fir shreb*' (*I need water*), or '*Fin wan mfouk*' (*You are my friend*). Naima delighted in being able to do the alphabet as far as M – with my promise that we would add two more letters a day.

When the hour was up, Titrit would arrive, Naima would give me a kiss goodbye, and I would have another two hours alone until dinner. I wish I could report that, during the many hours a day I was alone with nothing but my thoughts, I achieved some sort of resolution about the state of my life; resolving somehow to follow Maika's directive and move forward. But what happened frequently was panic attacks on a major level. A desperate sense of falling into a vortex. The agonising replay of everything that had happened in the desert. The barbarous image of my assailant after I had fought back. My sense of horror at what I had been forced to do. Had I truly killed someone? The accompanying terror of discovering that facet within me.

I knew I was still in shock. Whenever I thought of the world outside of this nowhere place to which I had been transported, I knew I couldn't stay here indefinitely. Just as I also knew that the thought of returning to life beyond the oasis seemed out of my reach right now.

I was pleased that the days passed at a languid pace. Just as I could see that, though Idir could actually communicate with me in the basic French we both shared, he kept his distance from me. He never indicated that I was a burden to him or his family. But I was a woman. Apart from the evening meal I was kept out of his life, and I accepted this polite isolation, just as I accepted the burqa when outside. He spoke little to me during dinner, though that was frequently due to the fact that, in the tent where we all ate, there was a small television with a wire antenna that brought in one Moroccan channel. The fact that our encampment had no electricity meant the television was powered by a car battery which they charged using jump cables from the small and ancient truck in which they took their produce to market.

One evening I came in for dinner to discover the five members of the family huddled around the glowing set, watching the evening news. Out of nowhere a photograph appeared behind the news-reader. A photograph of a Western woman. As the broadcast was in Arabic, and as the reception wasn't exactly brilliant, it took me a moment to realise that the photo onscreen was of . . .

But Naima beat me there. Craning her neck towards me, she pointed to the screen. Mouthing one of the English pronouns I'd taught her she said:

'You.'

THE NEWS REPORT: a mugshot of me. A mugshot of Paul. Footage of a crime scene in the desert, with police tape around an area showing scorched earth. And then – oh God, this was beyond bad – footage of Police Inspector Moufad from Essaouira, giving a news conference, holding up the same photograph of me, shaking it vehemently, as if to say: *Here is our prime suspect.*

You.

Me. Now wanted by the police.

Me. Now revealed to these good Samaritans as someone who was on the run. Wanted not just for the disappearance of her husband, but for the death of another man in the desert.

My mind began to race. How were they tying the burnt corpse in the desert to me? Did the goon who'd assisted in my rape drive back to Tata? In his panic did he concoct a story which he fed to the police? He was worried about the welfare of his friend who'd met an American woman last night and invited her on a romantic drive at dawn into the Sahara in her hired car. The discovery by the cops of his pal's charred body – and no sign of me – would lead them to presume that I had turned on him at some juncture, things got out of hand, and I immolated his body before driving off into . . .

No, that's ridiculous. You arrived by bus. You didn't hire a car in Tata. The guy from the hotel would remember, under police questioning, that the two little shits were loitering by the stairs as we headed up to the hotel. So how, why, were they bringing the desert corpse into Paul's disappearance . . . and the fact that I too had now vanished? What incriminated me even further was that I had fled virtual house arrest in Essaouira, much to the fury of Inspector Moufad. He was stabbing my photograph on television with his index finger, as if I was a public health hazard or an escaped war criminal. Apparently they had some sort of evidence to link me to the incinerated body in the Sahara.

Another possibility: the goon got back to Tata, tried to work all day, was in a state of escalating panic as he had my backpack hidden away somewhere, and then suddenly came up with an ingenious solution to his problem. He drove back into the desert, tossed my backpack out near the corpse, returned to Tata, reported his friend missing, said he was cruising an American woman . . . and didn't fill in any further details. How we ended up in that nowhere spot in the Sahara . . . would that truly matter when compared to the smoking-gun evidence of my backpack near the corpse? It would directly link me to the events that culminated in a young man being torched alive in the desert. That had to be why I was now being pursued for the disappearance of my husband, and my link with that gruesome find amidst all that empty sand.

'What are they saying?' I asked Idir. He waved away my question, keeping his attention riveted on the screen. This was worrying. So was the even more hardened look of Maika and her husband. Titrit, meanwhile, was betraying all emotions, appearing both shocked and distressed. When she actually put her hands over Naima's ears, so she could hear nothing more of the broadcast, I sensed trouble.

The news item ended. There was an immediate heated exchange between Immeldine and Idir. When Titrit tried to say something she was shouted down by both her husband and her mother. Naima started crying. I began to panic.

'Please tell me what they said,' I asked Idir.

Out of nowhere Immeldine barked something so fierce at me that Naima hid herself behind her mother.

Then Idir said to me:

'You go. We bring the food to you.'

'If I could just explain—'

'Go!'

I wrapped my face in the burqa and crossed the few steps back to my tent. Once inside, my fear turned into a crazed panic attack, in which I found myself pacing manically around the tiny space, all sorts of extreme scenarios taking over, including Idir and

241

Immeldine deciding that they had to turn me over to the police, and me being thrown into a squalid cell in which I would be repeatedly abused by the guards, and Inspector Moufad from Essaouira conducting an all-night interrogation designed to break me, and me signing a confession that yes, I had killed Paul in a fit of rage on the beach and dumped his body in the Atlantic, and yes, I had agreed to go on an all-night joyride with those two monsters, and when the little shit got a bit fresh with me I lashed out and . . .

Stop this insanity, I hissed at myself. But my brain was on overload. In moments of lucidity I told myself that all the repressed mental trauma of the rape was now finally coming to the surface. But those nanoseconds of clarity were soon subsumed by a full-scale sobbing. All those terrible childhood moments of our family being evicted from a series of houses and apartments came flooding back, with the realisation: *It's happening again. I am being forced out from a place of safety; a family who have given me more love and acceptance and sense of shelter than I've ever had. Now this new family is about to reject me, turning me out into a malevolent world that will engulf me as soon as I am beyond this little oasis.*

My sobs became so convulsive, so out of control, that I felt as if I might become unhinged. My pacing was so frantic that I was literally crashing into corners of the tent, endangering its stability. Suddenly Maika and Titrit rushed in. Titrit had me in her arms in a moment, firmly settling me down on the cot, cradling me, whispering consoling words that had no meaning for me except that they were soothing. She held me as I buried my head in her shoulder, and Maika kept her distance as the grief came cascading forth. Perhaps she knew – given what I had been put through – that this was long overdue. Perhaps she also understood my fear of the world beyond. Whatever the reason she let me cry myself into exhaustion. When I briefly subsided she stepped in, helped Titrit to undress me and get me into the white nightshirt I'd been sleeping in. Laying me down on the cot she rubbed a different kind of balm (it smelled of patchouli and chamomile) across my forehead and into my temples, then massaged the same substance deep into my feet before sitting me up and making me drink an extra-large dosage of the nightly tisane.

Just before surrendering I grasped Maika and Titrit's hands and said one word:

'*Shukran.*'

When I came to I glanced at my watch and was shocked to discover it was almost eleven a.m. Had I really been out for over thirteen hours? When I got off the cot and changed out of the nightshirt and back into the djellaba, I noticed a certain physical stability that had been absent for a long time. Then I started wondering again what would happen if Idir turned me over to the cops and the shakiness began to reassert itself. But I managed to get dressed, wrap the burqa around my face and make it to the toilet without succumbing to another panic attack.

When I returned to my tent I found Idir standing outside.

'I would like to speak to you,' he said.

'Of course,' I replied, motioning that we should go inside. He shook his head vehemently. I instantly regretted my faux pas – there was no way he would enter a tent alone with a woman who wasn't his wife, mother or daughter. He pointed to the tent where we ate dinner. I followed him over, removing my burqa once inside. We had company, as Titrit was chopping vegetables in preparation for lunch. She didn't look up once at me. Idir bent down in front of a little gas stove and lit it, boiling a small kettle of water, opening a tin and throwing a large handful of mint into a pot, filling it with hot water, waiting several minutes for it to steep. Nothing was said during the tea making. Pouring out two glasses he handed one to me and nodded gravely as I thanked him. He motioned for me to sit down on one of the two stools. Then, in his hesitant French, he said:

'I know what happened to you. I am very sorry for that and I do not want to judge you. But . . . the police are looking for you. If they find you here, they will accuse us of hiding you. This will be bad for us. So you have to leave.'

I acknowledged his decision with a nod of my head. He continued:

'I know all your money and papers were stolen.'

I said:

'I don't know what I should do next. I was so unwell after the attack – and for the rest of my life I will never forget the kindness you and your family have shown me. But I haven't really thought about how to proceed.'

He scrunched up his lips.

'The man who drives the rugs and things that the women make . . . he should be here late this afternoon. I will ask him to take you with him. He will be going to Marrakesh, but usually makes many stops along the way.'

'You have to tell him I am wanted by the police.'

'Of course I will tell him that. He is my friend. Go back to your tent now. Think how you will get money and papers – because you will need both. I will get my wife to fetch you when the driver arrives. His name is Aatif.'

With a final nod he left the tent.

A few minutes later, back in the tiny space I was going to be vacating in just a few hours, I tried thinking through a solution to my immense problem. I had no easy answers. The accountant in me reasserted herself for an hour or so, weighing up all the checks and balances available to me. They were virtually non-existent. Say I found a phone and called Morton in the US, and told him he needed to wire money to me. Say that my disappearance had been picked up by international news services, and was also being monitored on the Internet – no doubt a small item, but a husband and wife separately missing in a North African country, with overtones of foul play, would cause interest. Even if Morton wired the funds to a bank or some outpost of Thomas Cook, I would have to show ID to collect them. I had no ID. Then there was the little problem of the previous night's television news bulletin. It is a strange experience, watching a missing person's report in which you are not just the individual the police are trying to track down, but also the chief suspect. Remembering how Moufad had jabbed that photograph of me I was in no doubt that if I simply turned myself in I would be burying myself alive.

So wiring money from overseas was out of the question, especially as the Moroccan version of the FBI and Interpol were probably now monitoring any potential wire transfers in my name. As they had shown my mugshot last night on television there was a good chance that it was going to be a regular feature of news broadcasts until I was apprehended. Would the Moroccan police also put a *Wanted Persons* poster up in post offices and banks and, indeed, anywhere foreigners could collect money? Were they sophisticated enough in their surveillance techniques to have found out my email address and flagged any messages sent or received from it? When Paul first proposed this trip I had quietly googled 'Moroccan terrorism' just to reassure myself that the security situation was as good as he said. Bar the terrible bombing of a Marrakesh tourist café in 2005, and certain warnings about travel in the extreme south, all the reports I read noted that the country was stable. But like every other place on which the spectre of terrorism had fallen, Morocco had very sophisticated intelligence and anti-terrorism apparatus at work – which surely meant the monitoring of telecommunications and the Internet. The fact that a national manhunt was under way for me . . . I was absolutely convinced that the moment I sent or received an email, alarm bells would go off and the geographic location from which it was dispatched or read would be flagged. Yes, I could borrow somebody's cellphone to call the States, but if I couldn't physically collect the money without photo ID, why would I risk a call? Especially as the Moroccan *Sûreté* and the US Embassy here had undoubtedly alerted the NSA and the Feds to my disappearance, and they too were monitoring calls to my office, my home, my professional colleagues.

As I pondered the lack of options open to me I kept twisting the two rings on my left ring finger. Which is when the penny dropped. When Paul proposed to me three years ago – it was during a romantic weekend in Manhattan – he took me to Tiffany's to choose an engagement ring and wedding band. He'd just sold a few lithographs and insisted that I choose a very beautiful single diamond ring and white gold wedding band which together cost

$17,000. When I worried out loud that this was far too much money to be spending on rings he made an amused comment to the very gracious, very formal saleswoman to the effect that 'my wife-to-be understands the bottom line far better than I do'. I could see her smiling politely, taking in Paul's long grey hair and his leather jacket and black jeans, and also telling him the two rings were an elegant choice, and him slapping down his credit card, and me thinking how wonderfully romantic and impetuous my man was, and how I hoped he'd have the funds to clear the bill next month (he didn't).

But now . . . now I had on my left hand one negotiable piece of currency. Surely, if this driver was heading to Marrakesh, there were several serious jewellers there who would be willing to buy my rings. I wouldn't raise anything close to their original value, but I would, at the very least, come out with a decent sum. Perhaps I could then find another driver to get me up to Casablanca. I would barge in on Ben Hassan. I would wave the money in his corrupt face and get him to make me one of his false passports. Then I would find yet another driver to take me to Tangier and the boat to Spain. Once I was on the other side of the water – and out of the shadow of the Moroccan *Sûreté* – I could call Morton and a lawyer and see about persuading the US Embassy in Madrid to issue a new passport to get me home.

So there it was. A plan, of sorts. Getting from here to Marrakesh might not be the simplest of journeys, but I didn't want to consider any of that until I had met the driver, sized him up, and found out his price. I also figured that, if I had plenty of cash in hand, Ben Hassan would provide me with a passport on the spot, and might even get Omar to get me to the ferry up north. With Ben Hassan money always seemed to talk.

But first . . .

There was a terrible moment when Titrit and Naima paid a visit, bringing me an early lunch of pitta and couscous. Naima ran to me, threw her arms around my legs and started to sob, putting together three of the English words I'd taught her:

'You no go.'

When I crouched down beside her she buried her head in my shoulder, weeping. I looked up at one point and saw Titrit also in tears. I held Naima for several moments before loosening myself from her embrace. Keeping my arms around her I said:

'I don't want to go. I don't want to leave you. But I must go home.'

I touched my head and my heart.

'You will always be here and here.'

Naima smiled a sad smile as she too touched her head and heart.

'Here and here,' she repeated, pronouncing each word beautifully. Now I felt tears. I reached beneath my djellaba and unfastened the silver chain around my neck. Bringing it out I showed Naima the sterling-silver horseshoe that had been a gift from my great friend Ruth on a weekend visit to Brooklyn just after Paul and I had decided to try for a child. When I announced this to Ruth she couldn't have been more thrilled, and returned that evening with this small, elegant good-luck charm. No charm could have much luck against an operation guaranteed to render pregnancy impossible. But maybe, just maybe, it had brought me the good fortune to survive my ordeal in the desert and land me here.

I put the chain around Naima's neck, explaining that my best friend had given it to me. And as we were now best friends – I signalled this by pointing to the two of us and then touching my heart – I wanted her to have it. Naima had the horseshoe in her little fingers, looking at it with wonderment. When her grandmother entered the tent a few moments later, holding my clothes in her hands, Naima ran over to her and proudly showed off her gift. Maika smiled gravely at her granddaughter. Approaching me, she handed me my freshly laundered pants and underwear. She also brought a fresh djellaba and a burqa, indicating that I was to keep them – and, through more gestures, also letting it be known that I might need them en route to Marrakesh. Then she did something completely uncharacteristic. Out of nowhere she embraced me. Taking me by both shoulders, she touched one of her leathery hands to my face and said:

'*Allah ybarek feek wal 'ayyam al-kadima.*'

It was a phrase I had heard regularly in Morocco. Here it was a benediction, a maternal prayer: *May Allah bestow his blessings on you in the days to come.*

Outside I heard the sound of a vehicle pulling up into the oasis. We all stiffened as the engine idled, then cut out. My driver had arrived.

Twenty-three

HIS NAME WAS Aatif. At first sight he did not inspire confidence. A short man with a small but pronounced paunch, thinning hair, a handful of brown teeth left in his mouth, world-weary eyes. I judged him to be around my age, but the victim of a hard-scrabble life. His vehicle was a Citroën four-by-four, at least fifteen years old, once white but now scuffed and dented, with two front seats and a reasonable cargo area in the back. It looked as though it was being run into the ground. What struck me immediately about Aatif was his immense shyness. Unlike Immeldine he wasn't taciturn or distanced. Nor did he exude the sort of detached authority that Idir displayed. Rather he seemed almost ill at ease around others. An innocent. And an unsure, timid one at that.

There was a rather strange, awkward moment when Idir called me over. I briefly lifted the burqa and could see Aatif flinch. Was this due to the fact that he wasn't expecting a Western woman (though surely Idir had explained that I was American), or owing to the still-battered nature of my face? I couldn't tell. Without thinking I extended my hand in greeting. He looked horrified, as if I had exposed a breast to him. When he took my hand in return his was cold and clammy.

One positive detail: Aatif spoke French. A somewhat simple French like my own, but with more fluency than Idir. When we started to talk it was clear that we could make ourselves understand each other.

Idir explained that he had informed Aatif about the circumstances that landed me in the oasis. Just as he also understood that I had been robbed of everything; that I had no papers or money; that I would settle up with him when we reached Marrakesh.

'Do you understand that the police are looking for me?' I asked him.

He nodded.

'Does this worry you?'

He shrugged.

'As long as you are willing to take the risk. I don't want to put you in any jeopardy.'

Another shrug. Then he said:

'Two thousand dirhams to take you to Marrakesh. *D'accord?*'

It seemed a very reasonable price, considering the potential hazard for him.

'That's fine – but I am going to need to sell some jewellery in Marrakesh to be able to pay you. I promise that I will pay you.'

A shrug, then:

'*D'accord.*'

'How long do you think it will take to get to Marrakesh?'

He thought about this for a moment.

'Three days.'

'Three days! But it's only a few hours by car from Ouarzazate, and Ouarzazate is perhaps seven from here.'

'I have many goods to pick up before I go to the souk in Marrakesh and deliver them to the merchant who will buy them. Many stops to make, many people dependent on me. Like your friends here.'

'But . . . if we are going to be three days on the road, where will we sleep? I have no money for hotels or food.'

'I have no money for hotels either. I have two bed rolls in the back. We will sleep by the car at night.'

I didn't like the sound of this at all. I gave Idir a telling look, asking with my eyes if I could trust this guy. Idir gave me a quick nod. Aatif noticed this visual exchange. Looking half-away from me he said:

'You will be safe.'

'All right.'

With that Idir and Immeldine spent the next ten minutes filling up around a tenth of the Citroën's cargo area with rugs, lace napkins, lace doilies, skullcaps. I could see Idir negotiating with Aatif, clearly hopeful that he could return next month with a good sum for them. From the way he was indicating his pockets and the sparse garden that was tended beneath one of the trees, I sensed that money here was urgently needed. How I wished I could reach into my pocket and hand them 5,000 dirhams right now.

'When I get to Marrakesh and sell my ring,' I told Idir, holding up my hand, 'I will ask Aatif to bring some money back for you.'

Immediately Idir waved his hands.

'We took you in because you were in need,' he said. 'There is nothing to repay.'

'I cannot begin to thank you . . .'

Again Idir waved his hands, but then thought about it for a moment and made the smallest of bows in my direction. Naima was standing near him. He touched the horseshoe pendant which she was now proudly wearing around her neck and bowed again towards me.

Aatif closed the cargo door of his vehicle. It was time. Titrit started to weep again and held me for several moments. Maika also seemed to be fighting tears, but was absolutely determined not to cry. As she squeezed my shoulder I noticed she had made a fist with her right hand and was, I sensed, demonstrably making it clear that she approved of the way I'd hit back at the men who'd attacked me. Naima glanced up at her father for approval before coming over to me. I knelt down. She kissed me with great delicacy on both cheeks. Intriguingly there were no tears, none of the sense of impending loss that we had shared with the other women in the tent that had been my refuge. Here, in front of her father and grandfather and a visiting man, she was conscious that she needed to act with restraint. After a moment she went running back to her father, looking up at him for approval – which he gave with one of his characteristic nods.

Idir's goodbye was also a nod. So too was Immeldine's.

'OK?' Aatif asked. Now it was my turn to nod. Moments later I was inside the cab of the vehicle. The three women gathered by my window as Aatif slammed the driver's door behind him, turned the key in the ignition, put the van into gear. With a lurch we began to drive off. My eyes met Naima's as she raised a hand and tried to look brave. Behind the burqa I began to weep. The daughter I always wanted. The daughter I would never have. The wondrous little girl whom I would never see again.

Aatif drove the hundred or so yards to the edge of the oasis. I looked back once more at the small plot of quasi-arable land in the great sandy vacuum. Their entire world. My entire world for a spell. And now I was going to have to negotiate the malevolent world beyond.

With a bump we crossed through the stone archway that separated the oasis from the desert. Aatif pulled out a lever and said:

'Four-by-four. We will need it now.'

We started crossing the sand, following a track discernible by the grooves of past tyres. After a minute I craned my neck and tried to spy the oasis. But it had vanished, its pale wall melding invisibly into the bleached horizon.

The cab of the vehicle was a mess. The seats were torn, there was trash strewn on the floor, the windscreen was streaked with sand and dead flies, the ashtray was brimming. And the heat was ferocious. I rolled down my window. This was a serious error. As the vehicle gained momentum, sand blew in everywhere. Immediately Aatif slowed down.

'You do not have to wear the burqa here,' he said.

'Are you sure of that?'

'It is fine with me. Especially as I do not have air conditioning. So if you also want to get out of the djellaba . . .'

I was instantly post-traumatic defensive.

'What do you mean by that?' I asked.

He looked startled.

'I meant no offence. I just thought you might be more comfortable in your own clothes.'

'Where I am going to change out here?'

He stopped the vehicle and got out, then went to the back and pulled out the bag containing my laundered clothes; the ones I'd been found in all those weeks ago. He brought it over to the passenger door.

'You can get out and change behind the car. I will take a walk and have a smoke. When you are dressed call me.'

He said all this in his quiet, shy, matter-of-fact way.

'Thank you,' I said, getting out.

Aatif circled around the bonnet and walked out quite a distance into the desert, lighting up a cigarette. He was dressed in a loose shirt, loose brown trousers, sandals, a skullcap on his head. I watched him walk for about a minute, then stop and not turn around once in my direction. Quickly I pulled off the djellaba, the relief of being free of its entombing weight countered by the immediate exposure of all my damaged flesh to the Saharan sun. Within a moment I had slipped on the linen pants and simple white shirt I had bought in Casablanca, then shouted that I was ready. Aatif turned and walked back slowly towards me. At that instant I began to feel shaky. For the first time since I'd woken up violated, battered and near death I was back in the Sahara's terrifying enormity. I felt as if it was about to swallow me whole and I slumped against the door of the jeep, blindsided by a full-scale panic attack. At which point Aatif – walking towards me – saw what was happening and came running. When he reached me, out of breath and drenched in sweat, I was clinging onto the door handle as if it was a life belt in treacherous seas.

'Can I help you?' he asked.

I nodded.

'May I take your arm?'

I nodded again.

He took hold of my hand that was gripping the door handle. His other hand supported my right arm.

'Let go, please,' he said. 'I will get you inside.'

I did as he told me to, all but collapsing against him. He might have appeared short and squat, but when it came to disengaging my grip from the car door and settling me into the passenger seat, he had surprising strength.

Once I was safely inside he went to the cargo area, fished something out and returned with a bottle of water, still dripping wet, making me wonder if he had some sort of basic cooler in the back. He handed me the bottle.

'Drink,' he said.

I drank half the litre before handing it to him. He took several judicious sips, then gave it to me again.

'You need to keep drinking water.'

'Thank you,' I said. 'Thank you so much. I am sorry I snapped at you before. I had a terrible experience out here.'

'I know. Idir told me. Terrible. I am so very sorry for you. But . . .'

He turned the ignition on. The Citroën reassuringly fired back into life. He put it into gear. We set off. And he finished the sentence.

'. . . I will get you to Marrakesh.'

I fell back against the seat, the agitation and anguish still coursing through me. Aatif lit up a cigarette and said nothing as we drove for almost an hour along the desert track, the sun beginning to dip, bathing the Sahara in a blue-hour glow. How I wanted to be dazzled and exalted by its frightening beauty. But all I could do was try to stop myself from sinking into a chasm in which all the recent horrors loomed large.

To his credit Aatif said not a word as we barrelled across the sands. He just smoked one cigarette after another, occasionally glancing over at me to make certain I wasn't going into meltdown again. I appreciated him giving me the space to somehow push the nightmare away . . . for an hour or two anyway.

That's the problem with the worst sort of trauma. You can will it elsewhere. You can tell yourself you will somehow 'manage' it. But you also begin to realise very quickly that, once subjected to its ghastly contours, you are now going to live with it for the rest of your life. Even if, somewhere down the line, you might come to terms with it, reach some sort of accommodation with its abhorrence, it will be with you for ever. Your world has inexorably changed because of what it has visited upon you.

With a bump we left the sand and returned to a paved road. Seeing a sign ahead for Tata, I shuddered.

'Do not worry,' Aatif said. 'We are not going there. But I am going to pull over in a moment and you are going to have to change back into the djellaba and a burqa.'

'Why?'

'Because two, three kilometres ahead of us, there is a police checkpoint.'

'How do you know that?'

'I passed through it a few hours ago.'

He slowed down. We were on an empty stretch of the road leading to Ouarzazate. He pulled over, telling me that, thanks to nightfall, I could change outside without being seen. But if a car came down the road, headlights blazing . . .

'I'll be quick,' I said, and was out of the car and grabbing my backpack, changing into the djellaba and burqa in under a minute. As soon as I got back in a truck came up behind us, its high-beams illuminating us.

'You did well,' Aatif said as it passed by.

'What happens if the police demand to see my papers?' I asked.

He reached over into the glove compartment and drew out a Moroccan identity card of a woman around my age – attractive in a severe sort of way, but like all mugshots capturing disappointment in grainy, institutional close-up.

'Is that your wife?' I asked.

'My sister.'

'Doesn't she need her papers?'

'Not any more. She's dead.'

'She was so young.'

'Cancer doesn't care how young or old you are.'

He lit another cigarette.

'Anyway, when the police stop us, I will tell them that you are my sister.'

'And if they ask me any questions?'

'They won't. Because you are behind the burqa, and they would have to think us terrorists to ask you to remove your veil. I drive these roads frequently. I can't say I know all the policemen, or that they know me . . .'

'But if you are from around here . . .'

'I live in a village many hours from Ouarzazate. If we were going through that *département* I wouldn't dream of passing you off as my sister. Everyone knew her. Everyone knows she's dead. But here – no problem.'

'But if they do still question me?'

'Say nothing. I will tell them you are deaf and dumb.'

Five minutes later we were at the checkpoint. Two uniformed cops had their squad car half-blocking the road. They greeted Aatif and asked to see identification. He handed over the two sets of papers. One of the cops shone a flashlight on me. I kept my eyes – barely visible through the slit of the burqa – fixed on the road ahead, and after a moment the beam of light snapped off. They asked Aatif to step outside the car. I heard him answering their many questions, then opening the cargo door and letting them search inside. The mounting terror I felt was immense. If the beam was turned on me again I knew I would go under. And reveal very quickly that I was the woman all of Morocco was looking for.

But within moments Aatif was back in the car, the officer was wishing him a good night, and we were driving off.

A fresh cigarette lit, Aatif exhaled a huge cloud of smoke, his relief tangible. Finally he said:

'The first checkpoint behind us.'

Twenty-four

WE SLEPT ON the outskirts of a small village, which Aatif told me was around thirty minutes from Tata. This village, a nowhere place off a semi-paved track from the main thoroughfare on which we were travelling, was called Sidi Boutazart. It was en route to the first stop Aatif would need to make early tomorrow morning. I didn't want to stay anywhere near Tata, so he suggested we camp here.

'I know a little area that is quiet and where no one will see us,' he said.

This area turned out to be a small plot of arable ground, shaded by a single meagre tree. A few cows and goats grazed nearby. As before Aatif wanted to assure me of his correctness when it came to our travel arrangements. He took out the two bed rolls and lay one down on either side of the car. Each was a thin cotton mattress with two light sheets, and some netting that he suggested I put over my face when I slept in case the sand flies came out early. When I'd been in the oasis sand flies had been an ongoing problem during daylight hours. At night they vanished into the ether. But come sunrise they were on the attack again. Which is why, as Aatif explained, it was essential to get to bed early and rise just before dawn.

'You don't need an alarm clock out here,' he said. 'The sand flies provide that.'

With the light fading he moved to his own bed roll, positioned himself in what I presume was the direction of Mecca, prostrated himself on his knees, and with his head touching the mattress, spent several moments saying his evening prayers. When finished he opened the back of the four-by-four and retrieved a small styrofoam box – out of which came a small gas burner, a pot, two plates, two forks – and made us a simple dinner of bread and couscous with a few carrots thrown in. Over dinner – which we had on my side – I asked him about himself. He told me he came from a village called M'hamid, around four or five hours' drive from here. It was at the end of a paved road that started at Ouarzazate, then passed through an important Berber town called Zagora, before dead-ending at his village, beyond which was the Sahara. He considered himself very much a Berber and therefore had decidedly mixed feelings about the government in Rabat.

'I deal with the police politely,' he said, 'the functionaries who regulate our *département*. But I also like being able to work around them, not to let them control me. I am not alone in this sentiment. Which is one of the reasons why I said yes to getting you to Marrakesh. If you are on the run from them—'

'They think I harmed my husband.'

'It is not my business whether you did or didn't.'

'I promise you, I didn't.'

'If you say that I believe you.'

'But what you also need to understand . . .'

Out came the entire story in one exhalation. I kept it short, and didn't get into the reason why Paul vanished – except to say that I had discovered a betrayal on his part. I also explained about the police inspector in Essaouira who was determined to frame me. And the friend of my husband in Casablanca who had cheated him. Then the events in Tata and beyond.

Aatif listened in silence. When I had finished he lit one cigarette off the other.

'That policeman in Essaouira . . . I've known people who have been persecuted by men like that. They decide you are guilty. They will run you to the ground, changing evidence and everything else to ensure they can win the conviction. They are not Berbers.'

I then explained my plan about selling my rings in Marrakesh, getting to Casablanca and bribing that shady former friend of my husband to give me a false passport and get me out of the country.

'I want to be direct with you. I don't want to hide anything. I want you to understand all the risks here.'

'I saw your face on television before I came out to the oasis,' he said. 'So when Idir told me it was you I was to take to Marrakesh . . .'

A pause, then the smallest of smiles crossed his face.

'Now that I know we need to outsmart that police inspector – well, a game is a game, *n'est-ce pas*?'

The night sky above us was astonishing. In the oasis I was put to bed most evenings at sunset. Here I got my first proper glimpse of the celestial floor show on display. The clarity in the desert was dazzling. Such density of constellations. Such a sense of heavenly potential. Even deep in the country, just ten miles from Buffalo, on a perfectly clear night you could never discern even thirty per cent of what was apparent here. It was like discovering an entire added component to the universe. My dad always said that looking up at a constellation underscored our insignificance. But tonight, seeing such immense radiance – particularly in the light of recent events – was galvanising. I looked to the stars and they told me that since nothing, in the great cosmic scheme of things, is important, everything that defines us is vitally important. What else do we have but our lives, our stories?

'It is an amazing sky,' I said to Aatif.

'Nice, yes,' he said, sounding less than overwhelmed.

'I wish I could believe in heaven, in some sort of eternal paradise. I thought about that when I saw you praying earlier.'

'It is important to believe in paradise. Especially when life is hard.'

'Faith is a complex thing.'

He thought about that for a moment.

'No, faith is simple. And good.'

'Do you have children?'

I saw him tense and apologised for asking what was clearly the wrong question.

He lit another cigarette. After several long drags he asked me if I would like tea – and told me that Maika had given him several days' supply of the tisane that had repeatedly knocked me out. This was welcome news, as I had been wondering how well I'd sleep out here under the desert sky.

'A mug of that would be wonderful.'

He went off to fetch water from a big plastic container in the

259

back, then boiled it in a pot on top of the stove. Knowing how swiftly the tea induced sleep I told Aatif I was going to change into my nightshirt before drinking it. He stood up and walked a good distance away. I retrieved my bag and quickly changed, then hiked in the opposite direction from Aatif, lifted up my nightshirt and baptised the sand. How strange to think that everything I had once taken for granted – like a toilet or the Internet or even a phone – had been out of reach for so long. And how I had adapted – because I'd had no choice but to do so.

As soon as I'd finished the mug of tea I wished Aatif goodnight. Crawling in between the two sheets, I placed the netting over my head and stared up at the luminescent heavens above. Just before sleep overtook me I glanced over at my companion. He had walked out into the middle of the nearby unpaved road to smoke another cigarette and he too was looking up into the great lustrous unknown. I saw him wipe his eyes. Was he crying?

But then the tea did its magic and the world vanished for a spell.

Aatif was right. The sand flies, arriving with first light, were a pernicious outdoor alarm clock. At least ten of the wretched creatures were dancing on the net covering my face. Light was cleaving the sky.

Aatif was already awake, making tea. He wanly waved hello.

'Sleep well?' I asked.

'OK.'

'Where are we headed today?'

'We go back to the main road. I have stops in several villages. You will need to cover yourself. There may be roadblocks.'

So I changed yet again. By the time we hit the road I was already bathed in sweat.

'First stop is Tissint – about an hour from here,' Aatif said.

We headed back to the main road. The sun seemed even more ferocious this morning. When I pulled down the visor to try to mitigate its blinding effects Aatif reached over and opened the glove compartment, pulling out a pair of sunglasses with red plastic frames.

'You can use these.'

I thanked him, but when I unveiled myself in order to put them on, he hissed:

'Get the burqa on now!'

I looked up. We'd hit a bend in the road. Right in front of us was a roadblock with a police car parked so as to only allow one car through at a time. Fortunately there was a big truck ahead, but I saw one of the officers glancing in our direction just as I got the burqa back in place. Had he seen me? If so, was this the beginning of the end?

The police were being very rigorous with the truck, demanding to see the driver's papers, opening up the rear of his vehicle, searching thoroughly inside.

'If he asks you a question say nothing,' Aatif whispered.

'And if he makes me take off the burqa?'

'Say nothing.'

The inspection of the truck completed, we pulled up to the squad car. Taped to one of the rear passenger windows was a poster in Arabic and French with my mugshot adorning it. The French words needed no translation:

Personne disparue – Recherchée par la police.

Aatif also saw the poster and gripped the steering wheel tightly as the young policeman – he couldn't have been more than twenty-two – stuck his head in through the window and demanded identity papers. Aatif had them to hand. Meanwhile his older colleague was at the rear of the vehicle, opening it up and pulling out all the neatly stacked rugs and lace goods. The young officer seemed super-vigilant, asking a considerable number of questions, demanding the vehicle registration papers – which Aatif supplied – then repeating questions thrown from the other officer about the goods in the back. Aatif answered these politely. But when the young cop got tetchy, Aatif's voice also became just a little defensive. Then the older officer sidled up to my window and began to question me in Arabic. Fear coursed through me and it was a good thing he couldn't see how much I was sweating. But I kept my eyes fixed on the road ahead and, as instructed by Aatif, said nothing. The officer, irritated, reached in and tapped me on the arm. I turned to face him, but remained silent. Aatif was now saying something angrily to him, and whatever it was the cop backed away from me. Aatif continued, gesturing to the back of the four-by-four, tapping himself on the chest, pointing to me. The young officer exchanged a glance with his older colleague, then they both walked to the squad car with our papers. I glanced at Aatif. He refused to look at me, instead gripping the steering wheel, trying to remain calm. He looked over at the police car and saw again the poster with my photo on it. He closed his eyes, clearly regretting that I was here with him. I wanted to say something, but knew I had to stay silent. After what seemed like an eternity while the older officer read out the ID details over a police radio (would the centralised system register that the woman whose identity I was travelling under was actually dead?) he came marching towards us.

But instead of ordering me out of the car and uncovering my face, the officer handed back the two cards to Aatif. With a dismissive flick of the wrist he informed him that we were free to go.

Aatif muttered a thank-you, put the car into gear and drove.

Five minutes later, with the checkpoint far behind us and the road empty of cars, I turned to him and said:

'I'm smothering in here. I have to take this off.'

Aatif said nothing but I could see he was not pleased. Pulling off the burqa I caught sight of myself in the rear-view mirror. My hair was drenched, my face beet red, terror in my eyes. Aatif handed me the bottle of water.

'Finish it,' he said. 'You need it. We'll get more in the next village.'

'I am so sorry.'

'For what? You did exactly what I told you to do. The police – they were just being difficult. When the officer asked about you I explained that you were mentally disabled, and could not understand him. He asked for proof. I told him to pull off your burqa and interrogate you – but that he would face serious consequences afterwards. That was when he backed off. But you saw the posters. Roadblocks are normal, but there are not usually so many. The police are looking for you and that makes using the main roads difficult. There will be no more checkpoints between here and Tazenakht, and all the villages where I pick up goods are on that route. We will have to find a back way for tomorrow.'

'We were lucky with your sister's ID.'

'We only buried her two weeks ago. They probably haven't registered her death as yet on their computers in Rabat.'

'But that's terrible. You should be having some time off.'

'I have to work. My sister left two children. Their father is in the army stationed in the Western Sahara, near Mauritania. He sends back little money. My mother is looking after them, but she is a widow and elderly. So I have to work.'

'Listen, that was a close call back there. I don't want you to get into trouble, lose your livelihood—'

'I said I would get you to Marrakesh. I will get you to Marrakesh.'

Ten minutes later we pulled into the village of Tissint. A row of low-lying buildings, dusty, fly-festooned; a butcher's with bleeding carcasses, a few cafés, a mechanic's shop, idle young men everywhere, the stench of rotting sewage amidst the blast-furnace heat. Aatif's client was a large cheery woman who lived in a tiny lean-to house on the outskirts of the village. She insisted on offering us tea. I could hear Aatif explaining about me, using, I presumed, the excuse about my mental state. She smiled sheepishly at me as she helped him load up the intricately decorated velvet bedspreads and cushion covers that she made. Before we left she clutched his right hand with two of her own, apparently making some sort of plea.

When we were back in the car and heading to our next stop I asked him what her entreaty was all about.

'She was telling me that her husband has been unwell. They have two young children. Because he is in hospital – and not expected to live – they are entirely dependent on the sale of what she makes, which I will sell to my merchant in Marrakesh.'

'Do you have to negotiate with him for your clients?'

'Of course. He is a businessman and he wants to buy at as low a price as possible.'

'So you fight on their behalf?'

'It is on my behalf too. I get thirty-five per cent of all their sales. The more I get for my clients the more I get for myself.'

'How much did that woman back there ask you to get for her?'

'She told me she needs fifteen hundred dirhams. That will get her and her two children through this month. Which means I need to sell her items for a bit over two thousand dirhams. This is not easy, as the merchant tells me the market is very bad right now. Not as many tourists as before – even though there is little trouble in Morocco. But I still argue hard for them.'

'Can you make a living out of this?'

He seemed a little taken aback by the directness of my question. But then he said:

'I can support myself. Trying to support a family . . .'

'Do you have a family?'

'Just my other sister who lives in Zagora. A schoolteacher. The only one of us who got a proper education. She is married to another teacher and they have two children. So I am an uncle.'

'But no wife or children of your own?'

'Not yet. But I have met a woman I like very much. Hafeza. She is a bit younger than me. Twenty-eight. A seamstress. Very kind with a good heart. And she would like many children like me. She's also from my village – which means I know her family. I also know that several men before have asked for her hand, but she is very choosy. So, alas, is her father. He has told me that, though Hafeza wishes to be my wife, I cannot have her unless I can buy a house.'

'He wants you to buy a whole house outright?'

'Not outright – but he wants me to make – how do you say it? – a payment up front?'

'A downpayment?'

'That's right.'

'And how much would that cost?'

'I've found a little place. Four rooms. Simple, but enough space.

264

The price . . . one hundred thousand dirhams. I have saved over the last year maybe ten thousand. But the bank wants me to put down forty thousand before they give me a loan.'

'And Hafeza's father is adamant?'

'Until I can move us into that house she will not be my wife.'

'That's a little rigid of him.'

'I wish I could make more money faster. When I am back in my village I repair bicycles – a second trade. But it maybe brings in three, four hundred dirhams a month.'

Forty thousand dirhams. That was just under five thousand dollars. Which meant the house itself cost around twelve thousand four hundred dollars. Less than a very basic car back home. The sum standing between Aatif and his dream of a wife, a family.

'You've never been married?' I asked.

He shook his head.

'That's surprising.'

'Why?'

'You are an extremely nice and honourable man – and there are few of that species out there.'

His reaction to this was a touching mixture of embarrassment and embarrassed pride.

'You shouldn't say such things.'

'Why not?'

'It will give me a big head,' he said, all smiles.

He lit up a cigarette. The smile quickly faded.

'Ten years ago,' he said, 'I proposed marriage to another woman from my village. Amina. She said yes. Then a man came through one day from Ouarzazate. A baker named Abdul. He owned three bakeries there. He met Amina. One week later he returned to see her father and propose marriage. Of course the father said yes. Because he had money and I have none.'

'I can see why trying to find that forty thousand dirhams is so important.'

'I will never get it. Her father has given me a year to do it, no more.'

'And the bank won't loan you more?'

265

'I have a cousin who works at the bank in Zagora which is why I am getting the loan. But I make so little . . .'

From the look on his face I could see that Aatif wanted to get off this subject quickly; that even speaking about all this was, on a certain level, a voyage into territory he rarely discussed . . . especially with a woman.

We stopped at a village called Melimna, where an elderly woman loaded up the van with several dozen white linen tablecloths and napkins. I got to use a proper flush toilet for the first time in weeks. There were additional stops in Foum Zguid and Alougoum – tiny, sandstruck villages, with a few local shops, a café or two, and many men, young and old, loitering in the streets. At each stop Aatif was greeted in such a warm and welcoming manner that it was clear that the women whose goods he delivered to market trusted him as an honest broker. Again I could see everyone's interest in this woman travelling with him – someone who clearly needed a lot of water behind her burqa. At every stop I entreated him to score us an additional two litres as I was seriously dehydrating encased in all those clothes. Aatif was adept at explaining away my presence, and also telling everyone that a defect at birth had robbed me of both speech and reason.

By the time we left Alougoum on a sandy half-paved side road, it was late afternoon and I could no longer stand being imprisoned in the strict Islamic dress.

'Surely we can risk me getting out of these clothes for a while.'

Aatif thought about this.

'We are going to get to Tazenakht – a town, not a village – by nightfall. I know a place beyond it where we can sleep for the night. Until then – this road is not much travelled, because it is unsurfaced. The police rarely set up checkpoints here. So, if you must change . . .'

He pulled over and went for another smoke as I got out of the burqa and djellaba, slipping back into the linen pants and shirt that were still sweat-stained from yesterday, but a complete liberation after the confinement in which I had been living.

Back in the car he had a question for me:

266

'You have no children. Is this your choice?'

I paused before explaining the problems I had with my first and second husbands. I was certain that Aatif would think I was damaged goods if two men didn't want children with me. But what he said instead surprised and disarmed me:

'So you've had bad luck with men.'

'Or maybe my choice of men . . .'

'. . . was not worthy of you.'

I was about to thank him for such a lovely comment when, out of nowhere, we both heard the sound of a motorcycle approaching us from behind. Aatif immediately tensed. As did I.

'Pull over,' I hissed at him, thinking I could jump out and hide behind the vehicle until the bike had passed.

'Too late,' he hissed back, as the motorcycle sidled right up by our vehicle in the process of overtaking us. There were a man and a woman aboard, both in their twenties, both in jeans and denim shirts, both Caucasians. The woman smiled as they drove by. But seeing me she poked the guy steering the bike and said something urgently to him.

'Accelerate,' I told Aatif.

But it was too late for that. The bike had stopped directly in front of us, and the man and woman had dismounted and were pulling off their helmets. They both looked super-fit, well-heeled. They waved at us to stop. Aatif looked at me, wondering what to do.

'I'll deal with this,' I said.

Aatif slowed the car to a stop. I got out. The couple approached me.

'*Parlez-vous français?*' the man asked in an accent which made it clear he was French.

I nodded.

'Are you all right?' the woman asked.

'Yes, fine. Why?'

'Aren't you the American woman everyone's been looking for?'

'We've seen your picture everywhere.'

I had a decision to make – deny it and arouse their suspicion, or . . .

'Yes, I'm that woman. And yes, this man is driving me to the nearest police station to let everyone know I am all right.'

'What happened?'

'That's a long story.'

'We could come with you.'

'That's very kind but there's no need.'

I could see them staring at Aatif, trying to size up if he was dangerous or holding me against my will.

'I would feel better if we accompanied you to Tazenakht,' the man said.

'Again, my thanks for such a generous offer. But I can assure you – I am not in any danger here. On the contrary, this man has got me out of a great deal of danger.'

They exchanged a glance. I could sense that they were wondering about my mental state, especially as I was clearly trying not to be nervous.

'I can talk to your driver if you like,' the man said.

It was time to end this.

'I'm grateful for your kindness. But—'

'Will you agree to meet us at the police station in Tazenakht?'

Damn these good Samaritans. Damn myself for taking off the burqa. I had to think fast.

'I'll tell you what – I'm sure there's a café on the main drag. Say I meet you there in an hour? Then you can make sure I'm all right.'

'We should follow them,' the woman said in an undertone not meant for my ears.

'And I have to phone Paris in thirty minutes. So we'll go to the police station, tell them that we've seen her en route to Tazenakht and put it in their hands.'

'By all means tell them,' I said. 'But the thing is, I'll be seeing them as soon as I pull into town . . .'

The couple exchanged a look, and glanced again at Aatif.

'OK,' the man finally said. 'See you in Tazenakht.'

'The café on the main drag,' I said, hoping there was one. 'We can have a beer.'

The man checked his watch. He clearly had a scheduled call to make. Reluctant to leave me they walked back to the bike and shot off towards the horizon.

As soon as they were out of sight I rushed back to the car and climbed in. Aatif could tell that the conversation with the French couple hadn't gone brilliantly.

'We have to get off this road,' I said. 'Now.'

Twenty-five

AATIF THOUGHT FAST. If we headed south back to the main road at Foum Zguid, we would hit something of a dead end, as the road east was unpaved. He knew this because his own village, M'hamid, was a fifty-kilometre straight line from here. But the desert track passed through treacherous sand dunes. Vehicles got bogged down in them – and at this time of year, with temperatures ferociously high, a horrible death was not out of the question.

'Even if there was a direct road to M'hamid, it would be very hard to bring you to my village.'

'Understood.'

'But if we go west for Foum Zguid the road brings us very far south. Then we would have to head north through Agadir. Big tourist town. Many police.'

His solution: he had one more pick-up of goods to make in a tiny village of Asaka, only around ten kilometres inland from here down a narrow desert track. He had a client there whom he was planning to visit in two weeks' time. But she always had goods on hand.

'I'll tell her that I have a little extra room in the back. There is another track near her house. We can sleep there tonight.'

'Mightn't the police come looking for us there?'

'They will have been told by the French tourists that you were in a car with a Moroccan. If we are lucky they won't mention the make of the car. But even so there are many vehicles like this here. You will have to go back behind the burqa. It's the only way we can make it to Marrakesh. If we leave early tomorrow the police in Tazenakht will probably think we headed south. There may still be a roadblock, but my hope is that if they see me driving a woman in a burqa it will fool them again.'

Stepping behind the car I cloaked myself again. Then, with the light receding, we drove slightly north before turning right down a desert track. Unlike some of the other unpaved roads on which

I had travelled this one was treacherous – an uneven surface featuring many ruts and the sandy equivalent of potholes. We bumped along at less than fifteen kilometres an hour, our progress slow, torturous. The landscape here was a return to the absolute remoteness of the oasis, only there was not the same sense of wide-open space. Rather it felt as if we were moving towards some cul-de-sac, from which there was no way out. There was a narrow barrenness to this route; a sense of heading to the end of the line.

'I can see why the cops wouldn't want to follow us out here,' I said.

'Which is why we need to stay here until sunrise.'

It took us almost an hour to reach the village of Asaka, which had just four houses. The one at which we stopped was lived in by a man in his fifties with a young wife and four children, all of whom seemed to be under the age of six. The wife was still pretty, but clearly beaten down by life. She barked at her children. She barked at her husband who sat on a stool, smoking and looking quietly disconsolate. She barked at Aatif, berating him for something while getting her two oldest kids to load up his van with the djellabas she had made. When her husband offered tea Aatif declined, pointing to the road and making some excuse about needing to get north soon.

As soon as Asaka was behind us, Aatif steered the vehicle down a track so narrow, so hemmed in by sand on either side, that it was just wide enough for our one vehicle. We bumped along for about quarter of an hour until we reached a small clearing by which there was a pump. Here we parked and set up camp for the night. Aatif said that, with a full load in the van, we could cut short the trip and get to Marrakesh late tomorrow evening, but only if we left before dawn. That was fine by me. The sooner I could get to Marrakesh the sooner I could sell my jewellery.

'The water, it is not good for drinking,' Aatif said as he got one of the jerrycans of water out of the rear of the vehicle; a cargo area now so jammed with goods that there was little room for the spare cans of fuel and water that he carried. He used the clean water to make tea and couscous. I asked him if I could wash at the pump. He told me that I shouldn't use more than four or five pulls, as water was so scarce out here that we mustn't use much. Especially as the next person coming along might be in desperate need of it.

He put the couscous on to boil, then walked off. I stripped down and pumped the water. The first dispatch of liquid was revoltingly brown, the second a little more neutral. The third looked relatively clear. I had no soap, no toothbrush (I hadn't brushed my teeth since that last night in Tata), no basin. Still, the feel of water against my bare skin was restorative. I got into my nightshirt, my skin still wet.

'That woman, she is always complaining, always bitter,' Aatif said as we ate. 'But that is not my Hafeza. She is far too kind to turn into such an angry woman.'

I thought that trying to raise four kids in the middle of nowhere, and in poverty, would make anyone bitter.

Instead I said:

'I am happy for you that you have found someone nice.'

'I will be happy if I can give her father what he wants. You have dowries in America?'

'No, not exactly. But trust me, when it comes to the end of love, it's all about money.'

'Money is not everything,' he said. 'But without it . . .'

'What else would you like, besides a house for you and Hafeza?'

'A mobile phone. It would be very useful for my business. I had one for a while, but it was expensive. Then I had to start saving for a house. So I could not afford the phone any more. Beyond that, a new television maybe. Mine is fifteen years old, and the picture is very bad. And of course, Hafeza will want to furnish the house.'

The hope in his face was so touching. I feared for him if he could not find the money necessary to win her hand. Not that he would fall apart, but that he would know further disappointment.

Night fell. I opened my bed roll, but found the ground near the car far too uneven. So I told Aatif I was going to move behind a small dune just a few feet from the vehicle. I wished him a good night, carried the bed roll over and laid it out. Then, after downing my evening dosage of knock-out tea that Aatif had prepared, I crawled between the sheets, placed the mosquito net over my head, and lay staring up at the stars, thinking: *Tomorrow I will be in a city. Will I ever again see a night sky so vast and clear as this?*

Sleep descended quickly. But then, out of nowhere, I heard voices. Angry, threatening voices. I stirred awake as they grew louder. It was still night. I glanced at my watch. Four-twelve a.m. I crawled out of my bed roll and crept to the edge of the sand dune. Poking my head around it I saw four men – I couldn't determine their ages – surrounding Aatif. Two of them were holding him while the other two were emptying his van of all its goods. When Aatif pleaded with them, one of them slapped him hard across the face. I ducked back behind the dune. Frantically digging a hole in the sand I pulled off my two rings and my father's Rolex and buried them, finding a rock on the ground to mark the spot. Then I sat very still, terrified of what might happen next.

More voices, more entreaties from Aatif. The sound of a punch and Aatif now crying. Then vehicle doors opening and slamming, Aatif issuing one last plea, a car engine rumbling into life, wheels moving away along the sand. I waited a good five minutes just to be certain that those men weren't coming back. Then I dug up my rings and watch and dashed over. I found Aatif lying in the sand, holding his stomach, crying loudly.

'Thieves, thieves . . . they took everything.'

I tried to put my arms around him to help him up, but he recoiled at my touch.

'Are you OK?' I asked.

. 'They slapped my face, they punched me in the stomach, they took everything out of the van. They even found my wallet and stole my four hundred dirhams. The only money I had . . .'

He got himself to his knees, put his face in his hands and started weeping again.

'I have no luck,' he sobbed. 'No luck at all. Life . . . it is too hard.'

I reached out and put a steadying hand on his shoulder.

'You're alive,' I said. 'And there is always a solution.'

'A solution? A solution? I'm ruined.'

'You're not ruined.'

'Those thieves . . . they have wiped me out. All the goods in the car, gone. I have no money to get us to Marrakesh . . .'

'You filled the tank today. And you also filled the two jerrycans you keep in the back. Did they steal those?'

'I don't know.'

I scrambled over to the vehicle, praying to some almighty force in that brilliantly lit sky above to let me find those two full jerrycans. I threw open the back door. Bingo! They were there, along with two full cans of water.

'We've got fuel,' I said. 'Two full jerrycans, plus the near-full tank. Will that be enough to get us to Marrakesh?'

He nodded.

'That's one good piece of news. Here's my next question – how much were the goods you were transporting likely to make for their producers?'

He did some quick calculations in his head.

'If I was to get them the best price . . . maybe eight thousand dirhams.'

'And you would be getting thirty-five per cent of the total price, which means that you would have needed to sell them all for twelve thousand dirhams.'

Aatif looked at me, bemused.

'Why are you so you with numbers?'

'It's my job. Anyway, if we get on the road for Marrakesh now, how long will it take us to drive there?'

'Maybe ten, twelve hours.'

'Do you know a good jeweller there?'

'I know people who know people who know jewellers.'

'So here's the solution. We give those bastards half an hour to get out of the area, then we'll get on the road, I'll wear the burqa all the way to Marrakesh to get us through the checkpoints. When we get to the city we'll find a jeweller who will give me the price I want, and I will give you the two thousand dirhams I owe you

274

for driving me . . . and twelve thousand as well for the goods stolen from you. So all your clients who are so dependent on you will get paid. And you'll get paid too.'

'I can't accept this,' he said.

'You're going to accept this. Because it was my stupidity that made me take off the burqa and let the French couple see me. Which led us down the back path. Which led you to being robbed. So you have no choice but to accept the money. Are we clear about that?'

He stifled a sob, rubbing his eyes with his hardened hands.

'I don't deserve such kindness.'

'Yes, you do. We all deserve kindness. And bad luck, *monsieur*, can change.'

He stood up, taking several deep steadying breaths.

'*Thé à la menthe?*' he finally asked.

'That would be very good right now,' I said, my adrenalin only beginning to subside after that chilling wake-up call – and the terrifying thought that history might have repeated itself out here, had I not been hidden behind that dune. I felt a shudder coming on and hugged myself. Aatif saw this attack of nerves – and did something unexpected. He reached out and put a hand on my shoulder.

'OK, *le thé*,' he said, trying to smile. 'And then . . . Marrakesh.'

IT TOOK US almost thirteen hours to reach Marrakesh. It was a hellish drive. When Aatif first got behind the wheel after the robbery his hands were shaking. He started to sob. I took hold of his arm until he subsided. Then, lighting a cigarette, he put the van into gear and hit the accelerator. We bumped along the rutted sand tracks for almost an hour. The relief at feeling actual paved road beneath our wheels was massive. So too was the fact that there was no police blockade awaiting us. When we started to head north to Tazenakht, I asked Aatif if he was going to report the robbery to the police.

'That would just get us into even more trouble. There aren't many roaming thieves in Morocco, though I've always been warned never to take back roads. But if I let the police know what happened, even if they apprehended these men, then what? They'll do a year in jail. Then they'll come out, looking for me. It's not worth the risk.'

'I feel so guilty about making you take that road.'

'Don't be. I've slept near that village several times and never had any trouble. We were unlucky.'

We got lucky, however, in Tazenakht. Yes, there was a police roadblock, but we got through it in minutes. The cops looked at our identity papers, glanced at the empty cargo area, asked a few questions and sent us on our way.

Four hours of non-stop desert followed. We stopped once to funnel one of the jerrycans of gas into the vehicle. We drank a little water and ate what pitta bread we had left. I ducked behind an abandoned house to relieve myself. We were both very conscious of the fact that we had no money whatsoever and we simply had to get to Marrakesh by night.

At the checkpoint before Ouarzazate, when the young police officer started asking me questions, Aatif had to do his spiel about me having mental challenges. Even so, the cop continued to address me. I stared blankly ahead, willing the interrogation to be over. When I didn't answer he got a little vehement until Aatif again seemed to be explaining that I was deaf (he kept touching his ears). The cop was clearly suspicious and called over an older officer, explaining the situation, motioning to my burqa, clearly indicating that he wanted me to remove it. The older officer – he looked well into his fifties – sidled over and had a chat with Aatif. Whatever was said seemed to do the trick, as the older cop motioned to his colleague that there was no need to continue the interrogation. He waved us on.

When we were clear of the checkpoint I noticed Aatif gripping the wheel, trying to forestall another panic attack.

'That was close,' I said.

He nodded agreement. Many times. And noted that, with any luck, the next checkpoint wouldn't be until Marrakesh.

As we negotiated the Avenue Mohamed V in Ouarzazate, I kept scanning the streets in some vain hope that Paul would suddenly materialise. Aatif, meanwhile, seemed so pained to be here. He spent much of our time on the main boulevard with his eyes focused downwards. Just as I was desperate to lay eyes on my missing spouse, so I assumed he was desperate not to come across the woman who broke his heart by running off with the bakery tsar of Ouarzazte. We are all haunted, in our own various ways, by our romantic past and present.

'The road ahead – it is complicated,' Aatif said. 'Are you afraid of heights?'

An hour or so later I certainly was, as we had gained almost six thousand feet in altitude and were driving on a single-lane switch-back road, hugging the edge of the Atlas Mountains.

Every hundred yards or so there was a blind corner, behind which lurked assorted obstacles: an oncoming lorry, a shepherd with a flock of two dozen goats, a young Moroccan daredevil on a motorcycle who nearly ploughed into us, shouting abuse before speeding off along another hairpin turn.

But what made this drive across a mountain pass called the Tizi-a-Ticha even more terrifying was the fact that one small mistake would send us into free-fall. On the passenger side I had a dizzying view of the deep ravine that began around a foot away from our right-side tyres. There was no wall, no guard rail, nothing to stop us from going over the side.

'In winter, with snow, it is terrible,' Aatif said.

In high summer, it was still something of a roller-coaster ride, each turn presenting a new navigational challenge, or some potential oncoming onslaught. Aatif smoked non-stop during the most taxing stages of the drive, humming to himself at the same time. As his humming increased, I was suddenly transported back to a drive with my father when I was fifteen and we were moving from Chicago to Minneapolis. We got caught in a huge blizzard on the interstate. Despite the fact that the visibility was zero Dad kept driving at 60 mph and hummed to himself throughout ('Fly Me to the Moon', of all things), ignoring my mother's entreaties to slow down. Aatif wasn't driving dangerously; on the contrary, he was a pinnacle of prudence. But he did tell me that, even though he drove this road twice a month, it never ceased to get to him.

'There is at least one terrible accident here every week,' he said.

'But we're not going to be this week's tragedy.'

'Insha'Allah.'

There was an awful moment when, as we passed through a mountain village, a young boy of seven or so chased a ball into the road, right in our path. Aatif slammed on the brakes. We skidded frighteningly towards the precipice on which the village rested. I screamed and had my hands over my eyes as Aatif somehow managed to stop us just before our front wheels went over. The boy ran off, spooked about almost being run over and almost sending us over the edge into the valley below (a fall of at least one thousand feet). There was a moment of terrible silence. Aatif did what he always did when stressed: he gripped the steering wheel tightly for several moments, trying to regain his equilibrium. Then he lit up a cigarette.

After several drags, he backed up the vehicle and we were on our way.

'That was nearly the fatal accident of the week,' he said.

The road began to improve as we lost altitude. The woozy verticality – and the potential for mortal danger – diminished as we started heading through flatter ground. Night fell. We filled the gas tank with the final jerrycan of gas and ate the last of our bread.

'Where's your jeweller?' I asked.

'We first have to go to my merchant in the souk because he is expecting a delivery from me and will be disappointed to see my vehicle empty. But he might know someone.'

'The way we're going now we should reach Marrakesh at what time?'

'Just before eight . . . if there are no roadblocks.'

There was a huge one on the outskirts of the city, backed up for quarter of a kilometre. It took us over forty minutes to edge our way to the front.

'They are not just looking for you,' Aatif explained before we reached the officers. 'They're also looking for terrorists.'

But everything was so clogged up with cars that, after a cursory glance at our ID cards, the police waved us through.

Marrakesh. I was expecting something mythical. I wasn't ready for all the new housing developments. Or the shopping malls with big international stores. Or the chain hotels. Or the congealed traffic. Or the hyper-tourist economy. We parked near the famed souk – an amazing open square on which snake charmers were frightening visitors with their vipers. Monkeys were running wild. A camel stood forlornly as people climbed on it for a photograph. Men were bothering every foreign woman who was walking alone. Tour guides were offering an exclusive tour of the souk. I saw a fellow American – late forties, preppy businessman clothes, very button-down with a wife wearing khakis and a matching blue Oxford shirt – losing it with a man who would not leave him alone, blocking his path, trying to hassle him into submission.

'Leave me the fuck alone!' he shouted.

His wife glared at me as I walked by, shrouded in the djellaba and burqa – so disapproving of this encasement of women.

We dodged all the tourist stands, the rug shops, the carved

goods and leather store, and entered a passageway, whereupon we came into a bazaar within a bazaar. Here there were men in suits, elderly gentlemen in immaculate djellabas; venerable establishments dealing in gold, a smell of old established Marrakesh money hidden away from the bleating, cheap commerce of the mercantile arena which Westerners saw.

Aatif steered us into a warehouse in which a young guy of around thirty – dressed in a black sweatshirt and sweatpants adorned with the Armani label, Versace sunglasses, and a lot of bling on his wrists, including a big Breitling – greeted him with a curt nod. He had a cellphone in one hand and another on the table in front of him, on which there also lay a calculator, a packet of Marlboros and a lighter that looked as though it was made of solid gold. He eyed me warily, pointing to me while asking Aatif why I was here. Or, at least, I presumed that's what he said, as Aatif began to explain (and I'd heard it so often I could almost follow the Arabic) the sad story of this poor girl behind the veil. Then his tone shifted and became plaintive, and I sensed (from his gestures and the sadness in his voice) that he was recounting the robbery and the reason why he had arrived empty-handed. The guy lit up a cigarette, made a point of not offering Aatif one, and blew smoke in my friend's face. I loathed his arrogance – how dare that preening little man use his petty power to lord it over Aatif? Why should an honest man's struggle to survive be seen as a sign of weakness? I could only begin to imagine what this guy was like around women, how he treated them as contemptuous objects, and how perhaps (this was wishful thinking on my part) he was inadequate with them. How I longed to pull off my burqa and attack him for his cruelty. But I knew that would be a disastrous call so I sat there silently as he berated Aatif and, with a dismissive hand motion, as if swatting a fly away, told him to leave his office.

Aatif looked broken by this and slunk out, his head downwards, tears in his eyes. I followed but turned and simply stared directly at the guy. He made contact with my accusatory eyes, showing him contempt through the veil. He shouted something at me in

Arabic. I continued to stare at him. He pointed to the door and seemed to be telling me to get lost. I continued to stare at him. He became nervous, stammering a bit as he stubbed out a cigarette and lit up another, then barking at me again to leave, but in a manner that betrayed his jitteriness. I continue to stare at him. He picked up his phone and marched to the other end of the room, trying to engross himself in the emails on his screen. I continued to stare at him. He turned back at me, now looking truly spooked. I raised my hand and pointed at him, using my index finger as a weapon of accusation. He stood there, not knowing what to do. Except to do what all bullies do when they are stood up to. He turned and fled out a back door.

I left his office and found Aatif outside, his eyes red, a cigarette alight.

'What did he tell you?' I asked.

'He said he thought I was stupid to get robbed, that I had left him short of goods, and he wouldn't care if I came back next week with a van full of new things. He also said, if I wanted to do business with him again, I would have to pay him five thousand dirhams as an apology.'

'Well, you don't have to do business with him again.'

'But he and his father have been my contacts here in Marrakesh for the past five years.'

'I'm sure you can find a better contact – and one who doesn't behave like a spoiled little boy.'

'But he has been reliable.'

'I bet he's argued over every dirham.'

'He is not a nice man. But . . .'

'No buts. You can ask around here and find another merchant who will gladly take your clients' goods and treat you with respect. Which you certainly deserve.'

He thought about this for a moment, then pointed to a small shop across the alley.

'There is a jeweller there.'

His way of changing the subject.

Aatif had to accompany me into the shop, as I feared removing

281

the burqa and causing a great deal of unwanted interest. The man in charge was hefty, brusque. Aatif explained what I wanted to sell. The fellow held out his fleshy paw and I handed over the two rings. He screwed in a jeweller's magnifying eyeglass and gave them perhaps ten seconds of his attention. Then he announced a price in Arabic to Aatif – who leaned over and whispered it in my ear.

'Five thousand dirhams.'

I held out my hand, palm up. The fellow dropped the rings back into it. We left.

There was another jeweller next door. This fellow in charge – around sixty, in a shiny brown suit, with equally brown teeth – was more polite. But he was also taking me for a sucker. When Aatif whispered his offer of ten thousand dirhams (I presume he told the man that I had limited hearing) and I shook my head, he upped it immediately to fifteen. A second shake of the head, and he said:

'Twenty thousand, final price.'

Once more I held out my hand for the rings. Slipping them back on, I nodded goodbye and we left.

I was beginning to despair of having to let my jewellery go at an absurdly low price. But then I saw a small, upmarket shop at the corner of the alley where we were now standing. Over the front was the name: *Abbou Joaillier*. I'd read somewhere, during my pre-trip research, that there was a small Jewish community in Morocco. Abbou Jeweller's – with its mosaic tiled decor, its mahogany counter, and a large solid desk behind which a well-dressed man in his sixties was weighing diamonds on a small scale – had a Star of David featured in the tiling above its entranceway. When I entered the shop the gentleman stood up. He wore an old-school double-breasted pinstriped suit with a well-pressed blue shirt and black tie. He had a most paternal face. Bifocals were perched on the end of his nose. I noticed photographs of his younger self in front of a jewellery store on New York's West 48th Street (he was standing under the actual street sign). He addressed me in Arabic. I decided to take a risk; a potentially huge risk, but one that might just get me a good price. I reached up and pulled off the burqa. I could see him just a little stunned to discover that behind the veil was a Western woman.

'I presume, from the photograph, that you speak English,' I said.

'Indeed I do, *madame*.'

He motioned for me to sit down. Aatif was standing in a corner, nervous that I had revealed my face. I turned to him and said that if he wanted to go outside for a smoke that wasn't a problem with me. He was happy to comply, bowing to the jeweller before leaving. Once he was out the door the man handed me his card: *Ismael Abbou*.

'And you once worked in New York?' I asked.

'I lived there for fifteen years. I still have an interest in my former shop there, and go back once a year.'

'What made you return to Morocco?'

'Family,' he said with just the slightest roll of the eyes. But then he studied me for a moment. I sensed what was coming next.

'Excuse me for asking, *madame*, but haven't I seen your face before?'

I chose my next words with care.

'You may have . . . but does that matter?'

He thought about this.

'May I offer you some tea?'

'That's very kind, but I would rather get down to business. Might I ask if you wouldn't mind lowering the blinds in your window while we discuss my proposed transaction?'

I could see him considering this. Just as I could sense him deciding whether I was worth the risk. I also saw him glancing at the diamond engagement ring and diamond-studded wedding band on my left hand.

'As you wish, *madame*.'

He stood up and went to the door, turning over a sign that I presume said he was closed. He lowered the blinds on the door and window, turning on several lights at the same time. Then he sat down opposite me again.

'How may I help, *madame*?'

I took off the two rings and placed them in front of him.

'I need to sell these, and I need a good price. They were purchased for me by my husband at Tiffany's.'

'Fifth Avenue and Fifty-Seventh Street,' he noted with a smile.

'Indeed. The engagement ring is platinum. The diamond has a one-point-one carat weight. And as I see you have a computer over there you can check the list price on the Tiffany's website, which I did recently when I got it reinsured. The engagement ring retails at thirteen thousand dollars. The wedding band is an Etoile style in platinum with seven diamonds, carat weight of point seven five. List price—'

He interrupted me.

'I would surmise four thousand dollars on East Fifty-Seventh Street.'

'I'm impressed.'

'It's my métier. Likewise I am impressed with your knowledge of such things. Are you in the business as well?'

'Actually, I'm an accountant.'

Pause. He put his fingertips together. Then he said:

'Yes, I did read that somewhere.'

So there we were: he knew exactly who I was, and he was still going to do business with me. Or, at least, that was my hope.

'Might I inspect the rings?' he asked.

'Of course.'

He spent the next ten minutes examining them minutely with his jeweller's eyeglass, weighing them both on his scales, going to his computer and onto the Tiffany's website, then excusing himself as he picked up a cellphone and had a hushed conversation for several minutes. *Oh God, he's calling the cops.* But, as if reading my mind, he smiled reassuringly at me. Concluding the call he explained that he needed to speak to his business partner before making an offer.

'So, indeed, those are Tiffany diamonds on platinum. And yes, the actual retail value in the United States for the two combined would be seventeen thousand dollars. But we are here in Marrakesh, and there is no possibility whatsoever that I could offer you anywhere near that.'

'So what could you offer?'

'Forty-five thousand dirhams.'

'Seventy thousand.'

'Impossible. Fifty thousand. That is close to six thousand dollars.'

'And if I went to one of those jewellery exchanges in the West Forties I would get at least twelve thousand dollars.'

'But you are in Marrakesh. Fifty-two thousand five hundred.'

'And I know you will sell these rings for at least one hundred thousand dirhams in the next few days. Sixty-five thousand.'

'Sixty thousand – final offer.'

'Sold,' I said, holding out my hand to shake. Mr Abbou took it and made a small bow. I could also see him eyeing the watch on my other wrist.

'Might that be a vintage Rolex Explorer from the 1960s?' he asked.

'It's the 1965 edition. It was my late father's. I had it valued recently at fifteen thousand dollars.'

'Might I please see it?' he asked. I slipped it off and handed it to him. He studied it, then explained that he was going to open the case and inspect its workings. This he did expertly, using his magnifying glass to study its mechanism. Again he went over to his computer to run a check on current market value. Again he excused himself to make a second hushed call. When he came off the phone he told me:

'The most I can offer is fifty thousand dirhams.'

'Eighty.'

'That is impossible. Sixty.'

'I am certain you have a rich client somewhere who has been waiting for a watch like this and will pay you at least one hundred and thirty thousand.'

'Sixty-five.'

'Seventy thousand,' I said, adding, 'and that is my final price.'

Now it was his turn to offer his hand.

'We are agreed, *madame*. And now I insist that we have tea.'

I nodded agreement. He stood up and opened a door, speaking to someone in the back. As we waited for the tea he asked if I needed help with anything else.

'I need to get to Casablanca – but without being seen.'

'Do you have any ID papers?'

'The man who drove me – he has been letting me use someone else's papers. And because I have been behind the burqa . . .'

'Understood. But why not ask this man to drive you to Casa?'

'Because I don't want him further involved in any of this.'

He tapped his fingers on the counter, thinking, thinking.

'I may be able to help you.'

The tea arrived, carried by a studious-looking young man in his twenties, also dressed in a double-breasted suit. He too did a double-take on seeing this Western woman in a djellaba, with a burqa on the table in front of her. Mr Abbou spoke to him in Arabic, clearly explaining various matters. They exchanged a few more words, tea was poured, glasses raised.

'I wish you a safe return home,' Mr Abbou said. 'How, may I ask, are you planning to actually leave Morocco?'

'I need to find a new passport. I don't suppose you would know anybody who specialises in that sort of thing?'

Because I so wanted to avoid having to have any further dealings with Ben Hassan.

Mr Abbou smiled sympathetically but regretfully.

'I am happy to send my assistant Mahmoud here with you to Casa. He will drive you in one of my Mercedes, so you will have a comfortable ride up to the big city. And if the price of three thousand dirhams is reasonable for you . . .'

'I bet I could get a taxi around here to do it for half the price.'

'Indeed you could, *madame*. But in my Mercedes, sitting in the back like a well-heeled woman with a driver – you will fly through whatever checkpoints may be in force tonight. With a normal taxi driver . . .'

'OK, fine, three thousand.'

'We will, of course, need to speak with your own driver and see if he is willing to entrust you with the ID card for another day or so.'

'Yes, that will be crucial. But before we go any further, might you be able to show me the one hundred and thirty thousand dirhams? I am sorry to be so direct about this, but—'

'No need to apologise. Business is business. And your rings and your Rolex will be left here in front of you while I go to my safe and retrieve the funds.'

As Mr Abbou disappeared into a back room Mahmoud kept an eye on the merchandise and also on the front door. I asked him if he spoke French. He nodded yes.

'How long is it from here to Casablanca?'

'What *quartier* are you going to?'

'It's called Gauthier.'

'I know it. Very nice. At this time of the evening, it will be two and a half hours. There's an *autoroute* that is direct most of the way.'

Mr Abbou returned with several large bundles of bills, all still with bank wrappers around them. He placed them in front of me. I counted them thoroughly, separating them into two distinct piles, one of which I put in the pocket of my djellaba. Then I asked Mr Abbou if he would mind me using his shop for a moment to talk to Aatif.

'No problem,' he said. 'Would you like me to call him inside?'

'Yes.'

'Aatif is a very good name. Do you know what it means in Arabic?'

I shook my head.

'Compassionate.'

Mahmoud stepped outside, calling Aatif in. Mr Abbou asked if we'd like to be alone but Aatif waved that away. I motioned for him to sit down in the chair next to mine near the desk. I could see Aatif taking in the considerable pile of money in front of him.

'That is for you,' I said.

He looked beyond astonished.

'That can't be right. We agreed two thousand dirhams to get you to Marrakesh.'

'Yes, and I also promised you twelve thousand for the goods that were stolen. But I have also decided that you deserve a bonus. So the total there is one hundred thousand dirhams.'

He stared at me.

'But . . . why?'

'Because, once you pay off your clients, it should give you enough – along with the money you've saved – to buy the house and marry Hafeza.'

Silence. Aatif put his face in his hands.

'This is too kind,' he eventually said.

'As I said before, you deserve kindness.'

'But . . .'

Mr Abbou reached over and put a hand on Aatif's shoulder, whispering something in Arabic. Then, out of nowhere, Aatif took my two hands in his own and said:

'I have finally got lucky.'

To which I replied:

'So have I.'

Turning to Mr Abbou and using French because I wanted Aatif to understand, I said: 'Aatif needs a new merchant in Marrakesh to sell goods that he brings from the south. The man he's been dealing with is awful.'

Mr Abbou asked Aatif for the merchant's name. On hearing it, Mr Abbou rolled his eyes.

'A nasty, stupid child,' he said. 'Will you be around here tomorrow?'

'I could be,' Aatif said. 'We got little sleep last night, we've been on the road for hours . . .'

'Where are you sleeping tonight?' Mr Abbou asked.

Aatif shrugged.

'We have a small guest room in the back. It's very simple, but clean. You are most welcome to stay. And I would be honoured if you were to eat with me. There is a nice restaurant just two minutes from here. Then, tomorrow morning, I can introduce you to one or two merchants I know. We can discuss all this over dinner. *D'accord?*'

Aatif smiled his trademark shy smile.

'*D'accord.*'

I asked Aatif if I could borrow his sister's ID card for a few more days, but said I would mail it back to him if he gave me his address.

288

'Please keep the card. My sister would have been pleased to know that her identity was put to such good use.'

I glanced at my wrist and realised my watch was no longer there. The last vestige of my father. My sole inheritance. Gone now for good. But being someone who appreciated life's manifold vagaries – 'You gotta play the hand you're dealt,' as he so often told me – he would, I was certain, agree that the money raised on his one and only asset had ended up in the right hands.

'It's eleven minutes past nine,' Mr Abbou said.

That would mean Casablanca by midnight. I reached for a pad on the desk and wrote out my email address, handing it to Aatif.

'Here's how to contact me,' I said. 'Send me the wedding photographs.'

He stood up and again took both my hands in his own. Saying:

'Allah ybarek feek wal 'ayyam al-kadima.'

I smiled and repeated the benediction back to him.

May Allah bestow his blessings on you in the days to come.

Ten minutes later, I was back beneath the burqa and speeding towards Casablanca. Mr Abbou had insisted on walking me to the Mercedes that Mahmoud would drive. As we reached this venerable black vehicle – it dated from the early 1980s, I was told – I handed Mahmoud the slip of paper on which Ben Hassan had scribbled his address.

'No problem,' Mahmoud said. 'We have GPS.'

Mr Abbou handed me his card, telling me his mobile phone number was written on the back.

'If there is any problem whatsoever you call me,' he said. 'I can't get you a passport, but I have connections should difficulties arise. And by the way, the drive to Casablanca is on me.'

'That's very kind of you.'

'Consider it a mitzvah,' he said.

Mitzvah. Jewish karma. I laughed.

'I never thought I'd hear Hebrew being spoken in Marrakesh.'

'Life is surprising.'

'Yes, I am somewhat aware of that.'

'And a mitzvah should always be rewarded with a mitzvah.'

'How true – and how rare.'

Now I took his hands in my own.

'Very good doing business with you, *monsieur*.'

'And you, *madame*.'

With that he opened the back door of the Mercedes and ushered me out of his life.

Fifteen minutes later we had cleared Marrakesh and were on the *autoroute* heading north. We had agreed that if we were stopped by the police or questioned at a checkpoint, Mahmoud would explain that he was my father's driver, and that I was a woman with mental challenges etc.

But in the two and a half hours I was in this vehicle we were never stopped once. Sitting in the back, drinking in the air conditioning, I fell into a subdued daze. There was one checkpoint on the outskirts of Casa but the officer simply looked in, saw a besuited driver and a veiled woman in the back seat, and waved us on.

At around midnight we pulled up in front of the apartment building that Ben Hassan called home. I handed Mahmoud two thousand dirhams – despite his protests that his employer had said I wasn't to pay him – and asked him to wait for me outside for an hour.

'If I don't come downstairs within an hour, you can head back to Marrakesh. But if I do need you before then . . .'

'I'll be waiting.'

The truth was that without the false passport I hoped Ben Hassan would provide, I would hit the end of the line. But just in case he was out for the night, or if the situation turned tricky, at least Mahmoud might be persuaded to drive me to Tangier. I would then have to find a black marketeer for a way out of the country. My hope was that, if I flashed ten thousand dirhams in front of him, Ben Hassan would come up with the necessary goods and even get me north to the ferry for Spain by morning.

I got out of the Mercedes and loitered by the front door until a young couple came out of the building. Before the door could slam behind them I had raced inside and up the five flights of twisted stairs to Ben Hassan's apartment. I rang the bell. No answer.

I rang it again. No answer. So I held it down for the better part of a minute.

Then, out of nowhere, the door opened. Ben Hassan, his capacious kaftan stained with sweat, looked as if I had got him out of bed.

He seemed just a bit confused to find a woman in a burqa standing in front of him. I pulled the veil back. The shock on his face was considerable but he swiftly wiped it away.

'So . . . the most wanted woman in Morocco drops in to say hello.'

I pushed past him into the apartment, saying:

'I need a shower and a passport.'

HOT WATER FROM a shower spray. Proper soap and shampoo. A toothbrush and toothpaste. A large towel. A bed with clean sheets. And before that, a late-night supper and several very welcome glasses of wine.

Basic comforts can seem like tremendous luxuries when you have been denied them for a considerable length of time.

As cautious as I was about being in Ben Hassan's presence I also knew from before that he had a nurturing side. Seeing me exhausted and rank, he roused Omar from bed and set him to work. On my way to the bathroom I was handed one of Omar's freshly laundered light cotton djellabas. Given his slightness – and all the weight I'd lost – it actually fit me. He also saw to it that the clothes I was carrying with me were thrown into the washing machine. When I emerged from the shower (having spent almost twenty minutes under its blessed downpour), dried and changed into the clean djellaba, I found that a small supper had been laid out for me.

The wine was balming. And the pastilla – a pie made with cinnamon, harisa, almonds and a very dead pigeon – was quite delicious. I had decided on the way from Marrakesh that my strategy with Ben Hassan would be to say nothing about Paul and the entire fraudulent loan for Samira's apartment. My desire here was to get a new passport and make it to Tangier as quickly as possible. But when Ben Hassan offered hot water, clean clothes supper and a bed for the night, my debilitation won the argument. While drying off in the bathroom I inspected the marks on my face and legs. The bruising from the beating had virtually vanished but my cheekbone felt fragile to the touch, and the deep rings under my eyes made me look like a haunted insomniac. The facial sunburn was still apparent but subsiding, but there were still severe scars on my legs. I knew that I had to see a doctor as soon as possible about STDs and any lasting vaginal injuries. Just as I probably needed an MRI on my face and head, and to deal with the slight ringing that was still omnipresent in my ear. Had he burst an eardrum when he'd slammed his fist against my left ear, then kicked me in the head?

I wondered: How much did Ben Hassan know of all this? As he'd called me 'the most wanted woman in Morocco' he was evidently aware that I was still being sought in connection with the disappearance of my husband. No doubt he'd also seen the television footage of the charred body in the desert.

But I was going to mention none of this. I would accept his bed and food for the night, and clean clothes. I would negotiate a price for the passport, and would hopefully be on my way by midday tomorrow.

So I ate my pastilla and drank my wine and let Ben Hassan do the talking.

'I must say, from what I've learned of your exploits, you've been quite resourceful,' he said. 'Sorry about the abuse you received. Though I am no doctor, my untrained eye tells me you might have a bone or two broken around your left eye socket. Still, your attacker did get his comeuppance, did he not? And as I am not the police, who am I to pry into how you burnt that man to death. Or what you were doing with him in the desert.'

I stared straight at his corpulent face.

'That young man and his accomplice seized me off a street in Tata, drugged me, drove me out into the middle of the Sahara, raped me and left me to die.'

'And you struck back.'

'I never said that.'

'Of course you didn't. Nor did his accomplice.'

'So he has been found?'

'That's for you to find out. But as your hope is, I presume, to be out of the country tomorrow . . .'

'Can you facilitate that?'

'For a price.'

'And what is your price?'

'Let's discuss that in the morning.'

'I'd rather discuss it now. I need a false passport. You are the one person I know in Morocco who can provide me with such a document. Here I am.'

'Availing yourself of my hospitality.'

'I can leave, *monsieur*.'

'And go where? Back into your native garb? How clever of you to go behind the veil to get through all those tiresome checkpoints. How did you manage the identity-paper problem?'

'I found a solution.'

'I'm certain you did.'

'So how much for a false passport?'

'We are all business tonight.'

'I need to know your price.'

'I presume you were robbed of everything.'

'That's right. And I am not going to take out a loan with you.'

'Smart woman. But if you have no cash to hand . . .'

'I have a little.'

'And how did you manage to obtain that?'

'I sold what jewellery I had in Marrakesh.'

He made a point of carefully studying my left hand.

'Indeed. All vestiges of your marriage vanished.'

'Except the mental scars.'

'You must have done well, given that your most collectible Rolex is also no longer on your wrist.'

'I had some debts to settle.'

'Ah yes, I figured that someone must have aided and abetted you in evading the police. And he must have cost plenty.'

'Actually, he might have been the most honourable man I've ever met.'

'I'm so pleased for you – honourable men being so infrequent in your life.'

'Present company included,' I said.

'So . . . I am right in presuming that you have little money.'

'You told me your standard price for a false passport was ten thousand dirhams.'

'I also told you that was my rate for friends. If the individual is problematic – as in, wanted by the police – the price trebles. So I am afraid thirty-five thousand is the amount needed.'

'Twenty thousand is what I can pay – and that must include transport up to Tangier. I'm certain you can get Omar to drive me.'

'That will be an additional five thousand dirhams.'

'It's only a few hours' drive.'

'But think of the risks involved in getting you there.'

'I can put on the burqa and use the ID papers I've got. Then, when we're at the port, I'll change back into my normal clothes and use the passport you've given me to leave.'

'My, my, you have this all worked out already. Most impressive. But there is still risk involved for myself and Omar. Still, as a way of showing goodwill, twenty-five thousand dirhams all in.'

I put out my hand.

'Deal.'

He seemed supremely uncomfortable taking my hand. As before his felt like a hot, damp cushion.

'What time can I get the passport tomorrow?' I asked.

'As it is now almost one-thirty in the morning I will want to sleep until ten. It will take an hour or so to put the passport together. I have the camera for the photograph. I will need to get the appropriate entry stamp made in the document, and also have it logged on the immigration computer system. That involves me contacting an associate who does this sort of thing. I have decided, given your facility with the language, that you will be French. But even at the Port of Tangier the immigration officers now have computers. My associate has a way of ensuring that your date of entry will pop up when they scan your passport . . .'

'And does this cost extra?'

'Of course not. It's all part of the overall fee. Tomorrow we can choose a name for you. Nothing too absurd. We'll sleep on it.'

'Fine. I could certainly use some sleep.'

'Your bed awaits.'

'One last question – in my absence have there been any sightings of my husband?'

'None whatsoever since you tried to chase him down in Ouarzazate.'

'How did you know about that?'

'I have my sources.'

'Like his other wife?'

'Perhaps. And I know full well that you are desperate to ask why I didn't give Samira the money that Paul borrowed for her apartment? And whether I contacted Paul, telling him that, by helping buy his daughter and grandson an apartment, he could atone for his absence from Samira's life?'

'Did I even indicate that I was concerned about this?'

'My source in Ouarzazate informed me that you certainly seemed vexed by it. The truth is—'

'The truth, *monsieur*, is that dealing with you is like walking through a hall of mirrors. Nothing is ever real. So be it. I don't need to know why Samira didn't get the money. Or if you set all this up as a trap to ensnare my now vanished husband. Let that be on your conscience . . . if you have one. You will be getting two thousand seven hundred dollars from me tomorrow for one hour's work and a five-hour drive to Tangier which you yourself won't have to make. Our business is therefore done for the night. I thank you for the hospitality.'

A very long silence followed, during which Ben Hassan got up and poured us both an *eau de vie*. Then he finally spoke.

'I don't entirely agree with your character assessment of me, *madame*. Yes, I do have my tricky side – and a very long memory for wrongs rendered. But I am also an excellent friend. As I was to your husband all those years ago. And the result . . .'

He held up his two battered, deformed hands.

'We all have our ways of dealing with the injustices and sorrows piled upon us, *madame*. We all have our ways of getting through the day. And we all have our moments of malevolence . . . even if, in your recent case, the malevolence you meted out on your attacker was wholly merited. Pushed to the wall, some of us surrender to the inevitable. Whereas there are others – like you, like me – who turn feral. And who fight back with the same brutality as that visited upon us. Because we know that, in life, the central preoccupation is still the same as it was when we all lived in caves – survival. You're a survivor. I salute you for it. But don't try to take the moral high ground here. You are exactly like me. You killed to stay alive.'

'There's a difference here – you killed as an act of revenge.'

'No – the difference is that, unlike you, I didn't have the opportunity to strike back immediately. Two crushed hands leave one at a profound disadvantage. But I did strike back eventually, to prove I would never again be cowed by such animals. And to let my little community here know that too . . . not that I ever actually admitted to such acts. I didn't need to. Everyone knew. Everyone also knew they could never pin the crimes on me, because I was too shrewd to get caught. But the real lesson that everyone around here gleaned from my strike back was: *Now you know that I will kill to stay alive.*'

Five minutes later, I was alone in the living room. As much as my analytical side wanted to take apart the skewed logic of Ben Hassan's attempts to draw a parallel between us, another part of me simply thought: *By this time tomorrow I will be in Spain. Ben Hassan will cease to have any impact on my life, unless I allow myself to be haunted by his version of morality.* The truth is, haunted I would be. And by so much. But why add Ben Hassan's toxic reasoning to the mix on a night when I was crawling into the first proper bed with proper sheets that I had slept in for weeks?

Having started the day at before sunrise, hearing my friend Aatif being beaten and robbed in the dark, sleep did not take long to overtake me.

Then I was awake and wondering where I was, feeling as though I had been unconscious for a very long time. Getting up and wandering out into the hallway I passed by Ben Hassan in his 'office'.

'My, my, you certainly needed your beauty sleep, didn't you?' he said.

'What time is it?'

'A few minutes before midday.'

'Oh my God . . .'

'Not to worry. Have your shower. I will tell Omar to arrange breakfast for you. Meantime I have a few phone calls to make, and then we can get down to business.'

'Will there be enough time—?'

'To take care of everything and get you packed off? Absolutely. Now go. The sooner you are showered and dressed . . .'

I hurried into the bathroom, noting with pleasure that, as before, a hairdryer had been left out for me, as well as my freshly laundered clothes. Ben Hassan was a dangerous customer, but he also knew how to play the thoughtful host. Twenty minutes later I was sipping proper coffee and eating two croissants in Ben Hassan's kitchen. At which point I heard his front doorbell ring. As Omar went to answer it Ben Hassan came into the kitchen.

'Enjoying your breakfast?'

I heard voices down the corridor.

'Do you have visitors?' I asked.

'*We* have visitors. Last night, after you went to bed, I thought about our little exchange. I also considered the complexities of risk, and the fact that there are some clients who are just too hot to handle. Which, on reflection, is most certainly the case with you. Another little matter entered my thinking – I need to keep my friends and associates happy. Helping you flee the country would certainly anger several of the men now down the corridor, all of whom want to talk with you. They are members of the *Sûreté*. Or as you Americans put it – the Feds.'

'You bastard,' I hissed.

'I won't contest that. At least be thankful that I allowed you a shower, a good meal and an excellent night's sleep before calling them.'

Then he shouted something in Arabic. Moments later I was surrounded by three men in suits and a uniformed police officer. One of the detectives spoke to me in French, asking me to confirm my name. I told him what he wanted to hear.

'Now, we would prefer not to use handcuffs . . .' he said.

'I'll go quietly.'

'Very wise of you, *madame*.'

With two men in front of me and two behind, I was marched out. Ben Hassan insisted on accompanying us to the front door.

'Do say hello the next time you are in Casablanca,' he said as a parting benediction. 'And do remember the subtext to all this – survival is everything.'

I was marched down the stairs and into a waiting unmarked vehicle, accompanied by two police cars blaring their sirens as we shot at high speed across the city. Neither of the detectives with me said anything. I shut my eyes. *Why am I surprised it is ending like this?*

The windows of the car were virtually blacked out, allowing me no view of where we were heading. After quarter of an hour I saw through the windscreen that we were entering a modern block of buildings, then driving down a tunnel into an underground garage. Once there all the officers exited their cars before I was allowed to get up. The same deal as before: two in front of me and two behind. I was marched to a door which only opened after one of the cops had punched in a code. The walls inside were painted an institutional green. I was taken up a set of stairs, and then down a concrete corridor until I was steered into a room furnished only with a metal table, four chairs and a mirror – which, no doubt, was two-way, allowing those on the other side to look in on the suspect under interrogation.

The cops deposited me in this room, then turned and left without saying anything. The door slammed behind them with a formidable thud and I heard a bolt sliding into place outside. *Do you really think I'd try to make a break for it?* I felt like shouting. Instead I sat down on one of the chairs, put my face in my hands and thought: *Whatever you do, insist on a lawyer, and refuse to answer any of their questions.*

But then, out of nowhere, I heard the bolt being slid back and the door opened. In walked a Western woman, late thirties, dressed in a crisp linen suit and a pressed white blouse, a bulging leather briefcase in her left hand. She came over to me, her hand extended.

'It is so good to finally meet you, Robin.'

I accepted the outstretched hand, trying to work out who this woman was and why she was here in a Moroccan police station.

'Alison Conway, Assistant Consul at the US Consulate here in Casablanca. We don't have long, as Inspector al-Badisi and the translator will be here in a moment. But what I wanted to explain before he got here—'

She had no time to finish that sentence, as the door swung open and in walked a man of about forty-five. He had thick black hair, a groomed moustache, and was wearing a light brown suit. He shook my hand and informed me that he was Inspector al-Badisi. He had a dossier of documents with him, which he put down on the table. I asked for water. He shouted out to someone in the hallway. Meanwhile another woman joined us – late forties, severe features, dressed in a dark suit with black hair tied in a tight bun.

'This is Madame Zar,' the inspector said, 'who will be translating for me today.'

'But we are speaking in French now.'

The assistant consul, now seated next to me at the table, put her hand on my arm.

'I felt it was better, for clarity's sake, if everything discussed here was translated, so there would be no ambiguities.'

'What's going on here?' I whispered to her in English.

'Just let the inspector speak,' she whispered back. 'All will be explained.'

The water arrived. The door was closed. The inspector sat down and opened his dossier, bringing out several copies of what seemed to be the same document. Then he looked up and regarded me with formal severity. As he spoke the translator waited for a pause every few sentences before rendering his words into English for me.

'*Madame*, on behalf of His Majesty and his government, I wish to offer you our sincere condolences for the ordeal you have been put through. We have, as Assistant Consul Conway can attest, been working very closely with the US Consulate here in Casablanca in the search for you. We are immensely relieved and pleased to have you here, alive and, I hope, reasonably well.'

I said nothing. I just nodded acknowledgement of his very civil words.

'Now I regret that we must discuss the events that occurred in a sector of the Sahara some forty-three kilometres from the town of Tata. We do know what happened out there—'

I flew off the handle.

'How can you know what happened? I was there. What happened there was inflicted on me.'

The assistant consul gripped my arm tightly. I shut my eyes for a moment, gathering myself, then opened them and said:

'I apologise for interrupting you, Inspector. It has been a very long few weeks.'

'There is no need to apologise, *madame*. On the contrary, it is we who should be apologising to you, considering what you've been put through. As I was saying . . . we are aware of what happened in the desert.'

With that he pulled over what was clearly a prepared statement and began to read it to me. In it he recounted the 'facts' of the case. How I had been searching for my missing husband in the Sahara and had been drugged with chloroform while leaving my hotel in Tata to catch the early bus to Ouarzazate. The two 'criminals' were named Abdullah Talib and Imad Shuayb, both twenty-one, both from Marrakesh, both working on a road work project in Tata. They beat and robbed me, knocking me unconscious. But after that, the two thieves argued over how to split the money and goods stolen from me. A fight between them broke out, with Imad stabbing Abdullah to death, and then, in a panic, setting fire to the body and returning to Tata. When he tried to sell my laptop and passport some days later in Marrakesh, a merchant notified the police. Imad Shuayb confessed everything after his arrest and was so ashamed of his crimes that he hanged himself in the prison cell in which he was being held while awaiting trial.

When the inspector reached this part of the narrative my shoulders stiffened. I was about to say something – but again Assistant Consul Conway put her hand on my arm, letting me know that silence was the best option. I knew immediately what the inspector was reading me: the official version of what went down, eliminating the nasty public embarrassment (in such a tourist-based economy) of the revelation that a Western woman had been abducted and raped and left to die under the Saharan sun. I could only begin to wonder if, having had his 'confession' beaten out of him, my abductor had truly taken his own life or was conveniently suicided to close the case. While part of me was outraged that the rape had been left out of the official statement, the other forensic part of my psyche (the eternal balancer of profits and loss) also understood what the authorities were doing. They were giving me a way out, and one in which no possible legal charges could ever be directed at me, or an investigation demanded by the assailants' families (because even in self-defence, a murder is a murder and must be investigated). The loose ends were being tied up in a manner in which the case would be permanently closed.

The inspector continued, explaining how a Berber family had found me lying unconscious in the desert, nursed me back to life and eventually helped get me to Casablanca. Again I wondered whether they actually knew the names of my saviours or whether this was just more official speak. I interrupted him.

'That is what happened, *monsieur*. I owe my life to those people who saved me and the man who drove me here.'

The inspector's face twitched, as if he had been caught unawares by this revelation. That's when I knew that they knew nothing of Maika and her family, or of Aatif and the way I had been smuggled here behind the burqa. They had just invented the Berber part of the story as a way of explaining why I had gone missing for several weeks. As such my Berber friends would not be receiving unwanted visits from the *Sûreté* posing all sorts of questions. They would be left alone.

Assistant Consul Conway shot me a look, telling me that I should let the inspector finish.

'I am pleased that you were helped by our citizens,' he said. 'And I would like to say – those men who attacked you, those criminals . . . they are not us.'

'Believe me, *monsieur*, I know that,' I replied. 'I know that so well.'

'We have prepared an official statement in English, French and Arabic which Assistant Consul Conway has examined in all three languages to confirm they are one and the same, and which we would like you to sign . . . after, of course, you've had the chance to peruse them. We would appreciate it if you would pose for a photograph with myself. It will be released to the media to show that you are alive and well, as there has been considerable concern here and elsewhere about your disappearance. We have been in contact with the hotel at which you and your husband were staying in Essaouira. All your clothes were packed up and sent here to Casablanca, where they will await you tonight at the Hotel Mansour. It is an excellent hotel and you will be our guest tonight. Anything that you want there you can just sign for. When Imad Shuayb was arrested we recovered your passport.' He pushed this across the table to me. 'We also discovered that you had a reservation back to New York on Royal Air Maroc some weeks ago that you never used. We have contacted the airline and they have changed the reservation, at no charge whatsoever to you, to tomorrow at midday. We will arrange for complimentary transport to the airport.'

So Ben Hassan had probably called his police contact early this morning while I was still asleep, telling them he had me at his place, but to wait until I was up and ready before coming to take me in. In the meantime the assistant consul had been contacted and everything put in motion to wrap this story up as quickly as possible and get me out of the country tomorrow.

'That's all very thoughtful of you,' I said. 'One important thing remains outstanding, though. Have there been any sightings of my husband? Any sense whatsoever of his whereabouts?'

The inspector pursed his lips and reached for another file.

'On the day in question your husband checked out of the Oasis Hotel early in the morning, and was seen walking out of town. A local tour guide named Idriss was going to work in his jeep and saw Monsieur Leuen walking directly into the desert. He stopped and asked your husband if he could offer assistance, as he was heading into a barren area without oases, and was wearing no hat and carrying no backpack or canteen. Your husband told the guide he was fine and kept walking into the Sahara. That was the last sighting of him.'

'And that was at what time?' I asked.

'The tour guide said it was around seven-thirty a.m.'

'But that's impossible,' I said. 'I arrived in Ouarzazate at seven and caught sight of my husband at least three times that morning.'

'Did you speak to him?' the inspector asked.

'No – he always eluded me. And the woman at the hotel told me he returned briefly at two o'clock before heading to the bus depot to catch the bus to Tata. I followed him. I saw him in front of me. I missed the bus and took the next one.'

The inspector pursed his lips even further, mulling over some more documents, scrutinising them with care.

'I have here the statement from the tour guide and the woman at the hotel. Again I repeat – she said your husband checked out at seven, and the tour guide confirmed that he had his conversation with him at seven-thirty. It's all here.'

'But I saw him.'

'If you saw him,' the inspector said, 'then why didn't he answer you?'

'He was avoiding me. But that woman at the hotel . . . I remember so well the conversation with her when I came back from seeing . . .'

I stopped myself from saying anything more. Because to do so would, I sensed, begin to raise questions about my sanity; questions which I myself didn't want to answer. I closed my eyes. There was Paul, running away from me on the streets of Ouarzazate. There was the scene at the hotel reception desk, after I'd visited his other wife. Yasmina told me that I'd just missed him. And the sight of his bobbing grey hair and his tall frame in the distance as I raced to catch him before he boarded the bus. Everything else that had happened to me after that was so real. I still had plenty of physical scars from the attack. They'd found the burnt body. Opening that passport in front of me I saw that it was, truly, my own. All tangible, all real. I had lived this story. It was all verified. But those hours in Ouarzazate when Paul was everywhere and nowhere . . . surely that couldn't have been a spectre, a hallucination, a mirage?

'Are you all right, Robin?' Assistant Consul Conway asked me, her hand on my shoulder.

'No.'

Leaning towards me she whispered in my ear:

'I cannot give you official counsel, as that is not in my diplomatic remit. But speaking personally, if I were you I would sign the statement. I had one of our legal people and one of our translators look at all three versions. They all match up, and they all let you leave Morocco with the matter entirely resolved.'

So she too suspected (or, indeed, knew) that the burnt body in the desert wasn't the handiwork of the accomplice who was then 'suicided' while in custody.

'Give them what they want,' she continued. 'Put your signature on the statement, pose for the press photograph, spend the night in the five-star hotel they've arranged for you, take the flight home tomorrow. They are being very smart about all this. Very conscientious. I strongly advise you to do the same.'

I shut my eyes again. Paul was there, sketching away on the balcony of our room in Essaouira, flashing me a seductive smile as I brought him a glass of wine, telling me he loved me. I blinked. Paul was gone. I blinked again. There he was dashing down that back alley in Ouarzazate, eluding me as always – but still so tangibly there. I blinked again. Nothing. A void as empty as the Sahara.

I opened my eyes. The inspector was staring at me concernedly.

'Would you like some time to think about all this, *madame*?' he asked.

'No,' I said. 'I want to go home. Where do I sign?'

Twenty-eight

AT FOUR O'CLOCK that morning I sat up in bed. I could not remember a single detail of the nightmare that had snapped me into consciousness. All I felt was a dangerous, oppressive presence. Undefined. Entombing me.

But then I opened my eyes and found myself in this heavily over-upholstered hotel room. Hours earlier, upon being checked in here, I was brought upstairs to find the two suitcases that had been dispatched from Essaouira. It was a shock to see all my clothing intermingled with that of my vanished husband. Whoever had packed up our room there had not separated his from hers. It took me just ten minutes to repack all of my clothes, and to lay out the items I would need until the flight tomorrow. While handling Paul's things I felt neither rage nor trauma, just a profound numbness. Assistant Consul Conway – she insisted on me calling her Alison – had accompanied me to the hotel in the unmarked police car that the inspector had ordered after I had signed the official statement and posed for a photograph with him. *Case closed*, it told the world. I had extracted one promise from the police – that the photo would not be released to the press until I was en route to the States the next day. I didn't want stares at the airport tomorrow. I wanted to be home by the time it was revealed that I'd emerged safely from the wilderness.

'You handled that all very well back there,' Alison said when we reached the hotel. The management offered us tea while the room was being made up. 'They wanted to wrap this up quickly, without fuss. They're pleased you played ball.'

'What else was I going to do?'

'After an experience like yours . . . well, most people would already be showing signs of post-traumatic stress disorder. I am very impressed that you didn't break down in front of the inspector, and kept yourself so contained.'

'I've had several weeks to sort through the worst of it. And I need you to do me a favour.'

I explained about the desert family who had taken me in, and the vague location of the oasis which they were calling home right now. I gave her the remaining 28,000 dirhams, then asked if she could perform a minor miracle and get the money to them.

'I can't promise anything,' she said, 'but I'll try.'

'I don't want the law involved. They're a bit wary, I sense, about anything to do with the government.'

'Berbers?'

I nodded.

'It will be an interesting challenge finding them.'

'May I ask you a direct question?'

'Of course.'

'Have the police conducted a search of the desert near to where my husband was last seen?'

'Absolutely. And they've found nothing so far.'

By nothing I knew she meant no body, no desiccated corpse, burnt by the sun, fed upon by vultures.

'And that tour guide who saw him – he clearly identified Paul?'

'I read the report from the Ouarzazate *Sûreté*. He described a Caucasian male, around two metres tall – that's six foot five – thin, with long grey hair and several days' growth of beard. Does that sound like your husband?'

I shut my eyes and again saw Paul's hair slapping the shoulder of his white shirt as he raced for the bus in Ouarzazate, my entreaties to him to stop only accelerating his pace.

'Yes, that sounds like him.'

'Of course, there could have been another Caucasian male of a similar age and build and hairstyle who went out hiking in the desert that day. And I have checked with my colleagues at all the other Western consulates and embassies here. There's no one else of that description missing.'

She chose her next words with care. 'You still do maintain that you saw him on the streets of Ouarzazate, later that same day, several hours after he allegedly disappeared?'

'I saw what I saw. But what any one of us sees . . . is that ever the truth? Or is it just what we want to see?'

She considered this for a moment.

'Trust me – and I know this, because I lost my sister five years ago in a car accident where I was the passenger – it's when you are beyond the initial trauma that it jumps up out of nowhere and grabs you by the throat. Don't be surprised if, now that you are out of danger, it begins to get tricky for a while.'

At four that morning the 'trickiness' began. That sense of a dark force in the room with me, about to encircle me and wreak havoc. I couldn't pinpoint who or what it was. What I found myself doing, after getting up and pacing the room, was throwing on something to wear, heading downstairs with a suitcase containing all my husband's clothes, and giving them to a homeless man in his forties who was lying near the gutter. I just put the case in front of him and handed him 500 of the 1,000 dirhams I'd held onto for tips and incidental expenses. His eyes widened when he saw the sum of cash I had pressed into his palm.

'Why me?' he asked.

'Why not you?'

Back in the room I ran a very hot bath and sat in it for the better part of an hour. A long soak, during which I started to cry and then couldn't stop until I was so wrung out that, after drying myself, I forced myself back into bed with the hope that sleep might overtake me again. But I was wired now and very wide awake. So I turned on my laptop and saw that Morton had answered the email I'd sent to him after checking in to the hotel, informing him that I was alive and would definitely be landing tomorrow (now today) in Buffalo. I also mentioned that Paul was missing, presumed dead. Morton's reply was all business:

Will be at the airport. Very glad you are out of harm. Re: Paul. You should know that, under NY state law, a missing person cannot be declared dead for seven years. But there are some legal things we can do to protect you. More when we meet. Best – Morton. PS – I can finally sleep now, knowing you are OK.

Trust Morton to practise ultra-pragmatism at a difficult juncture.

The rest of the day passed in a strange blur. An unmarked police car picked me up at the hotel, as arranged, at nine-thirty. At the airport I was checked in and taken through a special security line by the two officers charged with getting me on the plane. A representative of the airline met us and escorted us to a private lounge. The cops stayed with me until the flight was called, taking me to the gate and watching me board the plane. They wanted to make sure that I was leaving the country.

Eight hours later I was in front of an immigration officer at Kennedy airport in New York. I had expected to be bombarded with questions – but it seems that my 'gone missing' status hadn't been filed against my name on the Homeland Security website (or maybe the US Consulate in Casablanca had already arranged for it to be pulled). The officer scanned my passport and asked me how long I had been out of the country. When I told him, he asked:

'Were you only in Morocco?'

'That's right, just Morocco.'

'Working?'

'No, just travelling.'

'That must have been quite an adventure.'

I paused for a moment before saying:

'Indeed it was.'

When I finally landed in Buffalo, Morton was there to greet me. He gave me a paternal hug and said I looked a lot better than he had expected.

Morton being Morton he didn't push for details. En route to my house he did inform me that the *Buffalo Sun* had reprinted international press service reports about my being found alive and well in Morocco. He showed me the clipping, which featured that official photograph of me shaking the hand of Inspector al-Badisi in Casablanca and looking the wrong side of shell-shocked. Morton said that there had been several calls at my office for interviews from former colleagues on the *Sun*.

'I took the liberty of telling them you wanted to be left alone,' he said.

'That was the right call.'

That first night back I found I couldn't cope with the sight of all the detritus of my life with Paul spread around our dusty, shadowy house. Sleep evaded me. The next morning I called the manager of a downtown hotel whose accounts I had helped to straighten out. I asked him if he could give me a rate on one of his apartment suites for a few weeks and he got back to me thirty minutes later with a very reasonable price. I moved in that afternoon. I then contacted my doctor who told me to get over to her immediately. Dr Hart had been my physician for a decade. A smart, no-nonsense woman in her late fifties; direct, canny, but also sympathetic. I could see her taking in the state of my face when I walked into her office. I asked if she had followed my disappearance in the press.

'Of course, not that there was much in the way of detail, except that you and your husband had gone missing. And then I saw the report yesterday in the paper that you'd been found.'

I told Dr Hart about the insomnia and the sense of oppressive darkness that had taken hold of me the last few nights. I came clean with her about the revelation that had seen me indirectly confront Paul with his betrayal of me. I also told her about the abduction and rape. But I stopped short of revealing what I had done in response to this attack. That was a secret which I knew I couldn't share with anybody. Not just because the Moroccan authorities had conveniently excised it from the narrative, but also because a secret shared (even with the most trustworthy of friends or professionals) is no longer a secret. Even Assistant Consul Conway who clearly knew the truth of the matter – reiterated her advice when she left me:

'Speaking off the record . . . if I were you, I would be very selective about revealing what happened in the desert. The Moroccans have made it easy to do this – they have provided an official version of events on which you have signed off. Silence on everything else might be a wise strategy.'

I concurred with her reasoning. But by the time I saw Dr Hart – only forty-eight hours after this conversation – I kept having ongoing image explosions in my head, in which the moments from my being forcibly penetrated to my grappling the jerrycan open were replayed repeatedly. Just as I reviewed, in relentless slow motion, the instant when I grabbed the cigarette lighter from his accomplice's hand and tossed it on his gasoline-drenched body. And how – I'll admit this now – a huge sense of furious vindication came over me as I watched him ignite, writhing and screaming in agony.

Ben Hassan might be a bloated moral black hole of a man – but he did characteristically touch a very exposed nerve when he said: '*Don't try to take the moral high ground here. You are exactly like me. You killed to stay alive.*'

That knowledge was hardly comforting. It was stalking me day and night. Especially the night. In fact, all night.

Dr Hart was beyond sympathetic about Paul's secret vasectomy, because we had talked at length months ago about the fact that my husband and I were going to try for a baby.

'I cannot begin to imagine the shock and dismay and sense of devastation you must have suffered when you discovered what he'd done. For that revelation to lead to his crack-up and disappearance, and your pursuit of him around Morocco, ending with that rape in the desert . . . it may not be very professional of me to say this, but I have little sympathy for your husband's fate. How guilty are you feeling about all this?'

'The guilt is exacerbated by the insomnia and the panic attacks, and also the fear that I might have been infected with an STD.'

Over the next week I endured an entire battery of tests. I got lucky on several fronts. No parasites parading through my system. No sexually transmitted diseases. The gynaecological exam showed near-full recovery from internal trauma. I did not have a burst eardrum, but had suffered a sort of concussion to the ear canal which would subside in a few more weeks. A CT scan did not point up any damage to my left cheekbone. Nor did I have a dreaded 'zygomatic fracture' of the eye socket (as the specialist called it), even though I still had a semi-dark ring beneath my left eye. 'It will fade with time,' he assured me. The dermatologist whom I saw next said that, though the facial scarring would largely heal, there might be some subtle but potentially discernible reminders of the damage done to my legs.

When my friend Ruth flew up to Buffalo the weekend after my return I put her up on the sofa bed in the living room of my hotel suite. I told her just about everything that had occurred in Morocco, leaving out that one crucial detail. She listened wide-eyed and horrified, amazed by my fortuitous rescue and survival. When I mentioned that sleep was now an issue, she said:

'You're back in the land of pharma-psychology. And you need to sleep. So ask your doctor to prescribe some pills. If I may say so, you should also consider talking to somebody professionally who can help you—'

'What? Find a degree of *acceptance* about what happened? *Closure?* I know that talking to a shrink can help. It's just . . .'

I didn't want to complete the sentence. Because what I would have said was: *I am not going to sit in a therapist's office and somehow fail to mention that I burnt my rapist alive and, in the moments before his accomplice kicked me in the head, I felt a frightening sense of avenging triumph.* I was unwilling to share that hidden facet with anyone. It was a deeply troubling component within me which I was determined would stay just that: a secret, concealed for good.

I did accept Dr Hart's offer of an anti-depressant that also served as an aid to sleep. She told me it might take a week for its effect to be felt. Actually it took ten days, during which time an ongoing sense of oppression – a menacing sense of foreboding – stalked me. There were the flashbulb-like shards of memory which appeared in my consciousness without warning, and had me seriously skewed.

Finally sleep took hold.

Dr Hart saw me once a week to check how I was faring, especially when it came to sleep and the spectral zone into which I frequently retreated. She did suggest counselling on several occasions.

313

'Surely if you had a massive toothache you'd consult a dentist,' she reasoned. 'So won't you at least try a session or two with a therapist I know who specialises in trauma cases?'

I wanted to blurt out: *Get off this subject now!* Instead I tactfully said:

'Let me handle it at my own pace.'

I threw myself into work. Twelve-to-thirteen-hour days. A determination to function and cope and keep moving forward that saw me land a big corporate account – a chain of upstate New York hardware stores – the month after my return. After six weeks at the hotel, I moved back home. But it was another ten days before I finally walked into Paul's studio. On the draughtsman's table where he worked was the package that I had sent back to my office from Casablanca; a package which Morton had brought with him to the airport on the night of my return, and which I had tossed into the studio when I got home. Now all these weeks later I finally opened it, staring down at the notebook he'd left at Fouad's, forcing myself to turn the pages, looking at his supremely accomplished, intricate take on Essaouira and '*la vie marocaine*'. Seeing them all again slammed home the loss, the betrayal, the guilt, the horror of his disappearance, the horror of what had been visited on me, the fact that I was here alone in our house, regretting so much, trying to keep trepidation and rage and sadness at bay. I broke down and cried for a good half-hour, accumulated grief rushing forth.

When it had finally subsided I went into the bathroom, threw some cold water on my face and looked at myself in the mirror. I knew at this juncture that, though the wounds both physical and mental might always be there, my work was to somehow achieve, in time, a degree of accommodation with their attendant agonies.

An hour later, nursing a glass of wine, I went online and found a cottage for rent deep in the Adirondack Mountains on the shores of Upper Saranac Lake. It was available as of tomorrow – and the owner (with whom I had an Internet chat) lived in nearby Lake Placid and said he could have the place cleaned and ready for my arrival by nightfall. He told me that it lacked Wi-Fi and that cellphone coverage was, at best, spotty.

'Fine by me,' I said – and we then agreed a price for one month's rental. Negotiations completed, I packed a bag with clothes, another with a dozen or so books from around the house which I'd promised myself to read over the years. My last piece of business before I fell into bed was to send an email to Morton:

> *Sorry to drop a little bombshell on you, but I have decided this evening to disappear to somewhere rural and hidden for four weeks. I will drive to a café with Wi-Fi every few days to see if there's anything urgent to deal with at the office. Otherwise I am going to be out of touch. Are you OK with this?*

His reply arrived moments later.

> *Stay out of touch – and don't look at your email or cellphone for the next month. You evidently need this time away for all sorts of reasons. Go hide and think.*

Hide I did. The cottage was simple, clean, idyllic. And isolated. It was located at the end of a half-paved road with no neighbours in sight. The nearest village – to which I drove twice a week for supplies – was ten miles away. I slept. I read. I cooked. I listened to classical music and jazz on the radio. I didn't open a computer or touch my cellphone for one entire month. There was a narrow walking trail just steps away from the cottage that followed the lake front. Every day I did a three-hour hike along its shoreline. And I thought. About a certain rigidity that, prior to Morocco, had frequently made me look at life as a giant balance sheet, on which I was endlessly obsessing about reversing the loss column. About how I was always wanting to put things right. About how my wonderful, maddening father cast a shadow over so much. And about how rational, hyper-organised me chose men whom I thought I could rescue from the impulse to self-destruct – something I had been unable to stop my dad from doing.

The search for love – especially when it's been withheld by one parent – can lead to all sorts of tricky rationalisations. Had I always gone through life expecting to be, on some level, betrayed? And why, when it came to the commitment that is marriage, did I pick individuals whom I instinctively knew would not be able to give me the stability so denied me as a child?

'Life can change on a dime' was one of my father's favourite sayings. He was always hoping that the dime would finally come his way. Life changed utterly for me in the Sahara. It sent me to the darkest places imaginable; the absolute limits of endurance. But I did just that: I endured. No one would ever know that I killed in order to live. That secret would stay with me for ever. Along with a new-found knowledge that almost everything is survivable if you choose to survive. The only way forward after great pain is fortitude.

So in those weeks alone by the lake, there was a slow diminution of that dark presence which had hovered over me from the moment I was free of danger in Casablanca. It wasn't knocking repeatedly on my psychic door as it had done so virulently in the first months after my return. Which, in turn, gave me the space to examine that most telling and thorny of questions: *What do you want?*

And I began to formulate an answer.

When I finally did return to Buffalo, among the vast number of emails there was one which delighted me. It was from Aatif. Written in simple French, it arrived with a photo attached.

Hi Robin! Just wanted you to see a picture of my wedding and of the house we now live in. I will always be eternally grateful to you. I even have a mobile phone – number below – and an email address now. Allah ybarek feek wal 'ayyam al-kadima.

The photos showed Aatif and a petite young woman who – if the snapshot was anything to go by – was clearly outgoing and spirited. They were both in formal Muslim wedding attire in front of a simple squat one-storey house: concrete, painted that wondrous aquamarine blue which was so essential to the Moroccan decorative palette. I noted that laundry was already hanging on the line outside.

I sent back an immediate reply:

Happiness is a wonderful thing, Aatif – and it is splendid to see you and your wife so happy.

As I hit the 'send' button and glanced once more at the photo of the proverbial happy couple I couldn't help but feel a stab of loneliness; the sense that I was flying solo, but with a phantom still in the adjoining room.

There was also an email from Assistant Consul Conway in Casablanca. As promised she was keeping me abreast of the ongoing search for my husband. She told me that the Moroccan army had recently been doing military exercises in the desert, in the vicinity of where Paul was last seen. They'd been conducting a comprehensive sweep of the area as part of their manoeuvres but had found no body.

She also said, with regret, that the search for Idir and his family had turned up nothing. But now I had a means by which to make contact with them – and immediately replied to her email with Aatif's details, explaining that he knew the family and might be able to assist with their whereabouts. I then shot Aatif a second email, letting him know that he might hear from a woman at the US Consulate in Casablanca about trying to locate my saviours – she had a sum of money for them, and if he could help her locate them I would be hugely grateful.

Weeks went by, then out of nowhere a further email arrived from Alison: she had finally heard back from Aatif after several attempts to contact him. He told her he was heading to the oasis in ten days' time – so yes, he could deliver the cash to Idir and his family. The money had been dispatched by registered mail to his home and she had had confirmation from Poste Maroc that it had been received and signed for.

A month or so later I got a one-line email from Aatif:

Money delivered!

There was a photo attached of Maika and Titrit and Naima – the latter two laughing and waving at the camera, Maika as stone-faced as ever. The men were clearly elsewhere. I printed the photo and put it alongside the one of Aatif and his wife that I had pasted near my computer. The only family I now had.

When I reached the six-month anniversary of my return home I had a second HIV test. Negative. Dr Hart also did repeat swabs for all other potential STDs: all negative.

'You're in the clear,' she told me.

On one level this was true. The discoloration around my left eye was now a thing of the past. And the facial scars had reduced to a point where you would have to examine me closely to really notice them. Still the door to Paul's study at home remained closed. The house had gradually lost some of its hushed eeriness – but there were still moments when I could feel his presence within it.

My determination to push through the worst of the post-traumatic stress did pay off to the extent that I weaned myself off the pharmaceuticals, finding the one and only Chinese herbalist at work in Buffalo and switching to a strongly effective tea to help me sleep. At first, after I went off the prescription pills, there were moments of deeply unsettled regression and five days of complete insomnia. But eventually the herbal formula kicked in. I could function professionally. I could sleep. A few weeks later, on a morning noteworthy for its cold clarity, I presented myself at a fertility clinic attached to the State University for a psychological evaluation. It was an interview and a series of tests that lasted over an hour. I was just a little nervous in the run-up to this crucial hurdle. *Think of it as an audit*, I told myself. Much to my surprise I passed the evaluation. A few days later I returned for a series of examinations to determine if, now that I was forty-one, I would be able to hold a pregnancy to full term. Again I was approved – though the doctor at the clinic with whom I subsequently spoke did inform me that, at my age, the chance of a miscarriage or other attendant problems was considerably higher. Just as he warned me that, once I had

318

chosen a donor, it could take at least three to five tries before I fell pregnant.

The donor. I spent a good two weeks going through the thousand or so possibilities on file, reading up details about their family and educational backgrounds, their professions, their hobbies and interests. It was so surreal, on manifold levels, delving into the personal profiles of these men who had all masturbated into a sterilised dish and were now potential fathers for my much wanted child.

Eventually I narrowed the selection down to four candidates – and scanned all their details to Ruth in Brooklyn. Her choice was the same as mine: a thirty-three-year-old man listed as Michael P. An academic with both undergraduate and doctoral degrees from the University of Chicago. A published writer. Athletic. His interests included classical music, cinema, chess.

'I worry about the "chess" part,' Ruth told me. 'Chess freaks tend to be obsessive compulsive.'

'It's absurd, isn't it, choosing a potential father the way you choose food at a Chinese restaurant? This attribute from Column A, another from Column B.'

'And if you get pregnant you get a fortune cookie.'

'If I get pregnant it will be a miracle.'

'You've had one miracle last year. You got out of the Sahara alive.'

'So why should the gods smile on me again?'

But they did – on the third try.

It's a deeply lonely experience, having your legs up in the stirrups of a doctor's examination table, watching a nurse approach you with a tube filled with the sperm of your chosen donor. Lonely and immensely modern. No need to establish a rapport; to dance around each other at the outset, deciding whether to cross the frontier into sex; working out whether there is the chance of something more promising; the decision to set up house together (or not); the decision to reproduce (or not). There will never be a memory of the intimate coupling that led to this conception. But I had no doubt whatsoever that I was making the right decision in going this route. Too much emotional debris in my past. Too much trepidation about trying to get involved with anyone right now. Maybe, in time, that would change. Maybe there would be a point in the future when I wouldn't be so closed off to that possibility. But for now . . .

The first artificial insemination didn't take. Four weeks later I was back for Round Two. When my period arrived two weeks after that the disappointment and despair I felt were acute. But dogged as ever I returned another fourteen days later for Round Three.

This time . . . bingo.

When my period was one day late I bought a pregnancy test. At home that night I peed onto its chemically treated strip . . . and watched as it gradually turned blue.

So there it was: positive proof that I was pregnant. But being ever conscious of checks and balances I ran a second test five days later. When it turned blue again I called Dr Hart. A week later she gave me the official confirmation – and hugged me at the end of our consultation.

'I know this has been your dream for so long.'

And most dreams can only be fulfilled by yourself. It's a bit like happiness: you can never depend on someone else for that elusive state of being. In the end we are all directly responsible for our own happiness . . . or lack thereof.

I told nobody else but Ruth for the first three months of my pregnancy, reading up extensively on everything and anything to do with baby and child care. When twelve weeks had passed – and I was out of the initial dangerous miscarriage zone – I decided the time had come to inform Morton and my staff that I was expecting a child. And that after the birth I was planning to take some time off work. Because, perhaps for the first time in my life, I wouldn't be flying solo any more.

But I forestalled that announcement for a few days, as I suddenly had urgent business in New York. Business to do with my missing-presumed-dead husband. A week previously Jasper Pirnie, the owner of the gallery which showed his work, got in touch, telling me he knew about Paul's disappearance from the Internet and regretted not contacting me before now.

'I won't give you any sort of mealy-mouthed excuse about being too busy,' he said. 'It was bad form on my part, and you have my apologies for only contacting you all these many months later. But the reason I'm calling you now is because I have some interesting news.'

The news was that one of Jasper's clients – a wealthy Korean industrialist – had, while on a visit to Manhattan, paid a visit to the gallery and spied one of Paul's early drawings – a Maine seascape, shaded by omnipresent cloud. He loved it.

'He asked me what I wanted for it, and when I said twenty thousand he agreed on the spot. So congratulations – you'll be receiving fifty per cent of that.'

As if reading my thoughts he added:

'Or, at least, Paul's estate will be receiving that. But here's the thing – this gentleman is quite the collector. Since returning to Seoul he's shown off the drawing to several of his high-spending colleagues. There is now a market for Paul Leuen's drawings. So my question to you is—'

Now it was my turn to jump in. I told him about the sketchbook of Paul's final work which he left behind just before disappearing, and how the thirty or so drawings were, in my opinion, absolutely extraordinary.

By the time I'd finished my spiel I could almost hear Jasper palpitating at the prospect of something significant and lucrative about to come his way.

'Might you be able to FedEx the sketchbook to me overnight?' he asked.

It went out that afternoon. By the time he got back to me thirty-six hours later, Morton and I had already put into action a plan devised some months earlier for dealing with any possible sales of Paul's future work: a trust in his name that would revert to me after seven years from the date of his disappearance, at which point he could be declared legally dead. When Morton brought this up, we thought that maybe a few thousand dollars might trickle in over the years for Paul's remaining work. But now . . .

When Jasper rang the next night he was no longer masking his excitement.

'You have given us a treasure trove. The brilliance and uniqueness of the composition, the absolute assurance of his line, the exceptional density of detail, the fascinating contrast between the representational and the abstract . . . and, dare I say, the tragic nature of his story which will be a fantastic selling point when it comes to generating press and critical interest in the exhibition we plan to mount of these final works . . . I think we are looking at a major public triumph, and one which will, of course, translate into a significant escalation of our asking price per drawing.'

'Any sense of what that asking price might be?'

'At this point, I would probably be conservative about it and say, once we have drummed up the journalistic and collector interest I know we will generate . . . perhaps, forty thousand per drawing.'

I sucked in my breath. Fifty drawings at 40,000 apiece . . . $2 million. Half to the trust set up in the name of Paul Leuen.

'That's impressive,' I said.

'Might there be more of Paul's work left behind?'

'There must be a good sixty to seventy drawings in his studio upstairs.'

'Could you get those packed up and dispatched to us immediately, please? And were I to offer you a flight and a hotel room and an excellent dinner, might you be willing to come down and meet with me early next week?'

I had my iPhone out and was already scrolling through my calendar.

By the time I flew down on Tuesday afternoon to meet Jasper I already had in place a Manhattan lawyer who specialised in art contracts. Morton, meanwhile, having been fully appraised of this windfall in the making, had found a super-smart trust and estates attorney who was finding a wholly legal modus operandi by which the funds from the sale of Paul's work could be made accessible to me. If, as suspected, I was coming into $2.5 million net of Jasper's commission, besides setting up a trust for the child growing within me and perhaps moving house, I wanted to honour Paul's desire to buy an apartment for his daughter in Casablanca. Only this time I would be sidestepping Ben Hassan.

But talk is cheap. And talk about serious money coming your way is even cheaper. So until the drawings started to sell I was not doing or promising anything. One thought did strike me as the town car sent to collect me from LaGuardia airport emerged from the Midtown Tunnel and cruised into the epicentre of Manhattan: what was about to happen to Paul Leuen – his post-humous discovery as the major American artist I always knew him to be – was the reverie he always carried within himself. He had such exceptional talent. But when it came to that other crucial ingredient – having the talent to have talent – he was living proof of a great central truth: the biggest impediment we all have in life is ourselves.

I was checked into a hyper-stylish boutique hotel located diagonally across from Jasper's gallery. The room was a monument to minimalist chic. There was a bottle of champagne awaiting me which I would take as a gift for Ruth, as alcohol was currently off the cards for me.

I surveyed the room, and the cityscape beyond its immense windows. I thought how he should be here, revelling in the fact that, after decades of silently accepting his status as a creative also-ran – someone who had never achieved the critical or commercial success he knew he deserved – the door had finally swung his way. He was now being summoned inside, with all the attendant fanfare accompanying his entrance into the realm he so craved.

But instead of being here with me, he was out there, in the endless void that is the Sahara. The beckoning infinity into which he had run. A vanishing act from which there is no return.

I blinked and felt tears. I went into the bathroom and washed my face, reapplied my make-up, grabbed my leather jacket and headed out into that upscale hipsterish quarter known as the Meatpacking District. Once I reached the pavement I could glimpse

Jasper's gallery just yards away on the opposite corner. I awaited the changing of the lights. And that's when I saw him. On the other side of the street. Dressed in a white shirt, loose canvas pants, his grey hair cascading to his shoulders. I gasped. I told myself: *This is not real, this is not him.* I blinked again. Several times. And then focused my sight even more acutely on the man standing on the pavement directly opposite me. A man in his late fifties, six foot four inches tall, lanky with a distinctive French pencil in one hand, a sketchpad in the other. Without thinking I shouted his name.

'Paul!'

He turned and stared directly at me. And smiled. So happy to see me.

Out of nowhere a cab shot between us, blocking my view for a second or two. When it raced away Paul was gone.

I stood there, scanning all four corners of the immediate horizon. No sign of him. I dashed across the street, thinking he might have ducked into a shop or an apartment building. But there were no immediate entrances into which he could have vanished. Again I visually raked every niche and recess of the area, running back to the hotel in case he had crossed when I wasn't looking, then racing across diagonally to see if, indeed, he could have headed down the street or into Jasper's gallery.

I ran right into the gallery. There was a woman at the reception desk: hip glasses, a too-cool-for-school demeanour.

'Did someone just come in here?' I asked her.

She surveyed me wryly.

'Not unless he has a double act as a ghost,' she said.

'I'm here to see Jasper.'

'Oh really?' she said, not buying that line. But when I told her my name her attitude shifted. She became nervously respectful, telling me I was awaited inside.

'I'll be back in a moment.'

I rushed outside, certain that as soon as I hit the sidewalk he'd be there in front of me. Smiling. So happy to see me. So happy to embrace all the good that was to happen to him, to us.

But the street, though brimming with an early-evening crowd, was not harbouring Paul. I looked east, west, north, south. Only a minute ago he'd been right in front of me. And now? Back into infinity.

It wasn't a delirium. An apparition. A mirage. He was there. I'd seen him. With my eyes wide open.

But when do we ever fully open our eyes?

ALSO AVAILABLE IN ARROW

Five Days

Douglas Kennedy

How long does it take to fall in love?

For twenty years, Laura has been a good wife and a good mother. She's supported her husband through redundancy, she's worried about her son, she's encouraged her daughter. She's stopped thinking about all the places she'd like to go and all the books she'd like to talk about.

She's not unhappy, exactly. She's not that self-indulgent. As anyone would tell you, Laura is wonderfully constant, caring, selfless. She's certainly an expert at putting on a brave face.

But a chance meeting in a hotel lobby – and the five days that follow – remind Laura of the young woman she used to be – and the woman she could have become.

Is it ever too late to have the life you wanted? Or do we owe it to ourselves to pursue the promise of happiness?

'This modern Brief Encounter asks what it is that stops most of us from instigating change. Throughout we are kept in exquisite suspense, waiting to see whether the beleaguered pair will seize their chance of happiness' *Independent*

'Totally, blissfully absorbing' *The Times*

arrow books

ALSO AVAILABLE IN ARROW

The Moment

Douglas Kennedy

Thomas Nesbitt is a divorced American writer living a very private life in Maine. Until, one wintry morning, his solitude is disrupted by the arrival of a package postmarked Berlin.

But what is more unsettling is the name accompanying the return address on the package: Petra Dussmann. For she is the woman with whom Thomas had an intense love affair twenty-five years before in a divided Berlin, where people lived fearfully under the shadows of the Cold War.

And so Thomas is forced to grapple with a past he has always kept hidden. For Petra Dussman was a refugee from the police state of East Germany. And her tragic secrets were to re-write both their destinies.

'Kennedy is an absolute master at love stories with heart-stopping twists . . . The Moment is simply sensational.'
The Times

'His most ambitious to date and most deeply felt.'
Daily Mirror

'The storytelling is served up thick and meaty . . . the result is a big, satisfying read.'
Daily Mail

arrow books

ALSO AVAILABLE IN ARROW

The Pursuit of Happiness

Douglas Kennedy

Manhattan, Thanksgiving eve, 1945. The war was over, and Eric Smythe's party was in full swing. All his clever Greenwich Village friends were there. So too was his sister Sara – an independent, canny young woman, starting to make her way in the big city. And then in walked a gatecrasher, Jack Malone – a U.S. Army journalist just back from a defeated Germany, and a man whose world-view did not tally with that of Eric and his friends.

Set amidst the dynamic optimism of postwar New York and the subsequent nightmare of the McCarthy witch-hunts, *The Pursuit of Happiness* is a great tragic love story; a tale of divided loyalties, decisive moral choices, and the random workings of destiny.

'A compulsive read'
Kate Atkinson

'This is the novel against which the rest of the year's output demands to be judged'
Sunday Express

'Kennedy cannot help but write grippingly, and he weaves threads of love and betrayal into a thrillingly masterful ending'
Observer

arrow books